LIBERATING PERSECUTION

BOOK 5: ARMOUR OF LIGHT SERIES

DONITA BUNDY

JOURNEY
PRESS

Print: 978-0-6486387-3-5
EBook: 978-0-6486387-4-2

Editor: Belinda Pollard
Proofreader: Alix Kwan
Cover Design: Donita Bundy

Cover Images Copyright ©
Model by faestock via Shutterstock
Model hair by mimagephotography via Envato

Sword by fxquadro via Envato
Armour Left by fxquadro via Envato
Armour Right by fxquadro via Envato
Chainmail skirt by SergioPhotone via Envato

Stage by wirestock via Envato
Stage lights and speakers by salajean via Envato

❀ Created with Vellum

For the girls in the wings, whom I couldn't do this without.
Bel and Alix, thank you.

AUTHOR'S NOTE

Dear Reader,

As the story continues, the crew relocate to the city of Sardis. In researching for this book, I have used actual historical circumstances.

However, I have also set the story in the context of what was happening for the early church at the time the letters we read in Revelation were written to the Churches.

This is a work of fiction set in the not-too-distant future. It is not historically accurate; it merely draws on historical and biblical evidence for inspiration.

My hope is that you will enjoy the story and the journey of the family and people who live between the pages. But my prayer is that you are encouraged, no matter what lies ahead for the Communities of Light, and that you stand strong.

Sincerely,

db

TO THE CHURCH IN SARDIS

"To the angel of the church in Sardis write: These are the words of him who holds the seven spirits of God and the seven stars. I know your deeds; you have a reputation of being alive, but you are dead. Wake up! Strengthen what remains and is about to die, for I have found your deeds unfinished in the sight of my God. Remember, therefore, what you have received and heard; hold it fast, and repent. But if you do not wake up, I will come like a thief, and you will not know at what time I will come to you.

Yet you have a few people in Sardis who have not soiled their clothes. They will walk with me, dressed in white, for they are worthy. The one who is victorious will, like them, be dressed in white. I will never blot out the name of that person from the book of life, but will acknowledge that name before my Father and his angels. Whoever has ears, let them hear what the Spirit says to the churches."

Revelation 3:1-6 (NIV)

PROLOGUE: THE SARDIS HERALD

Crowds outside Sardis Courthouse erupted this morning when renowned businessman, Balashka 'The Big Man' Graves, was convicted on one hundred and forty-three counts of fraud and mismanagement of invested funds. The jury took thirty-six minutes to return a guilty verdict. The result was announced to a deafening roar, both within and outside the courthouse, as many celebrated the fall of "The Mighty Midas".

It took Her Honour Judge Cannell several attempts to bring the court back to order. However, the restraint was short lived as the scene turned violent after Her Honour vacated the room.

Graves was removed from the dock through a side entrance, in chains and under guard. Some members of the public gallery broke through the cordoned area, hurling abuse, and attempted to punch and spit on Graves.

Outside the courthouse, victims of the The Big Man's schemes and scams hugged, celebrating the guilty verdict. When the convicted felon was spotted being escorted to an Enforcer's van, the mob broke through the guards' ill-equipped protection and Graves was absorbed by the crush.

Witnesses say they heard him yelling for help as the guards stood by. "But after a while I couldn't hear nothing except cursing and yelling as his head sank beneath the scrum," one woman reported.

Another bystander added, "Yeah, them guards weren't in no hurry to help him. But from what I hear, so they shouldn't. Scum, he is. Deserves everything he gets."

An older woman said, "He took me for everything I had. All my savings, investments, superannuation... all gone. It's all gone. I've got nothing. Nothing."

"He was my mate... it didn't mean a thing. Still stripped me bare," said another.

Enforcers dragged Graves' inert body from the horde into the back of their wagon where he was reportedly transferred directly to the Ephesus Penitentiary hospital facilities.

The angry mob was slightly appeased by the prosecutor's statement that Graves' personal finances and multiple properties would be sold to reimburse all victims and that his Sardis residency status had been revoked.

Later, sources revealed Graves had been treated for multiple wounds, broken bones and severe concussion. When and if he recovers from his injuries, this Masthead is reliably informed he will spend his first six months in solitary confinement in a maximum-security cell for his own protection.

Mr Smithe, one of the one hundred and forty-three victims, and spokesperson for the victim group, stated from the court steps, "The extent of Graves' cruel schemes are far reaching, and the effects have been both debilitating and devastating. The ten-year sentence awarded to the accused was far too lenient."

JEMIMAH: THE SCENE OF THE CRIME

That sweet blend of generator fumes and street food made my senses reel and my heart sing. Tonight was going to be good. Guaranteed. A multitude of possibilities lay before me; all I had to do was choose which one I was going to indulge in.

Hunkering down in the shadows, my hoodie pulled low over the tender skin of my scalp, I prepared myself. Waiting was an important part of the relatively new game I'd learned to play: hide from the Enforcers, and seek whatever I needed to survive on the street. This shouldn't have been my life. I should be in school fretting about exams, not whether the authorities were going to find me and drag me back to my mother. But for now, I had to focus on the game. Facing me were the workers' entrances to a selection of food vans: tacos, burgers and kebabs. My mouth pooled, and my empty stomach kicked in painful anticipation.

The Benevolent Society Shelter's food was alright.... Who was I kidding, that was an outright lie. I had a theory about it, actually. The Shelter—as it was known by the locals—occupied prime real estate in the Cultural District and was a pain in the establishment's butt. Started decades ago by the previous, much-loved Gerent, the majority of Sardis's citizens didn't want it removed. But it was seen as an encouragement to the unsightlies to linger in the heart of the jewel of our city. So I reckoned, as a compromise, the management had been instructed to make the food nutritious but unpalatable. The bedding clean, but uncomfortable. The showers accessible, but cold. That way the undesirables only hung round when they were desperate for a night off the streets. So, for the likes of me, festival nights were a smorgasbord of opportunistic delight.

The senseless chaos of the crowd, the hum of the motors and the clash of utensils inside the vans all danced a chorus of white noise that sang a sweet lullaby. Despite the hunger, anticipation, and my best intentions, I slipped into a doze. I tell you what, I walked a constant tension of exhaustion and alertness. What with being a girl on the street without backup or a lookout for the Temples' Catchers, I was constantly sleeping with one eye open. Even at The Shelter. But, sometimes, your defences dropped and there was nothing you could do but steal some zzzs.

Thankfully, the loud curse of the worker sitting down just across the pavement roused me and kicked me into action. They went back inside for something they'd apparently left in the van and, more importantly, they left their meal unattended. My legs were stiff, but my need and instincts were limber.

Within moments I was waltzing through the shadows down the mountain road leading to the biggest temple of the lot, burger in one hand, fries in the other and a cold bottle of water stashed in the huge pocket in the front of my hoodie. The chill and condensation worked wonders to steal some of the heat from under my bulky clothes on this summer night.

After a few minutes I increased my camouflage by diving in and swimming with the crowd. The grease of the burger lined my stomach, which was now happily gurgling its way through a week's worth of carbs. I plucked a fry from the pack and savoured that luscious, salty seasoning. I reckoned there was no better meal in all the world.

Now, here's a life lesson I have come to respect: to be drunk on alcohol leads to stupid, senseless acts. But to be drunk on the contentment of a full stomach and sated hormones is far more dangerous.

The crowd was being guided, and managed, by the overhead drones. Not only did they flash arrows to direct the crowd and play music—specifically chosen by psychologists to control the mood they filmed everything. That way, as soon as there were any disruptions, the ground crew sorted it out before it got out of hand. All so that nothing could interrupt the highlight of the city's social calendar, the Festival of Feasts: a celebration, by way of free concerts, excessive feasting and partying to excess, of the wide assortment of gods who had chosen Sardis as a footstool. It was a totally wild time and perfect pickings for the likes of me.

Tonight was the first night of the two-week Temple-crawl, so, inevitably, the crowd was guided to the first cab off the rank for the whole shebang. Which was also the largest and most prominent temple, belonging to Artemis: the moon goddess and goddess of the hunt. My mother's favourite. Not that she was particularly loyal to Artemis. Like all others in this ambidextrous city, she worshipped and practised any rite of any god she was in the mood to play with.

Trouble was, we had already entered the floodlit arena. I would draw attention if I broke away from the revelry and ran for the hills— like every nerve in my body was screaming at me to do. Like I'd done ten months ago. But I knew for a fact my missing person's picture was still up in a few places, and I was confident it was still on the Enforcers' database. If I was captured on film I would be in real trouble. Caught up in the swell of the crowd, it looked like I was going to be a mouse in the claws of the great huntress once again. My scars itched, and my fight fought with flight whilst freeze did its best to intervene. In a daze of fear fuelled by my overactive imagination, all I could see was the worst possible outcome.

The group I'd journeyed the path with caroused and cajoled each other, me included, in time with the "happy, peaceful" vibe pumping out of the overhead drones. They hadn't even noticed I wasn't one of them. Or my extreme body odour. See above, regarding drunkenness and stupidity.

The worm of a thought started gnawing away at the alarm bells of my imagination. What if I could fool those inside the temple as well as

I had fooled those standing right beside me? If I continued to swim in the middle of the herd, would I be seen? Could I trust the safety of the pack? Would any dangerous predator peel away the unsuspecting fools on the outer of the group, thereby giving me more time to escape... if need be?

Yeah, I reckoned need would definitely be.

But what if I could actually go back and gauge the situation... and not get caught? The beat and pressure in my heart from my fear was nothing compared to the full-body pounding going on as I considered the possibility. Could I return to the scene of the crime and make it out alive... a second time?

The bloke beside me threw an arm around my shoulders and raised his beer in salute to the great goddess as we crossed the threshold of her dominion. Gulping, shaking, and kicking myself good and proper, I raised my water bottle in a dim imitation, and pretended to be drunk on the high of the night.

Idiot. Stupid, fracking idiot. What the hell was I doing?

Obviously, we couldn't enter the temple proper with alcoholic drinks—Artemis's temple that was. Pity we weren't at Dionysus's. My crowd was ushered to the side where all drinks were binned in the appropriate receptacles, apart from, "That's okay, miss, you can keep your water."

Praise be to whichever one of you gods can be bothered listening, and who gives the first flying frack.

With unease growing in my gut, I nodded a weak smile in response and kept my head down and my water bottle close. My hood had shifted as my new "friend" dragged his arm away, trying for a grope on the way. I tell you what, it didn't matter how baggy the clothes or tight the strapping, even at fourteen, my curves refused to be dominated and guys always felt they had the right to handle... with or without care. However, I am glad to report, due to my backpack, the inebriated idiot was neither smooth nor successful in his attempt to cop a feel. I gave him the flick with a quick side-step and pulled the hood back up over my yellow stubble. The soft fabric still irritated my red, inflamed skin but it was better than standing out like a yellow-headed matchstick.

Here's a life lesson I have come to respect: peroxide needs to be well diluted before applying it to your skin, because otherwise it burns like unholy fire.

It was at this point I realised that my extreme unease had met up with the junk food in my gut and was forming a volcanic eruption of titanic proportions. The fireball working its way through my bowels had "painful-ugly" branded all over it. My body then informed me it was going to forcibly eject all that skrat in a matter of moments. Thankfully, I knew the lay of the land. This was not my first dance through the temple's maze.

Here's another life lesson I had picked up along the way: yell "rape" and people look the other way; yell "fire" and people will run with you, if not trampling you in their bid for self-preservation; yell "I need the bathroom" people will stop and stare and do nothing to help; but yell "vomit" and people will move out of the way and leave you to yourself and your need to escape. So, with my bowels on fire and my hand over my mouth I ran, mumble-yelling, "Vomit, sick, move."

I bolted down the outside of the temple and found the closest public toilet. The door ricocheted off the wall, but I was already in a cubicle slamming and locking the door before the outer door could whisper back into place. Then I wept. Silently. I had made it. Again, I threw a word of thanks up for any of the Capricious to catch if they were so inclined.

From memory, I knew the classy crew who worked here stocked the bathrooms with nice-smelling things to cover the stench of the undesirables and unsightlies who happened through their sanctuary. All the temples were open to the public and, by rights, couldn't block entry to any who wanted to worship the goddess. But they didn't have to put up with the smell. And, right now, this undesirable was all in favour of nice-smelling things.

I couldn't believe I'd made it this far into her sanctuary. But it was far enough for me. Sense returned in the cool, well-lit solitude of the bathroom. As soon as I'd finished up here and had a bit of a wash, I'd be back on the road heading to the other side of Sardis's great wall. Never to cross this twik's threshold again.

The air changed and some background noise entered the room just before a voice: "Are you okay in here, honey?"

I froze.

I felt the pressure readjust as the outer door silently swung shut. She was standing outside my stall. Waiting for a response.

"Um, yes...?" I had to get rid of her. "Ummm... but I didn't quite make it. I... um... am a bit of a mess." That should give me enough time to scarper if she went off to get som—

"Oh, you poor thing, I thought that might be the case. I've brought you a change of clothes. I'm afraid it's an acolyte gown, but I've got a bag for you to put your dirty clothes in." The woman's voice was young, and sweet, and... genuine? That was one for the books. Not that I'd trust her as far as I could throw her. But it was a pretty cool gesture.

However, I almost climbed onto the back of the cistern as a hand appeared under the door with the items.

I managed to cough out a thanks. Then, with the gifts in hand, I was bowled over again as a damp cloth was passed under the door.

"This is to help you freshen up. I'll leave you in privacy and make sure you're not interrupted." And true to her word, the angel of mercy silently left the room.

I just sat and stared at this gift horse sitting on my lap. Clean clothes. A clean, fresh, damp washer. A bag... but I could hardly make it to the streets in a white acolyte gown. I had options but little time. First, I stripped down to my undies and strapped chest. Grabbed the cloth and wiped myself down. Next, I dashed to the sink, rinsed the cloth, added some smelly stuff and raced back into the cubicle and washed again. I tell you what, there was one thing I could not adjust to on the streets, and that was rank personal body odour.

Fear and lack of time had me scrubbing the top layer of skin as I smashed out a cleaning routine in record time. Using the inside hem of the gown, I scrubbed the rest of the soap off, then threw the robe on. I put my runners back on over my stinky socks, stashed the rest into the plastic bag, then put the lot in my backpack. I checked the stall, went back into the main area, washed my face and hands again, topped up my water bottle, then stared at myself in the mirror.

Large dark eyes, high prominent cheek bones and full lips. No matter how I tried to hide my curves, there was no way I could make my face look like a guy. However, the red, inflamed scalp covered in yellow stubble was a good distraction. With naturally thick, dark-brown hair, I looked too much like my mother. And since she was so well known in some parts of the city, and my missing person's case still quietly bubbled away, I had to do all I could to change that.

In the mirror I saw the door to the bathroom edge open. I flicked up the hood of the gown and dropped my face before the acolyte came back in. "There you are. How are you feeling, honey?"

"Um, better thanks. But I might just head home now if that's okay. I can return your clothes tomorro—"

"Hush now. Come with me and I'll call your family to come pick you up. We can't have you walking home when you're so ill."

"I don't have a family." What can I say? It was a knee-jerk reaction and one of the dumbest things I had done that night.

"You don't have a family?" The young woman just stared at me... or what she could see of my face. "Well then, we'll call you a ride to take you home."

This time I didn't blurt it out. I didn't have to. She read it all over me like I was lit up in neon. She glanced at the ratty backpack on the floor next to my holey shoes. "Right. Well then, let's get you a nice cup of soothing tea and have one of the staff check you over." I opened my mouth to object, but she had already darted in and grabbed my backpack. The sweet, maid-of-mercy mask dissolved with a flicker of insightful determination. Her dove-grey eyes narrowed as she considered me, head to foot. "I do believe," she paused and tilted her head, "a cup of tea and a medical check is called for." And with some crazy ninja move the tiny woman stepped in, spun around and clamped my arm to her side with surprising strength. She looked back up at me, mercy mask back in place. "I'll just help, shall I?" I could try to run for it. But as soon as I made a break, she would have security on my butt like the boys from school on a pizza-day feeding frenzy.

We were moving along the back pathways before my brain could process what had just happened. The noise of the carousing crowd dimmed as we crawled further into the heart of Artemis's coven. All I knew... all I felt was the woman's arm, her hip brushing my thigh, and my heart fluctuating between tremors, body jolts and stopping altogether. Further along the walkways, reflecting the soft-gold of the warm-toned lights, gliding—the woman glided, I jolted like a stiffed-kneed scarecrow—silently along smoothly paved paths, further and further into the heart of hell.

There was nothing I could do to stop the shaking. I couldn't hide it from the woman shackling me to my doomed fate. I couldn't stop the sweat soaking the no-longer fresh, clean robe. And I couldn't stop the foghorn going off in my head: "Doom. Doom. Doom. You're going to die."

My stilted steps stalled, the closer we got to the private buildings, the private area of the priestesses and acolytes: the kitchenettes, the sleeping quarters, the medical rooms...

"Doom. Doom. Doom. You are going to die."

2

JEMIMAH: THAT'S TWO LIVES DOWN

Heat flushed my body and all rational—and irrational—thought fled. No longer was there room for a debate between fight and flight. Freeze had body-slammed the both of them and we were all out for the count as my memory was dragged kicking and screaming back to that night ten months ago.

"Doom. Doom. Doom. You're gonna die."

I couldn't breathe. The walls spun, then jumped out to hit me upside the head and body. I slid to the floor. Firm pressure was placed on the back of my head and it was pushed between my knees. I didn't hear a thing, but I felt absence. I was alone. Gulping air, begging the ground to stop swaying and vaguely grateful that my system had emptied itself earlier, and I had nothing left to throw up.

Cool, fresh air assaulted my sweaty, swollen scalp as someone ripped the hood off my head. I was too late and unsteady to stop it. Everything happened at once. I looked up into the face of the acolyte; the woman gasped, and a blessedly cool, damp cloth was dropped across the back of my neck. I felt a crazy blend of pain, fear and relief. It stopped the panic long enough to allow the foghorn back into the game. "You're gonna die."

The woman let me pull the cowl back into place, but I left the cloth at the back of my neck and buried my face between my knees, wrapping my arms around my head. This was it. I was now going to be held accountable and punished for my significant sin of stupidity. The running and hiding had ended. The game was over. My warped mother was on the precipice of a win and she didn't even know it yet.

I commanded my heart to calm. I forced my breathing to slow down. If I was going to face my nemesis, and my death, I would not do it like a slobbering, blithering victim, damn it. I may have been an absolute idiot coming back here, but I was no coward. And I fracking well wasn't a victim.

With one last severe talking to, I inhaled, exhaled, and slowly unwrapped myself. I turned to the woman who had slid down the wall to sit beside me.

But she wasn't there.

Wildly, I searched the pathways. My ears strained, desperate to hear any sound of approaching danger. All I could hear was my own increasing heartbeat clanging in my ears and the distant revelry of the crowd. Beside me was a bottle of water, an apple and my backpack. I grabbed the stash and shoved it into my pack. Waiting another beat, I strained to hear anyone, any noise, any threat, any thing? Nothing. Time to move.

Testing to see if the ground had sorted its skrat out and could be trusted, I edged my way up to standing. So far, so good. Keeping my hand out to steady myself, and to make sure that kret of a wall wasn't going to jump out and hit me again, I stumbled my way to the back of the building. Everything was flood-lit and there was nowhere to hide. My adrenaline kicked in and flight got back in the driver seat. I forced myself not to look into the medical rooms on my way past. Head down, I shuffle-ran, not wanting to draw any new attention but desperate to escape.

One last turn and then I was out of line of sight and into the final run of the surrounding bushland. At the corner, however, I couldn't stop my instinct to check for pursuit. A swish of fabric disappeared into the kitchenette area next to where I had collapsed. For the first time since this nightmare started, I dared to believe I was going to make it out alive. I hit the ground running and burst into the sanctuary of the night.

The day's heat had faded and at last I could let the evening's cool breeze soothe my burning head. I hid behind a cluster of shrubs, stripped out of the garishly white gown and sat in the dirt sipping icy water. In the darkness, I allowed myself a few silent tears and shot another arrow prayer of thanks to the Capricious for getting me out of this mess. And for that beautiful angel of mercy who had helped me escape the most idiotic of ideas: that I could ever return to the place my mother had offered me as a sacrifice to appease the goddess Artemis.

* * *

WHEN YOUR LIFE is on the line, there isn't much you won't do to survive. Which is funny, actually, since I'd hated life most of my early days on the street. I'd hated this city. And I'd hated my circumstances. Plenty of opportunities came along for me to end it all, but despite the pathetic "victim" identity I wore, I still wanted to live.

First thing I did was step out of that useless headspace. As much as I hated my mother, I had to give credit where it was due: I got more than my looks from the woman. She had clawed her way to the top of the ladder in her industry by sheer willpower, cunning, and smarts. I was her daughter, so I could, and had, matched her at every turn. And I tell you what, she and the Enforcers still hunted me, but I had evaded her, them, and everyone else.

I was no victim; I was a survivor.

But I missed my dad. So much. Where my mother had cultivated me, my dad had loved me. Understood me. Chalk and cheese they'd said, but we'd fit. His absence was a never-healing wound. I hadn't seen him since the night my mother had deceived him and tried to sacrifice me. He'd never have gone along with it.

* * *

THAT NIGHT WAS STILL A BLUR, but I did remember the swell of nausea, the pounding ache behind my eyes and the all-consuming fear. I'd managed to get out of the straps and off the table. Road base sliced my hands and I fought against the robe I'd been dressed in. Tangled in it, I couldn't crawl—I was just as restrained as I had been on the table in the medical rooms.

A wall of hopelessness and frustration collapsed on top of me. But I'd be damned and dead if I gave up. And I wasn't done yet. Gathering the volume of the robe in one hand, I continued crawling, bare-butt and vulnerable, knees bloodied but the pain dimmed by the drugs they'd given me and the desperate urge to escape. To live.

And, just like tonight, ten months later, I'd made my way into the shelter of the surrounding forest and hidden. That night, I didn't stop at the dumpster, I crawled deep into the scrub and kept going until my body collapsed and I physically couldn't move.

Later, I awoke stinking of vomit and sticky from dried blood and dirt. Not a great start to my new life. But at least I wasn't naked: I had the robe.

I guess we could all trash talk The Shelter. But I tell you what, when I stumbled in there, the cold shower, the clothes and the bed on offer were luxuries I would forever be grateful for. The only thing I had in my possession that night was that wretched acolyte gown.

No way was I keeping tonight's gown. Slipping back into my old smelly clothes, I folded the robe and left it near the bin. I made my way back towards my hideout outside the city gates by way of the external ring-road that hugged Sardis's low side.

Keeping to the shadows, I stopped by the old tip to see what they were up to. This place was in the process of being transformed into a garden paradise. The whole city had an upgrade after The Quake, but none as amazing as here. I couldn't investigate during the day, but at night I was a free agent. The gate was closed but it was only intended to keep cars out, so I took my daily... nightly stroll around the land-scaped property, washed in the stream leading to the huge pool of water at the bottom of the garden, lay on the grass and watched the stars, somehow confident the Catchers wouldn't find me here.

But they might find my friends if I didn't get a move on.

Farewelling the garden, I crossed the road to my home: the shanty town locals referred to as The Wreckage. Unlike the tip across the road, and the rest of the city, it'd never been repaired after The Quake. Out here, outside the wall, we were all non-citizens. We didn't count. Which is why this was prime hunting ground for the Temple Catchers. Some here, though, weren't capable of watching, or guarding themselves.

I slipped through the broken window of the first house and crept through the pitch-black rooms. At the back, where part of the roof was missing, I heard shuffling and mutterings. Using barely a whisper, I breathed, "Hello?"

A rush of movement, steps lurched, arms came at me and wrapped me in a fierce vice. "Hello. Hello. Hello. Late. Late. Late. Hello."

Prising his arms from around my neck, I tried to calm my friend. "It's okay, Richard. I'm sorry I'm late. But I am here now and you're safe. I'll keep watch."

I waited till his fear ebbed and his beautiful, innocent, good nature returned. He went back to his spot directly under the hole in the roof and lay down in the circle of moonlight on the worn, filthy carpet of the dilapidated house. Petrified that another quake would trap him inside a building, Richard only felt safe under the opening. But, even more terrified of the Catchers, he needed to be able to hide. I left Richard and went in search of my other friends to let them know I was here, and they were safe.

Here's another life lesson I learned pretty quick on the street: you might think your circumstances are skrat, but compared to others doing it tough, you're good as gold.

3

ALARIO: RETURN

I stood at a wall of windows scanning the world stretched out below me. Flashing lights pulsed in colours that bent reality and denied comprehension. From my vantage point, I could see most of the city below. And over the whole lot, Dark disfigured creatures scaled walls and infested lives like a virus on steroids. Climbing... crawling over themselves, to taste, take, tease and steal. In Sardis you could find the height of human depravity and the depths of human despair. The city screamed gaudy extravagance whilst exposing its depraved intentions, leaving nothing to the imagination.

I hated this city. I don't know how she lived here... in this infested wasteland...

"It's good to have you here, Al." Her voice echoed around her apartment, making it hard to pinpoint her exact location. This haven, pure and clean, clear of clutter, was a reflection of her: classically classy; warmth camouflaged by minimalistic sharp lines.

Wordlessly, in the muted lighting, I watched as she made her way over to me from the open-plan kitchen. I steeled myself and finally swallowed my pride, trying not to choke in the process. "Listen, Cissa, thanks for letting me stay. I don't want to put you out, but..."

"I know, I know, you had to... *finally* get out of Philadelphia." She didn't try to hide the snark.

"I don't want to fight, Cissa. Not tonight. I'm spent and I know you're done-in, too." I didn't have it in me to pick at old war-wounds right now. I wasn't doing a very good job of digesting the truth. For just over three years I'd been wrapped up in caring for my best mate, Jonathan, and his girl, Ruby, but I'd just been given my final marching orders. He was in a new relationship with Daisy, a young woman living at Sanctuary, and was moving on to the next chapter in his life. He had made it pretty clear that I should too.

It was pathetic really. He'd been telling me since I was seventeen to grow a pair and man up. Said I had responsibilities, commitments, made promises, yada, yada, yada, something about pulling my head out of my backside and starting to live in the real world.

So here I was, cut loose without a cause or a purpose. A skin tag on the rear end of life. I still had my job—alongside my estranged wife, the other half of Black & Light Architectural Designs—but I could do that anywhere, half the time with my eyes closed and only one hand on the keyboard. But I mustn't be doing too bad a job. Our buildings hadn't failed in The Quake that wiped out most of the region. But I guess that's why we charged the big bucks. We built with substance.

"Hello?" Cissa stood in front of me, holding out a tall glass of something cold.

"Sorry, what were you saying?" I took the glass from her and focused on the woman in front of me. Still a knockout at forty-four. Fit, tall, and breathtaking. A total contrast to the cesspit she called home.

"I said, you're welcome to stay for as long as you need... or want." She dropped her eyes and played with the condensation pebbling on the side of her glass. "What are your plans?" Before I could answer she continued, "I don't mean to pry, I know it's none of my business. But seriously, you can stay as long as you want."

"Thanks, Cissa. I mean it. I'm happy to pay rent, help ou—"

"How about doing me a favour instead?" The gleam in her eyes should have had me running for the door. Living on the street or going back to Philadelphia to face Jonathan's wrath... worse still, Daisy's... anything would be better than what was brewing behind those emerald eyes.

"I'm almost too scared to ask. Do I want to know? And will it involve donating a vital organ or major limb?"

She roared with laughter. "Worse. Father and Mother are hosting a charity ball, and I'm expected. I want you to be my plus-one." At the look of complete shock and fear on my face she raced on, laughter still evident but dissolving to reveal... vulnerability? Nerves? "Harry will be there." Again, she dropped her eyes and, for the first time in... eons, intentionally or not, the mask came off. Vulnerability was her lethal weapon. She only released when it was life or death. Usually requiring my life to save her from death. But she knew I was power-less against it.

I gulped down my drink, coughed as the bubbles burned my throat and tried to find the cojones Jonathan accused me of not having. "Sure. I can do that." We both knew I was lying. But I'd give it my best shot. At the end of the day, there was nothing I wouldn't do for this woman.

In a rare display of affection—public or otherwise—she hugged me and whispered in my ear. It was so quiet, I was not sure she intended me to hear. "Thank you, Al." She kissed my cheek. "Welcome home... husband."

* * *

"I DON'T WANT to rush you, I know you're doing me a favour, but seriously, Al, if you don't get your butt into gear and get yourself out here, we're going to be late. We will never live it down. You know Mother."

I was ready. Had been for a while. It wasn't that hard: shower, shave and don the monkey suit she'd supplied. It may have been one of my old ones, but I doubted it. Knowing the hubbub we were heading to, and the war zone we were entering, there was no way Cissa would have dressed me in anything but the newest and latest.

I wasn't dragging my feet to annoy her. Or even to delay the inevitable. I was just trying to figure out... what now? Where did I go from here? Not Cissa's apartment, or even this hellish dinner event, but here? Now? I was lost. I still had my business... our business. But I needed to figure out who I was when I was no longer caring for Jonathan and Ruby.

The door opened and soft lighting silhouetted the perfection of my wife. "Al? Are you okay? I don't want to rush you... but I need to rush you. Our lives will not be worth living if we leave it any later. Please don't tell me you've changed your mind. Anything, I'll give you anything, pardon everything, if you come with me." Her flawless form glided across the carpeted floor; she dropped to her knees and rested her hands on my thighs. She looked up at me and I almost fell into the bottomless pools of her eyes. "Al?"

I traced a finger lightly across her cheek. All doubts and uncertainties momentarily locked away. "Ready when you are."

Cissa let me take her elbow as we exited the limo and walked the red carpet into the hideously extravagant event. I didn't even try to figure out which charity this was supposed to be in aid of. It was all a joke. Well, I'm sure it wasn't, for those who received the dregs leftover after the bill from tonight's excesses. With a mild case of PTSD, I remembered the training Cissa had given me in the early years of our marriage. "Eyes ahead. Avert your gaze from the camera flashes. If someone calls your name"—they never did—"turn, smile, raise your hand and keep walking. Do not stop moving. If you get flustered, turn in and pretend to whisper in my ear. I have your back. Just keep walking until we're inside."

I was grateful for the rain falling in a soft mist. It meant the least ardent photographers stayed home and, despite the inadequate shelter of an awning constructed last minute, we had an excuse to hurry along the red carpet. In the relative safety of the foyer, Cissa looked me in the eye—her heels were so high that I was lucky I didn't have to look up to meet her gaze. "You did well, Al." She leaned in and brushed her lips across my cheek. It was so brief and light, I may have imagined it.

"I had a good coach." I smiled back, releasing her elbow and resting my hand on the small of her back. She let me guide her to the main doors where the usher was ready to take us to our places. As was the expected custom, we were seated with Cissa's parents on the main table. Not to put Douglas and Babel Chalmers on the head table would have been professional and social suicide, whether they were hosting or not. There was only one way you could make it in this city… region… state, and that was with the Chalmers' blessing. They were even on first-name terms with the Gerent. That sick kret. At least they didn't run in the same social circles; they had that going for them.

Harry rose as we approached the table. "Thank frack you made it, Cissa. I was thinking you were going to leave me high and dry." He embraced his sister, who was trying to tell him off for swearing. He ignored her protest and my proffered hand and embraced me as well. "It's fracking good to see you, Al." He winked at his sister before she could tell him off again. I'd always liked Harry. Apart from Cissa, he was the only good thing to come out of this family.

"Oh, how terribly cosy." The voice sent icicles though my eyeballs and a rapier through my heart… and shrivelled cojones. Babel had arrived. Half a glass of champagne in one hand and a vape in the other. Her skeletal form was draped in some form of sparkly gold fabric. I wondered if her plastic surgeon had supplied it. It let everyone get an eyeful of his work.

"Mother." Cissa rounded the table and air-kissed her mother on both cheeks.

Harry lifted his glass toward his mother as a form of greeting.

Following Harry's lead of informal, I just nodded my head. I learned, early on, not to give the enemy a foothold. Words… your own words, were Babel's weapon of choice. "What is it, Mr Black? Cat got your tongue as well as your manhood. Naughty kitty." She challenged her daughter with a raised eyebrow.

Cissa countered with her own sweetly-delivered barb. "Where's Daddy, Mother? Did you arrive separately?" Whilst Douglas Chalmers only had one daughter—whom he adored—he struggled to contain his physical affection to just one woman.

Babel's mouth contracted, her face too pumped full of toxins for her expression to change much. Instead, her anger poured out through her eyes and bounced harmlessly off Cissa's merlot-coloured armour. I knew better than to smile, so I turned to survey the room, thereby missing Douglas's entry.

The man kissed his daughter. "Darling, so glad you could make it. Harry, my boy, good to see you." Slapped his seated son on the shoulder and turned to me. "Alario, you are looking well. How long are you in town for?"

"I'm not too sure at this point, sir. For a while, though."

Cissa returned to my side and linked her fingers through mine. This time I didn't imagine her leaning into me. Something had come over my wife and I had to admit, whilst it was hitting me for six, I was not opposed. But of course I'd made the cardinal mistake of opening my mouth and Babel made quick work of me.

"I must say it's good to see some things don't change, Alario. You are as unreliable and impotent as ever." She downed the dregs of her champagne and took another from the tray of a waiter passing by.

I ground my teeth and bit my tongue, did everything I could to stop myself showing any sign of response. It's what fed her.

"Come now, darling, that's unfair." Douglas rounded the table, air kissed his wife, then pulled her chair out and placated her by playing the gentleman. But we all heard his quiet rebuff, "And put that disgusting thing away."

"I will if you will." Babel countered by nodding her head to the starlet who made a show of walking past our table grinning like a Cheshire cat at Douglas.

The man roared with laughter and kissed his wife soundly on the cheek, "Touché, darling." A hint of colouring leaked out from under Babel's warpaint, but she conceded and put both her vape and her viper away... for now. Considering the speed with which she was downing the champagne, I suspected the asp would be released again soon in all its vitriolic glory.

Our table filled with other guests and conversation was peppered with perfectly aimed and timed sniper-barbs at Cissa from her mother.

"… little *Black* sheep, so determined to go her own way."

"… arrogance. Thinks she's better… above them… us."

"… ignorance, thinking she can achieve anything by herself…"

"… without her family name, she is nothing… hopeless…"

Each remark was made with a snide tone, increasing hostility and slurred edges.

We'd managed to pretend to ignore her until the entrees arrived. Cissa had told me one of the best ways to wound her mother was to remove her platform. So, I hunkered down in my armour and focused on Cissa to my right and another woman—the wife of someone important—to my left. As the waitstaff laid the plates on tables around the room there was a universal lull in conversation.

Babel's cue for sniper fire. "Cissa, darling, I have heard there's a new fertility program being developed in Laodicea. Apparently, you don't require a young womb or a man. Since you have neither"—her eyebrow attempted to rise in my direction—"I booked you an appointment." The alcohol not only added volume to her attack, it removed any ounce of subtlety or feigned concern.

Everyone at our table stared in open shock at the woman. The rest of the room tried very hard to look like they weren't fully invested in hearing what happened next. The gentle humming of air conditioners was the only sound in the room.

Until I pushed my chair back. "Douglas, it's been good to see you again." I nodded to Cissa's father. "Clara, it's been a pleasure." I inclined my head to the woman to my left, then stood. "Harry, I hope to catch you again soon." I shook his hand. Then looked to my wife and spoke quietly. "Cissa, you are the most amazing, independent, resilient, resourceful, creative… incredible human being I know. I respect your ability to fight your own battles. But staying at this table, and continuing to listen to the constant froth of toxins dribbling from your mother's reptilian mouth, not only condones what she says, it encourages her. I am stepping outside to get some fresh air. Let me know when you're ready to go and I'll come by and see you home."

Before I could beat a retreat with any shred of pride intact, Cissa laid a hand on my arm, warmth bursting from her eyes. "I believe a breath of fresh air sounds perfect. Perhaps a walk? Oh, I know a darling place we could grab a bite to eat?" The smile on her face could have lit up the night city.

My heart swelled. I don't know what had happened to her, but never before had she stood with me against her mother. I pulled her chair out, she kissed her brother's cheek, blew a kiss to her father, nodded to the table in general and took my offered elbow. We navigated the packed space, her tall body leaning in and clamped to my side, the only two people in the silent room. Or at least, that's how it felt.

I didn't know who this woman was and what she had done with my wife, but all of a sudden my time in Sardis wasn't looking quite so bleak after all.

4

ALARIO: MAKING PLANS

Cissa didn't release my arm as we made our way down the streets of Sardis. It was still my least favourite city, but now I had to wonder if part of that was because Cissa's family... her mother, was based here.

A more vile woman I had not met. I often caught myself staring at her to check if she had the shimmering that Jonathan had told me about in the final months before the attack in Philadelphia. They had been harassed by "Hosts", humans willingly open to the Dark, allowing demonic access to the more physical world via their own bodies. Apparently, they gave off a dark shimmer. Babel definitely gave off a dark shimmer, but I am pretty confident it was just her warped attitude rather than the Dark's direct influence.

Tonight, however, now that the light rain had ceased, the bright lights of the city reflected and shattered the darkness, giving a veneer of positivity. People still rushed around pursued by demons. Darkness still pervaded every life and aspect of this city. But for once, the woman beside me and her declaration to choose me above the rest seemed to make the vileness fade into the background. I hardly noticed or cared as we neared the heart of the Cultural District, and the crowds increased as the night's revelry unfolded.

Three years on from The Quake that not only devastated Philadelphia to the core but also Sardis and a number of other cities, there was minimal work left to do. Sardis would never need financial help from anyone, least of all the Gerent. This city prided itself on extreme wealth, evidenced by the speed with which everything within the arms of the great walls had been cleared of debris. Any buildings not capable of withstanding the devastation had been demolished and all evidence deleted post-haste, as if they'd never existed in the first place. It was almost like an air of shame hung over the now-empty cavities where beautiful, ancient relics had dominated the city for hundreds of years. Classic style, modest grandeur, ageless class... all gone, forgotten, repurposed. Another Sardisian character flaw that irked me.

The Quake was now considered ancient history after three years, much like the people, buildings and culture that fell. For now, it was all about the new: new projects on the rise and new partnerships being forged. The city and its people had moved on. Much like I had to do, too. In Philadelphia, Sanctuary was going from strength to strength as the Community of Light burrowed underground, very much alive and healthy, and Jonathan and Daisy were forging their own path with Ruby and Jet.

Since the day Jonathan and I had met, fought, and become best friends, I had taken a back seat. Nothing could compete with Jonathan's innate charisma. He had a relentless magnetic aura that he point-blank refused to turn down. Then Cissa arrived. She always commanded, and lit up, her own universe. She'd spread her wings early and escaped her mother's clutches, demanding her father send her to school in Philadelphia. Something had happened in Sardis which set her on her current course at odds with Babel.

Her father agreed and, halfway through Year Ten, Cissa waltzed into our school. It was quite a show, watching all the pubescent teens fall over themselves to be her peers... satellites... lackeys. Yet this wonder of a young woman had surveyed what was on offer and, not long after, chosen Jonathan and me to hang out with. And then, she'd selected me, above all the others, for a boyfriend.

I didn't want or need to compete with her or Jonathan. I mean, who could possibly be seen in Cissa's aura? I didn't mind. I loved them both. I was happy to stand in the background—the spotlight was definitely not for me, thank you very much. I learned early on that in the background, out of the public eye, you could get away with a great many things. I took it on myself to be their chief problem solver. Half the time they didn't even know there was a problem. And, after I saw to it, there wasn't. Bullies, the rumour mill, jealous troublemakers... none of them stood for long.

It became a bit harder to justify my actions the deeper I grew into the Light. But every now and again, a bit of forceful self-defence on behalf of others was a sign of brotherly love, right? And that's what we were all about. So, I figured, within reason, it was all good.

And that's why it hit like a diesel truck when those you loved and cared for didn't need you to fight for them, or stand up for them, or clear up their messes. I knew they hadn't ever really needed me. Jonathan found Laura. And Cissa didn't need anyone. A fact she proved time and again. But I felt they'd been happy to have me hang around.

Not only am I a great fighter, I am an excellent engineer for Black & Light Architectural Designs. That's not pride speaking. It's a fact. I bring skilled and natural insight to assist the creative genius that is Cissa and her concepts. But this job, or role, or day filler was not my motivation. It paid the bills... abundantly. But it wasn't my purpose. To help hold and stay the fort for them, was.

"Al?" Cissa shook my arm.

"Sorry, what were you saying?"

"I asked if you were going to join me on this walk, or whether I was just a tether."

"I've been thinking—"

"I can hear." Before I could get impatient with her for interrupting me, I caught sight of the light-hearted tease flitting across her face.

I gave her shoulder a slight shove with mine. Then, with eyes ahead, I blurted my idea before I had a chance to second-guess myself... or even fully think it through. "I'd like to stay and work from our Sardis offices for a while." I waited for a response, a jibe, a retort, some form of snark. But nothing came.

So, with eyes locked ahead so as to steer us through the growing crowds meandering the streets, I continued. "And if it's okay with you, I'd like to stay at your place." I shifted my eyes to gauge her response. Her body hadn't given me any clues as to what she was thinking. She even hid her face from me by feigning interest in the footpath just in front of our feet, her short, bobbed hair falling forward to hide her face, trusting me completely to guide her through the pedestrian traffic.

I waited a block and still she had not responded. *Idiot.* I had taken her stand against her family, her body language, her attention this evening as a sign that things could be different. *Idiot.* Of course it was all for show. Once again, I was a pawn in her ongoing war with her mother. It was all a show. Just like our marriage. I am confident the only reason she married me was to annoy Babel.

The only reason she stayed married to me was to make it harder for other men to encroach on her space. And harder for Babel to line up others to take her daughter's hand. I was such a bleeding fool.

I couldn't help shaking my head. My frustration at myself had me being a little less subtle navigating the crowd. A good shoulder barge right now would really hel—

"Al." Cissa pulled me up short by planting her feet and causing me to spin. We stood as an immoveable island in the middle of the hideousness of the humanity swimming around us.

I didn't growl like I wanted to. I counted to three then replied. "Yes?"

"I said, that would be great. I would really like that."

"Oh?" I searched her face for a hint of falsehood. I might live in the background but that didn't mean I was blind. I knew this woman and could read her like a book. Even though we'd lived apart almost as much as we'd lived together, I could always read her. Right now, she opened her face to me and hid nothing. Her eyes were a touch glassy and they dared me to see her without the mask. "You mean it?"

"Yes, Al. I mean it. I want you here with me." Her gaze didn't waver. "Things have been really tough here and, I won't lie, I am drowning." Her voice hinted a crack, but the mask stayed off. "I don't know how much longer I can stand on my own. Quite honestly, I feel the only thing holding me up are all the opposing forces coming at me from every side. I could really use another person in my corner." The glassiness evolved into pools.

There was a roar building in my ears and a heat burning in my chest. To see her so vulnerable sparked a furnace of rage. But then I doused it with a dose of reality—*you weren't here. You were never here; you were too busy looking after Jonathan and Ruby.* "I didn't think you needed me. Or even wanted me. I thought I cramped your style."

The pools filled and a tear escaped, but no expression invaded her face. "I have always needed you. I have always wanted you. But you always chose Jonathan. I wasn't going to beg, Alario. I will never beg you to come home. To be with me. You are a free man to do as you please. I had hoped at some point it would please you to be with me. With. Your. Wife." The mask was still down and raw hurt and brokenness cracked her stoicism and my heart.

I pulled her into my arms and pinned her to me. She was never one to demonstrate personal feelings publicly. But on that street, in the middle of the city swimming in Darkness, Cissa allowed me to hold her as she wept silently. Her hands clenched the front of my suit and her face burrowed into my neck, her tears soaking my shirt.

Forgive me for my selfishness and bratty attitude. I have been so wrong. Forgive me. Right here and now I vow to never make this mistake again. I was, and will always be, to my dying day, my wife's wall and shield.

My armour flashed and ignited with new life and fire. Cissa inhaled and stepped back. Her eyes were red and swollen, but all the more beautiful for those slight imperfections. "What just happened?" All openness disappeared and the mask was back on in an instant. She stepped away and looked around, her eyes ranging for the enemy, readying for a fight. Our Guards didn't move, they—hers and mine—both just looked to me, nodded their heads and... smiled?

"What? What was that? Al, what's going on?"

Now that the heat of the moment had passed I felt like a bit of a goose. But like a dog mauling a bone, she locked on. Her focus narrowed and she stepped in closer. I couldn't look her in the eye.

"What did you just do?" The accusation was tinted with fear.

"I... ah... just made a promise to the Light."

She looked to our Guards. They both nodded and smiled at her. She looked back at me with squinted, calculating eyes. "And what exactly did you just promise, Al?" Not only was her mask back on, but her cold, hard, facade was locked and loaded. This was the Cissa I knew. The self-reliant, completely capable, uncontainable, fully independent, Cissa.

Immediately I was tempted to go on the defensive. But as a breeze ghosted down the street, the dampness of my collar sent chills down my neck. This woman had been brave enough to show me her brokenness. I had the choice of having the shortest-lived vow in the history of... forever, or I could once again dig deep and find the cojones I needed to own, to live in this world beside my wife. I stood tall, took Cissa's hands and returned her fierce gaze. The look of shock on her face almost made me laugh. But I am not suicidal so, I didn't. "I made a vow to the Light."

She waited for me to go on. But I made her work for it.

"And?" She didn't stamp her foot, but I could see it was taking extreme self-control not to.

I smiled at her frustration. "And, I think He was happy with me." Using my eyes I indicated my emblazoned pale-blue armour and the Guards who had returned to scouting the perimeter.

"And?"

"I will do what I can, with the Light's help, to fulfil my vow." I leaned forward and brushed a kiss against her lips. This time I didn't hold back the laughter at her shock. Before she could respond, I swung my arm around her shoulder and steered her down the street. "Now, where are we going to get food? I'm starving."

"Al." She tried to stop me and plant her feet again. My wife is strong... and determined. But it turns out that I am stronger and can be just as—if not more—determined. "Come on, eat first, talk later. We have all the time in the world."

I did let her stop me this time as she stepped in front of me. "Do we?" She searched my face. "Do we really have all the time in the world?"

I kissed her again, mainly because I had rediscovered just how much I liked doing that, then whispered, "Yes."

Back in Cissa's apartment, we sat on the couch looking out over the city below us. Empty take-out boxes littered the table and we each sat in mutual, silent contemplation. Cissa's head was resting on the back of the couch, her eyes were closed, and for the first time in years, I took the time to study her. To really take her in. Even in her casual wear for around the house she looked like she would light up a runway. The woman was stunning. Once again, I pinched myself. How was it possible that she wanted me? That there was room in her life for me?

"You're thinking awfully loud over there." She didn't open her eyes or move her head.

"I was just thinking of Jonathan's friends from Sanctuary and their plans to come here."

"Liar."

"Quite. But it is something we could help with."

Cissa rolled her head and curled up on the end of the couch to face me. "I have already offered an apartment. The tenants are leaving next week. As soon as the cleaners have gone through, they can move in."

"I appreciate that. But I was thinking of the two guys. You know they pretty much built that place. I mean they had help, but the kid... it was all his idea. The older guy was fully on board and brought some of the younger ones on as well. They had two pros onsite, teaching and mentoring, but... there's potential there. Sardis could really use that kind of initiative for the outer suburbs."

She sat up, took a sip of her drink, and, as she placed it back on the side table, I saw deep dark circles growing under her eyes. "Are you thinking of our program?"

Concern for her tiredness started pushing the thread of thinking from my mind. "Yes, but we can talk about it later. You look exhausted. Are you okay?"

She smiled a sad smile. "Yes." Raggedly inhaling and dropping back into the elbow of the couch she confessed, "I do find time out, with family… people… exhausting. I will be fine, but I need to spend time in the cave"—she raised a hand and waved vaguely to indicate her dimly lit apartment, soft jazz playing in the background, but then let it flop back onto the couch—"to recover."

Fearing I had overstepped my welcome, I raced to stand. "Do you need me to go? I can find somewhere el—"

"Al." The utter exhaustion and deepening circles stopped me faster than if she'd hit me. "I want you here. I find peace in your company. Please stay. But excuse me, I just need to rest." Her eyes fell shut again and she didn't move. I feared she may have fallen asleep already. But the groan that escaped her body as she attempted to heave herself from the couch had me racing to her side.

"Here, let me help you." Sitting next to her, I wrapped an arm around her waist, and together we stood. I walked her down the hallway to her bedroom. Soft, warm lighting illuminated the way. Deep, lush carpet cushioned our feet and with Cissa's arm around my shoulders, and my arm firmly around her waist, she let me help her to her room. I sat her in the neo-classical black-lacquered armchair angled toward the wall of windows and pulled back the bedcovers on the side that had a table with a clock, papers, pens, a glass of water and a box of tissues. I gathered her up and walked her to bed, laid her down and pulled the blankets over her.

The external wall of the room was completely made of glass. I knew for a fact it was timed to block out the rising the sun, but for now, I stood and contemplated Sardis as it pulsed with nightlife.

Cissa's whisper wrapped around me like a promise. "Stay with me?"

I climbed behind her and lay on top of the covers and held her to me. Together we looked out the window and, from this angle, all we could see were the heavens revealed in all their glory.

The weight of the night settled on me and my heart squeezed with the truth I had to confess. If I had any hope of fulfilling my vow, of starting life with my wife in this place, and seeing how the Light would use us, I had to speak before I exploded from the pressure. I was a coward, I admit it. But lying at her back, looking out to the night, it was the perfect opportunity.

Please help me do this right.

"You still awake?"

5

ALARIO: THE CONFESSION

Cissa squeezed my hand wrapped around her middle.

"I need to... I want to... apologise." Her body froze and I raced on before my conviction faltered. "For the past twelve years, I have been selfish... and it has skewed my thinking."

Cissa rolled to face me. It was best. I'd have much preferred confessing to the back of her head, but I acknowledged this needed to be said facing my victim and judge.

"I always saw my place... my purpose in helping... supporting." All of a sudden my mouth dried, I tried to swallow. It didn't help. "First, I was Jonathan's prop. Then yours."

Cissa's hand cupped my cheek, then ran down my shoulder and rested on my waist.

"From the moment you walked onto the school grounds, like everyone else I was in your orbit. But you chose me." I ran my dry tongue over my dry lips. "The invisible guy at the back of the room. You made me visible—hated, but seen. They all thought it was a joke." She went to speak, but I shook my head and continued.

"I was king of the world. I was ten foot tall and solid titanium. Then, when we turned eighteen, you wanted to get married. I wasn't an idiot. There was no way I was going to say no."

I couldn't hold back the memory of the day I'd won the jackpot. There was no place big enough to contain my joy... or my head. I was "The Man". "You made me brave enough to take on your mother." Just thinking of the woman gave me an involuntary shiver. "But we were kids. We didn't even know who we were as individuals, let alone as a couple. Wait. No. *I* was a kid who didn't know who I was. *You* knew exactly who you were and what you were doing." I swallowed again and brushed a stray strand of black silk from her face.

"I came to believe you married me to skitch your mother off. Then stayed married to keep yourself legally unavailable for any of the other puppets she wanted to politically align with." Again, she made to protest and I touched her lips with my finger. "I believed the gossip. What would a woman like you see in a boy like me? What could a woman like you want with a boy like me? What could a boy like me offer a woman like you? The answer? Nothing." She was shaking her head, but I continued. "University was a blur. Starting our business was all-consuming. We worked well as partners. When it came to design, we were a perfect match. But always at the back of my mind, all I heard on repeat was, 'Nothing.'"

I swallowed again. I was on a roll now and nothing could stop me. I had to get this out. "I watched you move through the world, deal with people, problem solve, create deals, work around the clock, take on new challenges... challengers. Nothing stopped you or stood in your way. You were... are... irrepressible. Amazing. Explosive. Creative. Dynamic. And I just couldn't see how you needed me. Yes, as a partner in the business, to do my side of the work, but as a partner in life...?"

I shrugged my shoulder. "I felt useless. So, I started to look at who might need me. And I focused on Jonathan." Her tightened mouth and raised eyebrow that often accompanied his name almost made me laugh. It was inevitable and, I suspect, a Pavlovian response.

But that was my fault. It sobered me and I continued, "And that was wrong. I was wrong. If I felt I wasn't needed I should have talked to you about it. I... should have done something about it. I didn't talk to you, and I am sorry. I left you, and I am sorry. I have let you down and forsaken my wedding vows, and I am sorry. I have let you down as your husband and life-partner. And I am sorry." With each confession more weight pressed on my heart and more air squeezed out of my lungs. More heat burned my eyes, and more emotion choked my voice. "You know how much I love fighting." A ghost of a smile graced both our faces. "Yet, the most important fight of all I walked away from and surrendered. I didn't fight for us. I didn't consider you, and I am sorry. I was wrong. Please, forgive me."

Cissa had disappeared behind my tears. I sniffed and brushed my face on my shoulder, took a shuddering breath and finished. "If you could... would... forgive me, could... would... you consider letting me try again? Would you let me please try to do better and prove that you weren't wrong when you picked me?" I shut down then and folded in on myself. I had been so fracking weak.

Cissa's arms came around me and through her own tears she sniffed a laugh. "Oh, Al, I'm never wrong." At that we both laughed. She was right. To a point. Mostly, Cissa was always right. Except when she was monumentally wrong. Raising my face with her hands, Cissa laid the softest kiss on my forehead. "The Light has been working in me too, my love. And... I, too, need to ask for your forgiveness."

Everything stopped. My brain. My heart. My breathing. "What?"

Again, she laughed. "I was... am so arrogant. I know this. The Light is working on me to help me break the facade. I am gifted, intelligent and totally capable." Coming from anyone else, in any other situation, this would have sounded high-handed. But it was the simple truth stated without flourish or self-aggrandisement. "Not only has the Light blessed me in this way, I was granted the boon of being born into a very wealthy family, and cultivated in a culture of entitlement."

I couldn't hold back my scoff. That was putting it mildly, but also understating the struggle she lived through. With an arch of her eyebrow, I ceded and let her continue. "I grew up believing I didn't need anyone but my intellect and my family. But then I learned the truth about my family and the fallibility of my intellect. As you know, this is when I met the Light and ran away from my mother. And met you. You and Jonathan in your armour, not needing anyone around you, not needing to be pumped up by peer hot-air, acceptance or protocols. You were free. Just living life and loving it."

She paused and we both slumped back. I suspect she was, with me, meandering along memory lane through those days of wild abandon and fun. Nothing terribly illegal, just hijinks, testing boundaries and mainlining testosterone, and a few too many fights on the side. I looked over to Cissa and saw my smile mirrored on her face. "Good days."

"Heady days. I wanted to capture it forever. Never leave."

"So, you married me."

Her smile was sad, and warm, and true, and wry. "I married you. Loved it. Hated it. Wanted it. Didn't know what to do with it. So, went to my default and the walls came up."

"We were so young."

"So naive," she said.

"So in love," I replied.

Another pause, another shared smile. Cissa took a long, slow, deep breath, rolled back onto her side and took my hands. "I shut you out. I knew you and Jonathan were inseparable. It was a package deal. But he had the world—I figured I could have a part of you." Cissa stopped my imminent protest with a quick shake of her head. "I wasn't going to schedule time with you. Like a child in joint custody, work out an arrangement with Jonathan for which weekends and holidays I got to see you. I wasn't going to demean myself by begging my husband to be with me. I figured if you didn't come willingly, I didn't want you."

She dropped her face and took three deep breaths, then looked me in the eye. "I never told you how hurt I was. I never communicated how I felt. I wanted you to read my mind, to understand my feelings, to fill the gaping hole and love the sadness and loneliness out of me. And when you couldn't do that, I surmised you didn't really love me."

Pain pierced my heart like a lightning rod. Gobsmacked. No thoughts formed. I had no idea. Cissa ran a hand over my frozen face. "That was horribly unfair and completely unrealistic of me. Like I said, naive." She took my hand again. "The more incapable you were of reading my mind, the thicker I built the wall."

"Why didn't you say? Why did you stay?"

"Pride kept me silent. Love kept me put. I love you, Al. I want to love you. I am constantly choosing to love you."

Again, my fried brain was incapable of processing thought.

"You are an amazingly loyal, strong, fierce... good-looking man. There is depth and integrity in you that is rare and worth fighting for. Your love and obedience to the Light inspires me. You make me laugh like no one else can. I am so proud to have you by my side in our business, and I would like to have you by my side again in my life. And to be honest, your passion for battle is... stirring." The hint of a heated smile climbed into her eyes.

If she kept this up, I would need a lobotomy. I was struggling to process anything she was saying. All that kept cycling through my brain was: *I had no idea.*

Cissa laughed and gently closed my jaw with her finger. "But for that to happen, I need to apologise for shutting you out. For expecting you to be perfect; to fulfil the Light's role in my life, not my husband's role. For presuming you could read my mind." Tears had worked their way through her voice and onto the pillow, but still her words were clear enough for me to hear. "Can you forgive me?" A deep, ragged inhale then, "Do you want to do life with me again, as my husband, by my side?"

I searched her face. She wasn't breathing. Her bottom lip disappeared between her teeth. Was she genuinely fearful I would turn her down? I pulled her to me and pinned her to my chest. She released a heavy sob, and I rubbed circles into her back and slowly rocked her. I just couldn't believe the revelation. There was so much to process. Like I said, all I could think was, I had no idea. No idea what she'd thought, felt, suffered...

"Al!" Pain broke through my musings, Cissa was gently... but not too gently pinching my chest.

I pushed her back a little. "What?"

She shook her head. "You are not a cruel man. Absent-minded at times, but not cruel."

"I think we need some ground rules here, Cissa. First rule, use words. What are you talking about?"

She huffed, laughed, gently pushed me with both hands and wriggled herself up to sitting. I joined her, genuinely confused. "Al, I asked you a question. Two, in fact. And you haven't answered me."

"Yes, I did."

"No, you didn't. You hugged me and rubbed my back… which was very nice, thank you, but it was not an answer."

"Yes, it was. I wouldn't do that if I didn't love you and forgive you and want to start again." Fresh tears ran down her beaming face. "And anyway, you never answered my questions either… with words."

She tilted her head, her focus on the corner of the ceiling. Then with wide eyes and her hand covering her open mouth, she looked back at me and laughed. "I am so sorry, Al. How are we ever going to make this work? We are as bad as each other."

"So, just confirming"—I shuffled back against the headboard and pulled Cissa beside me, my arm around her shoulders, her hand on my thigh—"we are going to have a go at being married like regular people. Living in the same home. Doing life together. And just to be super clear, we've both stuffed up, we're both sorry, and we're both forgiven"—I looked her in the eye—"right?"

Cissa bowed her head and nodded, tears splotching her dark, silk shorts. Leaning over, she grabbed several tissues, handed me a bunch, blew her nose and wiped her face, then ducked back under my arm, still with her head bowed. When she was ready, she tapped my leg and I continued. "First thing I think we need to do is ask the Light for help."

She nodded.

So I began, "Thank You for breaking our walls and hearts and bringing us to this place of mutual readiness to start again. We don't know what You have in store for us in this place… or any place, but we ask that You help us work out our part in Your plan. Help us work out our way of being married, of being a team, a partnership in life, in

You. Show us how to communicate, humble us to connect, enable us to forgive, gift us strength and grace for each other's failings, and please... please help us keep You at the centre. So, be it."

"So be it."

We sat in silence and let the peace pummelling into the room have the priority and prominence it deserved. Wave after wave of love, and peace, and forgiveness, and grace pulsed into me. I felt as if the chains that had been holding me down for years had cracked and fallen away. Tears flooded from my eyes, and even though I still held Cissa, I felt alone in that moment, being completely held and comforted by the Light. I had come home and I was incapable of anything but over-whelming, un-communicatable, incomprehensible gratitude.

The moment ebbed and, in unison, Cissa and I inhaled and exhaled deeply—washed, wrung-out and exhausted. I shuffled round until I faced her and took her hand. "So, Cissa?" She tilted her head. "I think you and me should go out. Like boyfriend, girlfriend."

Her body collapsed sideways, and the deepest, richest laughter filled every corner of the room as I recited her original declaration of our relationship, twenty-nine years ago when we were in Year Ten. She sat up and looked at me. And nodded, yes.

"We'll take it slow. Learn to do this properly, as adults, as friends, as partners. We'll talk. And listen. And we'll petition the Light... a lot."

She nodded, yes.

6

ALARIO: THORN IN THE SIDE

"Remind again me why you choose to participate in this ridiculous farce of Community." I tried to keep my voice down. I didn't want to start a fight I couldn't finish. And surrounded by about seventy people who would find my words offensive, I tried for discreet. The garishness and excesses of the city leached into every corner of this Community gathering. From the clothing people wore to their language—body and verbal—nothing was tasteful, let alone reflecting the Way of the Light.

Sure, they were generous and had a great reputation for helping people, especially after The Quake: clearing, housing, feeding, relocating, helping to find jobs, donating to the hospital, aged, widows, orphans, those living with mental health challenges, stray animals, picking up litter. You name it, they'd done it. Their efforts had been noted and gratefully received throughout the city. So much so, they had a reputation for being generous, gracious and giving. But nothing about their current words or interactions reflected the Light.

"Look around you, Al." Cissa hadn't released my hand since leaving the car. Most people used free public transport to get here, but since I liked to be able to make a quick and convenient getaway, today I had chosen to drive. Cissa used our combined hands to pull me close and continued to whisper. "How few are there here who represent the Light in truth. If I were to leave, who would stand to challenge those whose minds are closed, whose hearts are sleeping? There are so few of us, I will not abandon this sinking ship until I am the last standing. And even then, I will not abandon hope. If I do not stand for Him in His house, who will?"

"But Cissa, to what end? What do you hope to achieve? How long have you been coming? What has changed by your presence?"

Anger? Frustration? flashed across her face and the grip on my hand tightened to painful. I liked to think it was not intentional… an outworking of her emotion rather than a true desire to hurt me. "What can I do? I am one of so few. Should I just leave them to their certain judgement?"

Our conversation had risen past a whisper, and we were drawing more than a few hostile glares. I tried diplomacy. "We will finish this later. I am not judging you; I just want to understand." The grip on my hand slackened to comfortable and Cissa's shoulders relaxed. Once our spectators' attention had been snagged by other gossip-inducing behaviour, I leaned closer and continued our private conversation. "Tell me again why they meet in the Temple of Artemis, not in their own building?"

"The High Council feel it's safer to hide from the Gerent in the shelter of 'recognised' religions. Whilst we have built a quality reputation in the sight of the citizens, we are still in the Gerent's grey area. We definitely have the money to buy our own place, but…." Cissa looked me in the eye, grief eclipsing everything… *Philadelphia*.

Philadelphia.

Shock waves were still reverberating around the region. The Gerent was to the Community of Light what The Quake was to this corner of the world: indiscriminate carnage. The tyrant was using my beloved city, Philadelphia, as a poster child for those who stepped out of line. Thing was, the man was so deranged, his lines were as haphazard as a child's game of pick-up sticks. But it was working. He had everyone second-guessing and falling over themselves to look like "good citizens".

But it was also working for the true Community of Light: those who understood they had to decide. None of us could stand with a foot in each world anymore. We had to pick a side and back it all the way: Light or Dark. Only the most ardent of believers had the cojones to stay the course.

There was movement at the front and a hush settled across the crowd. We both turned and watched as the performance began. I meant what I said, I was not judging her for being here, but neither was I making any effort to belong to this group of actors. It frustrated me no end that she just kept putting herself in this situation where she was the odd one out, the one who suffered because she wouldn't bend. She refused to comply, and she refused to leave. Stoic, solid and stubborn, she was the thorn in their side that no amount of picking or digging could dislodge.

Once again, I was filled with equal parts frustration and admiration for my wife and the battle she waged. But I just couldn't see the sense of it. There didn't seem to be any foreseeable outcome or conceivable result to her solo assault on the mountain of the institution… and its witless members. And yes, even I had enough sense not to mention that in their—or Cissa's—hearing. But seriously, I struggled to see the point of her needless suffering. There was so much more she could be—

"Al." An uncomfortable squeeze of my hand and a raised voice in my ear had me back in the present. "We're finished. Are you ready to go?" Cissa tilted her head and assumed a wholly-fake look of innocence. "Or would you like to stay to meet and mingle?"

My repulsion was instinctive and demonstrated before I thought to mask it. Which made her laugh all the more raucous, which had more people staring. "Ah…" I looked around at our immediate audience who were eagerly awaiting my response to their invitation. "As enticing as that sounds, dear, I do believe we have another engagement"—I tapped the pocket where my phone was—"which we are late for." I gave my own look of mock disappointment, nodded to the group, then spun my wife to face the door and exited the building post-haste.

"You know the Light frowns on untruths… *dear.*"

"I was not lying. We do have an engagement. I have it in my diary." I retrieved my phone, pulled up the entry for today and sent it off to Cissa. She stood straighter, read the message on her phone, then grasped her waist. Genuine joy and happiness danced through her laugh and dug its tendrils even deeper into my soul. Right then, I decided I would do everything I could to make that happen more often. The world needed a lot of things, and one of those was laughter… Cissa's laughter.

"We had better make a move then. I would hate to keep the coffee machine and daily headlines waiting."

"Don't forget the couch and sound system. It's a full meeting of the board, all members are required to be present and accounted for."

"Well, it would be irresponsible to keep them waiting any longer." Cissa wrapped her arm around my waist, and I placed an arm around her shoulders.

I knew she thought it was all a joke, but I had learned a very important lesson since we'd been reconnecting after the battle of Philadelphia. My wife shone brightly in public. She appeared to be an inexhaustible force not to be reckoned with… and she was. But it came at a cost. Behind closed doors she had allowed me to see the price she paid.

Cissa needed her battlegrounds. She was a passionate woman who lived life fully, embraced causes wholeheartedly, and gave everything in her to make a stand. All the more so, on behalf of those who couldn't speak for themselves. But she was also a solitary being. Giving passionately, publicly, socially, drained her. The deeper the passion, the greater the cost.

I had first seen the savage results three months ago after the battle in Philadelphia. As the Gerent entered through the front gates of Sanctuary, we took off out the back. We laid low, watched what happened to our friends and were torn. Both of us were desperate to go back. To stand with them. To continue the fight beside them. But a Warrior had blocked our path and told us to stay hidden. Our fight would continue but, for now, our place was out of the spotlight. That would change, but our long-term mission would be compromised if we revealed ourselves at that point.

So, broken and exhausted, we watched in sheltered silence as the nightmare of the kids' capture and the execution of Mary and Travis unfolded. I still couldn't think about it without fire and grief overtaking me. Under the cover of darkness, and with an escort of Warriors, we made our escape. After reclaiming our car, I drove Cissa back here to her base in Sardis to come to terms with the savagery and insanity we had witnessed, and I saw firsthand how completely she faded.

She hadn't improved with the morning and I was even more concerned. Her olive complexion was grey, her eyes sunken and listless, her body lethargic. I began to suspect she had been bitten by one of those demonic black snakes, or been poisoned, caught a virus... something... everything.

After arguing with me and convincing me not to call a doctor, she explained it was the norm. But considering the degree to which she had given over the past forty-eight hours, recovery would take a bit longer than usual. She begged me to give her a couple of days and she would improve. And she had.

Something had happened to us that day in Philadelphia. Not only had we lost dear friends, made new ones, and had our eyes opened to a new reality hurtling toward us, we had reconnected. But in a deeper sense than we had ever been connected before. A door had opened, and it was like we had both been given a shot of... something... adrenaline? I didn't know. But our lives shifted and started leaning toward each other.

I had started working out of the Sardis office more regularly. I was still visiting Jonathan and Ruby... and all of Sanctuary. But there was a pull... a compulsion... to be with Cissa. Normally I would have fought it. But I had noticed a dropping of her defences that matched the dropping of mine. So, a week ago, when Jonathan gave me my final marching orders, I wasn't as angry as I had been the last time he'd done it, when I'd delivered his skeletal, frail frame, with nothing but one of my suits, to the hopeless situation that was Sanctuary just over a year ago.

Since the battle, I had been meeting with Cissa face-to-face for business meetings rather than online. And so, the final step to join her here in Sardis… and my new home, was inevitable. We had been growing towards reconciliation since the battle. I still slept in the spare… my room. And only on bad nights, like the first night, when she was totally wiped, did she invite me to stay. I always accepted.

I'd seen the pattern of her collapse after a public event repeat itself with disturbing regularity. So now, I blocked out my schedule after every outing and made space for her to relax, implode and recover in comfort and within the safe, private, space of the cave. I wasn't blind to the fact that, if this had been an issue for her earlier in our marriage, it hadn't been nearly as bad as it was now. Something had triggered this greater response. Maybe it was fighting so hard, so long, solo.

Help me make that up to her. Show me how to be the man she needs me to be.

And I was fully aware of the compliment and trust she offered me by allowing me back in… to see her like this. It only made me reaffirm my vow to be a shield for this woman. I knew the Light was going to… was… using her in a great way. I could help by being the stay at her back and the lintel at her front and supports at her sides.

7

BALASHKA: IT IS WHAT IT IS

Down the hill, the food truck door screeched open like a violin played by an ape. It was as unwelcome as the first spears of light shattering the remnants of my sleep.

I pictured her, frozen like a garden ornament, waiting to see if the noise triggered a response. After a count, I exhaled, knowing she would have, too, as she quietly clicked the offensive door back into place. Contemplating the morning light as it gained significant victory over my thin curtains, I waited until I was confident she'd had time to vacate the premises before I stirred. Jemmy lived securely within the belief that I was clueless of her residency.

Silly girl. I knew everything that went on in my garden—my realm. She'd been sneaking in and sleeping over for months. Obviously, I'd thrust out the welcome mat. But like every offer of help, she rejected it. So, for now, I feigned ignorance whilst ensuring the food truck was stocked, clean and readily available as accommodation.

Embracing a new day filled me with great anticipation of both good and bad. My family would visit, as too would the pain. There was great beauty to immerse oneself in, as there was ugly truth. Yet, playing the market always demanded the risk of the roll. One wouldn't be a true addict if one didn't honestly believe, this time round, one would be swimming in sixes.

Tearing pain matched the suitably discordant screech of the rising roller-door of my shed. But the searing ache was eased by the glory of the morning and the warmth of welcome offered by my constant companion, Sweetie. The name suited the mutt much like one called a redhead "blue": sweet-looking she was not. Although, if one spoke of nature, then the title fit like a glove. After petting her uniquely disfigured head, and clutching my cane, we were off on our morning circuit.

I took with me the red flags that would warn regulars an outsider was to grace our presence this morning: Harry was coming by to collect my latest commission. After positioning the warnings around the perimeter of the public area, I replenished the water and snacks for my guests, two-and four-legged alike.

Whence the cloak of talent evolved, I do not know—the creation of art that is, not the purveying of food. One did not dabble when growing up. The absurdity of the thought forced a wry chuckle to burble. No, in my family, one did not fritter one's time with frivolity. If it did not make money or climb ladders—preferably using the knives you'd placed in the back of the person above—it was a worthless and unworthy pursuit. Money and status were the only commodities we dealt in.

The delicious irony of the situation was, I'd accumulated far more wealth and earning capacity with art than I ever had legally in my previous life. Far more than I needed. But in this lay the heart of the matter: what did one actually need? From personal experience I can tell you, it is far less than what one may think. The more valid question, "What is the greatest human need?" was more deserving of consideration. One thing I can assure you, it was not wealth, fame… infamy, or status. Bars, stripes, and scars had taught me this.

My home was a testimony to my newfound truth: a massive shell frugally equipped with the barest of necessities. My creativity and work reigned dictatorially over the entire space, delegating a mere quarter allotment for sleep, ablutions, and sustenance to squabble over. One area, however, that I was no miser in was light: skylights dominated the ceiling, windows embraced the walls. After ten years preserved in a specimen jar of solitary confinement cells, hospital beds and kerchiefs of grass labelled "exercise yards", I could not bring myself to recreate the experience for my home. No. Large open rooms, big open windows, and space... space... space were my oxygen.

Yet, it was from within the "specimen jar" that my conscience had no diet other than self. It was as inevitable as it was unpalatable. The acidic mirror confirmed I was a cheat and a liar, an untrustworthy, weak, and insatiably greedy human being. As a resident of the justice system, I also learned the valuable lesson that corruption, intimidation, and injustice are far less palatable on the other side of the "Entitled" line. A hard yet necessary pill to swallow for one to learn the greater lessons: compassion and forgiveness.

A visitor frequented me. How he gained access, or who he was, I could not tell you. My prolonged time in solitary confinement stripped my grip on reality with one hand whilst feeding my imagination with the other. My loneliness begged I not challenge his presence with reason and logic.

His first visit was during a prolonged stay in the infirmary. I had sustained a severe injury to my hip which had necessitated a trip, off-site, to the Ephesus public hospital. This, too, had been an ordeal of neglect, abuse and savagery. Back in the prison infirmary—exhausted from constant pain, constant abuse, constant fear—the assured knowledge that this was my new, lifelong reality consolidated my resolve. It was time to leave. By their hand or my own?

Finally, I had a say in the situation: input, a choice, a voice. The realisation and power were intoxicating. I would need to harness this rush to see the excruciating deed done. I wasn't unaware of him until he was standing next to me. His eyes arrested all thought and action. Wordless, he gently laid a hand on my hip. An internal jostle was followed by immediate release. And oh, the relief: instant weightlessness of absent pain. The swell of freedom burst the dam wall of my emotion. He sat out the tsunami—ever calm, exuding peace, tangibly present. The storm inevitably passed and eventually I could speak. "Who are you?"

"A friend." This reopened the floodgates. Loneliness was the black hole that consumed my soul, rendering my existence null and void. Yet, this "friend" indeed sat with me through the night, his hand resting on my hip. Comfort and warmth spreading out from that point of contact until I was reacquainted with the sleep bestowed only upon the young and naive. When morning arrived, the nurses noted the change and were relieved they could return me to the safety of my solitary cell.

From that point on, he became a regular feature of my life. At first, we just shared the space in silent companionship. Eventually, I discovered the courage to petition him. Might he… perhaps… remove the residual pain in my hip? Whilst I had been healed enough to leave the infirmary, it still gave me grief and made walking difficult. Not impossible, but definitely painful.

"In time, yes. I will send someone to you, and they will remove your remaining suffering. When they come, you will know they are from me. Listen to what they say."

I am not proud my behaviour resembled a petulant child. But there it was: the honest truth. When I grew tired of my sulk, he started talking about general things: life in prison, life before, hope for what was to come. It was here I had to draw a line. Those two topics were forbidden: hope and the future. Neither existed.

Speaking of the past was nothing but painful and hollow. Speaking of life inside was barren and grey. Subsequently, we spent a lot of time not speaking. But he wore me down and offered me the greatest gift— greater than the healing. The gift of moving on. The most significant stumbling block confronting me was my own self-loathing. But he offered me a treasure, the knowledge of how one could forgive oneself. I had made some monumental errors—I refused to blame others for my actions. I alone had chosen to plant my feet in the well-worn tracks of those who'd gone before me. It just so happened I was better skilled at deception, and less adept at discernment.

Letters penned in genuine remorse, with heartfelt apology and generous reimbursement, did little to make things right. Dissolving all my assets and doling everything out to pay back the multitudes I'd wronged was not enough. Volunteering all my hidden bank accounts and investments to finance recovery programs and protection software achieved naught. In the end I paid back four times what I took, and still it wasn't enough to stem the tide of hostility.

It wasn't enough for them. It was, however, enough for The Man. He said if I chose to maintain this attitude and perspective, I could move forward in peace—knowing I had done all I could to make amends. Therefore, I vowed this would be, from that point on, my life's mission.

Which brings us to here and now where I continue to make amends and do my bit to see the unseen, love the unlovable and enhance the beauty of the world's detritus. Because, now, I understood what that felt like. Still defrocked, unmasked, and transparent, yet no longer voiceless, helpless and hopeless, I had a platform.

The vehicle of my reincarnation came from so far outside left field it was like betting on dogs and winning the horses. Art classes were deemed suitable for me as no other of my erstwhile companions were so inclined. Much to my art teacher's joy, and my surprise, he declared I showed "promise". Better yet, after a few years, an audience declared my work "desirable". Agreeing that anonymity was the only assurance of continued success and a genuinely unbiased view, my art teacher, Gerald, came up with the pseudonym Little Man. I thought it a hoot and agreed.

As the years passed, and my one-on-one classes continued, I had to admit I could see an improvement. But more than that, regardless of my circumstances, one felt true freedom within the expanse of the boundless, blank canvas. My work gained popularity and notoriety as an anonymous convicted felon. And, since my teacher was taking a healthy commission, I felt confident my secret was safe with him.

By the time I was released, I had pooled enough of an audience that my list of commissions promised employment long into the future. So much so that Gerald employed the help of Harry, a well-known and prominently placed art agent. Despite moving in the same circles pre-conviction, I hadn't actually made his acquaintance. Astonishingly, the nondisclosure agreement and my true identity barely caused a wrinkled brow—him being one of the few who hadn't been scarred by my schemes.

His laid-back attitude and acceptance were a breath of fresh, life-supporting air—which I chose to believe did not stem from the significant cut he also received from my work. The relief to be outside, to have options, and to have friends was so valuable, it fuelled one's determination to be overly generous.

8

BALASHKA: GARDEN GAMES

The old dump had been the trifecta of perfections: perfect price, perfect location and perfect condition to match my new situation and worldview. But it needed significant work. The site had been selected by convenience and sport. A game of sorts had begun generations ago: pitching waste from the height of the wall into the bowl below. However, stormwater runoff, piped from under the city walls, converted the mess into a festering wound. Its convenient location outside the wall had relegated the issue to Someone Else's problem. But when it was slapped with health-code violations and the whisper of "structural damage", the issue was pitched back into Everyone's court.

Incinerating the consumables, throwing trucks of concrete at the substructure, then sweeping everything under tonnes of soil "carpet", with extra boulders thrown in the mix for good measure, worked in the short-term to reduce the eyesore and stabilise the foundations.

However, Mother Nature stirred the mix and lanced the boil by way of The Quake, thereby increasing my bargaining power tenfold. Either keep it, pay the fines and repair the damage... again... or sell it to me for a song.

Sardis's wall is imposing, make no mistake. When one stands, an insect, at the base, it blocks half the sky. A thug. Overwhelming, and more threatening than the mountain it moulds. Radiating the power of the sun: furnace by midday, hearth-fire by evening, fridge by morning, to start again.

With a mountain there is hope, there are tracks, passes, crevices. With the wall there is uniform denial. And I was forever locked out, barred from citizenship, no longer a member of society: entry other than by invitation was a fallacy. My mind entertained despair as it recalled prison. How could it not?

But to turn toward the plain beyond the foothills—the great expanse, a plateau, a boundless canvas—sent my soul soaring. No bars, no wire, no guards... emancipation. And I realised the truth: a worse fate it was, to be restricted behind the wall.

Like a child gathering armfuls of sand to hold back the ocean, I employed an army of worker ants to create my garden paradise. A protective layer of bamboo buffered the great wall. Hedges of natives were established to skirt the east and northern boundaries. Low enough to see over, high enough to block vision of any below. The cliff that bled into the wall to the south I left bare. It's ruggedness a reminder, a testimony, a work of art in its own right.

Throughout the sloped five acres, I mapped waterways to evacuate and decorate. Boulders were relocated to shore-up, highlight and punctuate. And soil, life preserving, nurturing, sustaining soil was laid and sculpted to enhance and receive the thousands of plants and acres of grass. Eighteen months was all it took. But the bones were set and the dressing done. All that was needed then was time: time for growth, development and maturity. My garden was complete, and my home was secure.

Regardless of time served, in the eyes of this city I was "guilty", sentenced to solitary confinement for life. But I made a vow to give back, to keep giving back, what I had taken. And if humanity would not accept what I was offering, I was hoping the wildlife would.

My home became a harbour of peace on the outer edge of the fractious city. After Sweetie, other stray animals made my haven their home. How they all got on without killing each other, I had no idea; I gave Sweetie full credit. Not too long after the animals, the people came. None I had encountered in my previous life... by choice. My choice. The imperfect, the broken, challenged, homeless fringe dwellers came to test the waters. Whilst curiosity enticed them, peace drew them back.

I tried to offer housing but, after The Quake, most had sworn off permanent shelter, making their lot even more arduous. They didn't live in houses because they couldn't... or wouldn't. But they had other needs I could fulfil, if they would let me. For a troubled mind that strained with finite understanding, trust was a limited commodity.

Food, clothing, facilities to wash, a place to be welcomed and people to care were always on the menu. So, with the constant flow of income from my art, I asked Gerald and Harry to help me purchase a food truck. Trouble was, once I'd set it up and established an agreement with a local company to keep it stocked, I couldn't find anyone who would work it. No one would come onsite once a day and feed those who came by. And heaven knew I couldn't do it. I'd be more likely to burn the place down.

And that's where Gerald's other job worked in perfectly. Not only did he teach at the prison, he instructed at TAVE (Trade and Vocational Education). He was in constant contact with people who needed practical experience to obtain their final qualifications. Those who either didn't know of me or didn't care—and were happy to sign the non-disclosure—were offered opportunity to experiment with and develop their newfound skills on us. Some only stayed for a term, or until they were fully employed. Others chose to stay on. Thanks to TAVE we now had Molly, our regular gardener, maintenance-handy person. Just as welcome and needed were Aran and Gabby, community nurses who came by at least twice a week to check up on everyone.

It's what gave me inspiration on how to help Jemmy. I still hadn't earned enough trust to learn all her circumstances, but it didn't take a genius to figure out the basics. She said she liked cooking and she... "guessed she could help out. If she had to." I tried not to laugh. The longing with which she scrutinised the paraphernalia in the van was similar to me poring over art supply catalogues brought weekly by Harry. It took an addict to identify an addict.

I told her I'd "let her help out," if she agreed to go to TAVE and learn proper cooking. The mix of fear, excitement, disbelief and mistrust came the closest to breaking one's heart since those early days in prison speaking with The Man. After learning my lesson with my other friends, I didn't presume to know what Jemmy needed, but I did want to give her this. And, like a child receiving a gift of a lifetime disguised as a venomous snake, she accepted.

After the first few months, she started sleeping over. I hated the thought of her sleeping rough. I knew she had survival skills, but I was glad she snuck in. The other members of our little community loved and accepted her as much as I did. And even though she worked hard at not showing it, I knew she loved us just as much. I made sure not to ever point that out.

She would be back this afternoon after Cooking School to prep a meal for us all. It was the perfect solution. I made sure all my meetings with Harry happened in the morning, ensuring my friends would be free to receive a meal without fear of someone new, or the unsettling change of routine.

But for now, it was time to make oneself presentable for Harry, who was going to hand over a large sum of money for my latest piece. I would then give him back a good proportion of that with which he would pay my bills. Without access to the internet or phones—apart from the ancient model programmed with two numbers—living life in this world was nigh on impossible.

For an extra fee, my art agent, Harry, was happy to be my life agent, fulfilling my needs in the outside world as well. I could have done it myself. Every so often I gave it a go, but the hate was now part of this city's DNA. At times, I just didn't have the energy to swim against it.

9

BALASHKA: MEET THE FAMILY

"Hello, hello, hello, hello."

Harry stopped mid-sentence and, with only a hint of an eyebrow raise, looked at the newcomer.

"Good morning, Richard." I rose to my feet but stayed within the bounds of my shed, standing on the concrete to meet with Richard who was now focused on Harry's car.

"Pretty, pretty, pretty, pretty."

Full credit to Harry, he didn't react at all when Richard started patting his "British Racing Green, thank *you* very much" Jag. I was constantly grateful to my friend for this and all the other accommodations he made when he joined us. Like parking his car perfectly perpendicular to my shed. Richard was not the only member of our community who lived with OCD. If Kirra, Eric or Sebastian dropped by this morning and the Jag was off centre, chaos would ensue.

"You have fine taste in motor vehicles, my man." Harry's easy smile encouraged Richard to join us. But at my raised hand he baulked mid-step, remaining outside at a pre-determined "socially acceptable" distance. He was learning about personal boundaries, but stared ominously at Harry, leaning forward with a glinty scowl on his face. My friend didn't flinch.

He'd obviously passed this morning's test as Richard deemed him worthy of a greeting. "Hello, hello, hello, hello."

Harry smiled and nodded in response, staying seated, as was his way.

"Did you see the flags this morning, Richard?"

He turned and pointed to the car. "Pretty, pretty, pretty."

"Ah, yes, the love of a fine vehicle is, at times, enough to prompt us into action and the crossing of boundaries."

Richard looked back at me. "Hello, hello, hello, hello."

"Richard, I am in a meeting with my friend at the moment. That is why I put the flags up. So that you would know someone was here. You are very welcome to go and have some food and I will come and join you soon."

"Dog skrat, dog skr—"

"Richard." I cut him off. "You know we don't swear here."

Richard dropped his head and his hands started fidgeting. "Hello, hello, hello."

"It's okay, Richard, we all forget at times."

"Dog poo, dog poo, dog poo."

"You're right. We do need to clean up and I will help you. But first I need to finish my meeting with my friend. Would you like to go and have a drink and some fruit while you wait in the Undercover Area? I won't be long."

Just before he made to leave, Harry tossed a spanner in the works: understandable, but unfortunate. "I hope you don't go hunting dog sk—poo in bare feet. Did you lose your shoes, mate?"

Richard froze. His hands knotted and he started rocking side to side. "Hello, hello, hello, hello, hello, hello, hello." His words rapid-fire staccato.

Harry half rose from his chair. "Oh. Skrat—"

"Skrat, skrat, skrat…"

Harry tried to finish his sentence over the top of Richards rising siren. "What'd I do? So sorry." Harry was visibly upset, but thankfully not as upset as Richard.

I took a step toward Richard. His eyes bulged, his head started shaking and his breathing had increased to shallow panting. But at least he'd returned to hellos rather than skrats.

I maintained my distance, and pointed to the tool shed, and yelled so as to be heard over the now-deafening chanting. "How about you go and sort the tools by the shed, Richard. I will be over soon, and we can put on our gloves and clean up the dog poo for Molly who's coming tomorrow. Don't want her to have to mow that, do we?"

"Hello, hello, hello." Thankfully he looked at me and locked his eyes on mine, his head slowly nodding.

With his full attention now on me, with over-exaggerated actions I began miming deep breathing. Soon, Richard started copying me. His breathing slowed, his chanting with it. His body now focused on the pantomime I was performing, which was a full body experience involving knees, elbows, wide eyes and puffed cheeks. I could hear Harry behind me trying desperately not to laugh. When Richard finally joined me fully, we looked like a couple of drugged chooks. Soon after, however, he was calm enough to make his way to the tool shed to start sorting, his trail of, "Hello, hello, hello," receding with him.

I went back to my seat, and we watched as the man addressed the row of tools left out for this very purpose. Richard then proceeded to organise the rake, shovel, hoe, another rake and a garden fork into every conceivable arrangement. All the while a faint mumbling carried across the clearing. "Dog poo, dog poo, hello, Molly, dog poo, pretty..."

"Sorry about that, mate. Seriously didn't intend to upset the fellow." Harry sipped from his takeout coffee cup. He knew this place well enough to bring his own when he visited. There was occasionally someone onsite who knew how to use the fandangled coffee contraption in the food truck, but it wasn't me. Thankfully, he was a generous chap and always brought one for me too. I only indulged in such luxuries when they were offered.

I took a pull from my own cup and savoured the intense flavour and committed it to memory. As my tastebuds came down from their little high, I responded. "I know it's tricky, but the main thing you need to remember while you're here is, everyone"—I turned to face my friend to ensure his full attention—"everyone... just wants to be treated like they're normal."

At his scoff, I challenged him. "Tell me, Harry, what is normal?"

He started to answer, then stopped. "I don't know."

"Normal, Harry, is not different." I looked back at Richard who was still rearranging garden tools. "Normal is feeling like you fit in. Like you're acceptable. Even if... when... you're radically different." I glanced back at my friend and grinned. "The biggest compliment I can give you, Harry, is that to us, you are normal. Your car, clothes, wealth, class, don't matter. You fit in." I used my cup to indicate Richard. "When you pointed out he wasn't wearing shoes, Richard *heard* you saying, 'You don't fit in, you're not like us, you're not normal, therefore you are not acceptable'."

"Okay, so what about that woman standing at the edge of the hedge posing like a tree?"

Making a point not to look, I smiled at my friend. "That's Cheryl, she's seen the red flags and knows you're here for your weekly visit. But her curiosity is as strong as her fear. She is pretending to be a tree so you can't see her. Knowing you can't see her gives her the confidence to check you out from the safety of the hedge."

"But she's wearing a bright pink cardigan and a fluorescent orange skirt."

"Great, isn't it? Cheryl loves colour. Harry?" He turned to look at me. "It would be very helpful right now if you ignored her and pretended she wasn't there."

He whisper-yelled his response. "She just picked her nose, Bal. Shrubbery doesn't pick its nose and eat it."

I couldn't hold in my laugh. "Normal, Harry. Perfectly normal, my friend."

"I do believe I might be a bit scarred after that."

"How about we look at the art instead and you can pay me ludicrous amounts of money, then take it all back to pay the bills, your percentage included."

"Now that, my friend, is more my kind of normal."

10

CONTESSA: DON'T RAIN ON MY PARADE

I loved my life. I adored my husband and our little house he built for us. I loved our family here at Sanctuary, Philadelphia. And I love, love, loved that I got to spend my days making all sorts of things to sell on Sanctuary's website. Not only home furnishings, but I'd been developing a new line of clothing. And children's clothing. They were so popular, I could hardly keep up.

But I was also seriously excited about our move to Sardis. It was *the* capital of trade in our region. The meeting point... launching pad... hub of all trade on the continent. And it was one step closer to Thyatira, textile capital of the world. There were strong links between the two cities, and Sardis in general was the hottest place to be, to make a start and become established in business. So, not only was I filling orders, I was trying to create the best of my best to have ready as a portfolio when we got there.

Of course, I'd be all kinds of sad to leave our family here. But I had grown to accept that as our lot: leaving. But the best thing was, Sardis was only forty-five minutes' drive from here. So... visiting... much.

Actually, Dan, Marcus and Val had already been making reconnaissance trips for the past few weeks. They'd started the search for the "Seeing Blind Man". Thankfully, Dan hadn't suffered the same constant dream message as he did when we were looking for the "Black and White Girl" in Laodicea. I think if he had the typical nasty-as dream hangover added to his recurring headaches, his head would explode. This time, it was enough to receive the one call. But today, everyone was home for a rest day and a special occasion.

I was very grateful on Dan's behalf. Despite the headaches—effects of the concussion he suffered from the vile Gerent—still lingering, his eyes had improved, and he could now read for short periods of time. Darling Raph kept trying to heal him. I think it was working? But in small increments. The main thing was that it *was* improving, he was okay, and he was now busy with something to occupy his mind. A bored Dan was a dangerous Dan.

Anyway, the twins seemed perfectly content to stay here with me and Kait while the others were away on their daily adventures. Riah was still madly in love with the goats and Miriam, the goat lady. Raph was up to his elbows in the garden with Tiger, his cat... and Ruby. Kait was spending as much time as possible helping Mr Berry with resources for the school so when we were gone he wouldn't be without help. I think the battle, three months ago now, pretty much did him in. Especially after losing Nanna-May and Travis. It seemed to have really knocked the wind out of his sails. He went through the motions of teaching, but really it was Kait who did it all. Thankfully our computer gurus, February and October, at Kait's prompting, were able to get access to a lot of online resources. Gemma, Tim's wife, had already stepped in with Marina, mother of three, and would do most of the teaching and schoolwork when we'd gone.

Felix had come to the rescue, once again, and brought a whole heap of laptops. Now the hut that hadn't been fully finished was the new schoolroom, hooked up with internet, cooling, desks and every-thing else our little school needed.

It was just perfect.

And my Dan built it.

I was so proud.

"He is here. He is here." Raph bounded through the door and, despite now being fourteen, the thought of seeing Felix had him jumping like a toddler on a sugar high. But then, it *was* Felix, and we all tended to get a bit excited when our friend from Laodicea arrived. And now he was here we could begin our celebration. It was a surprise birthday party for a very special person who hated being the centre of attention. Which is why we had to make it a surprise, so she wouldn't, like, run off to fight someone… or something… somewhere random.

"I'm almost done." I was just making the finishing touches to the gift I was sewing. This was not easy with one twin bouncing on his toes beside me and the other tapping my shoulder reminding me I had to hurry. I slipped the final piece in with others and sealed it all up.

Tucked under one of Raph's arms, and Riah pulling me along by the hand, we made our way to the Meeting Place—the central marquee that was a permanent structure at the heart of Sanctuary—to see what news he'd brought, over lunch.

Once he had suffered the twin's enthusiastic greeting with good grace, Felix allowed the rest of us to hug him. With discomfort warming his pale complexion to cream, he accepted his place at the table.

Then he began. "As you know, I have been visiting the Elders in Sardis in an attempt to… pave the way for you in that city. I know the Light has called you there and I know it is never easy, but it will be… particularly difficult. The Overseer… ex-Overseer, Achan, has gone before you." Felix's face normally looked a bit grim, but his eyes had taken on a particular "unhappy". "Ever since he expelled you from the Community in Laodicea, he has been laying a… foundation of lies in the other cities. The first to receive him and listen, after his exile, was Sardis."

Felix laid his scrunched napkin down and swivelled to face Val next to him. "I would never… presume to tell you where to go and what to do. I know you are obedient to the Light and His will is your… directive. But please, be careful." He looked back to the table and straightened his already straight cutlery and quietly continued. "I feel even this will fall on deaf ears. But know this, if there is anything you need… anything at all, please contact me."

Felix had managed to drown the party with sombre, and now *I* was wearing a significant unhappy. But Jonathan jumped in with the last word. "Kait has already received Word from the Light that we are to maintain business as usual here at Sanctuary. Considering the wall of Warriors who have not stepped down since the Battle of Philly, I know there is more to come." All our eyes were drawn to the impressive wall of protection the Light had provided. "The spare cabins will remain prepared for any who need respite. We will be ready to receive and assist all who come to us. We are self-contained, we have supplies, contacts and escape routes ready. We are here for you when you need us."

Daisy, who was never far away from Jonathan these days, had just placed a tray of food on the table and stood behind his chair. She placed both hands on his shoulders and looked to each member of my family. "We will stand with you no matter what. We will aid you, no matter what. We are family, and as the world around us dissolves into Darkness, we stand in the Light, for the Light, no matter what."

"Enough." I couldn't take one more word. I jumped to my feet. "This is a birthday party. I will not let that narcissistic psychopath interrupt any more than he already has. I hereby declare this a Gerent-Darkness-morose-depressing-talk, we're-all-going-to-die-horrible-and..." I still couldn't get the image of Mary and Travis from my mind. Tears stung my eyes, but I locked my stance and continued, "—painful-deaths free zone." Dan came up behind me and kissed the top of my head.

I think we must have all been thinking the same thoughts. Everyone was silent and swimming in their own memories for a while. Great. I had tried to create a happy space and now everyone was sad. I marched around to Val's spot and slapped my present on the table. Possibly... okay, definitely, far more aggressively than I had intended. But it was okay, it wasn't breakable. I forced a smile. "Val, happy birthday. We love you. Very much. So, these are from Dan and me."

"What?" It wasn't a shriek so much as an accusation fired first at me, then at the rest of us. We all laughed, and everyone lifted their own offerings onto the table.

"Oh, did we not tell you, me dear sister? Or are you getting too old to remember." The grin on Marcus's face was nasty. "It's your birthday and this is your party. Albeit a few weeks early. We could not celebrate with all and sundry if we weren't here, now, could we?"

Marcus then proceeded to be the focal point for Val's hostile glare. He merely brushed his shoulders. "Water off a duck's buttocksials, woman. Now, swallow your pride and follow your own teaching and get your grace on. Forty is too important to ignore."

Which she did. Get her grace on, that is, not ignore her birthday. Once her laser eyes retracted, we all relaxed.

Val smiled at me and all my sad-depressed-angry faded and I kind of melted at how much I did genuinely love this woman. She really wasn't one who liked to demonstrate affection, but I just didn't care. It was her birthday, so she'd just have to toughen up. I swooped in and hugged her fiercely. "I really, really love you, Val. Please be safe… and careful… Okay, so maybe not careful, but safe. Be safe." I don't know why, but tears came to my eyes. And I hugged her even harder.

Eventually, she gently prised me away, and stood. She held my shoulders, her laser-beam eyes searched my soul, and a sad smile warmed her eyes. "Tessa, it's going to be okay. No matter what, we're going to be okay. Things are going to be tough, we will suffer, but we're going to be okay." She ran a calloused hand over my cheek. My tears made her face blur and wobble in front of me but this time as I went to pull away, she pulled me close so our foreheads rested together. "You are such an incredible blessing to us all. I am so proud of you, more than words can say. Having you in my family, as a daughter, is one of the greatest treasures the Light has blessed me with. No matter what happens in the future, know this. You are mine; I am yours; forever, in the Light."

Yes, well, as you can imagine I was a complete blubbering mess after this and, yes, everyone was sitting around watching my pale face turn blotchy red with swollen, puffy eyes. But as was now common practice, Dan moved in and hid me under his wing and suggested Val open her present. I will admit that I felt a tad vindicated to hear his voice was a little roughened around the edges. Not that that was a criticism. He was doing so much better than me; I couldn't even speak.

Val did as was instructed and, as she peeled back the tissue paper, froze when she saw what was inside.

I mean literally froze.

Didn't move.

Didn't say a word.

I wasn't even sure she was breathing.

Oh, Lord, does she hate them?

I darted back to her to explain. "Val? Are they okay? I just thought, instead of always wearing those ghastly second-hand T-shirts and men's button downs, you could have some... colour... and something new... and pretty... but not too pretty?

"I know you don't do pretty.

"But... nice?"

She slowly turned her head to look at me, the wonder enhanced by the sheen in her own storm-grey eyes. My tears had dried enough to make that out. She still hadn't said anything. No one else was saying anything either, and all of a sudden I was feeling really... really self-conscious. In my rush to explain, words kind of just... tumbled out.

"So, an organic wool blend, right? It's so soft and lightweight with a bit of stretch. You can move really easily in them. I know sometimes when you're struggling with the Dark's blades, you may not want a button down, so I designed these loops and gorgeous big buttons. But discreet, right? To the side? So even your achy fingers could get you in and out of your clothes. Because, seriously, I know how much you like receiving help. Not." I waited. She still didn't speak but looked at the six shirts in front of her, running a hand over the lush fabric. I couldn't blame her; wool was all kinds of lovely.

"And, well, I just wanted you to remember us, wherever you are, whatever you're doing, so I made them in green, blue, indigo, violet. But I had to give you a different red to Sariah's, because you can't wear that red. And of course there was no way I was putting yellow in there. That's why I put Amber in… for Daisy. It was the closest tone you could wear to my yellow."

The shock on Val's face was almost comical. "I can wear yellow."

Kait's soothing caramel voice interrupted. "Dear heart, believe me, you cannot wear Tessa's tone of yellow."

"Don't tell me what I can and can't wear. I can wear yell—"

"Okay." I had to raise my voice. "Val, you shouldn't wear my yellow, it would… does… eat you alive. But look at all the other lovely colours you can wear. And"—I smiled—"they all go really well with your black cargos and workboots. See? Pretty, functional and tough."

"But what if I want to wear your yellow, Tessa?"

"You don't have to Val; you're wearing my shirts. Well, I hope you will. Dan searched high and low to find those exact colours." I thought I had better throw that in to remind her it was a joint gift. I waited while she lifted each one and ran a hand over the collars, seams, beautifully crafted buttons, loose cuffs. Each similar, but just a bit different. Still, she didn't say anything. "Do you like them?" I know I sounded needy, but seriously, I was.

I really needed to know.

"If she doesn't want them, I'll have them. I think they're brilli—"

Before Daisy could finish her sentence, Val cut in. "Thank you, Tessa, they are beautiful. Perfect. Extraordinary. And no, Daisy, you cannot have them. But I can put you in touch with my designer, she may be able to make room for you in her schedule. But I'm not too sure, she's pretty exclusive these days." She then looked back at me and smiled. "Beautiful, Tessa. They're beautiful and I love them, thank you." She pulled me into a fierce bear hug.

"Um, yeah, I helped," Dan said.

Val pulled him into a hug as well. "Thank you, Dan. I know Tessa couldn't do what she does without you doing what you do to support her, and the rest of us. So, from the bottom of my heart, my boy, my son in the Light, thank you."

Thankfully, Ruby was, like, totally unaffected by the emotion suffocating the rest of us and she barged between me and the table plonking her present down. "Mine next. I made you a pot."

Daisy laughed. "You're not supposed to tell. Let her open it first."

Val complied. Returning to her seat at the table, she peeled back the wrapping to reveal a beautiful indigo pot. It had this amazing glaze that looked dark blue in one light, deep purple in another. "I knew you would be leaving us, and I didn't know if you could keep a plant. So, I made it for you to put things in. And to remember us. We will miss you." And all of a sudden, the emotion hit her and she buried her face in Daisy's waiting embrace.

Now, the trumpet call of the elephant among us captured everyone's attention. In front of Felix was a small, beautifully wrapped box. Raph's excitement was the first to burst. "Now Felix's." We all knew it would be mega expensive. I was kind of thinking it was jewellery? But then, that would be dumb. Val didn't wear jewellery. But what else could be in a box so small?

Felix cleared his throat. "Happy... birthday, Valarie."

Very. Flopping. Slowly. Revelling in our impatience, Val eventually made her way into the box and folded back the lid to reveal a small white disc about a centimetre thick, roughly the size of one of the Gerent's newly minted coins.

To be perfectly honest it was a bit of an anti-climax. But then February and October's whistles of appreciation pulled us all back into the intrigue. "Is that a ShellCom?" February reached forward to touch it, then she withdrew her hand realising she was about to cross some social boundary.

Felix flushed. "Yes."

We all stared at him, as, obviously, there were only three people onsite who knew what on earth a ShellCom was.

"Lovely. That's just grand, Felix. You always were one for the flash and fancy." Marcus's sarcasm was lost on Felix. He merely dropped his flaming face and nodded his appreciation.

Val's quiet voice only made him flush more. "Thank you, Felix." His skin almost made it to the colour of peaches. "Could you please tell me what it is, and how to use it?"

October lost it and blurted, "Hologram." She was almost frothing at the mouth with excitement. I had never seen her express so much emotion.

As everyone looked around blankly when she offered no more explanation, Felix became the focus of our attention. Thankfully, he filled in the blanks. "It's the latest form of communication."

"It's actually not even released yet," February interrupted.

"Well, actually, I know a person who got me two. Wherever you are, you"—he picked up the disc and gave it a twist revealing two separate discs. The inner curve of one matched the outer curve of the other. Felix showed Val the scooped half—"hold this one up in front of you and press that indentation. This side houses the capture, hologram generation and transmission components. Hold this one"—he indicated the other half—"flat, and it will display the hologram of whomever you're communicating with. I believe, because it is small, and… unassuming… it might pass scrutinising eyes, and enable you to receive help, or provide updates in a time of emergency. It works off the city satellites and this battery cradle is in the box. However, the developers have partnered with Life Batteries, and its stored life is… significant. They are unsure exactly, it is still being tested." He handed the disc back, fleetingly looking her in the eye. "I want you to be able to reach me, anytime you need… assistance. I will do everything in my power to… see you have what you need."

We were all silent. That little disc sitting in Val's opened palm held everyone captive. Not only what it meant, but the heart with which it was given. Val reached over and squeezed Felix's hand. "Thank you."

"Right, next present." Marcus rescued his friend and sister from any more uncomfortable attention.

The rest of the afternoon progressed with presents, planning and quality family time. But seriously, it didn't take a genius to read the signs of the times. I couldn't shake the feeling that something horrible was on the horizon.

11

KAITLYN: DEJA VU

"So, I am both a weak woman who needs to learn my place, and I am single-handedly responsible for the collapse of the Laodicean Community of Light? I'm confused." Val was addressing the crowd at our latest attempt to "meet and greet" the locals at a new Sardis Community. We were meeting in a civic hall on the lower slopes of the city. Val stood on the stage behind a lectern with a microphone. Marcus and I waited off to the side in the wings. The Community hosting this event had been very clear on where we were to wait.

"Your forked tongue is testimony to your guile and deception. You are a child of Darkness."

"Now I am a snake *and* a wolf in sheep's clothing? Maybe it's you who is confused." The slight humour and refusal to be offended was doing more to enrage the crowd than if she had just labelled them for what they were: a bunch of blind, weak, transparent individuals masquerading as children of Light.

"We have been warned about you. We know we cannot trust you; you are full of deceit, wilfully preaching lies and tarnishing the Light."

And there it was. The incendiary that sparked the explosion. You could say anything about my dearest sister and it would bounce off her like a tomato hitting a hot Teflon wall. But infer her testimony was not genuine, or her love and devotion to the Light was less than all-consuming, and you may as well have drawn a blade and held it at her throat. It would be taken as a declaration of war.

Her eyes narrowed and her body relaxed. She loosened her limbs and dropped her weight ever so slightly to the balls of her feet. I must say, in her emerald-green bamboo shirt, jet-black pants and butt-kicking boots, she looked fierce, yet classy. She wasn't a ragtag, uneducated, random citizen hauled in off the street. She had an air of authority, which was nothing new, but now she had an air of styled authority. Tessa would be so proud. I wish I could take a photo. But... maybe later.

"I am intrigued as to why you invited me to speak. However, any time, any place I am happy to sit down with you to go through The Way and answer any questions you might have regarding my message. Are you willing to do the same with me?" Now, if you weren't there in person, it might sound like a reasonable response and quite possibly an intriguing proposition. But none in the room could see it as anything other than a direct, gauntlet-thrown-to-the-floor challenge. As was the norm, the room fell deathly silent as no one volunteered to take her up on her "invitation".

My heart was breaking for this city. It was nothing new. And perhaps that's what made it all the more disheartening. They'd had a golden reputation for their heart and dedication to the Light, demonstrated by serving the wider population. Yet, everywhere we went, the Community of Light was anything but. The Light had called us here to find the Seeing Blind Man. So far, all we had found was a haystack of Blind Seeing Men and Women.

After an uncomfortable eon of silence, Val finished her invitation to speak with an, "I didn't think so," disdain dripping from her voice. She turned to us waiting in the wings.

I didn't understand. Since Dan had received the Dream which revealed our mission in Sardis, Felix had been using his contacts and opening doors for us to join the Community here. There had been great interest and many invitations to come and talk. But as we soon learned, it wasn't to hear the message or welcome us into their boat to pull an oar. It was to see first-hand this woman who had caused so much damage in Philadelphia, Laodicea and Sodom.

In the past, it had always confused me as to how Achan—ex-Overseer of Laodicea—had any word from Sodom. Only seven of us made it out of that city alive. But since meeting Achan's advisers and inner circle, I realised he *did* have an eyewitness's perspective, warped as it may be: The Dark's.

So rather than genuine interest in walking The Way with fellow Community members, Val drew a crowd out of morbid curiosity. Sadly, they didn't bank on the message she came to deliver: "Wake up before your sleep becomes permanent. Turn from your Dark ways, there is much work left to do." Not only were these "seeing" people blind, they were deaf, and hardened against the Light's heart.

Val made her way to us, shaking her head. Marcus stood beside me, his anger making him unusually quiet and frighteningly still. I laid my hand on his arm and reached up on my toes, kissed his cheek and whispered, "Breathe, Bear," in his ear. He was not impressed, but it shocked him out of his fury coma. "It's okay, Bear, we knew it wasn't going to be easy."

"I tell you what, Kait, the wheel is spinning in this city, but the mouse is dead. There's naught but the sound of the sea ghosting between their ears. The—"

Before Marcus could build up a true head of steam, sirens pulling into the carpark had us all taking stock. We looked to each other—me, mid-action of collecting our bags.

"She's out the back. In the wings." A gleeful voice echoed through to us from the auditorium. I threw one backpack to Marcus, I donned the second, and the three of us stood ready for the next round of… what? We just didn't know.

"Valarie Benlukos!" Three guards approached, one from the stage, another two from the side stairs behind us.

Val raised her eyebrows at us, shrugged and turned to the one who had addressed her. "Yes."

"Come with us, please." He said "please", but we all knew there was no choice in the matter. Especially considering the way the other two had their hands resting on their side arms.

Val didn't move but she gave off an affable, relaxed aura. "May I ask why?"

"There won't be any trouble, unless you continue to be uncooperative."

"I'm merely asking why I am being... invited to join you? Where are we going, and why?"

One of the guards from the back spoke up. "Several complaints of being a public nuisance, disturbing the peace, and intentionally attempting to incite an anti-Establishment movement."

The shock of laughter that burst from my sister was not helpful. The guards became even more edgy when she finally responded. "May I ask who made the complaints?"

"No. Now come with us peacefully or we will be forced to use more direct methods."

I could feel Marcus's barely contained fury crackling along his skin. His armour was flicking with black lightning. Just as well the guards didn't have the Sight, or they would have seen that, in fact, their biggest threat at this point in time was Marcus and me. Not Val. But not being so disadvantaged, Val did see us. She tried to calm us with a nod, and her response. "It's okay. We'll come along. We don't want to cause trouble."

I heard one guard mutter under his breath, "Not what we've heard."

But the first one rebutted Val. "Not them, just you."

"It's going to be okay," were her last words to us as she was marched back onto stage, down the main steps and out of the building to a roar of cheering and catcalling.

I could not tell you what else happened after that, for a while anyway. I vaguely remember Marcus calling Felix, but I hardly remember what I said, or what he said. I was so angry, and confused, and worried, and... angry. I was having flashbacks to the day they took my kids from me at the checkpoint in Philadelphia. Feelings of being bound, inadequate and consumed by rage over my inability to do anything to help my family.

I knew Val could take care of herself. But she was at the mercy of a system that did not guarantee fairness or equity. We had learned that the hard way: watching via drone footage of Tessa, Riah and Raph being mistreated and thrown to the wolves in the sports stadium; the Gerent's personal guard beating and capturing our children; and his senseless, heartless murder of our dear friends, Mary and Travis, both defenceless, elderly, law-abiding citizens. Yes, we had experienced first-hand the reality of the law in a country ruled by a madman. Which only fuelled my fear about what was in store for my sister.

Please keep her safe. Please keep the Dark's blades from torturing her flesh... anyone from torturing her flesh. Oh Lord...

I was going to be sick. The things they could do to her. The ways they could hurt her.

I felt Marcus's arms around me and his whisper tickling my ear. "We need to get out of here, Kait. The crowd is still full of hostiles and they're high on seeing Val being taken away."

I let him steer me out through back hallway, following the fluorescent green signs to freedom, hoping our path didn't cross with any other members of this Community on our way. We'd made it to the fire door and Marcus had enough wits about him to check before barging out of there into the fresh air. The coast was clear from this front, but as we turned the corner to make our way back to the car, we saw a crowd had gathered around it, waiting for us. We turned and made our way back through the alley to a parallel street.

I was in complete and utter shock. How could things have become so impossibly hostile. We had thought things were bad in Philadelphia... and Laodicea... and Sodom. And they were. But members of the Community of Light turning violent against their own? In the past we'd been put out, asked to leave, jeered at and harassed, but never targeted and arrested for speaking about the Light to a Community of Light... who had *invited* us to speak, for crying out loud.

It was then it dawned on me. The previous meetings had been

lulling us into a false sense of security. This was all part of their... of Achan's trap. This was his plan of revenge from the start. And, like mindless sheep, we walked straight into it.

Why didn't You warn me? Warn any of us? How could You let this happen?

A new fire of rage ignited in me. The Light knew this was going to happen. And He had not warned us... me. He had gifted me with the badge of Hearing His direct Word. Yet, in this, He'd been silent. I could feel the fire crackling down every nerve of my body. We had been faithful. We had been obedient. We had been doing all that we had been called to do, going to whom we had been sent. Not once had we dropped the ball, and still, He let this happen? I could barely breathe, let alone see where I was going. I was so angry.

Once again, I felt Marcus's arms around me as he pulled me into the alcove of a closed shop. This time his voice wasn't a whisper, it was a command. "Breathe, Kait." I do believe I was going to ban that bleeding word from my family's vocabulary.

"Do not. Tell me. To breathe. Marcus." I stopped, spun on him and let him feel the full force of my anger fuelled by our abandonment. And, praise the Light, my husband was man enough to take it and not back down. I needed something to rail against, and he took the full force of it head-on.

"Do you think, me dear wife, the Light was taken by surprise by this?" It wasn't a question; it was an accusation... at me.

"Of course I bleeding well don't. He knew."

"Do you think the Light was powerless to stop it?"

"Of course He bleeding well isn't. But He bleeding well didn't. Did He?"

"Did the Light promise us an easy ride? Safety? A pain-free insurance policy?"

"No. He did not." I knew the reality. I knew it. But it just didn't stop the rage. The fear. The worry.

In a softer voice, Marcus continued, "Do you think He doesn't know what He's doing?"

"Of course I don't. But I do not have to like it."

"No, you don't, Kait. But you do have to accept it. That is if you're still in the game?"

Rage exploded in me again. "What do you mean, 'Still in the game'? Of course I'm bleeding well still in the game. Are you calling me weak?"

He chuckled in the face of my fury. Which, let me tell you, did not help. But it also did. "No, me dearest, most beautiful wife. I would never be so ignorant as to call you weak." He brushed some of my hair from my face and let his hand trail to my shoulder. "But we're called to trust. I know you know this. I fully suspect, by the time we figure out how to get to our new digs, without a car, you will be preaching the same message to our family." His other hand came up and repeated the brushing action against the other side of my face. Not only did it clear my vision... literally, it helped clear my thinking. He was right. Of course.

"I know He knows what He's doing. And I know we weren't warned for a reason. I know we need to trust Him. And that is the battle. To choose to trust Him in the midst of bleeding chaos and Darkness." And then the walls came down and the tears pushed through the anger. "What if they hurt her... really hurt her?"

Marcus pulled me into his arms and hid me in his embrace. He let me cry, holding me tight, then quietly he answered, "As well as I do, you know our sister. She'll stand firm. She'll fight. And the Light will see her right."

After allowing me time to pull myself together, we continued our way along the street, lost. Coming across a café with some vacant tables, we stopped and took refuge. Marcus was back on his phone giving someone details of where we were. Moments later, a sleek black car pulled up outside. One of the reflective tinted windows powered down and Cissa looked out from the passenger seat. I could see a fire in her eyes that matched mine, but there was a hint of a wry smile as she offered us a ride back to our new home.

12

DANIEL: UP WHEN I'M DOWN

issa was one classy chick. Not only did she rock every room she entered, she was a female version of Felix. Not that she was socially awkward or grooved to the beat of her own drum, but, due to her hard work and brains, she was loaded. Loaded and generous. Since meeting her at the top of the mountainous hell—literal hell—overlooking Sanctuary on DSDD-Day (Defeat the Seriously Deranged Dude Day), she had kind of adopted us as family.

Distant family. She didn't do "gush" or "physical contact" like we did. But she was definitely a fully-fledged member of Team Light. Not only had she provided this seriously sweet pad for us to camp in whilst we were in Sardis, she and Al offered me and Marcus a scholarship to study at the TAVE industry school in the city. Better yet, they'd worked it so Josh and Tim in Philadelphia could continue to be our supervisors. They'd also played the system so we could be a branch of their huge corporation: Black & Light Architectural Designs. And not only that, Cissa was so blown away with what we'd done with the recycled materials in Philadelphia, she'd signed me up for an extra course in design. Stoked didn't even come close to how I felt about it.

Tessa had been included too. Cissa loved her designs and how she'd dressed each of the cabins. She had also checked out her stock on the Sanctuary website and said she showed real potential and had a unique eye. So they signed her up for an advanced textiles course at the same campus as Marcus and me.

It hadn't stopped there. They'd been so buzzed with our whole family, she and Al had sat us all down and asked what we'd all like to study. The Blacks were sponsoring us all to take a "sabbatical"—a year out of the daily slog to learn, or relearn as was the case for Kait—anything we wanted. Kait was doing a nursing refresher. Raph had signed up for cooking, and Riah had taken her sweet time figuring out what she wanted to do. We had talked her out of fighting, and suggested she had a go at something new, or pursue something she was really into... other than fighting. She chose art.

Val had blown us all away by choosing writing. I guess she *was* one helluva a reader. And she did have a lot to say... about a lot of things. So, it made sense. In the end though, it wasn't the course she chose that really rocked me. I was still reeling from the fact she'd accepted the offer at all. Not that she was above learning a new skill, but we all knew her main focus would have been on scouring the streets looking for the Seeing Blind Man. The only thing that'd stopped her turning bloodhound was Kait's Word: the link we needed to find him was at TAVE.

But right now, I was pinching myself. My brain was numb. Surely this was a nightmare. Val had been arrested for speaking at an event she'd been invited to speak at. It was fralapping ridiculous is what it was. Felix had done the groundwork and officially vouched for us in the Communities of Light here in Sardis. But that dodgy kret, Achan, got his claws in here well before us—more than two years ago. Turns out, he'd run here after the battle in Laodicea. Sold some story saying Val was personally responsible for toppling the Temple of Ashera. And, as a result, Felix's introduction couldn't compete with Achan's fear-mongering groundwork, which had had plenty of time to take hold and bear toxic fruit.

We were thanking the Light that it was only Val who had been arrested and not Kait and Marcus too. And that the twins hadn't been with them this time. I don't even want to think about the mess that would've made: if someone had tried to take the twins from Kait... and Marcus... and Val, again. They would have all gone completely postal. The charges would have been far more serious than "disturbing the peace".

Felix was on his way from Laodicea, as were Jonathan and Daisy from Philadelphia. I didn't know what any of them would be able to do. None of them had real sway in this city, but I had to admit it felt better knowing we had friends on their way and our collective brains trust would grow significantly with them here—and Felix's aide, Marlene. Tessa, the twins and I had been petitioning the Light to get Himself in the mix as soon as we'd heard.

When Cissa had received the call from Marcus a short while ago, Al grabbed his wife and the two of them raced to collect our parentals. The four of us were left incapacitated by shock. I stood at the wall of windows in our new apartment looking to the city beyond and had to confess, the betrayal had soured the vibe. Tessa wormed her way under my right arm, and Riah came and stood in front of me. I wrapped my left arm around her shoulders. Raph, who was growing like a beanstalk, folded his arms around Tessa and me from behind, resting his chin on my shoulder. The four of us waited silently, petitioning wordlessly. What was there to say except, *Help. Please help?*

The front door flew open and before I could think, Kait had the four of us in her arms. Well, she tried, but she was too small, and her arms were too short. Marcus joined the scrum, and we shared a moment of grief and shock. But then Kait fluffed out her mother-hen feathers and took charge. "Right. How far off are the others? We need to petition the Light as a group and wait for answers, instructions... anything." Her voice caught.

Marcus hugged her trembling shoulders in a bear hug and took over the orders until she got herself back under control. "Raph, Riah, could you pop the kettle on. Dan, Tessa love, can you find some extra chairs and prepare for our guests. They'll be here in two shakes of a hen's foot." He then looked to Cissa and Al who stood just inside the door as if they weren't welcome in the apartment they owned. "Thank you for coming to collect us. Can we offer you a whistle-wetter while we consider how to swim through this swarm of vipers?"

They both came into the sitting area and gave their requests to the twins working in the open-plan kitchen. Al perched on the arm of the engulfing chair Cissa claimed. An image of queen, regal, calm and totally in control flashed through my head. I don't know what it was about her, but all of a sudden I felt like everything was going to be okay.

It reminded me of that day back in Philadelphia, at the top of the hill overlooking the battle at Sanctuary. We'd just defeated a group of the Dark's worshippers who were not only throwing some pretty ugly flies in the ointment of Sanctuary, they were waiting to welcome us into their kill zone. Fully equipped with a complete complement of their demonic overlords flanking their backs... sides... and fronts.

We'd just finished mopping up when Al, Cissa and Luke, Travis's son, arrived on the scene. Felix explained our plan—Tessa, me, Felix and six other friends from Laodicea—to take on the hordes of hell, and invited the three of them to join us. Cissa had roared the most joyous laugh and more or less asked where she could sign up. Turned out she was pretty handy with that blade of hers as well. The three of them had fought hell for leather that day. I for one was immensely grateful for them then. And now. At her party a couple of weeks ago, Val had insisted, no matter what, everything was going to be okay. But for the first time in the last crazy half hour, I started to believe it.

Moments later a bluish-pale Felix, accompanied by a furious Daisy and a stern Jonathan, marched into our apartment. Now that everyone was here the game could begin. I was confident that within this room we had the resources, intellect and faith to solve this disaster.

Felix started the ball rolling. "Has anyone been in touch with the authorities? Do we know what the situation is? The charges? How long is she being held? I have not heard from her. Does anyone know anything?"

Never in the years I'd known Felix, had I seen the guy so rattled.

We all knew he and Val had a special connection. But I'd just had a glimpse of how deep that went... for Felix, anyway.

Cissa spoke up. "I have been waiting for everyone to arrive"—she nodded in the direction of Jonathan and Daisy; Felix was too busy pacing to acknowledge anyone—"before I made the call. I was just debating which card to play."

Jonathan and Al both glared at her, the heat almost setting her chair to smoulder. Jonathan was shaking his head and Al, with his hand on her shoulder, spoke up. "Don't do it, Cissa. Please. There are other ways. If you reach out to them, it will be the end of all you have fought for. There is another way. We just have to figure it out."

Jonathan was in agreement. "We'll think of something. You don't need to make that sacrifice, Cissa."

Daisy, thank the Light, was as clueless as the rest of us, but not so backward in coming forward. "What sacrifice? What are you talking about? Is it really worth not considering?"

Al's hazel eyes burned and his free hand fisted. "It is not worth considering. I will not condone it."

"It's okay, Al." Cissa laid a hand on his thigh. "I think it's worth acknowledging, at least." Before Al could manage more bluster, she continued, "My parents are quite significant in this city. They have incredible influence and power."

"Sweet." Seemed pretty logical to me. "Can you ask them to pull some strings?"

At this, Al blew a gasket. "No, she bleeding well can't. Cissa has spent her whole life breaking away from the insidious web of her parents. She has slaved to make a name for herself independent of her family. I will not stand by and allow her to throw her life away and become a slave to them again for this. The cost is too high. There has to be another way." His rant had him on his feet and pacing.

Thankfully, Felix had been so surprised by the potential hope, he'd come to a standstill. Whilst this apartment was spacey, there was only pacing room for one. Felix, obviously not reading the heat in the room, made his plea. "But if it could hel—"

Al roared, "No!"

Cissa lifted her hand and the room fell silent, the tension as tight as a wire. My ears were ringing from the stress. Cissa's calm voice was oil on choppy waters. "Al, it's okay. I am not about to throw everything away. I will not use my family's name." Al's shoulders dropped and his face sagged in relief. "But I can use mine… ours. I have earned enough of a reputation in this city that I may have some influence in the matter."

I was shocked to hear Jonathan's response. "Are you sure you want to make that kind of stand, Cissa? You know what it will mean, once that door is opened."

I'm glad she knew, because I was as clueless as a monkey at a chess tournament. Al was once again by her side, seated on the arm of her chair. This time, however, he was silent. Almost absently, Cissa reached her hand out again and laid it on his thigh. Al covered it with his own.

After a moment, Cissa answered. "It is time. For so long I have been working in the shadows, not making waves. It is hard to intervene when you are a party of one. But recently, things have changed." Her eyes lifted to Al and she smiled. He, however, dropped his head, a red glow washing over him, and a weight had him sinking into a slouch. "I am in a better place to fight that battle. And now too"—she looked around the room—"our numbers have increased by one hundred percent. I think if we continue to grow at this rate, we will be unstoppable. I will no longer be a sole thorn in their side; we will be a barbed-wire offence." At this she laughed. It was a song of joy. The mood in the room lifted and hope peeked its head through the door.

A momentary flash of light ignited along Cissa's deep crimson armour. "And let us not forget whose battle this is. We are merely foot soldiers. Our General has a game plan, and I do believe He is assembling the troops. The battle line has been drawn and we shall engage." A savage grin broke out across her face. She made eye contact with everyone in the room, stoking our fires till we were ready and amped to take on not only the gates of Hell, but the Sardis police as well. "I shall make the call"—her dark, almost black eyes flicked to Al—"on our behalf."

* * *

VAL STOOD at the top of the stairs, her face raised to the heavens with her eyes closed, and filled her lungs. Then almost stumbled as she was pushed in the back. "Get a move on. You've darkened our doorway long enough." A bored-looking Enforcer used his chin to indicate the footpath below them. Where, as it happened, we'd just arrived to pick her up.

The collective fear and anger in our group was amping us toward a riot. We were stopped by Val's smile. First to us, then to the Enforcer. "Thank you for your hospitality."

The shock on his face was comical. But then his mask changed to a sneer. "Frack off, you smarmy twik." Once again, we were on the verge of storming the Enforcer, but Val merely raised an eyebrow in response and strolled down the stairs into a tangle of arms. And very awkward shoulder patting from Felix. Once we'd disentangled and disengaged the twins, we piled into two cars, ours and Al's, and headed back to the apartment.

"Seriously, everyone, I'm alright." Val was now standing in the living room with both her hands up, calling for a halt in the fussing. "I am in need of several litres of water, a bite to eat, and a shower." She smiled and looked to me. "After that, Dan, I would appreciate you making me a cup of pure luxury from that marvellous contraption." She pointed to the coffee machine in the kitchen. During our time in Philadelphia, we had been living on tea due to the lack of real coffee. There was instant, but... tea was preferable.

Val took the chilled water bottle Riah handed her, gave the girl a shoulder hug, then made her way down the hall to her bedroom we'd modified from the apartment's study. She called out over her shoulder, "I will tell you all about it when I am feeling more human."

Fifteen minutes later, we sat around in the living room as Val held court whilst eating a significant snack Raph had prepared, drinking another bottle of water. We tried to be patient whilst she ate and drank, but when she pushed the plate away and eased back into the couch, holding her coffee, we couldn't take it any longer. Raph's questions were the first to open the flood gates. "Did they hurt you?"

Releasing her left hand from the mug, she placed her arm around Raph and leaned in and kissed his cheek. "Not significantly. I am fine. I am well. All is okay." From there she faced, and answered, the barrage.

"I was put in a cell with two other women. One was unconscious, the other extraordinarily angry. When she realised I was not going to be intimidated by her fury, she dropped the act and returned to sitting at the far end of the bench, the curled-up sleeping woman separating us.

"They never got round to providing food or water, which in a sense was a blessing, as it meant I didn't need to use the bathroom.

"Apparently, I was detained for disturbing the peace. And since it was my first offence, and my fine was paid expediently"—she raised both eyebrows to Felix in question. He shook his head and looked to Cissa. Val nodded in gratitude—"they agreed I only needed to stay overnight.

"However, I have been warned: I won't get off so lightly next time." She smiled from the eyes and looked around to each one of us. "I am well. I am refreshed. I am unharmed. Everything is going to be okay." She put her empty cup down and put her other arm around Riah sitting on her right, and kissed my sister's cheek. "Now, are there any more questions? I do believe we need to get moving if we are going to make it to TAVE in time. I am looking forward to learning how to put words on paper."

13

ALARIO: AND SO, IT BEGINS

"So, what's your take on them?" We were riding down in the elevator to pick up the Philly family and head out for our Community gathering. Raphael had suggested they might all go to the Community meeting at Sanctuary and visit their friends there instead of going to another in Sardis. Val'd smiled at him, her grey eyes warm, and told him, "No."

Cissa interrupted my musing before I took off down a rabbit hole. "It's just been a bit over a month. A bit early to tell, don't you think?" I stared at my wife. Silent. Waiting.

She smiled from the depths of her soul, staring back. Silent. Head tilted.

I caved first. "You formed an opinion of the young couple the instant they stepped out from cover at the hilltop west of Sanctuary. You had everyone's number at the war council when Val was arrested. You form an opinion of every single person you meet within ten to sixteen seconds, max, from the time you lay eyes on them."

"My goodness, Al, that's very specific."

"So are you. What do you think of them?"

Cissa tilted her head in the opposite direction. Her eyes lost focus and slowly she started nodding, her sleek black bob catching and reflecting the bright blue-white light of the lifts. "I like them. A lot." She came back to me then with an impish grin. "Can we keep them?"

The lift chimed and the doors opened. I shook my head and ushered my wife along the corridor leading to the apartment we had supplied for our new friends.

They were all ready and waiting for us. Since they... meaning Valarie, had been shunned from a number of Community gatherings in the month prior to her arrest, and there had been no more "invitations" to speak, we offered to take them to the main Temple of Light in Sardis—or what passed for one—where we normally went. At least we could guarantee, on any given Sunday, there would be at least a couple of genuine brothers and sisters in the Light among the multitude of play actors.

Nervous energy pinged off every surface and, in the centre of the storm, Val sat reading a book, apparently oblivious to everyone else climbing the walls. I could understand their fear of the unknown. However, the dread trickling down my spine was of the inevitable.

Any chance you could hold this off? Is Cissa ready for the consequences? Can we survive the fallout? Could you just keep the fools at the temple silent? Or on a leash? Or maybe really ill so they stay home?

Cissa patted my arm and winked. "It'll be fine, Al. Stick close and get ready."

We all made our way to the Pod stop at the base of our building and, as usual, waited less than five minutes for the auto-conveyance to pull up on its circuit of the city.

The Community of Light met in the foyer of the Temple of Artemis. Unlike most of the other cultural spectacles of Sardis, Artemis's temple lay outside the city walls and there were two ways to get there. The most common was to catch a Pod to the city gates, then a bus to the temple. The other was a Pod to the Acropolis, then the Sky-Rail down the mountain directly into the complex. As we lived close to the summit anyway, this was the way we chose to go. Sadly, there were no road accidents, hold ups or protest marches. There were no earthquakes, floods or declarations of war, and we arrived fifteen minutes before kick-off.

There is still time for a miracle here. I have faith. I know You can pull one out of the bag.

As was to be expected, we drew everyone's attention. Normally, when it was just Cissa and me, it was bad enough. But this morning, with seven guests in brilliant armour, and one who came with a scandalous reputation, we were like a beacon on a hill... in the middle of a starless night.

"Cissa, darling." One sycophant greased up to my wife and air-kissed her. "Aren't you going to introduce us to your friends?"

Cissa did as she was asked. "Neelam, these dear folk are recently from Philadelphia. They are staying with us at Black & Light Designs."

The attention Val was receiving was ridiculous. People were gathering and staring. I made an effort to unclench my fists and jaw. My shoulders, however, remained solid. "Please excuse us." The crowd didn't take the hint so I stepped forward. "We'll go and get some seats." It was hard to ignore the configuration our friends formed: Val at the front, Kait and Marcus on the sides, the twins on the inside. Tessa just in front of her husband bringing up the rear.

We took our usual place at the back in the "cheap seats" alongside the few others who were genuine children of the Light. The higher up in the Community you were, the better and more comfortable your seating was. The more money you donated, the more deference you were shown. We chose to sit at the back with the dregs who couldn't afford to sit at the front. And alongside our true brothers and sisters. As far as we were concerned, the further away from the Altar of Artemis, the better.

Shortly after, we made quick introductions to those in armour around us. The first act had officially finished without too much damage. But the second act was about to begin, and my money was on this being where the skrat hit the fan. I leaned into Cissa. "You ready? You know there'll be no going back?"

She squeezed my thigh and gave me her scary-eye grin. "More than. Now you're here, and we're good, I'm ready to jump."

It didn't take too long for hell to descend and, under the guise of a Community Gathering, have its way in a Temple of Light in Sardis.

"Brothers, sisters, welcome. To our guests from out of town"—a head nod to our row—"welcome. Today as we gather in the Light, let us give thanks for all that He has blessed us with and enabled us to achieve for our great city. Thanks to the hard work and generosity of so many, the Food Bank and The Shelter are funded for another six months, and we have raised over six thousand dollars for the Hospital auxiliary." He stopped and waited for the smattering of applause to die. "We are doing great things in this city and by doing so, continue to fly under the Gerent's radar. Our gifts and good wishes were well received by him, and I have a missive here from his office thanking us for our generous support of his recovery."

The seven sitting around us froze. Their breathing stopped. I knew this because in my motionless, hyper-aware state, mine had too. I suspect there may have been delayed brain function as well, as they tried to fully understand what they were hearing.

But, as was the norm, the disgusting truth kept pouring forth. "We have been working with the City Council in alliance with the priestesses of Artemis"—his arm waved to the side indicating the entrance to the Temple we currently sat under the lintel of—"to participate in this year's Festival of Feasts. We have been offered a seat at the Table of Temples, which has the approval of the Gerent. And, as you can well see, this is a huge step forward for our growing family. We are blessed to be in the Light, to be serving as His representatives and enhancing the life of those unfortun—"

"What did he just say?" It wasn't a yell, but it wasn't a whisper either. Val's disbelief echoed around the stone enclosure and bounced over the fifteen or so rows of semi-filled seats between us and the front. Everyone stopped, turned, and stared.

"I'm sorry, do you have something to say?" The Lead, Cassius, was too excited to have been honestly caught off guard. He'd obviously been waiting for Val to show and possibly even baiting her. The sad thing was, he didn't even have to try too hard to get her to bite.

Val inhaled deeply and considered the man. Marcus and Kait dropped their heads and held hands. The twins' eyes flicked between Cassius and Val, whilst Tessa and Dan stared, open mouthed, at the fool at the front of the gathering. I squeezed Cissa's leg and she took my hand and held on tight. We were balanced on a knife edge. Did we fall through the doorway or fall out?

Val stood. "Is that an invitation?"

Cassius was vibrating, his eyes alight with glee. "If you have something you would like to say, the floor is all yours. In *this* Temple, we don't bar fellow children of Light from having their say... within reason."

Val inhaled again, kissed the top of each twin's head, patted Dan and Tessa on the shoulder and nodded to Kait and Marcus, then made her way to the front of the gathering. The energy and anticipation within the room amped up to electric. Some even had their phones recording before she got to the pulpit. Kait sank into Marcus's shoulder and the twins shuffled their positions to bracket them.

Then Val spoke. "You call yourselves a Community of Light. You say you represent the Light in this city. Yet you cower before the man who hunts and kills members of your own family? You shelter under the lintel of the Dark to hide from consequences of living in the Light. You declare your own praise and preach your own works. Where is the Light in this place? In your hearts? How is His truth demonstrated in your actions?" Val's eyes took a few moments to skirt over the crowd. She stopped and nodded to the few others who, like us, were cloaked in armour.

"You have achieved good things in this city. But it is the Light who has provided the resources, the finances and the opportunity. Everything you have is from the hand of the Light. And yet, you acknowledge neither His blessing, wisdom, nor guidance. For those outside the Light, this is to be expected. But from those who claim to be His children, it is unacceptable. Without His provision, you have nothing. Without His blessing, you will fail. Without His guidance you will stumble.

"Wake up before it is too late. The truth is in you, His seed lives in your hearts. But you are selling your soul-security for short-term gain. You will lose it all if you do not stop what you're doing, turn away from this fallacy and return to the Light. Finish the good work that has been started here. It's not too late. I beg you. Dig deep and return to Him. Time is running out."

Someone from the front yelled out, "Who do you think you are? Coming in here and telling us what we are and aren't doing. How would you even know?"

Val lifted her arm and indicated the temple we were in. "You have cloaked yourselves in Darkness for fear of human reprisals. Do not fear humanity, or the Dark. It is the Light you should consider. He sees your actions. He knows your motives. You will be held accountable for your actions *and* inactions. For your words *and* your silence. He will come at an hour you cannot know. Will you be found sleeping? For you are far from Him and your charade here is thin and inconsequential. You cannot worship the Dark and the Light. Grow up. Stand up. Wake up!"

The ring of her voice bouncing off the marble walls and floor blended perfectly with the sirens approaching. Their high-pitched wail was an incendiary call-to-arms sparking the crowd into a fevered hysteria. Yelling in outrage, they all raced to get to Val. All sense had left them when she had challenged them on their pretence of dual citizenship, when she dared accuse them of wrongdoing, demanding they turn from their ways. If only she knew—and she probably did—she was telling them they could not feed their disgusting vices and addictions at the many temples, at the same time as claiming to be in the Light. They had to make a choice. Telling anyone in this city to renounce their memberships of the other temples was akin to telling them to stop breathing. Participating in these disgusting practices was their lifeblood.

We stood as one with Val's family. Albert, Desleigh, and Laura and Kirt, our neighbours, joined us as we tried to make our way to the front to stand with the woman who was fending off the enraged crowd. The mass of swarming hostiles and the discarded, fallen chairs made it too difficult to get to her.

And, of course, our progress was also hampered by the sudden onslaught of demons, barring our way with intent.

14

ALARIO: THE FALLOUT

I was impressed with the lithe and catlike manoeuvres of Sariah as she darted, weaved, climbed and leapt her way over the chairs, dodging demonic blades and human limbs, fighting her way to Val's side. Dan and Tessa were hot on her heels: Tessa just as nimble, Dan more wrecking ball in his approach. It wasn't long before all three stood their ground in front of Val.

Seeing reinforcements arrive spiked the crowd's agitation. A fool of epic proportions made a grab for Sariah, possibly because she was the smallest and looked the most vulnerable. This, however, ended badly for the imbecile. Not only could the child defend herself, she was standing within reach of three fierce warriors, all of whom took great offence at the act of supreme idiocy.

Perhaps, though, the most frightening response was the bellow of rage that caused everyone to pause. "Get your hands off my daughter!" Kait, an acrobat like her kids, was leaping her way to the front over the chairs. Marcus, with Raphael pinned to his side, just barged his way through, demons dismembered and discarded like rotting toxic refuse in their wake, until they took their place in the ring around their sister, shoulder to shoulder with their children.

Never one to miss out on the opportunity of a good rumble, I followed hot on Marcus's heels, elbowing my way through my personal attackers to the outer perimeter, all the while clearing a path behind me for Cissa and our friends. Arriving on Marcus's coat-tails, I barely heard Val's roar over the madness of the crowd. "Get them out of here."

At first, I thought she was referring to the hostile Community members, but then realised she was semi-shielding and pushing both Sariah and Raphael into Kait and Marcus. Her eyes wild searching for someone else. They locked on Tessa. "Go. You all have trackers. You're already on the radar." She looked to Marcus and roared, "Get them out. Now!"

There was no denying the order. Both Kait and Marcus glared at Val, nodded, and made a grab for the twins. I'm not sure Tessa received the memo she was leaving. She and Dan still tried valiantly to block the arms and fists reaching through to grab their prey. But Val ignored it all, sheltering the twins retreat. Her head snapped back as someone grabbed hold of her ponytail. Swivelling so she now faced her attacker, still bent in half, she rammed her head into the body of the fool. He dropped his grip, winded, staggering, out of the fight. Val righted herself, caught my and Cissa's eyes then nodded and mouthed, "Go," before she was pulled back.

The lad, Dan, was doing everything he could to stand as a wall between the hate and Val, but also pushed his young wife away—not gently—and yelled his own instruction. "Run!"

With gritted teeth, red face and rage burning along her armour, Tessa nodded once. Being so slight, she seemed to melt through the feeding frenzy. One moment she was there, the next she was gone. So were the twins. And Marcus and Kait. Cissa, our friends and I took their place in the ring until we were sure they'd enough time to escape the building. Only then did Cissa intervene.

She righted one of the ridiculously ostentatious chairs from the front row that had toppled, then stood, one foot on each arm. "Stop this at once." Her voice rang like a clang of clarity. "Stop. Now." Authority and arresting power pulsed through her voice. The third call of, "Stop," brought ringing silence and blessed pause to the insanity. "Look at yourselves. You are behaving like thugs... ignorant, undisciplined, savage dogs."

She paused and her eyes bored into all who stood closest to Val. The sirens stopped but flashing lights still pulsed as three cars pulled into the courtyard beyond the foyer of the temple. "All this because someone says something you don't like? Pathetic!" She spat the word with such incrimination that, as one, the crowd flinched like they had been slapped. "Each of you consider yourselves elders of this Community, leaders in our city. Burn with shame at your actions. Today you have not only defiled this Community of Light, you have destroyed your own precious and pitiful reputations. Burn in the filth of your shame."

Enforcers made their way over to us. The moment was lost and Cissa's power over the group dissolved as the newcomers entered the arena. The crowd, sniffing a hint of vindication, burred and barked, each eager to tell of the great offence of our guest.

Because of where she was standing and the attention she had previously held, the Enforcers assumed Cissa was their target. I stood in front of her and made it clear she was not causing any trouble. "In fact," I continued, "the only people causing trouble is this crowd who have violently turned on a single, unarmed woman, a guest, who was invited to share her opinion. These people"—I threw my arm out encompassing the group of about fifty—"are the ones who have incited this violence and disruption this morning."

"She can't come in here and say things like that. It's downright insulting and... disgusting. She is a public nuisance," a voice trembling with wrath spat from the back. I suspected Neelam's "spurned woman's fury" was finding an outlet.

The Enforcers, as one, turned to consider Val. By now a small clearing had appeared around her as everyone was eager for the law to see their evidence. She stood tall, hair barely contained by her hair tie, with tracks of blood down her face, neck and arms. Her ears were bright red, but her focus was clear and calm. Dan, similarly marked, stood beside her, almost containing his fury.

With a sniff, bored expression and raised eyebrow, the lead

Enforcer drawled, "You again. This your thing is it? Enjoy causing a riot?" It was rhetorical as two other Enforcers flanked Val, pulled her hands behind her back, cuffed her and marched her to one of their cars.

"What are you doing?" Dan barked. "She didn't do anything. They attacked her." His bulging eyes and ragged appearance didn't help his cause.

"You in on it too, are you?"

Both Cissa and I chorused, "No!" Possibly with excessive volume.

I continued, "He's an innocent bystander caught up in their feeding frenzy."

The Enforcer considered first me, then Cissa. He wasn't an idiot, he knew who she was and decided to let it slide. However, I could almost hear the bell tolling for the closing of our time of grace in this city.

Seeing that our part of the show was over, the crowd rushed to the Enforcers' vehicles to farewell their victim with shouts of abuse and hopes of long, undue suffering. We collected an inert Dan and slipped away to regather with our friends, and petition the Light on Val's behalf, and to consider our next step in this newly declared war.

* * *

"She is alright." Without knocking or stopping, Felix marched into the room with his arm out straight, a small disc sitting on his palm.

All of us had convened in our friends' apartment where Kait had gone over everyone, dressing wounds, checking injuries, wrapping sprains. She was the only activity in the room. The rest, us included, sat in shock, each lost in our own thoughts. Felix's entry, however, brought the room to life with activity, noise and hope. The little image hovering above the disc in his hand flicked off with the eruption.

Confusion wiped his face and stole his voice. At this we all paused and waited. Within moments the disc came to life, and blinked, again, at the roar from the room.

"Quiet. We must be quiet. She has somehow managed to hide the

ShellCom, but it transmits sound as well as vision." Collectively, the room swallowed their words, breaths and motion. Frozen, mid-movement, like a child's game of sleeping tigers, we waited. Sure enough, the disc sprang to life a third time, and this time we were looking at a hologram of an unimpressed Val.

"Not helpful, people. Do you know how hard it was to get this thing in here? Thank the Light I'm in minimum security." Tiptoeing on the plush carpet, Felix made his way to the centre of the group and slowly rotated a second small disc, so Val could lay her eyes on everyone. I suspected there wasn't a dry eye in the room. I couldn't tell you for sure as I was caught up in the middle of it.

Cissa squeezed my hands and edged her way forward to... quietly... get some information. "First, are you okay? Are you hurt from the riot?"

Val shrugged and gave a quick tilt of her head. "I've had worse. They're not too bad in here at the infirmary. Patched me up okay."

Cissa continued, "Do you know where you are and how long you're expected to stay? What are the charges, and can we pay bail?"

"I'm at some minimum-security unit outside the city. I think, because it's my second offence, I'm in for eight months. I believe, can't be sure, but because it's not a major lockup, I'm not eligible for The Games."

There were a couple of whispered, "Fracks," accompanied by quiet gasps released around the room. I, for one, hadn't thought of that. Neither had anyone else by the sounds of it.

Val's image quickly looked over her shoulder and her image blinked out.

"Okay. Well. This is... bearable. We can keep the ShellCom under watch around the clock. We can take turns and make sure we don't miss any... communications. I will..."—Felix's inhale was ragged—"leave it with you. You will need to be able to know what she needs, when she needs it. You are in the best... position to help." All this he said whilst his eyes were locked on the small disc perched in the palm of his hand. His arm still, ramrod straight, unwavering. His breathing unsteady, the fingers of his left hand dancing a tattoo on his thigh.

"Hello everyone." Marlene, Felix's aide, walked into the room, her appearance immaculate, the waiver in her voice the only indication of distress. Her eyes locked on Felix and her face dropped. She then sought out Marcus's attention and nodded her head to the hallway. She hitched her right shoulder which held the straps of her handbag.

Marcus nodded and gently placed his arm around Felix's shoulder and guided him out of the room. All the while, the man's eyes never left the disc nesting in his palm, as his left hand became increasingly agitated.

"Okay, people." Cissa brought us all back to attention. The steel in her voice was mirrored in her eyes. The two simple words were a rallying cry that invigorated the rest of us. "Val is okay. She is not in imminent danger. We have time. We have resources. We have the Light."

With each statement, life surged back into the group. "We petition the Light, then wait for further updates from Val. When we have a better idea of what we're up against, I will phone the authorities and see if I have any credit left in the bank."

Marcus returned. "I've set Felix up in Val's room. Marlene brought his medication. He'll be out for the count in a beat." The sorrow pouring out of the big man drew his kids. Both Raphael and Sariah went to him and enfolded him in their arms. This of course turned into a family embrace. Cissa and I went to the kitchen to boil the kettle, rummage for comfort food and try to give them some personal space to start to try to come to terms with the new reality.

Marlene's quiet re-entry drew it all to an end. Her insistence that she should, "Go and leave them to it," was met with a, "Completely unacceptable notion. You're family and you're needed here more than there, so take a load off, park your purse and have a cuppa."

She cupped Marcus's cheek and did as she was told. "Yes, dear. I've told the office Felix is taking a long overdue break. And if necessary, he will work from Sardis for the short-term future. I will find accommodation for us."

"Nonsense. He can stay with us." Marcus had barely let the woman finish speaking.

Marlene's stare bored through Marcus. I'm surprised the man was still standing. "You know that will not do."

"What about Gem?" Raphael piped up.

"Dear boy, thank you for your concern. He is in his carrier in the car with Arty."

Cissa and I put everything on trays and placed our offerings on the centre table. Kaitlyn paused mid-stretch. "My goodness, please tell him to come up. And bring Gem. Tiger is around somewhere, but we could shut him in a room?"

Raph took off, presumably to hunt for his cat, as Marlene, once again, did as she was asked. I pulled an extra cup from the kitchen and when Arty arrived with Gem, we partitioned the Light for Val, for direction, and wisdom in working out where to, and how to, from here.

I looked around the space. A cathartic quiet had settled like a comfort rug. Things were not right, but we had handed everything over to the Light and were trusting He had the ability and will to do what needed to be done.

And so did I. "Thank you for allowing us to be here with you. But" —I looked at my watch—"I'm afraid we have a meeting we need to get to and it can't be delayed any longer."

"Of course, thank you for everything." Kait stood and embraced me. Her head only came up to my chest, but the woman had the ability to make a person feel encompassed. Her warmth and compassion were a full-body experience. She then waited for Cissa to stand, to offer her the same comfort.

However, just as we were taking our leave, the ShellCom came to life. We all froze, scared any movement or noise would cause us to lose the link. Sariah raced to pick up the second disc to show Val who she was speaking to. "Is Felix okay?"

Marlene stepped in front of the device and answered, "Yes, dear. He is resting. We will stay here in Sardis so he is near his support base." Marlene's eyes flicked to Marcus and the twins. "I will keep watch, and I am sure Marcus will, too."

"Too right." Emotion gravelled the big man's voice.

"Okay everyone, here's the deal. I am fine. I am safe. You need to carry on with the plan. Go to TAVE as organised and find the Seeing Blind Man. That is our mission here. Do not get sidetracked with this…" she pursed her lips and shook her head, "flopping inconvenience. Keep your eyes open and I'll see if I can check in regularly to let you know how I am, and I can see how you're all doing. But I don't know how long this battery will last. I am petitioning the Light on your behalf. I'm sorry I can't be with you or help you in the search." I think I actually heard her teeth grind. "I will help you as soon as they let me out of here."

Kait replied, "Dear heart, do not worry about us. We will do our best and see what we can do to get you out as soon as possible. But until then, stay calm and try not to make waves… too many waves. This isn't forever."

Val exhaled and some of the tension smoothed from her face. But then her head snapped to look over her shoulder and she was gone.

On that note, the room exhaled and stress was leeched like an unsavoury ancient medical practice. I took Cissa by the hand and, after we had another round of farewells, took her upstairs for some downtime to recuperate.

Cissa considered me. "You know, we could help Felix out. I believe we have an apartment he could have. We could even accommodate Marlene… and her cat."

The lift dinged and the doors opened. Within moments we were heading home. "Yes, we could. And tomorrow we will consider what options we can offer them. For now, we are retreating, taking stock, and recuperating."

My beautiful wife smiled, leaned into me and acquiesced. She was getting better at that. Maybe I was getting better at constructing and enforcing boundaries. Whatever the cause, the effect was rewarding. I locked our door behind us, and hit the remote that instantly brought a few dim lamps and soft music to life. The temperature was set to a comfortable twenty-four degrees Celsius. "Go have a shower. I'll hunt down something for dinner and be back in fifteen."

15

RAPHAEL: NEW KIDS ON THE BLOCK

At 4.00 am this morning, when we rose for our usual sets and preparation for the day, the ShellCom came to life. We all gathered around and quietly had a quick catch-up with Val.

"Do not be scared of the people in this city. Do not be scared of what they can do to you, or me. Take courage, be bold, keep looking for the Seeing Blind Man. I am sad I can't help you, but the Light has work for me to do here among this group of women. The search is yours. Each morning at this time, I will try to briefly communicate with you and join you for at least part of our morning petitions. If I don't activate the ShellCom, please don't worry or try to contact me. Be assured I am well, and I am confident this is all part of the Light's plan for us."

She then asked if we could arrange for Cissa and Al to join us tomorrow morning. She had been thinking of a plan and wanted to see if they were "amenable".

After making plans for the day, giving it all to the Light and seeking his guidance, she disappeared, and we went on to sets. I felt like I was missing something... an arm?... my leg? Without her I struggled to find my mental balance. But I trusted she was right: it was all part of what the Light had planned for us.

Please take care of her and keep her safe. And well. And us, too?

Felix insisted, after what happened to Val, we each receive a new technological gift from him: earpieces that were paired with our phones. But something I was still struggling to understand was their capacity to write and send messages purely by thinking what we wanted to say. First, the contact needed to be established, and in our case, a group chat created. Then, once the earpiece had been synchronised with the user, and the app activated on our phone, we could send a text message simply by thinking what we wanted to say to whoever we wanted to speak to.

WE COULD SEND messages to the group via voice to text, or voice to voice—the message was relayed by Artificial Intelligence, using an imitation of the sender's voice so we could know who was speaking without having to look at our phones. The fitting that secured the piece around our ears took a bit to get used to, but held the device securely in place. Even in battle. We all had fun teaching the device our voices. Riah had the option of picking from a "sample bank". I was very grateful, and it made me feel a bit better about going to TAVE. I could be in touch with my family at all times.

A more beautiful place I had never seen. Laodicea was an impressive city, but the TAVE campus in Sardis suspended belief. Even though there was still evidence of damage from The Quake, over the past three years the people of Sardis had been worker bees tidying up their city and putting everything right again.

The Trade School sat next to the University in what was called the Erudite District. Despite the damage, clear evidence of beautiful architecture, exquisite gardens and thriving cafes sprawled throughout the vicinity. No one could see the whole from one vantage point: each bend in the beautifully designed paths opened new vistas and mind-boggling arrays of gifted craftsmanship. I could see how it would be both an inevitability and a joy to get lost in this wonderland.

Thank you for the blessing... the gift of studying here.

Each of us had been sent a welcome app on our phones. It came with access to all the maps, schedules, an overview of our courses and an introduction to our lecturers. And lots of information. About lots of things. On call. All the time. It took a while to navigate and get used to.

There were no cars allowed in the Erudite District, but free public transport was available from all over Sardis to ferry students and staff alike. The apartment Cissa and Al had provided was within their own building. It not only had two floors of apartments, it was their business headquarters and offices as well. They lived on the fifth floor. We lived on the level below. It was close to the very centre of the city, so it was easy for us to catch the Pod to TAVE... and everywhere else for that matter.

Hydrogen-powered City Circuit Pod transporters ran day and night, offering automated transport for all citizens. It was not illegal to drive cars in the city, but it was neither common nor necessary: Pods were regular and free.

Despite its beauty, I was unsure of this city. I knew the Light had us here for a reason, and I was very grateful for Al and Cissa... and my family. I just did not know what to think of a Community of Light who would attack Val and have her arrested... twice.

And how were we supposed to find the "Seeing Blind Man" in a haystack of humanity? All I could do was what Val said: come to TAVE every day, do my best to learn as much as possible, and try to make friends. I was not too worried about me. But I was very worried about Val.

And Sariah.

She still chose not to speak, but for the first time ever she would not have me to translate for her. We had discussed what means she could use most effectively to communicate with others. Felix had offered an electronic tablet. Dan had suggested a notebook and pen. In the end, Kait had sourced a small whiteboard and easily wipeable marker pens. This seemed the quickest and most reliable form.

We made her practise all week, each one of us taking her by surprise and asking questions out of the blue. Riah would madly scribble her answer, then wipe it away with her sleeve, leaving the surface clean to continue the conversation.

Tessa was not happy with this method. She kept trying to give my sister rags to use rather than stain the sleeve of her shirt. In the end it became a game until Tessa gave up. The rest of us also surrendered when Riah's answers to our surprise questions had turned… uncharitable. But at least we were all confident she could communicate effectively. It helped give us peace of mind. Especially Riah.

As we approached the main Administration building, my nerves began to overwhelm me. Would Riah be okay? Would Tiger survive by himself in the apartment? He was not an inside cat. Cissa was very kind. Not only had she allowed us to keep him, she had offered to check in on him during the day when she could. I knew everyone else would be fine. But Riah, Tiger, Val, and me, I was not so sure about.

Marcus's excitement burst from him. "Here we are, heart of the maze. Time to find our arteries and move out." Dan was just as keen, his hands tapping on his leg, almost bouncing on his toes. They each kissed their wives, hugged the rest of us and speed-walked along the path leading to Construction.

"See you this afternoon," Dan managed to call over his shoulder as they disappeared around the bend.

I was an icy statue as I watched them go. I was confident I would wander the paths of this maze all day. Lost. The thought of which no longer brought me joy. I could feel the red haze growing, making it impossible to comprehend the map on my phone. Now was not an ideal time to sink under its waves. I tried breathing deeply. Counting. Imagining Tiger in my arms, his needle claws kneading my chest, soft warm fur vibrating from his noisy purr.

"Right, then." Kait's words made the haze intensify. She was about to leave me, too. Val was not here. Tessa would go. Even Riah would leave me.

Oh, Lord, help me. I want to be brave. I know I can do this. I am just a bit worried that I cannot.

Her next words broke the back of the panic rising in me. "How about Raph and I explore this side of the campus and see if we can find Health Care and Hospitality? And you two"—Kait hugged Tessa and Riah in turn—"see if you can find The arts?"

I tried not to weep with relief. But I fear a tear may have escaped. I will always be grateful to my family for their care and discretion. Tessa and Riah both embraced me fiercely, and consequently dried all evidence of weakness from my face. Riah pumped my hand twice and the day seemed a lot brighter as we took our paths leading to new adventures and possibilities here in Sardis.

The facilities were perfect: shiny, new, modern and spacious. Every conceivable contraption anyone could possibly want or need was on hand. In triplicate. Our teacher was a peanut shell: her almond coloured skin, pale brown eyes, dark-blond hair—pinned back under a chef's hat—and apron ties offering a slight indent to her blocky outline. Her welcome was both perfunctory and warm, which helped dim her intimidation.

Because I had experience with cooking, evidenced by letters Felix had arranged from Vashti and Akai at the Factory in Laodicea, I was allowed to start in the intermediate course. There were two workstations at each of the eight benches. The large room was set out in two rows of four, and huge monitors were spaced around the top half of each wall. In this way, whatever you were doing, you had access to relevant information, in the form of video demonstration as well as notes.

Most of the spaces were taken except one place next to an angry boy, whom I suspected was only a few years older than me. I made my way over. "Is this space free?"

It was not quite a snarl, but he did hitch his chin, which I hoped indicated, "Yes." I stowed my bag in the locker provided under the bench and tried to break his ice casing. "Hi." I held out my hand. "I am Raphael… Raph. This is my first day."

He stared at my hand, then back at my face. "I know."

"You know my name is Raph?" I let my ignored hand drop in surprise.

He rolled his eyes, reminding me so much of Riah it made me

smile. "No, that it's your first day, dum—" He rolled his lips, stopping mid-word. I tried not to show my hurt feelings and forced my smile not to dim. He then threw his hand out. "Jimmy... Jim."

We shook in the most awkward fashion I could imagine. It reminded me of how Felix used to hug... before he had had the chance of learning how. I then determined that I would not only do my best to learn everything about cooking, I would also teach Jimmy Jim how to shake hands.

Thank you for such a great opportun—

"Okay everyone. Time to begin. This week we are exploring Asian cuisine. Buckle up, there is a lot to learn."

$$* * *$$

OUR RENDEZVOUS CAFE was not only central to where we were situated throughout the campus, it was popular with every other student as well. I was drowning in the crowd and being swept along in the swell to the front counter. Swimming sideways through the rip, I made it to the corner of the room. It was so swollen with people, I could not see a thing. I stepped into the chilly autumn air and sent the others a message on my phone where to find me.

The paved courtyard was enclosed by a shoulder-high retaining wall. Several long bench seats were built into the wooden sides. Callistemons, ferns and the pink tips of bromeliad leaves overflowed from gardens on top of the walls. In the middle of the courtyard a fishpond with a burbling fountain took pride of place. Orange and white fish lazily coasted their way underneath large-leaved water plants.

Dotted around the courtyard were umbrellaed tables. But in the chilly weather and soft sunlight, the umbrellas were not opened. Thankfully the dappled light was not warm enough to entice others out here: I had the space to myself.

Warm and snuggled in my jacket, I was caught up watching tiny sparrows play in the water of the fountain spilling into the fishpond. I had not heard anyone approach. My heart stopped and my nerves exploded when Daniel's arm wrapped around my shoulders, and he ruffled my hair. "How did you go, mate? Meet any interesting people? Any 'Seeing Blind Men'?"

He laughed and released me. I knew I was safe, and I was glad they were here, but my nerves and heart were yet to settle into the comfort of confidence. Marcus gave my shoulder a pat. Then stopped, pulled me into a quick hug and asked, "How was your morning, son?"

A warm glow whitewashed all other feelings. No longer a twig in a flooded river, I was grounded. "Really good thanks, Dad." A matching grin broke out across Marcus's face and he pulled me in for another, tighter squeeze. I was glad no one could see my heating face. I was not embarrassed, but I still felt a bit awkward using that name. I guess Jim wasn't the only one who was going to have lessons in being less uncomfortable.

"Move aside and let me get some of that good hugging action." Kait arrived and took Marcus's place.

"How was your morning, Mum?"

Kait did not answer straight away, and when she did it was very quiet. "Wonderful, my dear boy." The warmth in her voice flowed right through me, ushering the last of the chill away.

Soon after, Tessa and Riah joined us and the flood of people at the counter had abated. Tessa and Dan went to buy lunch for us all as we sat at an outside table, rugged up, discussing our classes.

Steam rose from the frothed milk of my hot chocolate as it warmed my hands. I did not feel the need to talk, but instead basked in the joy and excitement my family exuded as they shared about their first morning at TAVE. Already our lecturers had started speaking of possible placements for the practical component of our courses. Because we had started in the second term of the year, the other students had already organised where they would do their work experience. It seemed there were just too many good things going on for us here in Sardis. That is, if I chose to forget Val being sent to prison.

So, even though I was excited, and a bit nervous about our new beginnings here, I was also not confident things would work out well. I was grateful for my family. I was grateful for Cissa and Al who had given us a place to live, and a place to learn. I was grateful to the Light for giving us jobs to do, and so, for now, I would cling to these blessings and lock them in a memory box for when times were highjacked by the Darkness again. And I would wait for Val to be released from prison and, until then, trust the Light would take care of her.

16

JEMIMAH: EYES ON THE GROUND

I'd never had pets or a large welcoming family before, so I couldn't suppress the warmth that crept from my heart to my limbs when I stepped foot into the zoo. Sweetie, Bal's little white shadow, was usually the first one to sound the alarm, followed closely by Richard's "Hello, hello, hello." But once he realised I wasn't holding any new clothes or samples from TAVE, he drifted back into the garden, much like the strays—cats and dogs alike.

Kirra, however, wasn't so easily distracted. My trust was something I guarded under lock and key, but these guys didn't understand the concept of duplicity. Or boundaries. I allowed Cat Woman one head swipe and one hug, then gently encouraged her to step aside. But since I'd known Kirra for a couple of years now, she knew the drill and wasn't offended.

I dumped my bag in the food van, switched on the coffee machine to warm, then went over to the bathroom to wash up before prepping dinner. I always served dinner early so these guys could get back to their hideouts at The Wreckage before dark. I didn't want any of them out and about when the Catchers did their rounds. I'd keep an eye on them—like always—but best to have them secure early so it didn't come to anything.

Another thing I made absolutely sure of was that we had good, nutritious and tasty meals. I knew that apart from a few bits of fruit and veg and a bowl of muffins, these guys didn't eat much during the day. There was no way they could make it through the labyrinth of hostility all the way to the top of the mount, where The Shelter still doled out its horrendous excuse for food, nutritious but disgusting.

But now, thanks to Bal, and my coaching at TAVE, I had the resources and the know-how to feed my family properly. Each week, I made a detailed meal plan and handed it over to Bal. He didn't even look at it. He approved it and handed it on to Harry without question. Bal was super weird, super loaded and super generous. But he had never done me wrong. And he'd kept my secret... so far. So—so far—I'd trusted him.

I figured he knew I was sleeping in the van. But since he didn't speak of it, I didn't bring it up. Why should I smack that silent gift horse in the mouth? It seemed to work just fine that we each pretended the other didn't know.

Back in the van, music from the radio humming away in the background, I was in the zone. Making up dinner for my family. If you'd told me three years ago, when I was living the easy life with my parents up near the heights of Sardis, that I'd be doing this, here, I would have laughed myself sick. Mixing with the likes of these... and Bal, was an impossibility. No way a blue blood like me should ever cross the very visible status line that delineated the elite district. Now, I was planted deep and fully converted. I was never going back.

Here's a life lesson I have learned to respect: to the rich and powerful, people were an asset to be used, bargained or sold... or sacrificed, to further their career, or already bulging pockets. To the low and needy, people were a lifeline, a safety-net and an anchor to sanity.

Bal came by after dinner to help with the clean-up. Even though he'd once been one of the obnoxious rich and powerful, he wasn't like that anymore. Said some bloke visited him in prison and changed his perspective and life. Seeing as I hadn't known him BP—Before Prison, as we liked to call it—I wasn't judging him. But just couldn't get my head around the fact he used to be people like my mum. Now he was a PLU—People Like Us. Maybe there was hope that we could all change.

Bal was always offering to be the one to clean up after meals, wash the clothes, clean the bathrooms, pick up the dog skrat—with Richard's help. He was always the one offering to do the dirty work and serve everyone else. I just couldn't put him in the same frame as my mum and her cronies. Yet, that's where he'd lived... BP.

"Are you heading out again, Jem?"

"Of course."

"You know you don't have to." His big brown eyes pleaded for me to be safe. I knew he worried. But he didn't understand.

I had to keep an eye on our crew. Bal never left this property; he had no idea how dangerous it was out there. I let my eyes follow the last to leave, one of the pretty spotted dogs on his heels. "No. Thanks anyway. I'll be back tomorrow to help out." It wasn't actually a lie. I'd be home tonight, but it would technically be tomorrow.

Here's a life lesson I'd learned to respect, if you wanted to stay hidden, you had to move slow. So, covered from head to foot in black, with rubber soled runners, I took to the streets creeping along my pathways, tunnels and well-trod alleys. Despite my body craving a run to stretch my legs, I kept low and slow. Over the past two years I'd learned all the shortcuts, escape routes and vantage points of this city's facade. I knew my way in and out of the temples... all of them. Well, except Dionysus's under the Theatre; that one was full-on freaky scary.

I knew how to access my old apartment block, and I knew how to keep tabs on my mother. I figured the best way to stay safe was to keep one eye on the enemy, and the other eye on the nearest way out of Dodge. I'd made it my job and number-one responsibility. That's another reason I'd agreed to sign up to the TAVE course. I knew it was dangerous. I knew she was there. But our faculties were on opposite sides of campus. And I wasn't there to socialise. I was there to learn. Life wasn't just about me anymore. It was about keeping everyone safe. No way was I ever going to end up a victim... vulnerable... or a useless slab of meat on someone else's platter, ever again. Nor would I allow any I cared for to end up in that boat either.

Circuiting the ring-road at the top of the city, I moved to check what Mother was up to. I was almost caught by the new kid and his huge family. I sank back into the shadows and followed the kid's tail. Not like I didn't have time to kill. I wouldn't finish my rounds till after midnight. But I lost him when they entered a huge building a couple blocks along from my mum's place. Interesting. I waited to see which lights came on up the wall of glass, but there was no sign of them. Must live round the back.

After that, I checked to see Mother was at home. She wouldn't be for long. It was a Thursday night. She'd be heading off to play at one of the temples. I'd noticed Dionysus was the flavour this month. The woman was like a bat, most active at night and rarely a sole trader. She tended to dole out her preferences and offerings to the most alluring bidder. After watching her apartment lights blink out, I waited. She'd be down soon, but, unlike the masses, she wouldn't be taking the Pods. Too common for my mother. She'd drive.

Once I saw her car did, in fact, head east toward the Cultural District where the Theatre was, and not west to the main exit of the city toward Artemis's temple, I continued my rounds of the other temples. Needed to keep an eye on what they were up to, who they were offering and, if need be, see if I had to intervene.

Strays around our golden city weren't a problem... ever. Animals, that was. The Temple Catchers did their job well. Although, I couldn't understand the appeal. Why would any god—a supposed supreme being—be happy with the sacrifice of a stray dog or cat? I couldn't imagine they were good eating. I've always suspected this was the reason so many of the beasts hung out at The Wreckage and Bal's... *outside* the city gates. With no access for the Catchers at Bal's, and too many escape routes and hideouts at The Wreckage, it was a perfect place to call home. For all of us.

Not often did the sickos at the temples offer up people for sacrifice. Special occasion, that. But they did have other depraved uses for the city's human expendables. Apparently, people paid good money to abuse innocent victims. First time I saw it, I had to scarper super quick, so I didn't give myself away heaving my guts out. I just couldn't understand how those sick fracks could come up with that stuff. And live with themselves.

And that's why I kept watch: for my family and companions who made The Wreckage and Bal's our home. Had to make sure none needed rescuing from becoming the sickos' playthings. Liked to think I would, anyway. Rescue any who needed it, that was. But in my gut, I just didn't know if I had the nerve. So, knowing what was going on, who the players were and what they were into, how to get out of every single building and district in town had become a compulsion. I had to know. I had to be sure. I also had to check that Mother wasn't on the hunt for me. I had to check and check again every night, before I could sleep.

And here's another life lesson I've come to respect. Repeat a lie long enough, you'll believe it. So, every night, whilst doing the rounds, I told myself I would. I would definitely rescue any of my family: people or animals, who got caught up in the temple's feral web. I was brave, I was a survivor, and I would make my dad proud. And one day, I would actually believe it.

17

MARCUS: THE DEATH OF ME

All this bleeding paperwork and study was leaching the life out of me bones and the passion from me blood. Hours upon hours of reading reams of text was driving me cross-eyed and giving me a burn to purge something... from somewhere... with extreme diligence.

At first, I'd naively believed our lecturers' tall tales of early release. Josh and Tim, our supervisors from Philadelphia, had laughed, slapped us on the back and encouraged us to "hang in there". But I tell you what, me fingernails were bleeding and me teeth were fully skinned. I was about done. It'd been almost two months since we'd started, and I was officially standing in the doorway of throwing the towel. I was stuffed full of carrots from the diet we'd been fed on fishing lines promising that we were coming to the end of the torture. "Soon as you're done, you can get outside and get your hands dirty." But the promises were Scotch mist and me patience was wafer thin.

The sky had been as heavy as a full udder hanging over the city and had started throwing cats and dogs at us before we got off the Pod at TAVE. It was sealing me fate for yet another day: in this weather, we'd not be getting outside. I'd protested and suggested: as carpenters and builders we'd need to work in all conditions. Me instructor hadn't said a word, just lofted one of the thickest theory booklets and pointed to the dreaded title, *Workplace Health and Safety*. "Do you need a refresher, Marcus? Would you like to spend the day going over the basics?"

I bit me tongue, swallowed me frustration and fear, and waved it all away. "Just pulling your leg, Garret." But inside I was crying and trying to hide so he wasn't tempted to follow through with his threat. I was a silent pressure cooker on the verge of something stupid. I'd much rather be out there soaking me soddens than in here any day of the week, rain or shine.

Me instructor gave me a knowing grin and went on to address the class. "Good news, everyone. Today, after our final theory exam, we're putting the books aside for the rest of the term. However, before we can send you on your practical component, we need to check the paperwork to confirm you're all squared away for your placement." Me groan at the thought of more paperwork was not supposed to come out. But when Garret gave me and me lad the thumbs up, saying we'd already been approved and cleared to work with Black & Light Architectural Designs, I wanted to buy the guy a coffee and give him a hearty slap on the back.

I was not proud to be the last in the class of about twenty to hand me paper in. I would rather be the last one through the gate, though, than the only one sent back because I'd got me answers wrong. Being the oldest in the group I liked to see myself as wisest, so didn't put on a show about being the fastest. Garret smiled as I handed me paper in and stage whispered, "Not long now, mate, and we'll all be out of here."

It was our faculty's tea break, so Dan and I took to the halls and raced around the campus to check on the kids. When we'd first arrived, it'd taken our whole break just to reach Tessa. Not only did we have to fight the demons lurking around the shrine to Timolus and Hermus—the local gods of the mountain Sardis was built into and the valley beyond... or some such rot—we had to then fight the demons blocking the path into the Textiles building around the shrine to Artemis.

Sardis was like most… all cities I had known, who enjoyed their gods like an all-you-can-eat smorgasbord. There was no rhyme nor reason to their worship or even clear lines between the gods. It all came down to which vice a person wanted to play with on any particular occasion.

It didn't take too long for us, and our Guard, to make an understanding with the local minions. We would come through every day and we would check on our family, every day. And if they stood in our way, we would kill them, every day. So, they could either step aside and let us pass, or things would turn ugly, every day. Because, I'll tell you now, the extreme boredom of being stuck in a classroom, reading eye-wateringly boring text, had me trigger finger itching and me fists ready to express me severe frustration. A bit of hallway skirmish was going to go a long way to settle me soul and bring me equilibrium home to roost. I was kind of hoping they'd object. After a while, they didn't. Which was just as well. Our classmates started to think we were as mad as two bags of spanners as we returned flushed and breathing hard after every tea break.

As was our habit, we went first to Tessa. Bursting through the doors of the Textiles building, past the Artemis shrine, we made our way to her room and saw her. Head down, tape measure around her neck, chalk in her mouth, she was working away at something on her huge table. Her Guard was at her side and hadn't drawn his sword, so all was good.

From Textiles we made our way to the Arts in order to check on Riah. Of all the "gods" we were exposed to daily, Dionysus was the worst. Me skin crawled and the hairs at the back of me neck danced whenever I had to pass his shrine. When we laid eyes on Riah, her back was to the door. Seated in front of an easel, leaning to the side so she could see her instructor, she looked to be listening. Her communication whiteboard was on a tall stool by her side within easy reach and, again, her Guard stood nearby with his sword sheathed.

We had to pass the shrine to Demeter to get to Raph. He was harder to see at the back of his class. He was still partnered with the angry kid. I could see me boy's hands working away, mixing something in a dish. I couldn't see his Guard clearly, but the room was calm and there wasn't a mass of trouble brewing.

Next, we raced past Persephone's shrine to find Kait's class. Her room was open, more like ours, with desks that could be easily moved and a huge screen at the front of the class. Set up around the space were models, and dummies. As we peeked in through the glass top of the door, she turned and winked before turning back to her lecturer.

Kait: You know you could just message us, Bear?

Marcus: Don't you be telling me how to parent me kids, woman.

Marcus: I mean, that is to say, I love you.

Riah: Love you too, Dad.

Raph: I love you too... Dad.

The messages came through our shared family contact group, and were read audibly via AI in me earpiece. The lump in me throat was like a knot of dry wood shavings. Dan and I nodded and raced back to our own class before the break was over. Everyone was okay, we could get on with the day.

Once again, I was reminded of how grateful I was to me mate Felix for sharing his ShellCom with us. Each morning I was reassured me sister Val was doing okay. All me family were fine and prospering in Sardis. This could be an easier assignment than normal. Apart from the chaos caused by Achan, and the extreme boredom of theory, we were all doing okay.

18

CONTESSA: THROUGH THE
LOOKING GLASS

F ar. Flaming. Out.
We had only been here, in Sardis—the biggest trade city on
the continent—for just over two months and I had already been
noticed by the Guild. I just couldn't believe it. I was seriously pinching
myself.

All. The. Time.

As far as industry went, Sardis was the centre of the universe. All
business in the continent—and textiles in particular—started and
flowed from here, straight down the mountain to Thyatira: textile's...
design's... fashion's capital of the world. It was so big and important,
there was a governing Guild that had a chapter here in Sardis. And the
fact that I had been noticed... before graduation... was, like, a
complete honour.

My lecturer was a big deal in the Sardis Guild, and she had
checked out my work on Sanctuary's website, and she'd asked to see
photos of other things I had made and designed. And she was all kinds
of impressed. Last week she called me into her office. I was, like, super
scared. Anyway, she said she'd liked my work and asked me a few
questions about my concepts and inspiration. And, I mean, I wasn't

name dropping or anything, but I felt I kind of had to acknowledge that some of my inspiration came from Achilles, back in Laodicea, who designed a whole line for his autumn collection based on my armour. And Kari and Jason? Even though they turned out to be horrible, I did learn a bit from them first.

Then, of course, I had been inspired and influenced by Kerm and all the time I'd been working with him and designing for my sisters at the Factory. Jolena, my lecturer, had wanted to see evidence of these designs. So, thankfully I had some photos on my phone from the wedding and I could show her those, and some of my other work, like Val's shirts, and then explain why I had designed them like I had. Why I had chosen the fabric, colours, and well, you know... all that. Not that I explained the colours matching our armour. Trying to elaborate to an Unseeing person was just a waste of time. And they ended up thinking you were a crazy. But, as far as design, colours, fabrics... once you got me going, I kind of had trouble stopping.

Anyway, Jolena was so lovely, she just let me talk and explain. She'd pushed a large-screened tablet across the table and given me a stylus to help me show what I was trying... and not doing a very good job at, explaining with words. With a tablet and stylus, I had so much more freedom.

Eventually I sat up and realised Jolena wasn't looking at the tablet, she was leaning back in her chair watching me... smiling.

And nodding.

And all of a sudden, I had a feeling in my gut that something wasn't right.

"Sorry." I put the stylus down and pushed the tablet into the middle of the table and folded my hands in my lap. Heat rose from my collarbones, and I knew that I would now resemble a sunburned daisy: white hair, dark eyes and ghastly red skin. "I do tend to get carried away when I get started on design. You should have stopped me."

Her smile didn't dim.

Nor did she say anything.

Like. Any thing.

At all.

She just stared.

I am not proud of my weakness, but there was just no way I could hold her gaze anymore, and I looked down and fiddled with the fingerless, skin-coloured glove that covered my ugly tattoo. 0046. The number burned like a black brand into the back of my hand: ugly, permanent and damning.

I was so lost remembering how I'd got it, I jumped when Jolena spoke. "Oh, no need to apologise, Tessa dear. On the contrary, I see you have a great future here in Sardis… in textiles. You really are an enthusiastic little thing, aren't you? I do believe your star is on the rise and I would like to do what I can to help you achieve greatness."

Gob.

Smacked.

Seriously, what could I say?

Jolena laughed at my response. "Surely you can't be too surprised. You know you're good?" She paused.

I realised she was actually waiting for a response.

That was a question.

Not rhetorical.

What could I say?

"Um. I like designing?" I gulped. "And people seem to like what I make them? So, I guess?"

Again, she laughed. "Too much, Tessa dear, you are too much. Listen, I run an extension program for my extra… gifted students. It will mean more work, extra assessment, and additional classes… night classes. There are only a handful in the group so, it is more… intense… intimate. One-on-one. No escaping the microscope, so to speak." Her eyes regarded me like I was a bug under a magnifying glass. A strange bug she was struggling to identify. "There is no obligation to accept of course. But…"

But…?

But what?

Oh.

Again, I realised she was waiting for a response. "Um, that is seriously incredible. Thank you. However, I am not sure I can afford that extra program. You see, we're sponsored here in Sardis. Our studies are being paid for by—"

Jolena laughed, collapsed back in her chair, threw her hand out, disregarding my argument. "It's free. Consider it a type of scholarship you have won due to your talent, work ethic and potential. All you need to do is say yes"—she took the tablet and stylus back and with a few taps and swipes she put it back in front of me, holding the stylus for me to take—"and sign here. Then it will all be done."

"Oh." That was fast. "Um... I guess it would be okay? I know Dan comes in for night classes. I could come with him... Maybe I should talk this ove—"

"Classes start tomorrow night. You've only just made the cut before this term's project starts. My students will feature their garments in the opening of the Spring Festival at the end of the term. Your work will be presented, not only to the Guild, but to all the buyers and suppliers in Sardis, the Seven Cities and... Thyatira. My students not only open the programme, the top performer gets a contract and special billing." Her sing-song voice was the perfect accompaniment to the huge sparkly disco ball she was waving in my face. I could feel my heart skip a few beats with just the thought of it. My own line, on show. I tried very hard to breathe steadily and command my heart to flopping well calm down. I was going to have a heart attack before I had the chance to sign.

I leant over and took the stylus with a shaking hand and started reading the form.

"Oh, don't worry about that, dear. That's just all legal talk. If you want to join the elite group, just sign your name at the bottom. I will sort everything and make a place for you." She shunted the tablet a bit closer.

I looked to her, then to the page in front of me. "How much extra time will be required of me?" I was having flashbacks to Laodicea when I went AWOL doing this precise thing. Then in Philadelphia when Dan was sucked into the "work" hole and abandoned us... me. I didn't want to start our marriage making the same mistake. "I need to know the time commitments and expectations to be fair to everyone before I can sign up."

"What a wise girl you are. You will be required to attend one extra class a week... at night. You may work on your assignments in regular classes and, if you would like to, or need to, you may do extra work at home. But that is entirely up to you."

I looked down. Between my rapidly beating heart and the crowded print, I couldn't make sense of the document. Except of course the blank line down the bottom waiting for my name.

Please let this be the right thing.

And I signed.

"Wonderful. I will ensure you have a complete set of equipment and workstation set up and ready to go by tomorrow night. Class starts at 6.00 pm on this floor, in the room at the end of the hallway. That way you can all leave everything set up as you like it and don't have to worry about anyone moving your gear. However, anything you want to bring to day class, you are more than welcome."

* * *

DAN'S THIGH was pressed up against mine. Our hands were entwined as I stared out the Pod window at the darkened city cruising by. My first night. I couldn't believe it.

Thank you so much. For everything. I'm not sure how effective I am going to be in helping to find the Seeing Blind Man, but I am so very grateful for the opportunity to learn and improve and help support my family doing something I love. Please. Please. Please help me get it right this time.

Not taking my eyes from the window, I pumped Dan's hand twice. I did not want to go backwards. I wanted to keep going forward and always consider my place in the Light and my family. But, it's just, I always seemed to be the one making mistakes.

Dan leaned over and kissed the top of my head. "It's going to be okay, Tessa."

"Tell me if I'm going wrong. If I'm losing sight of what and where I need to be? I don't want to leave you behind."

"I will, if you will."

"Deal." We sealed our pact with a kiss just as the Pod pulled into the Erudite District. Tonight was the start of something big. The promise of it zinged in my bones.

Help me get this right.

Jolena swanned into the room, her black, flowing top billowing like a dark cloud. Her long dark hair bouncing in layers around her shoulders only complimented the concept of an imminent storm. An electrical storm bursting with energy and potential. "Tonight, people, we begin to prepare the way for your future. Tonight, we start the hard work in defining your unique voice in textiles in Sardis, then into all the world. We only have three months, so get your head out of winter and get your heart into spring. And what will The Chosen be wearing in spring? That is what you are going to answer in the next few months. From each of you I require a three-piece outfit... accessorised. Tonight, you will find your inspiration. Next week, you meet your models."

Far. Flaming. Out.

Three months.

Three pieces.

Ready to show.

Accessorised.

Uniquely and tastefully. Well, that was my take on "unique voice".

Intimidating, much.

I looked around the room to the other six students. One blond guy was already madly sketching on his stylus. The rest of us just looked at each other, all equally in shock. I trembled a smile at the two other girls in the group. One smiled back. But it lacked warmth. I was not feeling the love. Obviously, this group was already out to compete.

So, You know how You're the Creator Light? Could You, like, maybe help me out a bit here with some inspiration? Please?

Thankfully we were not left in the cold. Jolena darkened the room and put a video on. With tablets and styluses in hand, we watched a timeline of fashion trends: a collage of concepts, favourites and flops. And it worked. Ideas started flowing and, as soon as I released the initial lines, sparks of ideas exploded.

Thank you.

19

ALARIO: CROSSED WIRES

"You're back." It wasn't a question. But then it wasn't a necessary comment, either. It was bleedingly obvious I was back.

"As are you." I dropped my keys in the foyer bowl and went to my room to drop off my gear, and change. The atmosphere was still chilly when I emerged into the living room.

Cissa was seated in the central lounge looking out over the city. She didn't even bother to face me when she shot, "Where have you been?" Another unnecessary question. I'd taken my car and there was only one place I needed to drive and that was out of town. Generally, Philadelphia.

"Out. Where were you?"

"What do you mean, where was I?" At this she swivelled and at least gave me the decency of her focus. "I've been here the whole day, working." The temp went from cool to slightly higher than comfortable.

So I thought I might add some more heat. "This morning, after my ride and shower, I heard you in your bathroom, and thought I'd nip out and get us some breakfast from the bakery downstairs. I was only gone fifteen, twenty minutes max. When I got home, you were gone. No note, no text, no email, nothing.

"I tried calling you, but your phone was on DND. I had breakfast, waited a few hours, worked from home, dropped into my office, worked there for a few hours, caught up with Charlotte—who also had no idea where you might be—and cleared my desk. Still no word from you. And, since I can't start the plans for the Sanders project until I have the details, I thought I'd head out... after work, and see how Jonathan and Daisy were going at Sanctuary." I stood perfectly still, hands in pockets, and spoke in a quiet, calm voice. Well, that was what I was going for. "Not one word from you, or a returned call. No message from your PA to mine, or any indication of where you were or what you were doing. So, I figured you were... busy." Calm sidestepped that last word and allowed sarcasm centrestage.

"I was in a meeting. Meetings," she amended. Her face was in shadow, but her indignation was almost comical.

I wasn't in a laughing mood, however. "A work meeting? One that was for Black & Light Designs, by any chance?"

"With the Saunders for most of the day. But when I went to tell you about it this morning, I thought you were still asleep, so I left without you."

"So, this meeting, with these difficult clients, the one I need to work closely with you on, just happened to be called on the spur of the moment. This morning. At 6:55 am?"

She spun away from me and faced the window. Twilight had blended with the lights blinking awake from the city. Cissa's voice was so quiet, I almost didn't catch it. "No."

"And you didn't think of telling me about it beforehand? Or returning my calls during the day? Or at least leaving a message with Charlotte? If I'd been in the Philly office, I would have been included via conference call. But, like our other complex clients, I would have driven over to be here in person. If it had been an early morning or late-night meeting, I would have stayed over."

"I'm not used to you being here. Within reach." She looked up at me as I rounded the end of the lounge, dark circles under her eyes evident on her olive skin. "I'm really sorry, Al." She dropped her head and swivelled her wedding ring. "When you were aslee— When I

125

thought you were asleep, I thought you didn't care. That this"—she raised her head and bounced her hand between us—"wasn't important."

"My bike wasn't here." I pointed to the little office space next to my room. "You didn't even give me a chance. Why didn't you return my calls?"

She looked down again and whispered, "I was angry... and hurt."

"I can relate."

"Please don't be angry. I am trying. I really am. But sometimes when I look at you, I have to remind myself you're not the enemy. For so long we've been hurting each other, it's my default mindset."

I huffed and collapsed at the far end of the lounge and repeated, "I can relate." It was an ugly but honest truth. I felt the same way. "I guess it was never going to be easy, or that we could just slip back into married life without hiccups." I made myself look at her. I was still significantly skitched off. "We've been single for so long."

"Communication was never really our thing, even when we were good. Was it." Again, it wasn't a question, it was another bleedingly obvious statement of truth. Cissa turned to face me. Her knee came up and rested on the broad, dark, leather cushion. Her arm lay on the back, she breathed in and out deeply, then spoke directly. "Al, I'm sorry. I made a terrible error of judgement and I feel terrible. Sick with guilt. I am asking you to forgive me, and for another chance at working this out. I will ask Freya to share my calendar with Charlotte, and, if you are willing, we can share each other's diaries." I was about to answer, but she raced on. "You don't have to share your personal calendar, just work. Maybe we could get Charlotte and Freya to work at making a combined 'work calendar' that both of us will share?"

The tumble of words slowed to a stop. I waited a beat just to make sure there was nothing else, then responded. "Yes." I tried exhaling some of the hurt. "Yeah, that sounds like a good idea."

She tilted her head and stared into the space over my shoulder as— I assumed—she reviewed what she'd said and what my answers meant. I could have been more explicit, but... I was still hurting a bit... a lot. I would... did forgive her. I knew I was going to stuff up sooner or later, so it would be helpful to have some credit in the bank. Because, at the end of the day, I did want this to work. I was just incredibly grateful Cissa had been the first to make the inevitable mistake. Things were going to be rough. How could they not be? We'd been apart for so lo—

"Al?" Cissa was sitting next to me, her hand shook my leg.

"What? I mean, yes?"

She leaned up and softly kissed my cheek. Her spicy fragrance tickled my nose and brought me back to my new reality. "Thank you, and shall we get dinner? Since I missed breakfast… and lunch."

"Are you crazy, woman? No wonder you're tired. What do you feel like?" I was on my way to the door before she had answered.

"You choose. I'll set the table."

20

BALASHKA: BUSINESS AS UNUSUAL

I shouldn't laugh, but it was impossible not to. It happened each week when Jemmy returned from her trawl of the opportunity shops. Like bees to honey, she drew our friends, desperate to inspect her wares. Without patience or any concept of waiting, however, it had the habit of turning troublesome.

"Hello. Hello. Hello." Richard was desperate to see what was in the multiple paper bags she carried but was very careful not to come within a metre of her. He was doing well practising appropriate social distance.

Cheryl was not afflicted with the same discipline. Personal boundaries were not within her worldview. "What did you get me, Jemmy? Show me, show me, Jemmy. Me first."

Kirra, expressing her delight at something new via her default persona of a cat, released a very impressive mewl. And, thankfully, the rest who were here demonstrated their feelings of something new by hiding or waiting in the shadows until they felt safe to emerge. Nevertheless, my poor Jemmy was struggling to battle her way through to the Undercover Area in order to offer her weekly find.

Fighting off the last vestiges of chuckles, I hobbled my way down the slope to help, Sweetie at my heels, to find, as per usual, Jemmy had brought home gold: fluoro for Cheryl, multiple shades of green for Richard, flowing dresses for Kirra who was currently purring as she held a floral number to her cheek, caressing the fabric. I also noted the few black items in the mix of multiple styles of fresh, clean, whole clothing. I was relieved to know that she was also taking care of her own needs as well as helping me care for the others.

Once she'd re-sorted the clothes after Cheryl, Richard and Kirra had swamped her, Jemmy handed back the drawstring bag we used as the kitty. "You need anything else, Boss?"

"I'm good thanks, dear—" Her glare cut me short. I looked around the property and couldn't see anyone out of the ordinary. "There's no one here, dear."

"You promised me you wouldn't tell people I'm a girl."

"I'm not. I haven't. I never will." I moved in and placed a hand on her shoulder and waited till she looked up at me. In a quiet voice only she could hear, I continued, "But you, my dear girl, are very precious to me. Like a daught—"

"I don't need a father."

"No, of course not. But we all need family."

"I don't. And I don't need you." Her eyes darted away before she'd finished the lie. She still preached the same message, but the heat was ebbing from her argument.

"You may not need us... me. But I value your help, your contribution and your company. In the presence of our... my family, I would like permission to express my fondness of you, as I do with all the others, and call you 'my dear'. Yet, I understand this makes you uncomfortable. Forgive me. I will work harder at remembering to watch my tongue and help keep your true identity hidden."

Jemmy rolled her eyes, shook her head and huffed in a manner, I believed, was consistent with teenagers throughout the ages. The normality of the response had me laughing again. *Now, let's see what you have bought to try to entice me out of old faithful.*

Prior to prison I had lived a life of excess in every area of my life. This led to owning far more than one needed and weighing far more than was healthy. Since my encounter with The Man, my life's perspectives had changed. As a result, I still wore the suit I was taken to prison in—despite it being multiple sizes too big—and the occasional new belt. That was the thing about buying quality: back then, it was made to last.

Jemmy, however, did not see the purpose behind my stubbornness in this. She saw I had means and an income and therefore couldn't understand my refusal to take on anything more than I absolutely needed.

I had not divulged the agreement I made with The Man. I would replace my current clothes only when they were too worn to be socially acceptable. I had, obviously, taken on several other shirts and another pair of slacks in my early days—from an opportunity shop. Thankfully, as my waist diminished I could just tighten my belt. As far as I was concerned, I didn't go out much… at all. And the people who came to my home knew the score: everyone's normal was completely acceptable here.

I stepped back and, again, tried to hold back my laughter. "Richard, how about we try to wear one pair of trousers at a time."

"Hello. Hello. Hello."

* * *

THE TWO NURSES found out about us via Gerald the art teacher. There was a constant rotation of students on placement at the Sardis public hospital. Aran was one of the nurses who was a liaison with TAVE. Through his contact with Gerald, he came to know about us. Now he and a colleague, Gabby, included us on their bi-weekly rounds of community nursing. Occasionally, if they came across a star pupil, one whom they thought had the compassion and humility to work with our family, they were invited to come along. After signing a non-disclosure, that was.

As far as I had heard, though, today it was going to be just them. Aran would supervise showers and do health checks for the men; Gabby would do the same for the women. Hence the need for new clothing. When our friends were having their showers, I would wash their clothes. They then had the option of choosing something new, or, when it was dry, wearing their usual until it was unfit for public appearances. It was all about giving them options and allowing them to make as many decisions for themselves as they were capable of.

This was an important lesson I learned in prison. The freedom to choose how I lived my life—even down to something as simple as what I wore—gave me dignity and ownership. Robbing someone of choice is the root of imprisonment. It's why I can live here, surrounded by a wall of plants, isolated from the world, and feel free: I have chosen to do so. At any point in time, I am free to walk out, to mingle with society. Although, why I would subject myself to such abuse is beyond reason. The thing is, I could if I wanted to.

There were many things my friends here couldn't do. That they were not permitted to do or capable of. The idea was to find out what each of them could do, then allow them the freedom to choose how they did it. Except when it came to being naked.

"Richard, my friend. Might be best to wait until Aran gets here for your shower and check-up before you take your clothes off. Show me what clothes you want to wear today. Then we can do some gardening till they get here."

"Dog poo. Dog poo. Dog poo."

Thankfully it worked. Richard put his pants back on and started toward the garden, ready to start picking up the offending parcels left by our other residents.

"Gloves first, Richard, remember?"

"Hello. Hello. Hello."

* * *

HARRY ARRIVED to collect my latest commissions and we caught up over delightful takeaway coffee he'd supplied.

Once we had completed our business, it was time to start work.

The flags came down, signalling to the less inquisitive that the coast was clear. As was normal, the first port of call for residents was the fruit and vegetable snack bowl and water station. Gabby and Aran made health and cleanliness education part of their regular visits. Continuing to remind our friends how to wash hands and toilet properly... in the provided facilities. Their efforts had greatly improved health and boosted immunity.

When all were ready, we headed into the garden. With disposable gloves and a bin on wheels, we strolled throughout the five acres looking for obvious weeds, sticks and dog poo.

Molly had allocated a small allotment for each of our regular family members to "tend". The space was a cacophony of colours and textures set out in a patchwork quilt. The only rule: your plot only.

Some were just green plants—Richard. Others were over-planted with bright stringy flowers—Cheryl. Kirra liked tall grasses, while Eric had a perfect square of level, rock-free dirt. His was the hardest to maintain as the cats saw it as the ideal place for toileting. In order to keep the peace, I tried to get down here before anyone arrived, to check for feline assaults on his happy place. Any hostility toward cats of any kind tended to upset Kirra.

We made an interesting ensemble as we strolled around the garden: an eclectic gathering of humanity accompanied by a collective of canine genetic soup. I was still in awe of how it had all come together. There was something about my new family that brought out the gentle side of the strays—cats and dogs—who had joined us.

Except Sweetie. A stranger mix of DNA I had never come across, with four long, spindly legs, a body the size of a loaf of bread, a tail that curled round and over her back, all covered in long, coarse, white wire. But her most defining characteristic was the gnarled face, bulging eyes and offset jaw. She did, however, have quite adorable ears. For some reason, the fur on them was short and soft. One often found oneself absently stroking them.

Sweetie ruled them all. The smallest of the dogs, and more fierce than any of the cats, she governed her dominion ruthlessly and impartially. I was very grateful for not only her control of the premises but her company as well. She was a dear thing and since my early days here, had become my constant companion. I had invited her to sleep inside my shed, but she had declined, choosing rather to sleep by the main roller door. We had compromised: I bought her a bed and she deigned to sleep in it. She also had her own water and kibble bowl. Yes, I played favourites. I believe this helped her keep her Queen Bee status and assisted her in enforcing the peace of our home. For the animals, anyway.

Once again, I was struck with how blessed I was to live in such a haven. The gardens, waterways and trees were simply beautiful. More beautiful than any residence I had ever lived in. I knew in some way The Man was responsible. He had enabled me to find my peace and healing and out of that had come thi—

"Hello. Hello. Hello."

"No. No, you don't. No. You horrible. You go now."

Chants and cries were accompanied by a caterwauling of feline perspective from Kirra, which started the dogs howling. Shaking myself free of my reverie, I looked to where my friends were gathered around a pile of rubbish. All the dogs had gathered and were showing great interest in their discovery. Why did people still choose to dump their waste here? It infuriated me no end. I tried not to consider the possibility of it being personal, an attack against me or my friends, but the thought did raise its ugly head every now and again.

I made my way through the melee to find burst garbage bags with grisly contents spilling out, assaulting all my senses. Three large bags of bloody rags and sheets, covered in gore and defecation, spilled out from the wall of bamboo abutting the mighty wall of Sardis.

Cold chills fried my brain as heat exploded along all my nerve endings. Too much blood. What suffering, torture had caused this result? To an animal? To a human being? Somebody's someone? I could not comprehend what horrors led to this. The grisly evidence stained black from dried... drying blood. My heart and soul were torn with compassion for the victim. I could not stop the memories of my own beatings and torture at the hands of my captors and those working to exact vengeance for my crime.

But that, at least, I could understand. I had acted purely out of greed and self-interest with no concern for those I was manipulating. Whilst I had no idea whom the victim... or victims of this crime were, whether they were in some sense guilty of crimes or not, I could feel only compassion for their pain and suffering.

The wailing and visceral distress of my friends brought me back to the chaos of my immediate situation. Richard wandered in circles, hands knotted, mumbling unintelligible mutterings. Kirra sat in a ball, her head between her knees, hands over her head, her long fingers pinching her skin as she rocked side to side. Cheryl, a concrete statue, her eyes saucers unable to pull away from the bloodied bags. Eric, pulling handfuls of hair on his head, paced furiously back and forth. The others who had been with us had run for the hedges, hiding in the shadows, too scared to stay within eyesight of our discovery.

I was lost. How was I going to protect my friends? How could I keep their anonymity and right to be free to be who they were, unmolested by our heartless society?

How could I keep my own identity and presence here a secret, maintaining my ability to earn an income to keep this place running? To provide safety and protection if we had to open our doors to the outside?

And even when the police came, how could I trust them to act fairly and respect our privacy? Whilst I was forced to live on the outskirts of the city I had hurt, in the hope of making right my many wrongs, I was in no way ignorant of the reality of the wilfully blind, purchasable legal system that ran our region. I had not only profited highly from it, I had been on the blunt end when it had been sold to a higher bidder.

However, one did not have the luxury of imagining the worst outcomes in the future. One had to gather one's friends and try to bring some normalcy and calm to their current inability to cope.

Since Richard and Eric were still standing and mobile, I guided them back to the Undercover Area into the care of the recently arrived Gabby and Aran, briefly giving them a rundown. Aran stayed with the two men and Gabby raced off to gather Kirra and Cheryl.

"Don't run!" Aran and I called in unison as Gabby laced her fingers under her very extended belly and took off down the path leading to the garden beyond. The last thing we needed was for her to go into early labour or do some damage to her unborn child. Content to see her slow to a speed-walk, I ran to my shed to unearth my phone. First, I rang the police. Straight after, I rang Harry, immediately followed by Gerald admitting to both, I did not have the wherewithal to cope with this new development.

Gerald, knowing my background and history of injuries sustained whilst incarcerated, heard my plea for what it was: a desperate and panicked cry for help. Harry, not having as much information but aware of most other aspects of my situation, was quick to respond and was the first to arrive.

21

BALASHKA: CHAOS REIGNS

"Please step away from the bags, son." An indifferent Enforcer was trying to break through to Jemmy. After hearing my news, Gerald had excused himself from his responsibilities at TAVE, found our mutual friend and shared the situation with her. Gerald rightly assumed Jemmy would be able to help us restore some semblance of calm to the established state of panic. What neither of us had counted on, however, was her extreme shock and paralysis at the sight of the discovery.

I requested she might make coffee and tea for our guests and ensure there was food and water available for our friends. Not only had she *not* complied, she had marched straight down to the untouched evidence and immediately transformed into a pallid statue. Her artificially dyed blue-black hair only made more of a contrast against her paler-than-normal pale skin. She did not respond to the officer's request; I suspect she had not heard him.

I knew better than to touch her, so I stepped between my dear girl and the vision that held her hostage and tried to break through whatever fog she was drowning in. "Jemmy? Can you hear me?" I waited a beat. "Could you possibly come back to the Undercover Area and lend me a hand? Kirra has eaten all the cat kibble and Richard is eating his way through all the orange peel… again." Still she gave no sign that she'd heard me. At the officer's growl indicating I get a move on and, "Get the kid out of here," I was resigned to using the big gun. I leaned in close, trying to avoid the officer hearing, and whispered loudly, "Come on, dear girl. Time we left them to it." It worked. But I was going to be paying the price for that wound for a long time.

Jemmy's attention snapped to me. Shock then fury burned from within. Her eyes darted to see who was nearby and who may have heard. The Enforcer, writing notes on his device, gave no indication he had picked up on the apparent discrepancy. The other officers, currently photographing the evidence and the surrounding area, were too preoccupied with their search. The call of, "Boss, you're going to want to see this," had all the Enforcers' attention focused like a laser, and my heart stopped. What other… more grisly discovery had they made?

With a snarl of hurt and disgust, Jemmy spun on her sneakered toe and headed back to the food truck. However, her seething was not enough to disguise the trembling. Water sloshed in cups and the contents of the tray rattled as she tried to get everyone to… do something other than… panic.

There had been a tussle over the garden implements outside the storage shed. But thankfully we had enough for me to pull out three sets of five tools, adequate for sorting and re-sorting. I was incredibly grateful to our four-footed friends who picked up on the distressed mood and made themselves available for enthusiastic petting and brushing. With Gabby and Aran doing the rounds talking to everyone, attempting to distract and settle, and Jemmy dropping fruit and water, there was enough chaos and disruption that both Gerald and Harry were welcomed as acceptable.

Well, Harry's car was going a long way to helping Richard and Eric find their calm place. I was immensely grateful to my friend who was thoughtful and, even in this chaotic situation, still managed to park his car perfectly perpendicular in the correct space. The classic lines of his Jag, the soothing colour, and the rightness of the parking angles was enough to bring peace to at least two very troubled minds.

With some of our number caught up with garden tools, Richard and Eric focused on Harry's car, and others hiding in the garden, there were only a few who needed to be distracted on short notice as the Enforcers made their way up the garden path with the bloodied discovery.

"Aran, Gabby? Maybe now would be a good time for some soothing showers and hygiene lessons?" My high-pitched, desperate plea sparked the two into action, but flew over the heads of the others. I helped herd them toward the washrooms and helped divide the group, ushering the women with Gabby and the men with Aran.

Then I remembered Jemmy. She needed a distraction too. "Jemmy, could you come and help? I had never put her in the situation where she had to accompany men into the washrooms, and I wasn't about to start. I marched to the adjacent garden shed and asked her to... "Can you please... help..." I was desperate to think of something. I knew the officers would be waiting to speak with me. My eyes raked the area, desperate to find something, some task to give her. *Thank you.* "...Kirra out of the tree? She's eaten all the kibble, and she looks a bit green. I'm not sure she can get down."

Of course, the girl saw straight through me and my baseless plea. Kirra had eaten all the kibble, but rather than green, she looked very satisfied. However, getting her down *was* going to be a challenge.

Jemmy rolled her eyes, but at least she didn't growl, or swear at me. Maybe there was hope for reconciliation after all. She climbed the stepladder, and with her back to the group approaching from the bottom of the garden and her attention on "negotiating" Kirra down, she had enough of a barrier to hide behind.

I made a quick surveillance of the area. Gerald had gone in to help Aran. Harry was, at a respectful distance, engaging Richard and Eric, talking about pretty cars. From what I could see, he was entertaining them by engaging and disengaging the locks, triggering the lights, and an accompanying quiet beep.

I exhaled. Everyone was occupied. Turning to face the Enforcers, I did my best to hide my anguished fear that they were going to end our lives as we knew it.

"Interesting lot you got here."

"Thank you, yes. They are wonderfully unique, but unfortunately a tad fragile. This is going to take some getting over."

"What can you tell me about the discovery?"

As I didn't have much knowledge, it was a short reply.

"Have you upset anyone? Do you have any enemies?"

I looked at the man. Blinked. And waited.

He froze, looked to his notebook, then back to me. "I mean, recently. Have you upset anyone… recently."

"Since I live in isolation, have a life manager who deals with everything for me in the outside world, an agent who sells my work, and TAVE students occasionally doing their practice here, I would find it very hard to see how I may have."

"Upset any of the students?"

"Not that I am aware of. I've not had any negative feedback from them, their instructors or the institution."

"Anything else you can think of that would spark this"—he looked over his shoulder indicating his fellow Enforcers holding the ghastly evidence—"activity?"

"Laziness? I often encounter rubbish thrown over the high wall." We both looked to the imposing wall reaching to the sky. "To some, we'd be closer than the new dump?"

The Enforcer slowly nodded his head. "We'll be in touch." And on that note, the rude intrusion into our peace made its way off the premises in the capable care of the Enforcers, accompanied by a chorus of, "Pretty, pretty, pretty," and cat mewling as Jemmy finally bribed Kirra out of the tree with the promise of more kibble.

"Jemmy, could you possibly make a round of coffee? We need to convene and discuss what happens now. I would like you to join us, if you would?"

She nodded, helped Kirra down the last steps of the ladder and folded it and took it with her into the food truck. I made my way to the washrooms, called out to Gabby, Aran and Gerald giving them the all clear, and stowed the excess, abandoned garden tools back in the shed. I couldn't hold in my laugh, however, as I turned to make my way up to my shed to gather Harry and saw both Richard and Eric lying on Harry's Jag: Richard on the bonnet, Eric over the boot. With unsynchronised chanting of "pretty" they drooled and patted the object of their affection. Harry, unperturbed, sat in a chair in the open doorway of my shed reading a paper. I plonked myself next to him and, once again, was overwhelmed with gratitude and admiration for my friend.

He folded the paper, shifted in his seat and looked me in the eye. Harry, a light-hearted man, usually gave the appearance of not really taking anything too seriously. But now, his focus and earnestness were almost frightening. "Are you okay?"

The thin veneer of coping dissolved as my matchstick scaffolding disintegrated. "Um…" I looked down the slope to my family, moving and gathering, less agitated but still heightened. "No, not really."

I couldn't stop the tremors as they slowly took hold of me. "What does this mean, Harry?" I looked back to my friend and tried to hold his gaze. "Have they found me? Will they hurt *them*?"—I tilted my head to the Undercover Area. "Will they hurt me… again? I don't know if I can do it all over again."

The memories of the aggression, the brutality, the vitriol… spitting… kicking… punching… helplessness to defend or fend off the abuse, flooded my senses as I was transported back to those times… many times… in prison where I had been attacked. The tremors turned to a blend of uncontrollable shaking and paralysis. The pain in my hip flared and became unbearable. It was all I could do to get air into my shrinking lungs.

Tears streamed and blurred my vision. My hands had turned to vices gripping the arms of the camp chair. My heart rate exploded. Once again, I was a prisoner. I could not escape the cell of my memories assailing me, taking me back in time to relive my worst nightmares. A wave of heat passed from the top of my head and travelled down my body. When it reached my stomach, I lurched forward as I vomited over and over again until I was dry retching. All I could smell was blood. Oceans of my own blood as it flowed from my many wounds.

Darkness swamped.

Lifted.

Moved.

Sitting.

Water.

Easing tremors.

Ebbing emotion.

Eroding grasp.

Washing away.

Nothing left.

Until I saw Aran.

I was in my shower.

Sitting on a chair, fully clothed, under a heavenly stream of hot water.

Aran squatted next to me, so I had to look down to maintain eye contact. Sweetie, standing next to him, shifted from foot to foot. Her presence and Aran's voice brought a semblance of calm. "You're okay, Bal. You survived. All of that's in the past. You're okay." Slowly, enunciating the two words carefully, he repeated himself. "You're okay. You are a survivor. You are okay."

I nodded. Yes. It was in the past and I had survived. I had changed. Worked hard at making a difference and healing the hurts. I was... okay. Not good. But okay. I was also wearing soaking wet, vomit-covered clothes. "But"—my voice croaked, and my throat burned—"I am in a bit of a mess."

Sweetie whimpered and Aran laughed. "Jemmy might finally get you out of those suit pants after all these years."

I looked at myself and conceded he might be right. "Could you ask her to pick something for me from the pile? It might help him feel a bit better."

With Aran's help I was able to wash and change and, with a nervous Sweetie at my heels and a cautious Jem at my shoulder, I called the meeting of the board to order. "I just want to lock the gate and stop anyone new coming in... forever. I want to remove the shrub border and make a stone barrier twice as thick that reaches up and over. I don't want anyone to be able to break through ever again. I want to lock everyone in and keep everyone safe. Forever." I inhaled a shaky breath and tried to stem the tide of the new wave of tremors that threatened to take hold. "But I realise that might be overreacting."

Harry's joyous laugh was a helpful response. "Just a bit, my friend, but..."—he looked me in the eye again with that frightening focus—"perfectly normal."

Once again, tears blurred my vision and stole my voice. His compassion and understanding was a gift I did not deserve. A nod was the only response I was capable of.

Aran moved us forward into a more practical plan of action. "You're not completely off the mark, however." He and Gabby exchanged a glance. Gabby absently rubbed her beautifully round belly and smiled at me as Aran continued. "I think if we were to put a hold on any new visitors for a while until things return to..."—he smiled—"normal. I had a new nurse lined up to come in, but we'll put her on hold."

Aran looked to Gerald who continued, "I'll make sure to let TAVE know that we're taking a break for a while. They'll understand. They don't know specifics, but they know the situation here is sensitive."

Gabby perched on the edge of her chair, her face still a mask of concern. One hand sat under her belly, the other circled the top. "I agree with the decision to hold off newcomers, but"—her eyes flicked to Aran and tears came to her eyes—"I need to do a handover. I don't know how much longer I have before the baby arrives. We can't just bring her in without me introducing her to our people. They won't cope. And I need to do it a couple of times—" She froze. Tensed. Pain etched across her face.

"Are you okay?" I reached for her but she waved me away. We had all moved forward out of our seats to... I have no idea what. Catch the baby? It was a very timely demonstration of our need to consider her concerns.

She breathed heavily. "Braxton Hicks."

I had no idea who this Braxton person was, but it didn't look good. I turned to Aran.

He filled in the blanks. "The preparation stage for the baby's arrival." At my continued confusion, he elaborated. "Gabby's body is having a dress rehearsal… like a false labour." I could feel my eyes boggling out of their sockets. Again, I wondered what kind of rehearsal we needed. It was all overwhelming. On this note, Aran continued, "Gabby has a point, but, as always, it's up to you."

I looked around my family and friends. Everyone's face was open and concerned. What to do? My eyes wandered past the group sitting with me, down the slope to the Undercover Area to "our people" wandering around, doing puzzles on the big table, rearranging garden tools—just the one set—desperately trying to climb a tree in a flowing gown and no ladder, lavishing affection on Harry's car. And I knew Gabby was right. "Okay. Just the one." At the flinch of pain on Gabby's face, I added, "Is there any way we could arrange for her to come a few days in a row? Could you fit that into your schedule? I know this in itself will be a change and a shock, but I want to make sure everyone is comfortable before you have to leave, Gabby."

She looked to Aran, they spoke wordlessly for a moment, then Aran answered, "I think we can do that. We'll check with the candidate."

At this decision, a wave of tension fell away from Gabby and consequently the rest of us as well. We had a plan.

Then it all returned, locking us in the reality, with a whispered, "What about the Enforcers? Will they come back?" Jemmy's quiet voice had come close to revealing her true identity.

I looked around the group. Did any of us know? I shook my head. "About that, I can't say." My poor girl was not coping. Something particular about the incident this morning was throwing her more than it should. Somehow, I thought it was personal. Of all of us, she was the most distressed and that was most concerning.

22

ALARIO: MARSHALLING THE TROOPS

"Friends, it is time for us to step out of hiding and into our calling." Cissa addressed the small crowd of about thirty faithful from every Community of Light that met in Sardis. Val—an enigma of a woman—via her ShellCom 4.00 am meetings, had encouraged us to gather genuine individuals and start being intentional about who we were and what we were doing as a Community in this city.

Addressing the locals of Sardis and our friends from Philadelphia in our ground-floor conference room, standing at the head of the table, my wife continued, "We have been silent, hamstrung by the 'powers that be' for too long. The High Council's fear of the authorities and love of the depravities of the temples have stifled any authentic ministry, and have led our Community into Darkness. It is time we made a stand and defied the status quo." Her intense focus scoured the strained group and stopped when she got to me. I was both surprised and impressed that I felt I could read her unspoken message: *I can't do this without you.*

I squeezed her hand and sent my own back, hoping she could interpret. *I'm here. Always.*

The warmth from her eyes amped my confidence that we might

actually make some success of this—the fight in the Light, and our marriage.

Cissa's pause had let the truth of the matter sink in. An electrical current stretched its tentacles, tempting and tethering each one of us to hope. Excitement, tinged with fear, buzzed and zinged around the room. If we did this, if we stepped out and made waves... ripples, even... would we face the same, widely publicised fate as Philadelphia?

Possibly.

And yet the stirring of the Light's Breath within was undeniably intoxicating. Life pulsed through my veins. Via Val's incarceration for her decision to do the very thing she challenged us to do, we were left standing on a pinnacle of potential: to flee our purpose and calling would have eternal consequences; to fly into the arms of the Light would bring certain ostracism at best. Torture at worst.

However, the lure to surrender our future into the hands of the Light was liberating, exhilarating and terrifying. "Rightness" aligned two disjointed halves of my spirit. The jolt was audible. Just like the night I vowed to stand by my wife and work my way back into her life. I looked across the table to my Guard, who held my gaze and gave me one slow nod, and a hint of a smile. I, for one, had been working on growing some cojones, and I petitioned the Light that the rest of the room did the same.

Now that the reality of Cissa's challenge had taken root, she went on, "For those of you who want to join us at the table to discern how best to do this, in and for the Light, we welcome you." Again she paused, looking around the room at our brothers and sisters. There wasn't enough room for everyone to sit at the large conference table; some stood around the edges. Having given everyone more time to make their decision, Cissa continued, "We have been gifted help from experienced brothers and sisters in the Light to prepare for the battle, and we would like to begin immediately. We have been offered warfare training—Seen and Unseen, teaching in The Way, and assistance in serving the needy in our city.

"Before we go any further, however, let us petition the Light. Then, those of you who choose to leave may do so. The rest of us will get to work." There was a murmur of agreement. "Marcus, would you speak on our behalf?"

My new friend and ally stepped forward from where he stood among his family, behind Cissa and my seats. "Would be me pleasure."

Some bowed their heads, some stared out the one-way wall of glass at the city bustling past outside, lost, alone and wretched in its ignorance. The Dark's minions trailed their prey, at times stopping to stare through the glass at our gathering, making obscene and violent gestures before moving on. But we weren't too concerned by their antics. The Light had provided us with extra protection for this meeting, knowing it would draw certain attack. The Warriors of Light on the outer perimeter had been busy. For now, however, the enemy was held at bay as Marcus kicked off.

"Your ways are right and true, and Your paths are narrow and straight. We ask You to guide our feet and plot the dance. Keep us close and reveal Your plan. We want to be Your salty hands and beacon-lit hills in this place, but acknowledge we're more likely to get it wrong if we're not in Your sights at all times. We've got no idea, yet, what You've got for us to do here. But that's okay, 'cause You know, and we trust You'll let us know, when we need to know.

"We ask for listening ears and stilled tongues. We ask You to strengthen our hearts, soften our wills and erode our pride. We know You love this city. We know Your heart breaks for its people. Show us the where, the what, and the how. And thanks for Your Guards who walk with us each day. Thanks that You have called us here, and thanks for those who've been planted here for a while. Thanks that, between the lot of us, You've given us the means to do the job. But I ask, from the bottom of me heart, that you protect me sister, Val, me family, me friends, old and new—this family—and You bring about Your victory in this place. So be it."

The room echoed, "So be it."

I didn't hide my grin. The man had a way with words that made you pay attention. He enfolded gold within riddles that were a joy to unwrap.

Cissa stood again, smiled to the group and said, "Friends, now is the time to declare your intentions. Are you with us? Or are you…"—the pause was pregnant with something sharp that, I guarantee, one hundred percent, took a great deal of self-control to withhold—"not." She was making a significant effort to be polite and gracious in the face of our guests' potential defection.

"Cissa, Alario." Albert, a wizened old man and long-time friend from our Community gathering, in blazing red armour, nodded to each of us. "I, for one, am grateful for your time, hospitality"—his arm swept to indicate the heavily laden table—"and invitation. It would give me great pleasure to join you in this overdue endeavour." He laid his sword on the table, then sat.

Desleigh, not quite so aged, encased in pale green armour, also from our home Community gathering, didn't bother with standing or a similarly wordy response. "Aye. Count me in." She, too, then laid her sword on the table.

Other friends from our Community, Kirt and Laura, merely nodded and placed their swords alongside Desleigh's and Albert's.

And so it went around the room. Like lightning flashing in the sky, indiscriminately without rhythm or sequence, members of our new True Community acknowledged their intent to join us in the fight for our city… until there were those who didn't. It was like the electricity was cut. Instantly a weighty pause charged with tension intruded, bringing silence so loud it wailed.

Cissa let the call hang in the air, unanswered by about a fifth of those present. A fissure was forming between the ayes and the nays.

My wife remained silent.

Heads bowed and fingers knotted. And still, Cissa didn't say a word. Until finally, one of them cracked. "Did you hear what happened in Philadelphia? Did you hear what happened to those people? The Gerent killed their children."

After a beat, the boy, Raphael, spoke up. He held his cat close and stroked it as it curled around his neck and shoulders. "We were not killed. But Tessa and Dan were beaten when they tried to protect us. When the Gerent's men came for us, we all fought. But Dan and Tessa fought the hardest and they suffered the most when they tried to protect Cyan. She was only a baby. But Nanna-May and Travis exchanged their lives for hers... for us all." His voice was quiet but truthful. The kid paused.

Then he continued, "They—Travis and Nanna-May—were beaten, then shot. If they had not stepped forward on our behalf, I am not sure the Warriors would have come. If they had not come, we would all have been killed." He nodded to his twin and Dan and Tessa.

The spokesperson for the nays stared, open-mouthed.

Looking around at everyone who was now staring at him, the boy seemed to realise, for the first time, he had spoken aloud. But then he continued speaking his mind. "You are right to be concerned. The Gerent has great power and an even greater dislike of us."

"So what's to say the same thing won't happen here?" The spokesperson argued the unconvinceds' case with the boy.

Cissa countered with just the one word. "Nothing."

"And you want us to sign up for that. For being a potential target for the Gerent's wrath?"

Kait took the floor. "I would say you are now standing at a T-intersection. You have to make a choice: face the Gerent's wrath and potentially suffer physical pain and death. Or face the Light's wrath and definitely suffer eternal pain and death." Her hands were on her hips. She tilted her head. "Tell me, are you aware of what is going on in the Temple of Artemis in your city? The temple in which one of the Communities of Light actually meets? Are you aware of what is going on in the name of worship? For all Communities of Light in this city? The abominations being carried out by members of Light in that place of filth?"

She gave her head a slight shake and a furrow creased her brow. "The Light has declared the acts of His people in this place abhorrent and unacceptable. I can give you an absolute guarantee: judgement is coming. Not only on this city, but on the Light's *people* in this city. That is why we are here. To help warn the faithful and wake His sleeping children. Open your eyes. He is coming and it will not be with a message of affirmation and encouragement. The sands in the hourglass are racing to completion. And we all need to make a choice."

There was, as I had learned to expect from Kait, a ring of truth about her statement. It brokered no argument. Sariah was tapping her brother on the arm. He looked to her and nodded and then turned back to the table in general. "Riah suggested you also needed to know before you make up your mind, that three of us have the Gerent's trackers in our arms…" He faltered. "On our hearts."

"What?" was the exclaimed consensus in the room.

"And his tattoo." He tried to fold back his cuff to reveal his but was having trouble juggling his cat. But Sariah thrust her fist into the air so everyone could see the back of her hand and the 0048 marked there. "It is both a tattoo and a brand. Even if we could get rid of the ink, we would still have the raised scar. Tessa has one too." She didn't seem to be as eager to show hers. In fact, she slipped her gloved hand up under her armpit. "So, you should all be aware that wherever we are, whatever we do, the Gerent could easily find us… if he wanted to."

Cissa stood again. "I apologise for not speaking of this earlier. Al and I had the privilege of fighting alongside our friends here for part of the Battle of Philadelphia and were aware of this from the beginning. I did not intentionally hide this information; we just accepted it as our new norm and moved on. Again, I apologise for not being transparent, it was an oversight, not intentional subterfuge. Of course, if any of you who have volunteered to stand with us now feel differently, you are welcome to withdraw your blade from the table." She surveyed the room. "But remember, this does not change anything."

"I would say it changes everything." Again, the spokesperson… I really should figure out their name, exploded.

"I'd like to know how you see it changing the way of things?" Marcus's rumble was not threatening, but there was a hint of judgement?… accusation?… frustration? in his voice.

"He will know where we are and what we're doing all the time. Every step of the way. We will have no ability to hide," the spokesperson said.

My friend countered the argument. "But surely our activity within the city, our teaching of The Way, our acknowledgement of why we are serving those in need, will also advertise what we're doing, every step of the way. We have no desire to… hide. You don't seem to understand. We were betrayed by our own High Council. We were attacked by our own people. In Philadelphia, we were working quietly to support the needs of the people, providing housing, income and food for those who had lost everything in The Quake. We lived in a private yet fully transparent community and were not making any waves. Except we would not bow to the Gerent and accept him as a god.

"The Battle of Philadelphia would not have happened if our own people had not turned us in. Do you think it will be any different here? Already, me sister sits in prison, for the second time, because people in our own Community—fellow children of the Light—have turned on her. None of us, not one, is safe in hiding. None of us, not one, can trust the security of human nature. We stand here, warned of what is coming, fully aware of the threat, unashamed of what we're doing, trusting in the security of the Light.

"Me wife is right when she says you stand at a T-intersection. It's not a crossroad. You only have two choices, left or right. You don't even have the luxury to dally on the way, because all who are not on the right path will be judged. Failing to choose is as bad as choosing wrong." I thought he'd finished the longest speech I'd ever heard the man speak, but then he sunk the boot in. "Are you ashamed of the Light?"

As one, the room lurched back at the accusation. In the affronted pause, he continued, "Are you in doubt of His power? Do you mistrust His promises?" He reached out and laid one arm around his daughter's shoulders, his other around her twin, Raphael, who was still clutching his cat. "There is no shame in being worried. But doubt? Bone deep, soul-wavering doubt? We'd be best off without you standing by us in the battle. And we'd appreciate your honesty to the truth. I don't want to risk me family's future, our armada's success to be derailed by your rudderless doubt."

Well, I guess that was one way to put it. But it did seem to galvanise the undecided. Two stepped forward and laid their swords on the table. Three stood, looked around the room, tried to maintain a guise of pride and left.

23

ALARIO: BATTLE PLANS

"Best to sort the sheep and wheat before we kick off a war, don't you think?" I couldn't help but chuckle at Marcus's take on the situation. It was the release valve we needed, and the temperature dropped to slightly higher than comfortable after our... former family members left the room.

I'll admit, Marcus's challenge had me questioning my own ability to stand. Would I be reliable when it came down to it? Was I harbouring doubt? I looked to those who remained. Some I knew, most I didn't. I considered their armour, and their blades laid out on the solid wood conference table. Each a different hue, easily connecting it to its owner. It was as good as signing their name to our resolve to be a thorn in the side. To intervene against the status quo. None of us were perfect, none of us were truly experienced.

I trusted the Light implicitly, and having Him station His specially trained, tactical soldiers here in our city, to lend their sword to our fight, to lead us and teach us, as well as having the extra Guard surrounding us, bolstered my confidence. When I stopped and considered what He'd done up till now, it enabled me to have hope for what He would do. I think it was to be expected we were uncertain of the unknown, but we were locked solid in the truth of the Known.

What I had witnessed—Seen and Unseen—will never leave me. It provided a very healthy dose of reality. It was not blindly that I stood beside my wife in this declaration of war. Now the remnant were aligned. Cissa continued, fire crackling along her deep crimson armour, "First order of business, we need to find a new place to meet. We cannot"—she slammed her clenched fist on the table, punctuating her emphatic declaration—"continue to meet in the doorway of the Abomination. We cannot"—another pause, another slam—"in any way be associated with what goes on in that place." There were murmurs of assent and nods of approval.

"Second, we need to work out a plan of preparation. Purely by meeting here today, we have drawn a spotlight onto our activities. The Dark"—she tilted her head, indicating our slavering audience outside—"has us in his sights. The Community will do so, soon." Again she was quiet and looked around the room, taking time to connect with every person present. "Friends, let me tell you, the threat is real, we are not just continuing our war with the Dark, today we are stepping apart from our Community and society. We are now without the illusion of shelter offered by their thin facade. We will find ourselves targeted on every side. We need to be aware and prepared. I suggest we implement a plan to ready ourselves for this attack, Seen and Unseen.

"Third, we still have a responsibility to the Light to represent Him in this city, full... overflowing with those who need all He is offering. I suggest we consider how we can meet the needs of those who are without, and make a stand for those who cannot do so for themselves. Let us continue the Light's edict to take His truth and Light into the Darkness and alleviate the suffering of those who are held hostage there. I know the Community of Light is very vocal and visual in supporting charities and donating to causes in the city. But I believe it is important we look further afield... in different places, to serve. Regardless of their intentions, and actions behind the scenes, the money they are contributing is meeting a need. But let us not be associated with their ministry, nor let us reinvent the wheel. Let us find those who have no one to meet their needs."

Again, there were... more enthusiastic... murmurs and nods of agreement. Until another venue was made available, we decided to continue meeting in the ground floor conference room of Black & Light Design—our building. Due to their experience, in both warfare and teaching, our friends from Philly's offer of teaching and training was enthusiastically accepted. And, as he was in a position to give us the best idea of the needs of those on the fringe, Albert shared his knowledge from working with the City Council.

"Brothers and sisters." Albert stood as he took the floor. "Our city's leaders, influencers and philanthropists have done a great deal to reduce the suffering and meet the needs of the most obvious of those who are still without basic needs after The Quake. They are all, our very own Communities of Light among them, very quick to throw money at the most obvious and well-advertised situations. But let me share the reality of those who are not visible, those whose plight cannot be used as one-upmanship and competition in the reputation ring. There are still people who do not have safe, suitable housing. There are still multitudes suffering trauma, depression, anxiety and grief from The Quake. There are many small businesses who still— three years on—cannot afford repairs, staffing and licensing fees. And, as a result, have not recovered. The flow-on from this is a good number of people are out of work.

"Our City Council is very generous in providing free and readily available transport for those who can afford to live in the city. But there are so many more who live further out who have no transport, who struggle to get themselves to the shops, their children to schools, and, if they have jobs, to get to work.

"I could go on. If we are looking for a place to serve and minister the Light, there are many who have fallen through the cracks and are not privileged enough to live on the battlefield of the Reputation Wars waged by the rich and richer." His sardonic smile, I felt, was fuelled by decades of working in a system that awarded deferential, obsequious preference to eyes that were privileged and blind, ears that were deaf-ened, and hearts that were hardened towards those who needed their help the most. How he kept going in that culture, I didn't know. But I did admire the man and was grateful for his insight.

Cissa took the floor again. "Thank you, Albert, for sharing your insight. Next, I suggest, considering our number, we pick one area we are best suited to start, and see how best we can serve."

"I can help out. Maybe teach some people to sew? Like, maybe, how to earn an income, or even make themselves some clothes?" The halting voice of the young woman—Tessa—was a breath of fresh air. Someone willing to jump in straight away with a practical idea. "I just need a little while, I have this huge assignment at TAVE, and it's like, crazy stressful. But give me a couple months and I'll be good to go."

Her enthusiasm sparked others to join the conversation and offer their ideas for the taking. Desleigh was next to jump on the bandwagon. "I have contacts with the community nurses who work on the fringes. I can touch base with them."

Even though we were small in number and most had come from the same city, the rest of the morning was spent sharing a meal and forging alliances. We found how and where the group was situated in the workforce, how we were experienced in life skills and how we were gifted with Badges. From there we would have the information to start our plan of attack.

DANIEL: SLUMMING IT

I t was all systems go. Council had signed off on the project. We were allowed to start negotiating with the folks outside the wall to help them restore their homes. TAVE had given their approval. Josh and Tim were authorised as our supervisors and Cissa and Al had both endorsed and agreed to be guarantors for our work.

City Council's main focus had been on the top of the mount. Then, as work was completed, interest and resources were trickled down through the city streets. Until everything had been exhausted—or everyone lost interest—by the time it got to the bottom. Let alone outside. Priority was directly proportional to tax bracket. It seemed everyone was blind to those who sheltered in the shadow of the wall. So, that's where we came in. We didn't want to be seen as trying to compete for brownie points.

Josh and Tim had driven over from Philly early this morning. Marcus and I had been approved leave for the day to assess the situation, interview residents, take notes and photographs and then start making a plan. This would be shown to our lecturers who were willing to both advise us on how to proceed, and grade us on our outcomes.

I won't lie. I was pretty excited. We were going to transform the lives and environment at The Wreckage by getting people out of the dirt and putting them into funky houses made from recycled building materials. I loved the challenge of finding ways to use what was on hand to create something new, unique and suited to the individual or family that were going to move in.

It was a long, hard road of learning from experience and problem solving in Philadelphia. I couldn't wait to bring all of that experience and skill to this project to achieve similar outcomes in Sardis.

As we exited the city on the north-eastern side of the mount, we entered hell. Well, it must have been some kind of hell for the people living there. It was far worse than Tent City in Philly when we first arrived. This place was disgusting. It stank from poor drainage that ran from broken pipes under the city wall out into the broken streets beyond it. It was hot and stifling as the sun beat back from the stone blocks of the city wall with no trees or gardens to absorb the heat or provide shade. The streets were still set out in some kind of order, but huge cracks and breaks in the earth divided roads, footpaths and houses. We saw evidence of life in semi-standing buildings and in makeshift lean-tos.

All of my excitement, bravado and expectations were torched by reality. This was far bigger than replacing tents with huts. This was far too big a job for us... for me. The size of the need was overwhelming. I was well and truly out of my league.

We drove as far as we could before the road was too damaged to continue. "Just breathe, lad, and remember to petition the Light for some sense, or plan, or place to start." Marcus was just as overwhelmed as I was, his voice a hoarse whisper. We parked the car and set out on foot. How could such an affluent city, whose streets were pretty much paved with gold, have people living like this? It was doing my head in. Three years since The Quake and these people still lived like this?

My initial thought was to bulldoze the lot and start from scratch. But even that was going to be too big a job without a literal army of workers and resources. There were a few faces peeking out from behind shelters. Where were we going to put them while we rebuilt?

Thankfully, the more we explored, the more I grew to believe that most residences were empty. A group of kids were playing with a tatty ball in a soggy green space. It flew toward us. I jogged over, grabbed it, and attempted to return it and have a chat. Marcus followed a bit slower. The kids looked pretty spooked. "Hey guys." I tossed their ball back. The biggest kid stepped forward and grabbed it. He flicked his shaggy, dirty-blond hair out of his eyes with a shake of his head.

He was young, probably about the same age as Raph, tall and guarded. He stared, his face and body language on alert, wordless, with the ball tucked under one arm and the other hand on his hip. The others, mostly younger, gathered around him. They didn't run away, but they didn't respond either.

Keeping a safe distance I engaged. "We're new to Sardis and interested in how you guys are doing after The Quake."

No one said anything.

"We've come from Philadelphia where it was pretty bad. We lost most of the city and the suburbs around it." I scanned the area in which we now stood. "Looks like it was the same for you guys."

The lead kid hitched his chin in agreement.

"Do you still have power down here? Water?"

The leader twitched his head to... I don't know what, and took it to mean that yes, they had at least one of those resources.

A little kid from the back stepped out from the group and called out, "My mum gets me to collect water from Parson's house twice a day. They have rainwater tanks that still work."

The leader glared at the boy, but it didn't stop a girl speaking up. "Yeah, so does Harris's old place."

"What about school, or shops, or... doctors? Do you guys have anything like that?"

The lead kid laughed, "Nah, we live beyond the wall. This is where they throw their skrat. And so skrat is what we live on."

"We were hoping we might be able to help out a bit. Do you guys mind if we look around?"

The leader twitched a shoulder and turned back to his flock. We

158

were dismissed, I think with his blessing, and they returned to their game.

Marcus murmured as I returned to his side, "I think we just stumbled across where the True Community can plant their shovels and plans."

We did a loop and went back to meet Josh and Tim. Using a drone TAVE lent us, we took photos before going door to door trying to find out who lived here, what situation they were in, and how best we could serve them.

What started out as a building project soon turned into an all hands on deck... and whatever else we could lay our hands on, community project. We still had a specific goal to help—I had no idea how—with housing, but any information we could gather to take back to our crew might be beneficial in helping them plan how else we could provide services here.

Again, the main thing I just couldn't wrap my head around was the absolute division between the two lives separated by the wall. The kid was spot on. These guys really were invisible out here.

In Philly we had resourced all our materials from a well-ordered, overstocked tip. So as we wrapped up our limited interviews, I asked directions to Sardis refuse and recycle centre. Taking a circuitous journey we were able to make our way to the western city exit and discovered what we hoped would be our main source of building supplies. Like Philly, there was a heap of materials we could use. Unlike Philly, it wasn't as well-ordered.

After asking permission and selling our idea, promoting how we would be purchasing what we required, we were granted access. The four of us scoured the store and roughly piled stock, again taking photos and drone footage of what there was and what we might be able to use.

We decided we could make a start with what was on offer. The worker got the boss on the phone, and we made a deal securing the rights to use what we needed. Obviously, we didn't have to negotiate too hard. They were getting money and clearing space.

I had no idea how long we were going to be in Sardis. I knew the

Light wanted us to find the Seeing Blind Man, but the job in front of us was huge. Having lived for a long time with nothing—belongings, income or hope—I just couldn't walk away from these people and leave them like this. Especially when we had the resources and knowledge to fix it, or at least improve it.

Thank You for bringing the crew online. For galvanising Your people here and showing us this need. Whatever we start here, please let Your people finish it if we're not here to do the job ourselves. This is just wrong. Show us how we can help these guys the most.

* * *

THE LAST OF the drone footage flicked off and the lights were turned on in the conference room on the ground floor of Black & Light Designs. The room was almost at capacity. Most people had been able to respond to Cissa's call for a special meeting. She and Al were still away, scheduled to return tomorrow. But she had said to start without them and to get the ball rolling.

Everyone continued staring at the blank white screen. Unmoving, yet obviously moved.

After allowing the reality to set in, I began our report. "We were looking for a place to share the Light. Well, we found a pretty dark and hopeless place to start." I waited a beat. "These guys have shelter but no security. They have some water and no power. They, like everyone else, have tax relief, but they have no income."

Marcus took over. "It's neither here nor there what your gift, experiences or expertise is. It's irrelevant what your schedule is. Whatever you have, whenever you have, it will be a cup of refreshing water to a thirsty pool. The four of us are trying to make a plan of where and how to start with housing. We'll be speaking with our lecturers, Cissa, and Al, and I hope with City Council about what is available to us. We'll then be doing further interviews with the residents to figure out what they want and how best we can serve them. But surely, housing, power, water, education and medical services are a priority."

I stepped back into the spotlight. "We are new here and don't really know who you are and what you do, but if there is anything anyone can do, please let us know."

I was expecting answers and calls of support, enthusiasm, but I wasn't expecting Kait to speak up with an excuse. "You know this is close to my heart. Those kids... they need direction and education. But I believe right now my priority has to be finishing my retraining. Also, I have been given an incredible opportunity to work with another group of people who have just as significant needs. Also outside the wall."

It was the domino that started the fall. One by one, around the room, people offered excuses rather than help. With each new apology followed by a perfectly reasoned excuse, my blood boiled a degree closer to full-scale eruption.

My patience was kicked to the curb. Cissa and Al were contributing truckloads—I wasn't expecting anything more from them. And I understood Kait's response, and I could kind of see other's reactions. It truly was overwhelming. But it still made me furious. "This is a fralping joke. You said you want to help, said we had a responsibility to the Light to represent Him in this city full... overflowing with those who need all that He's offering.

"You said you wanted to continue to take the Light into the Darkness and alleviate the suffering of those who are held hostage there. Well, we found a pretty dark place.

"You said you didn't want to reinvent the wheel, or throw money and resources to a cause that was already being met by others. Well, we found a helpless cause.

"You said, 'Let's find those who have no one to meet their needs'." I stopped and eyeballed everyone in the room. "And we found them. And you know what else we found?" No one said a word, everyone just sat silently, like stupid sheep. "A bunch of hypocrites who were no better than the bunch of two-faced actors who had Val thrown in jail." I turned to Marcus, Tim and Josh. "I don't know what we're doing here. This is a bleeding waste of time." I was just so fracking angry. I really needed to hit something really hard.

"Now hang on a second, lad." The old woman, Desleigh? who'd been second to lay her sword on the table two days ago spoke up.

I didn't swear out loud and I didn't hit anything. Instead, I breathed really deeply and tried to get a handle on my rage.

"You've given us a lot to think about. You've found a worthy cause and a need we can fill. But, to be fair, you've had time to consider the situation. You have seen how you can align this with what you do in the day-to-day. And we thank the Light for that." Others murmured agreement.

"But this is the first many of us have seen of it. I for one know how busy my schedule is"—she held up her hand, stopping my objection—"but I can see the need. All I am suggesting is that you email or text that footage to each of us. You acknowledge we need time to petition the Light as a group, and as individuals. You give us all time to discern what the Light would have us do and how we go about it."

She stood, leaned over the tables, placing her weight on her knuckles, and eyeballed me. She reminded me so much of Val at that point I almost wept for how I missed her. "You've got fire, lad, and that's good. We need a good dose of it. But may I suggest we take the time to absorb the information you've found for us, and allow the Light to lead us into battle, not your unrestrained... passion?"

And just like Val, I felt the old woman had served me my butt on a plate in a very public place. What could I do but nod, shut up and sit down.

Next the old bloke from council stood up and gave us some history of the area and, from what he knew, some understanding of how best we could approach this project: our new focus as the True Community of Light.

25

DANIEL: TROUBLE IN PARADISE

"I'm really happy for you, Tessa. I am. Seriously. But could you maybe tone it down a bit? I am very happy that you're kicking goals... scoring points and... winning hearts. But I am really struggling. Everyone thinks I can just go in and fix the problem on the outer wall like we did in Sanctuary. Like, 'You did it before, off you go, do it again.'"

"Well, why can't you?"

Some kind of switch flipped in my brain and all my fury and frustration came boiling out all over my wife. "Because I can't." She stepped back from my shout. "It's completely different here." I shouldn't have shouted at her, I know, but I was out of control with fear and... and... not knowing what the hell I was going to do. I walked away and just before my fist hit the wall, I remembered it wasn't our house. See, it wasn't that I couldn't learn stuff. It was just so much... too much to learn. All at once.

"In Sanctuary, it was just a matter of replacing a few tents with a few huts. Simple. We had access to supplies, we had help from the kids, we had permission from Mary, Travis and Daisy." I turned back to Tessa and tried with everything in me to stop the tears in my voice. "Here, it's a war zone. Houses, shops, buildings that are semi-standing, occupied by hostile, hurting people, and no clear place to start, no agreement from the owners to help, and the expectation of TAVE, Cissa and Al, and Council, that the four of us are going in there and we're going to be able to replicate Sanctuary for these people. And some sick person thought this would be great for an assessment piece. We have a deadline, and I am going to be graded on the results. Me. Just me. I will be marked on the efficiency and effectiveness of my designs. Marcus and I will be marked on the work, but some sadistic person decided I was the leader, so the buck stops with me."

Just thinking about it made me sick. I literally couldn't eat, or drink coffee. I couldn't sleep. It took every ounce of energy and focus I had to maintain civility to my family. The elaborate armchair I was growing to hate caught my weight as I collapsed into it. I was done. I had nowhere to go. I did not know what I was going to do. I hid my face in my hands and let the tears of frustration fall.

I heard the door shut quietly.

Great. We hadn't even made it to six months and already our marriage was done. Another nail in my coffin lined with failure.

I smelled her before I felt her arms wrap around my head and pull me into her stomach. She didn't say a word. She just held me. Her sniff drew me out of my misery party. I looked up into her swollen red eyes and blotchy face. Tessa made a small, helpless shrug. "I have nothing to say. There is nothing I can do to help. I feel useless. But I am here. And I love you." She ran her fingers through my hair. "And I will continue to petition the Light for an answer and a way forward. I know when I worked for Kari in Laodicea, I often felt that way. But then, the only people counting on me were you lot. I have no idea how difficult it is for you." She shrugged again and it caused two tracks of tears to run down her cheeks.

I pulled her into my lap in that horribly ornate chair and just held her. I was lost. Helpless and feeling overwhelmingly hopeless. But I was not alone.

26

ALARIO: ONE STEP FORWARD

A fter two weeks to consider the new information we'd received from Dan and Marcus, we called another meeting of the True Community to discuss possibilities. I got the meeting underway. "There's only one way I can see this working. We... someone... some organisation... purchase the land: a few hectares not inhabited. Or, we buy out the people who are currently living there, for a song. Then, bulldoze the lot, and start from scratch." I looked to Cissa. "If we bought it under our business, we could write it off on tax and establish our display village: our new, innovative, recycled, low-cost homes." I waited a moment and let her do the sums. "We could use this to reach a new audience.

"Then, in negotiation with the locals, we work out what they want, what they need, pull it all together with the Black & Light style, and sell it back to them at cost. We offer interest-free loans. Dan and Marcus come in and take each cabin or hut and design a plan for it, on a case-by-case, person-by-person scenario."

Our business had taken on extra expenses this year. Offering free accommodation, TAVE sponsorship, and living expenses for our new friends from Philadelphia wasn't a huge hit, but they were costs we'd had to absorb. In addition, word had spread that we'd made waves within the Community of Light, and fear of getting on the wrong side of the Gerent had caused our local projects to dry up. Thankfully, our business was spread throughout the Seven Cities, so we weren't too impacted... yet.

Albert indicated with a cough that he wanted to speak, and took the floor. "The City Council is open to what we propose. And, whilst they don't have absolute jurisdiction over the whole area outside the wall, the land within five hundred metres is their responsibility. They are happy for us to proceed as long as they are kept 'in the know', plans comply with their regulations, and all fees are paid accordingly."

Daniel was fidgeting in his seat and rearing to go. "Smaller. We can do that. We don't have to do the whole lot. What if we case out the best place to start... maybe the side closest to the road, heading west along the wall. That way it will be easier access for machinery to clear and trucks to deliver." And he was off, speaking about borrowing Old Faithful to start picking up loads from the tip.

As Marcus and Dan's bosses, Cissa's and my job was to oversee and help them break it down into manageable, affordable, practical tasks. Their supervisors, Josh and Tim, seemed sensible guys, but the scale of this was even, I believed, too big for them. Thankfully, we had TAVE onside and, as Albert had just informed us, City Council as well. This was the shot in the arm we needed, and the kid was the one to administer it to us.

His enthusiasm was contagious. Now we had a plan, others came forward offering bits and pieces. I guess the roadblock all along had been the sheer size of the problem. It was too overwhelming: the people, the buildings, the space. Everyone needed help, everything needed rebuilding, everything needed... everything.

Tessa jumped up from her seat. "Markets." We all stared at her. "The estate is right next to a gate into the city. Not a main gate but it's, like, a way in. People use it. What if we can help grow small trade industries and they could sell their product to passers-by. Like Sanctuary. Make a living from what they produce and craft." She had us hooked. "We could, maybe, ask our friends from Philly if they could visit and talk to them about it?"

Sariah's hands blurred with action. Her brother didn't bother interpreting. "I don't think they have room for goats, Riah."

"Why not?" Tessa interceded for her sister. "Why not goats, and veggies, and chickens and…" She looked around the room, at all of us just staring at her. Her pale skin flamed. She mumbled, "Sorry," and sat down.

"Don't apologise, Tessa"—Cissa patted the girl's shoulder—"they are very good questions. The land is outside of city zoning, we can check what's permissible. All ideas are worth airing."

A shy smile caused Tessa's red to recede to hot pink.

The rest of the meeting was spent petitioning the Light and, in smaller groups, brainstorming possibilities. Before we could hit the ground with a solid plan, however, like Marcus's youngest reminded us, "We have to ask them if they want help."

And as Dan repeated, "Then help them by giving them what they need, not what we think they want."

Now that we had a plan, goals and enthusiasm, I didn't think anything could stop us.

I took the floor again, looking at the potential in the room. Marcus had just opened The Way for us. His kids had led us in a time of singing in the Light. We were in the throes of enjoying a celebration meal within our new, true Community of Light and the wealth of knowledge, experience and passion threatened to overwhelm me. There was no reason why we couldn't get this dream off the ground.

27

ALARIO: TWO STEPS BACK

Could that woman *be* any louder? Something was obviously upsetting her. Aggression... and plenty of noise, were being played out in every movement she made. It was getting harder and more impossible to ignore her and focus on the news. When a glass hit the tiled floor and shattered, and swearing sirened from the kitchen, it was time to act. "Don't move, I'll get the... something. Where do you keep... cleaning... things?"

Cissa stood like a skyrise, red tingeing her face, ears, neck and highlighting her merlot armour. Standing in a sea of glittering, splintered glass, she was a stunning monument to fury. She raised one arm by infinitesimal degrees and pointed to the hall leading to her bedroom. Surely she didn't keep brooms in her bedroom?

"Did you hurt yourself? Are you cut?"

The woman's fury had stripped her of speech. My eyes raced over her and, when I saw no sign of blood, I dashed to find a cleaning device.

The floor was clean, as far as I could see—might be best if someone vacuumed again though. I cleared the carnage away, and still she stood seething in the middle of the kitchen.

"For goodness' sake, woman, what is the problem?"

She inhaled through her nose... noisily, and exhaled like a raging bull. Her eyes were burning holes through me and everything they grazed over, but I was the main target lined up in her crosshairs. With clenched jaw and fists she muttered, "Do you think... you might be able to... lend a hand... occasionally?"

"What do you mean?"

"You are living here. This is your... current... home." She had me worried with the growl that accompanied "current". "Do you think you might... consider... helping? Every now and then? Ever?" Her amazing chest still heaved.

Even I, however, was not stupid enough to take the time to admire her attributes at this particular point in time. "Help?"

"Do you understand the concept of the term?"

"That's a bit harsh, Cissa. Of course I understand what it means. But you, my dear wife, are always... were always telling me, you don't need help. You were perfectly capable of doing things on your own. And if, and when, you needed help, 'I will ask for it, thank you very much'." I mimicked her imperious—okay, previously imperious—tone. Possibly not my smartest move considering the current atmosphere. But there you have it. She asked, I delivered.

Her mouth dropped open and her eyes flew wide. Thank goodness she wasn't angry anymore.

"How can you possibly think what I said as a *teenager*"—her voice jumped an octave, and a decibel, with the word—"about fighting a battle with my parents, relates to every. Single. Thing. For the rest of my life?"

"Cissa, you are the most fiercely independent woman... human, I know. You never want help. You always... *always* want to do things for yourself."

Shock and rage married, and birthed some kind of outraged disbelief. This was not going to be good.

"One." To illustrate her point, she raised a finger. Thankfully it wasn't a weapon. "I do want help. With a lot of things. I just learned early on... and through my marriage..."—the tilt of her head and obvious effort to restrain herself was a savage reminder we had a long way to go—"help was not available. I have had to learn to manage by myself because there is no cavalry coming. There is no one waiting in the wings. There is. No. Help." Her eyes bulged then narrowed. "Any-where." Her burning orbs had morphed into deadly lasers. "I was on my own. Have always... been on my own. If I didn't figure it out for myself, I wouldn't have survived."

Before I could offer any form of rebuttal, she went on. "Two." A second finger went up. "Chores, Alario." I knew I was definitely in trouble now. Cissa knew how much I hated my name. She only ever used it when she wanted to get under my skin. "*If*"—the word was delivered with icy stress—"this is your home, for now"—more ice—"then I would have expected that you would help out with the chores without having to be asked. How did you live in Philadelphia if you didn't do your chores?"

"I had a maid."

"A *maid*?" The screech may have punctured an eardrum. I couldn't tell if my ears were bleeding, but there was definitely a lot of ringing and a lot of pain. "I am not your fracking maid, Alario."

Swearing? Cissa never swore? And this morning she'd crossed that line twice in less than ten minutes. Time for damage control. "Of course not. I would never think of you as a maid. How insulting. I'd never consider paying you to clean my house."

Her eyes popped. Her chest stilled. Her heart may have even stopped. And then, an almighty scream that could very well have broken every glass object in the house, was released. "So, I'm a servant? An unpaid slave who doesn't even warrant payment? What? So I have the privilege"—she spat the word—"to clean your house?"

"What? No. Of course not." Although, since she put it that way, it was a bit incriminating. The way I saw it, I had nowhere to go. There was no escape. Nowhere to run. I was cornered and out of ideas. Sadly, she was waiting for a response. With every millisecond that passed without one, the fire exploding in her eyes fuelled the growing inferno of her wrath. No doubt about it, this was going to hurt. "Ummm… sorry?"

Her jaw jutted, rolled and clenched again. She crossed her arms and tilted her head and in a very quiet voice asked, "For what, Alario? What exactly are you apologising for?"

Skrat, she had me.

Oh Lord, help me out here. Please! What can I say? How can I make it out of this alive, and keep my newly restored marriage? You know we've been apart for far too many years, but seriously, this is hard work! So, any help You could throw my way would be greatly appreciated.

I waited for inspiration to hit. Nothing. Not one idea. Not one word. So, I opened my mouth, and hoped like my life depended on it that something reasonable came out. "For misunderstanding the situation?" The involuntary hitch at the end of my sentence gave me away. But, at least it was an answer. Truthful too.

With arms still crossed, eyes now narrowed, Cissa's voice was, thankfully, a touch quieter. "Which part of the situation?"

Honesty blurted out before it had time to be filtered through my intellect. "The whole… situation?" Again, the inflection. I really needed practise in this husband-wife-negotiation thing. I was far too rusty. Now I jumped the gun before she had another chance to shoot me down. "Cissa, I am not perfect." She huffed and dropped her arms. Her hands settled on her hips and her shoulders dropped from next to her ears.

"I guess it was never going to be easy, or that we could just slip back into married life without hiccups. We've been single for so long." I repeated my words from our previous blow out. The one where *she* was at fault. I was hoping it would remind her I had credit in the wrong-doing bank. I also reminded her, "Communication was never really our thing." I tentatively took a step forward. I wasn't ready to pat the beast—not that I was calling my wife a beast, I was referring to her rage, please God I never let that slip—and in the most confident, genuine, conciliatory tone continued, "Cissa, I'm sorry. I made a mistake of assumption. I am asking you to forgive me and for another chance at working this out."

She sighed. I had her. *Yes!* She stepped forward and cupped my face with her beautiful strong hands. I stilled. Measured the pressure of her grip. Was this going to hurt? Was I going to have to fight for my life? But she didn't go in for the kill. Instead, she whispered, "We really have a long way to go."

"We have to work out this communication thing better. Maybe we could make it like work—"

She froze. Her eyes widened and sparked with fire again. Her hand was still on my face so I raced on, "Let me finish, woman." For goodness' sake, could she just give it a rest? For a breath, at least? "Like our weekly staff debrief. Go over what's working, what's not, how it went and what we need to prep for next week. Maybe we could do our own version of that. Over coffee? Or dinner? Out somewhere, or over a nice meal in?"

She relaxed again. "Sounds good."

"And, Cissa?" She stilled. "If you do need help, could you please ask? I know you said those words when you were a teenager, but you have backed them up with every action I have ever witnessed, ever since. I just don't know when you need, or want, help." Her eyes grew. "I'm not talking about chores. I'm talking about everything else." Well, I could have been talking about chores, but obviously that was not going to play out well.

"Maybe you could tell me what you'd like done? You have been living here as sole occupier, doing life by yourself since it was built. I love this place and I love living here with you. But, this is your home. It would be helpful to me if you could let me know what I can do to help. And when. Maybe we could work out... an agreement?... terms? What my responsibilities are, what yours are, what jobs around here I need to do and when?" I waited as she considered my suggestion. When she started nodding, I thought it best to finish with the embarrassing truth. "I'm not proud of it, Cissa, but I really don't have a lot of experience with housework. But for you I will do whatever it takes to make our marriage work."

I held out my arms and she stepped into my embrace. With her head on my shoulder she muttered, "I guess that makes us equal in the credit stakes... or debit stakes."

We may have an issue with communication, but my wife and I cruised along the same wavelength when it came to "life truths" and "negotiations".

28

DANIEL: DEAL'S A DEAL

"What are you doing here? No one invited you into our homes. I've seen you hanging around, filming with that drone. Walking around like you own the place. Well, you don't. So you can take your fancy car and get the frack out of here and leave us alone."

"But we just want to talk. To see how we can help—"

The dude turned his back and slammed his front door. Well, he tried to, but the thing wouldn't shut.

I was torn. Did I respect his desire for privacy, or did I use his dodge accommodation to make my point?

Before I could decide on my plan of attack, Marcus was at his broken door continuing the conversation. "So, you don't want to sell your house?"

"What are you talking about, you mad fool." The man didn't have to yell to be heard through his crumbling walls.

I was impressed by Marcus's lack of response, apart from turning and projecting his voice. "We are here to ask if any on this block are interested in selling their properties." Marcus paused and we watched as a few curtains twitched. He walked back out onto the street and continued the pitch. "We are here because we believe we can improve this space and make it liveable. We have an offer to buy your properties, and when the work is complete, sell them back to you for the same price."

We hadn't spoken about that and I didn't think it was part of the deal, but I guess if we wanted to help these people out, this was as good a way as any. And to be honest, I didn't think there were too many folks still living in this block of destroyed homes. There was no power and the drainage water leaking from broken stormwater drains was the source of an ugly stench.

A door a few houses down opened and a lady stepped out. A little kid clung to her legs. She was giving us a serious case of squint-eye, but edged forward to crumpled remains of a short, brick fence lining the property. The morning sun beat back off the high wall behind us, dissolving thick dew on the ground. There was a nip in the air as winter was in full domination. Yet the kid had no shoes, and the woman grasped a thin long-sleeved shirt around her. When she spoke her voice was low, quiet and hard. "You want to buy our houses, fix them up then sell them back to us? For the same price?"

She obviously didn't believe it, yet she wanted to. The offer had drawn her out of her house… shelter. "Where are we supposed to stay in the meantime? Live on the street? Out in the open for the Catchers?" She pressed the kid closer to her side.

The Catchers? I had no idea what she was talking about, but it was something I would look into. For now, though, we had a possible taker. That's all we needed. One person to try us out, give us a go and let us show them we wanted to help. "We'll provide temporary accommodation. It won't be huge, but it will be secure. We are doing a deal with City Council to arrange electricity and water. But we haven't yet got a firm date on that."

She pursed her lips, shot an eyebrow up and started to turn. I was desperate to get her approval. We needed her. "I give you my word." The look of cynical disbelief revealed a history of neglect, and hardly slowed her retreat. "I'll do you a deal." This got her. She stopped and stared. "How about…" I was thinking on my feet, no clue of what I could do to get her over the line.

Please help me!

"What if... I built you a temporary hut for... How many people live with you?"

"I got two boys."

"Right. What if I build you a temporary hut for the three of you. You move in and I pay you to give me feedback on the quality and liveability of it. Then... if you think you could live in it for a few months, we buy your house, build you a permanent home... then... you buy it back for half the price we bought it for."

"Careful lad." Marcus's low grumble behind me wasn't angry. I could, however, feel his nerves. They were jumping all over mine.

The woman turned back around to face me fully and the squint-eye returned. We all started when the kid spoke up. "He's that man what gave us the ball back, Mum. I seen him round. He's not a Catcher, Mum."

I may have had trouble with the woman, but I seem to have managed to win the kid. The lady considered her son and ran her hand over the boy's lanky hair. Then looked me in the eye. "Deal." She walked out to meet us and extended her hand. "Name's Sheila. And I want all that you just said written down and signed." Her eyes ran up and down the broken street. "I got witnesses."

A grin exploded from my heart. "Glad to meet you, Sheila. I'm Dan and this is Marcus. Thank you for trusting—"

"I want what she's getting." The old man who'd shut the door in our faces burst free from his house.

I could feel Marcus bristle, but his voice came out amicably. "Sorry, sir, that deal is for the first taker only. But we will be offering everyone a similar deal: we'll buy your houses, offer you somewhere temporary to live, then sell you back your rebuilt properties for the same price you sold them to us."

Whilst I spoke with Sheila, Marcus started introducing himself to the others who started creeping out of their shelters to learn more.

29

CONTESSA: GOLDEN TICKET

"Congratulations, everyone." Jolena breezed into the room as per usual, long, flowing, dark fabric pluming behind her. Tonight, she wore very dark red. Whilst the rest of us were dishevelled and stressed, with a million pins in our mouths. All of which I spat out immediately, because... you know... rules and workplace health and safety.

My gorgeous model, JJ, stood towering above me, patiently statuesque as I made the final adjustments to the hem of the dress she wore. Neither of us acknowledged Jolena's entrance. Me, because I was stressed out of my tree. JJ, because she was a professional.

There was one week until the Spring Festival. But we had to have our pieces finished tonight because they had to be marked—they were still our assessment pieces—and checked over to see if they were worthy of taking a place on the runway of this year's opening show.

Eeeks!

I could hardly breathe from the excitement when I thought about it.

So I didn't.

Think about it.

I focused on how much I had to get done to make my entry perfect.

Thank the Light they were allowing us to use accessories from their huge range of stock. There was no way I could afford to buy the pieces that I wanted to accompany my outfit. I had designed a classic sleeveless, empire waist, shift dress inspired by 1960s fashion. With lightweight, slightly stretchy wool. It sat about ten centimetres above the knee—on me. On JJ it was a mini. At the hem, the dress was off-white but the colour graduated to the most gorgeous yellow-gold. I'd dyed it myself. It had taken a few attempts, but I was all kinds of happy with the result.

And, yes.

It was my yellow.

Finally, I could design something, from scratch, with amazing fabric, for myself. Even though JJ was ten feet taller than me, I'd picked her because she had no shape, like me. When the show was over and our pieces were returned, it wouldn't take too much to alter it to fit me perfectly.

To accompany the dress, I'd made a coat which was also off-white. Its hem sat about ten centimetres above the dress. The initial effect was that the dress and coat were the same colour. But… it was lined with a soft, luscious satin in the same gold as the top of the dress. So, when JJ came to a stop at the end of the runway, she would do a bit of a flick and give a glimpse of the glory inside.

Yay. I loved it.

But what I absolutely loved, loved, loved the most, was the three-quarter sleeved, bolero top that could be worn over the slip dress. Its bottom hem, beaded with seventy-seven beautiful, individually made, beaded swirls, sat on the empire seam just under her mini bust. It was in the same yellow gold as the top of the dress. I had hidden the opening of the bolero behind more beading. Seriously, when it was on, you couldn't tell it was separate to the dress. It looked like one piece. I had also hand-sewn very subtle swirls… yes, just like those beaded on the hem—and on my armour—through the top. When you took it all in, it was one of the last things you noticed, like an extra little "Oh!" at the end of the show.

This outfit was totally me. And the coolest thing of all was no one would know... except those in the Light would see my signature all over it, just like I'd spray-painted it "Made by Tessa".

I decided to go with off-white, strappy-backed, low heeled, pointy toe shoes that had a hint of gold glitter, and a gold Kelly bag. Everything looked amazing against JJ's gorgeous dark skin. She was just perfect for the outfit. Not as perfectly suited as me, but the next best, ever. I loved everything about this design. It was one hundred percent different to everyone else's. And I was so flopping proud of what I had achieved.

I know You inspired me and helped me, thank You so much. I am just so happy. If I can just finish this hem, I can finally relax. I can't wait till my family get to see this. Thank You!

Our teacher slapped a folder on Travis's work bench to get our attention. "Come now, everyone. Down tools for just one moment and then you can finish off. But remember, you only have until 9.00 pm tonight. Then it's all over."

There was a quiet muttering and a few curses around the room, but we had learned not to keep Jolena waiting. We still had about forty-five minutes left. If everyone hurried up, she could say what she had to, then let us finish up.

I wasn't popular in the group. I think because I came late to the program, all the others had been working... and competing against each other, since they started the beginner course two years ago.

But in this, we all agreed: keep Jolena happy. She was our ticket to a future in the textile world. And, she had a world-class sulk if we didn't do as she instructed.

"I have wonderful news. As a reward for your hard work and dedication." Her eyes roamed the room, resting on each of our models who were wearing almost-completed outfits, and she smiled. "This is going to be a great show." She looked to me and nodded slowly, her grin growing. I knew it was probably wrong, but I kind of basked in her affirmation. I knew I would pay for it later from the others—another reason I wasn't popular, Jolena wasn't very good at diplomacy or subtlety when it came to playing favourites. But, if my lecturer... and an influential person in the Guild, was happy with my work, was that so wrong?

"Tomorrow night there is a Guild meeting. It is not official business so we'll meet at the Theatre, not the Guild Hall." She paused and looked to each one of us. "You are all invited to come along. Meet some people. Mingle. Considering your efforts and enthusiasm, I don't think it will be too long before you are all official members anyway." At this, there were, possibly for the first time, genuine smiles of joy shared among us. I beamed at JJ. She smiled back. Jolena continued, "This could be the start of something big. For all of you."

Frozen, I was completely frozen. We had just received an invitation... a coveted invitation... to a Guild meeting, at the Theatre, which was weird, but a Guild meeting none the less. Cissa had told me they were strictly for members only. And we weren't members... yet. My family would be so proud.

I put my hand up. Jolena liked protocol. She nodded again. "Are we allowed to bring a guest?" She tilted her head and furrowed her brow. I continued, "My husband?"

Her eyes flashed to my hands—still clutching my pin cushion—one wearing a fingerless skin-toned glove, the other a glistening rock on my third finger. She narrowed her eyes. Not in a nasty way, but as if she was weighing up her answers. "Sadly, dear, Guild business is for Guild members... and specific guests... only."

My heart sank.

Thankfully, the others continued the questions, our crazy, rapidly approaching deadline seemingly forgotten. Kayleigh, the more approachable of the two unapproachable girls asked, "Will they know who we are? How will we get in?"

This time Jolena's laughter was throatier, and that sinking feeling I'd been swimming in sunk a bit lower. "Be in the foyer by 8.00 pm. I will come out and collect you." As was usual with our instructor, this pleasantry was followed by a not-so-subtle threat. "If you are not there when I open the door, you will not get in." Meaning, if you miss my welcome, you miss your future. Her perfect white teeth glimmered behind her smile. "It will be my pleasure to introduce you to the other members. I do believe you will all be very well received."

"Do people discuss designing? And business possibilities here in Sardis? Will you introduce us to other designers? Will anyone from Thyatira be there?" My excitement pushed my nerves out of the way and took control of my mouth. I'd forgotten to put my hand up. Thankfully, Jolena was in a good mood and met my indiscretion with a slight frown, but graced me with an answer nonetheless.

She looked me in the eye and with great sincerity answered, "I promise to introduce you to everyone. And whilst there may not be a great deal of *business* discussed on your first night, there will be a great many possibilities. Believe me. This is just the beginning of a great future for you." Before she left she called over her shoulder, "And make sure you sign those agreements before you go. Can't have you kissing and telling, now, can we?"

30

CONTESSA: ALL THE FABRIC, NOT ONE DRESS

"Far. Flaming. Out. What am I supposed to wear? I forgot to ask."
I was storming around our room with clothes tossed over every surface. Dan sat on the horribly ornate chair at the little desk positioned by the wall of windows and watched me unravel. At first, he thought it was very entertaining. But his mood worsened as my frustration increased, and my patience fled the room with every ridiculous suggestion he made.

I mean, seriously, "What you've got on is fine," was not fine.

At.

All.

Or, "Jeans and a shirt always work for me. Maybe you could put some of those fancy shoes on and, bang, perfect."

Jeans?

Was he flopping serious right now?

When his third attempt at suggesting I, "just grab something clean from the wash basket," was met with a scream of fury, he yelled back, "Why do you even have to go?"

I couldn't believe what I was hearing. "What do you mean, 'have to go'? I don't have to. I want to. This is huge for me."

His eyes bored into me. I'd been so caught up in my desperation, I

182

hadn't seen the transformation. He was seriously skitched off. His growl of, "You can't even see what this is," grew to a raised, "or don't want to." Which then finished with a shout. "You're being so selfish."

"Stopping yelling at me," I yelled.

"I'm not yelling," he yelled back.

It was a stand-off. I was on one side of the room. He was on the other. Like two furious creatures facing off in a paddock, we both scowled and breathed noisily. I tried to maintain control by breathing very slowly. I held my hands up, fingers splayed. I just needed a moment to wrap my head around what was going on here. I knew he'd been stressed... overwrought. He'd been so caught up in his own struggles, he'd obviously not understood what was going on for me. "I know this is difficult, Dan. We knew that, heading into this. But we agreed it was just for a season. Three months. It has been really hard for the both of us, but it is almost over."

I couldn't believe I was so close to the finish line. After so much hard work, I was almost there. And now? Now? He decided to throw a hissy fit? I couldn't hold onto the calm. My exhaustion, fear, and anxiety took control of my voice... and its volume. "One week, Dan. Can you not hold it together for just one more week." Tears broke into my voice, but it didn't soften my resolve. "Is it too much to ask you to support me in this for just. One. More. Bleeding. Week?" I threw my arms up. I was so frustrated I didn't even know what to do with myself. After waving them around a bit I was at a loss for where to put them, so I planted them on my hips.

"Is that what you think?" Thankfully his yelling had reduced to a disbelieving loud speaking. "That this"—he shot my finger between the two of us and our latest standoff—"is all about. Me. Not support-ing. You?" His voice rose several octaves on that last note. My eyebrows matched it in shock. But then dropped very low at his last accusation: "Are you insane?"

"Don't you call me dumb. I am not dumb."

"I did not call you dumb, Tessa. I called you insane."

My eyes grew and my brain blanked. He said what? I inhaled, ready to release control and give my mouth free rein, when he jumped back in. "This is me being bleeding well worried about you." The very loud angry talk that wasn't quite a yell, but was far from conversation level, continued. "This is me seeing the bigger picture. This is me not happy about sending my wife off, by herself, into a feral mob, in the name of 'work', so that you can make your freakin' weirdo lecturer happy."

A bucket of ice water was pitched into the heart of my fury.

What?

Wait, I shook my head... what?

Again, before I could muster any words that made any sense, he continued in the same heated volume. "This is me being worried skratless that you're doing this. This is me terrified something is going to happen to you, and you do not seem to be able to see that this is a problem."

That threw me. I swayed back like his words had physically hit me. "Last time this happened, Tessa, I had to watch you being abducted, drugged, thrown into a pen of vipers and there. Was. Nothing. I could do. To help you. But at least I was aware you were okay because we had drones watching over you. We had Felix and Maurice, February and October breaking all kinds of laws to get you free. We had a whole team ready to get you when the opportunity rose.

"But here..." He faltered. For the first time I could actually see the fear etched deeply in his eyes... face... body. But he didn't stop, he slumped and continued, beaten, in a hoarse whisper. "Here, I will have no idea if you're okay. I will have no idea what they're doing to you. I will have no idea what's going on, and if you need help. I know you want to save yourself. I respect that, and I love you for it. But damn it, Tessa, we can't always save ourselves, sometimes we need help and I... I just won't know."

He came over to me, held my shoulders kissed my head and whispered, "I am not going to stop you. I want to support you. But, Tessa," he held me at arm's length and made me look into his deep, dark, grey eyes, "I'm worried skratless right now." He released me and slunk to the door, stuck his head out and yelled. "Kait. We need you." He then walked out and left me in a puddle of confusion and lostness.

Kait came racing in, and when she saw the room, and me standing with tears streaking my face, she made everything better.

Every.

Thing.

"Right, sweetheart, let's get to work. What are you trying to say at the meeting? What image are you wanting to portray?"

"I don't really know. I think it's casual. But they're designers." More tears threatened to fall. Now I didn't know if I actually wanted to go. "I wish Cissa was here and I could ask her." I would ask her why she didn't like the Guild. Was Dan right to be worried... to call me insane? Then inspiration struck. "Maybe I could message her?"

Kait mulled it over, then shook her head. "You know how Cissa feels about the Guilds. Not just here but... everywhere."

That's why I'd wanted to message her. But then lit Kait's face lit up. "You have Jolena's number, ask her. It's perfectly acceptable to ask the dress code."

The thought of Jolena had me remembering my classes, my work, my pieces for the show. Even though Dan was kind of right about her —she was a bit... off—this was my opportunity to make my dreams come true. "Oh, Kait, you are a genius."

With a cute, simple, but classic cocktail dress under a gorgeous black woollen coat I'd found in a charity shop in Ephesus on our honeymoon, and a lightweight emerald-green scarf, I strode out to the living area in my heeled mules. Kait had pinned my hair up in a simple updo and I had a light covering of make-up. I did a turn and everyone agreed I fit the bill of classy after-five attire.

Everyone but Dan. Silently he stood, gave me a hug: his smile fake and his eyes brimming with concern. "I wish I could go with you." He held up a finger when I went to speak and continued, "I know this is something you need to do. I know it's important. But, I'm worried. And nothing you say or do is going to change that." He ran his hands down my arms and took my hands. His thumbs running over the backs of my hands. My right one now permanently encased in the fingerless glove. "Do you have your earpiece?"

I nodded and raised my elbow and indicated the little bag that held the essentials: phone, bit of cash and lippy.

"Right then, we'd best be off." Dan went to the kitchen to grab the keys whilst I did the rounds, farewelling my family.

"So proud of you sweetheart." Kait embraced me. "Can't wait to hear all about it."

The car ride over to the Theatre was subdued and edgy at the same time. I was nervous, and a bit excited and also… very nervous.

"You look amazing, Tessa. You're going to rock this. Hands down."

"I'm sorry you can't come. I really would feel better with you there, but…" I looked to my husband whose eyes were focused on the road and the GPS showing him how to get to the Theatre. "This could be my big break, Dan. This could be all my dreams come true."

"I know, honey. And I'll be right here, all the way. Just let me know what you need. I am really proud." Dan pulled into a drop-off zone near the grand courtyard out the front of the Theatre. It was as close as he could get.

I checked my phone. 7:40 pm. I had fifteen minutes to make the three-minute trip across the paved area, climb the stairs and be in the foyer to make sure I was completely ready at 7:55. I knew Jolena would be early. It was her way. And I felt sick.

Totally and utterly sick.

And I wasn't sure why.

And I couldn't make myself get out of the car.

CONTESSA: DINNER WITH DEMONS

I reached across, kissed Dan, and forced myself to woman up. I saw Kayleigh and Emma step out of a Pod and start their way across the expanse. I had to do this or I would miss my chance. The late winter night air had a chilly nip to it, edging me on. I stood and took a deep breath, and just before I closed the door, leaned back in. "I love you."

"I know. You look great. Message me when you're ready to leave" —he tapped his earpiece—"and I'll be right here to get you."

We both looked to the grand entrance, crawling with demons, and then to my Guard, who had been joined by two others. This both encouraged me, and made me extra nervous. The Light didn't just hand these guys out like out-of-date catalogues. If I had extra, I was going to need them.

Thank You!

With my security detail in place, I quickstepped until I caught up with my classmates. I mean, I didn't actually join them, I hovered close by, just out of reach of their hushed conversation. Unnaturally unnerved, I didn't want to be isolated from human company.

Trust Xavier to already be there. Probably arrived at 5.00 pm. His stern eyes met mine and his scowl deepened as I climbed the stairs to the main theatre in the shadow of Kayleigh and Emma. His attention darted behind me at the same time I heard Wallace, Travis and Oscar skylarking their way across the forecourt behind me. We'd all made it. The three boys wore suits, but only Oscar wore a tie. Xavier wore an elaborately stitched waistcoat over a white shirt, top unbuttoned, sleeves rolled to expose his forearms, with suit pants. I had no idea what the girls were wearing, as, like me, they'd worn coats.

All six of them were buzzing with excitement and, as usual, I tried to blend into the background of the impressive, high-ceilinged room. Everything was cream marble shot with fine veins of gold, which matched all the fittings and edging of the room. Two men in matching navy-blue uniforms waited like statues at the internal doors. As we approached, they remained motionless, like we didn't exist, and as though three in our group hadn't almost knocked over one of the carved pedestals placed around the room holding huge vases of exotic flowers. Their scent in the heated air was heady and on the verge of being cloying. Everything about the place screamed excessive money. Wealth. Class.

And I wanted to go home.

I was so out of place—a trespasser... a play actor.

And I hated it.

All of it.

Sardis.

Not only because of what had happened to Val, but also because of the excessive demon action, their lurid behaviour, and the blindness of those around me. It reminded me of Sodom. This was a lot cleaner, but still, it was a haven for the Dark. I was growing more and more grateful for my Guard... Guards. Two more had joined me. Five in total.

I jumped when one of the statuesque attendants came to life and instructed us girls to leave our coats and bags in the cloak room. Leaving my coat wasn't an issue, the heat pumping through the place had me prickling with sweat. However, when I opted to keep my bag with me, the attendant was adamant I should leave it with my cloak. "Conditions of entry, miss." Kayleigh, Emma and I looked to each other. None of us were keen to abandon our essentials. In the end, Emma shrugged and handed hers over, Kayleigh and I followed. But as I reached in to grab my phone, or attempted to get my earpiece, I was told with a firm shake of the head, "Condition of entry, Miss."

I was the last to leave my name and belongings with the clerk, before we all turned as the huge doors of the foyer swung outward to reveal a mass of bodies, pungent smell—strong enough to override the flowers in the foyer—and heat pulsing from within. The lights were dim and the laughter, chatter and faint strains of music were loud. From the heart of the melee, Jolena emerged, sauntering toward us in impossibly high, red heels. Throwing her arms wide, she greeted us. "Welcome to the Textiles Guild, my wonderful young protégés. Tonight is your night to shine."

My six companions edged toward the door like children creeping toward a Lightmas tree laden with gifts, daring to believe the image wasn't a mirage. I on the other hand was teetering on the edge of flight. It wasn't too far to get home from here. I could catch a Pod, then come back later and collect my gear. No way I'd be leaving my coat behind.

But Jolena, quick as a snake, stepped forward and threaded her arm through mine and clamped it to her side like a steel-toothed trap. Which really was a feat, since, with her in her ridiculous heels, I only came up to her armpit. Yes, even though I, too, was wearing heels.

Pinned to her side—which was sheathed in a skin-tight, black, backless number that didn't allow for underwear... any... underwear —I felt a little immature in my outfit. Not that I could carry that look off. Jolena had all the necessary curves to keep that thing afloat. Her long dark hair was swept up in a loose bun and the red ornamental spike holding everything in place was the perfect highlight to her look.

I needed to get my head in the game.

I had nothing to be scared of.

Jolena was my instructor at TAVE.

They wouldn't let psychos work there. These folks worked with young people. Surely there was some kind of anti-psycho check.

Just breathe, and woman up.

Forcing myself to relax, I allowed my mentor to guide me into the main part of the Theatre and my brain froze. I thought I must have been in an alternate universe. "What...? Where...? How...? Business meetings?" I turned to my host and she laughed, handing me a tall glass of a bubbling drink from a tray held by a passing waiter.

The building was grand and the room was huge and ornate. All the seats had been cleared away to leave room for tables set up in a large rectangle and chairs placed around the outside. Even though there looked to be over one hundred chairs, there didn't seem to be enough to accommodate the number of people in the room.

However, all other details of the room were lost to me when I realised that all around the top several metres of the walls, holographic scenes played out. The crisp, pale-blue light giving life to the vision was in stark contrast to the dark, humid, suffocating atmosphere. It made the grotesque scene impossible to ignore. Each wall projected the same scene: the fake-god Dionysus, sitting naked, limbs spread wide, on his throne with hordes of women, blank-faced, coming to him, drawn by his spell. It was enough to make me gag. It was so dark, and noisy, and suffocating, no one noticed. I had to get out. This was all wrong.

Please help me.

"Come now, Tessa." With her arm still linked in mine, Jolena paused and I heard her call out, but couldn't understand what she said. Then we were moving again. Like parting a sea, the crowd stepped aside as we approached, and we were heading to some large doors. Attendants opened them and fresh, clean night-air rushed through. I almost ran to escape the oppressive atmosphere and Darkness pulsing through the room. I must have given my intentions away as Jolena pinned me more securely to her side. Her words sent ice through my veins. "Calm down, child, we will get there soon enough."

Next, we were ascending wide stone stairs. Moonlight reflecting off their cold, hard surface illuminated the frescoes on the walls. I couldn't make out the details, my senses were reeling, but gruesome depictions of people was all I could absorb.

We arrived into the open air on a rooftop balcony. A blazing fire was roaring in an open pit in the middle of the space. Men and women, barely clothed, stood swaying around the fire. The roar and buzz of the crowd behind me and—as I soon learned—my other class-mates, deafened me to all other stimuli.

My brain was shutting down.

Too many things were happening.

Waiters, swamped by the crowd, walked around the group with trays of dishes. As they came by, I saw the bowls were almost empty. The small, white pills within were consumed as people toasted each other with glasses of bubbling, golden liquid.

Jolena released me and I was left surrounded by my classmates. I looked side to side. Xavier stood in a space of his own, his face a blank mask. Kayleigh's eyes, much like mine, were darting all over the place. I was looking for any possible escape route. I suspected she was too.

The other four, however, were grinning, and looked eager to participate in whatever hell was about to break loose. Taking a tray from one of the waiters, Jolena herself served each one of us, making sure we each took one of the tablets. She merely chuckled when Travis took more.

"Drink up, my children, and prepare to meet our Lord, Dionysius." We were all then offered glasses. I looked to Kayleigh. She, wide-eyed and panicked, looked back at me. Our little group had become the centre of attention on the rooftop. The horde quietened and waited for us to participate. Some of them were removing their already minimal clothing. I desperately looked for my Guard. They, and others were involved in a savage battle on the perimeter.

I am in so much trouble here. I am so sorry. Please, tell me what to do.

As my classmates swallowed the pills, the only thing I could think to do was to copy, but fake it. I had to swallow the liquid. I couldn't hide that. Sweet, burning bubbles set my mouth singing and chilled my throat. Once the crowd and Jolena were satisfied, they all turned to face the fire. I dropped the pill and tried to step on it. No one took any notice as a drumbeat, slow and steady, pulsed through the air. Its tone so deep it resonated through my body. Music from overhead speakers vibrated and the crowd, as one, moved in synchronicity: a slow, rhythmic swaying.

Except Jolena.

Her eyes were wide and she was almost salivating.

I looked at Kayleigh.

Her eyes met and mirrored my fear.

We had to get out of here.

I scanned the rooftop.

My Guards, and more, were still fully involved in battle. I was overcome with guilt. I had caused this. I had put them in this situation. And I didn't know how to get out. My classmates were imitating the actions of those around us as they fell into a trace.

Except Xavier.

He watched everything with his permanent scowl.

We had to get out of here.

I had to get Kayleigh out.

With everyone focused on the fire, and drugged, I knew their eyesight and actions would be incapacitated. I knew of the doors we came in through, but maybe there were other exits? Fire escapes? My heart raced ahead of the drumbeat. Sweat prickled my skin in the chilled night air. Kayleigh edged closer to me and together we tried to fall to the back of the crowd.

Until people, carrying cages, joined us on the roof top. Were they... dogs?

I didn't understand.

My brain was not functioning.

Why did they need...

I turned and vomited.

"Oh, Tessa." Jolena's hand ran along my bent back and rested around the nape of my neck. "You are so predictable."

32

CONTESSA: FODDER FOR THE MASSES

"You are so wonderfully innocent, my dear. We are very much going to enjoy including you in our ceremony later tonight." I almost tripped as Jolena hauled me to standing and drew me through the crowd back to the main stairs.

I struggled to know where to look. By now people had removed what little clothing they had left. My classmates included. I threw my eyes around the space searching for Kayleigh. Emma was lost in her trance. But Kayleigh and Xavier had edged closer together and were following me and Jolena… at a distance.

But then I lost sight of everyone as Jolena continued to drag me down the stairs to another room. A stone-faced attendant opened the door as we arrived and Jolena pushed me forward. I stumbled into the darkness but found my feet.

This room was overpoweringly scented with musk and more-subtle music played in the background. The group here was smaller. I didn't have time to take much else in before my captor spoke. "Amand, darling, I want you to meet Tessa, a new student of mine. She shows a lot of promise." Shivers went down my spine. The way she stressed "promise" made the word sound rude, disgusting… sexual.

Maybe that was because Amand wasn't wearing any clothes.

None.

Nada.

He was semi reclined on a divan, one foot on the seat, knee bent, a rest for his arm. He looked like a parody of the statue at the temple of Zeus. Thankfully, a piece of fabric lay across the man's groin.

"Um… I think there has been some sort of mistake?" I couldn't look at the man. I tried very hard to keep my eyes on his face. But his intense gaze was stripping me and making his intentions blatantly clear. Heat raced to my face and my heart took off at a gallop. I had to get out of there. Quick.

"No mistake, dear. On the contrary. Our Lord asked for you specifically." Her head indicated the rolling, three-dimensional image that brought the tops of the walls and ceiling to life. "And because of that, I am introducing you to the most influential man in Sardis. Straight to the top for you, Tessa."

The horrid man on the couch leered and patted the couch next to him.

My eyes flew around the room. Some of my Guard had followed me and each of them were fully engaged with the enemy. Then I almost gagged… again. This whole situation took me straight back to Ashera's temple in Sodom. With no sense of shame, or decency… or taste, people were practising public… very public, displays of affection… very physical affection. Incense hung heavy in the fetid air. Everything was heavy, dark and dank. My heart took off again and in one part of my brain I had enough clarity to identify I was trying to discern the best tactic. Fight or flight.

I looked to the man in front of me, the woman beside me—once again her hand grasping the back of my neck—and the horror that filled the room.

There were too many to fight.

My Guard—all of them—were busy… very busy.

Flight it was.

"Please forgive me Jolena. Thank you for the invitation, but… um… I am a married woman and… um… this is not something I can… um… participate in."

Amand and Jolena burst out laughing. "You were right, darling," Amand said. "So naive and innocent. We are going to enjoy breaking her into the Guild. Thank you for bringing her to my attention." Amand leaned forward and kissed the back of Jolena's hand. They stared at each other for a beat, and with her attention fully on him, I took advantage.

And bolted.

Well, I tried to.

Jolena called after me. "Stop her." It was almost insulting how casual she was about it.

A shirtless man stood in front of me. I threw my fist in his face and tried to weave around him. An arm snaked around my waist and I was pinned. I dropped my weight, threw back my head and smashed him —definitely a male—in the chest... throat? Not sure, but it was enough for him to release me.

Another came at me front on. More came from the side. The music stopped and everyone quietened to watch the show. Time slowed and I prayed with the eloquence of panic.

Help me. Help.

A slow, untrained goon tried to wrap me in his arms front on. *Fool.* I ducked, whipped my shoes off and used the heels as weapons. One in the groin with an enthusiastic upward swing as I straightened, and another in the side of the head... because I was not happy.

I dropped into a fighting stance holding my shoes like the weapons they were. My unexpected actions, and the man lying on the floor groaning, brought the whole crazy scene to a halt.

Think, Tessa. Think!

My brain went to hyperfocus and I scanned the room. Then I saw it. At the back of the crowd. Kayleigh twitched her head and flicked her eyes to an opening and a possible escape route.

I bolted, dodged, weaved and leapt my way through the mass. Thankfully, most of them were too full of alcohol and mind-altering substances, semi dressed and—mere moments before—focused on other... strenuous activity. It all combined to give me a chance.

Some managed to get a hand on me, but with a few well-timed

spins, well-placed kicks and well-practised punches, I managed to elude them all. Kayleigh edged away from the crowd and was now trying to open the huge, imposing doors allowing me... and possibly her, to escape. I had no idea she liked me. Maybe she didn't, but either way, she obviously wanted to be gone from here as much as I did.

I almost collapsed with relief as a splinter of light broke through the darkness as she edged the door open. Fresh air diluted the oily poison of the Darkness the closer I got to the light.

The gap was wide enough for her to break through, and I was right on her heels when two arms of steel wrapped around me from behind. Before I had a chance to drop my weight, I was lifted off my feet. Before I had a chance to use my head as a weapon, I was spun and thrown over a shoulder. A shoulder covered in an elaborately stitched waistcoat.

Xavier.

Xavier, who hadn't had anything to drink, and was very unlikely to have consumed any mind-altering substances. Xavier who had hated me from day one.

"Why are you doing this? Let me go." I pummelled him with the heels of my shoes. The guy barely flinched. "Xavier, let me go."

I hardly managed to hear his growl over the cheers. "Two birds, one stone."

"What?"

"Earn my ticket without having to be part of this crap. And get rid of you."

I was just so angry. And a whole lot scared. And so unbelievably frustrated, I just couldn't get a good swing with my shoe heels, he was too close. I ditched them and used my fingernails, teeth, fists and everything else I could think of. He was squirming and grunting but his grip over the backs of my legs just increased.

I pulled up his stupid vest, and ripped his shirt out of his waistband so I could get at his flesh. I dug my fingernails in and raked his stomach and sides and any flesh within reach. All the while, I wriggled and fought every step of the way. When nothing seemed to work, or lessen his hold, or alter his course, I sunk my teeth in. I bit so hard I tasted blood. Then I bit again and again. Xavier yelled, slapped my butt hard.

So, I bit him again. Harder.

He swung me around and my head connected with a wall. Stars danced in front of my eyes, and I lost all focus as I drowned in throbbing pain. If my stomach wasn't completely empty, I would have thrown up again. Would serve him right if I puked down the back of his pants. Using his hips as leverage I tried to push myself away from his body to see where I was and what was going on. My sweat-soaked hair was blocking my view of everything except Xavier's back. All I could hear was the ragged huffing from my captor and the telltale click of heels on stone floor.

"Darling, well done. I always knew you had it in you." Jolena's oily voice transformed my now-groggy rage into serious concern. "We'll take her downstairs later. In the meantime, place her in one of the spare cages in the back hallway." She turned and instructed someone else. "Show him where to go."

The space fell silent and Jolena projected her voice. "I think Tessa has earned the right to the Special Room. Don't you?" All else was lost to me under the deafening cheers and roars of approval. A blood red fingernail traced down my cheek. "Such a waste." Jolena's final words turned my serious concern to genuine panic.

I threw myself back into my attack and did what I could to loosen Xavier's grip. He yelled and started another swing toward a wall.

Oh, Lord, please help me.

33

DANIEL: LIKE THAT WAS GOING TO HAPPEN

Yeah, right. Like I was going to leave her when she had five... *five* warriors accompany her across the forecourt of the Theatre. First thing I did was find a park. This wretched city was so opposed to cars—electric or otherwise—in the Cultural District, they made it almost impossible to park. I drove down dark alleys, got stuck in dead ends, but eventually found a space, that wasn't an actual carpark, but wasn't not a carpark either, around the back of the Theatre—I think—same stone, same design, same block—near some huge garbage bins in what may have been a delivery dock.

Then, I rang Marcus. "I'm worried. Something is seriously off and I need to get in there."

He grunted and I could hear him talking to Kait. "We've got to go. Tessa's pickled."

I yelled to interrupt, "She may not be, I'm just worried she may be."

"Hush, lad, we'll catch a Pod. Send me one of those pin thingys on the phone. The twins'll stay here, Kait and I will be lickety split."

"But Marc—" He'd hung up.

If I've overreacted, and I'm raining on her parade, sorry. I trust You... and Tessa. But... something's wrong. So, if I'm right, please help her. And help me help her. And get to her. And help us... if we need it, that is. If I'm not wrong.

But the fact that I, too, had been given extra Guards and there was a gathering of demons approaching, kind of made me think I was right.

I sent my location to Marcus, got out and started exploring the area with my sword drawn. The space reeked of the feral smells familiar from the undersides of most cities I'd been in. Good to know, in this instance, Sardis was just like all the rest. Sad reflection on me, but it kind of made me feel a bit more comfortable and less out of place. I inhaled the stench, strongly infused with sulphur, loosened my limbs and, with my Guard, started the search. Every time we were impeded by the enemy, some of the Light's rank broke off to deal with it, leaving me to keep hunting.

Every door I came across was locked, as was to be expected. But as more and more demons appeared around a short set of steps leading up to another door, we kind of had an idea of how we could get in. Or at least a place we could try.

This was going to get nasty. I quickly shot Marcus another pin in the hope he would identify the door I was going to attempt... after we got through that wall of ugly.

I was used to fighting surrounded by my family, or at least flanked by Tessa and Riah. I had never had to stand my ground against this many of the enemy by myself. Human or demonic. Needless to say, they were grinning, jeering and salivating as I, their dinner, approached.

Okay, Tessa's in there. They're standing in my way and You have sent me a whole lot of help. So, I'm guessing things are bad. I would be very grateful for as much help as possible here.

Almost immediately I was aided by spears shooting from the skies, which transformed to more Guards who were far more capable than I was of taking care of the growing number of hostiles confronting me. And, I suspected, that was my cue.

I shot off another pin to Marcus, letting him know which door we had gone through, just in case the growing wall of ugliness wasn't a dead giveaway. My Guard and I high-tailed it up the stairs, dodging some half-hearted parries, to gain access to the building through a —*thank You*—unlocked door.

The immediate heatwave made things a bit uncomfortable, but the roaring and cheering had me on high alert. I was in a hallway that was dimly lit by the green exit sign above my head, and the glow of reflected light coming from around the corner along the corridor. The floor was covered in a light-grey vinyl, which also helped reflect the light bouncing off the white walls. The taint of incense almost had me sneezing. But my flashback to searching the halls of the Temple of Ashera in Laodicea to find our friends, Iza and Amber, pushed all sensory overloads down. And the memory of finding Amber unconscious on the floor and Iza, naked, tied to an altar had me almost running. Surrounded by my wall of Warriors, I scuttled along hallways looking for clues of where Tessa might be. Desperately trying to convince myself she wasn't actually in trouble.

Then everything went quiet. A voice rang out. "I think Tessa has earned the right to the Special Room. Don't you?"

Bile boiled in my gut. The Special Room? What the hell was that? And more importantly, where was it?

The incense and laughter seemed to be coming from the same direction, so, staying in the shadows as much as possible, I moved on. The dim lighting of the hallways was enough to show me I'd arrived at an emergency gathering point. On the wall was a floor plan showing the exit along the route I had just taken. Not helpful. The rest of the map had sections of the two-storey structure laid out in blocks labelled with letters. Also, unhelpful.

I assumed the evening's event, considering the amount of noise they were making, was in the largest space, A, and the back room would be in one of the smaller spaces, any one of D through to H. Mildly helpful. However, the bloke carrying my wife over his shoulder walking down the hallway surrounded by a pack of salivating, semi-dressed thugs was just the clue I needed.

The hardest thing I had ever done was staying put. My Guard, who never usually intervened or really communicated with me at all, drew his sword and blocked my path. With one shake of his head, I received his message loud and clear: "Stay." Then, with a flick of his chin, most of his crew broke off and followed the thugs. That made it a bit easier to bide my time.

The guy who'd been carrying Tessa came back along the hallway without her, his face like thunder as he focused on inspecting his gouged stomach and trying to see his back.

That's my girl. Gave him one helluva lot of grief.

In his attempt to see his back, he semi-turned, and I saw bite marks. *You idiot.* She was never going to go quietly. As sick as I was at the thought of what had happened... was happening to Tessa, I was proud of her causing as much damage as possible.

I was pulled out of my brooding by the rest of the group following Bite Boy's path. They too were so focused on slapping each other on the back and discussing what they were going to do to my wife when she woke up, I was invisible to them, too. Their mild weaving and semi-slurred speech indicated they probably weren't too capable of seeing me at the moment, anyway. Again, I was almost sick, until my Guard gave me a gentle push on the shoulder and I took off at a jog with the three Warriors attending me to where Tessa was... held captive in a hallway?

Unlike Iza, she was fully clothed and stuffed in an... animal crate? Several empty crates were underneath hers and a couple held dogs. Tessa's Guard used his sword to unlock the door to her cage, his face a mix of rage and compassion. When he was done, he laid a hand on her head then looked at me and gave me one nod.

I didn't need another invitation. I raced over, lifted her tiny, inert body, so familiar to me now, and our significant Guard surrounded us as we bolted back down the hallway. But not before the other crate doors were opened and their prisoners released. Just as we turned the corner for the exit, I could make out the sound of shoes tapping and squeaking behind us. Torn between dropping Tessa and getting ready to fight, versus gripping her harder and running for our lives, my heart was jumping out of my chest.

Ahead of me, the door opened and Marcus and Kait stood fierce and puffing. Considering the bodies dissolving on the landing behind them, I wasn't surprised. I ran to them and whispered, "Quick, we've got to go. Any second, they're gonna find out we've got her."

No sooner had I said it than there was a scream. Fury, shock and frustration worked their way into every note of the cry. "Find her!" This was followed by barking dogs and cries of pain.

With bulging eyes and nodding head, I indicated the stairs and all of us turned and ran. I heard the door quietly close behind us. Thankfully, Kait was on the ball. I let her cover our rear and, since they'd cleared a path for a clean escape, I thrust Tessa at Marcus and dug the car keys out of my pocket. The beep unlocking the doors screamed in the silence, the pulse of the lights a beacon declaring to the world, "They're here."

We tumbled in and, without lights, in my dark-coloured electric SUV I crept out of the space behind the dumpster and, keeping my speed agonisingly slow, hardly breathed until we'd made it onto the ring-road. I turned the opposite way to the way I'd brought Tessa to this nightmare, flicked on my lights and hid myself in the minimal traffic, mainly made up of Pods.

In the back seat, Marcus still cradled Tessa, and Kait was speaking. "Hi Audette, sorry to trouble you so late, but we were wondering if you knew of any doctors we could trust in Sardis? We need to get Tessa checked over and we need to do it quietly." There was a pause. "You don't have to do that." Another mini pause then, "Thank you, but seriou—" Then silence. Kait tapped her earpiece. "She's on her way. She will call someone local who will meet us at home soon. When she gets here, she'll check Tessa herself. But we have to try to wake her up." Next, she was talking with the twins, giving them an update, letting them know we were heading home.

As I pulled into the underground carpark of Black & Light Designs, I was again so grateful for the people the Light had brought into our lives. The dim glow of relief started to work its way into my consciousness. I hadn't yet been able to think about what state Tessa was in, what had happened to her, and definitely not what had been going to happen to her if we hadn't got there in time. It was bad enough feeling the egg-sized lump on the side of her head and finding her limp as a rag doll.

If she has concussion, please don't let it be as bad as mine. Please make her alright. Thank You... just... thank You.

I could inhale just a tad deeper when the secure gates rolled into place behind us, and I eased the car into our designated spot. But nothing could stop me launching myself out of my seat when I heard Tessa's quiet weeping. I raced around and carefully took her from Marcus and let him and Kait lock up and summon the lift. Tessa clung to me just as brutally as I held her. I acknowledged both of our Guards as we entered the lift, relieved we only had our usual detail. Nothing was going to take her from me.

"Okay now, put her down and let me examine her, lad." The old woman from the True Light Community was waiting in our apartment... With Cissa and Al? I had trouble putting two and two together. What was she... they... all doing here? How did they get in? Why did the woman want to look at Tessa?

Kait came to the rescue with some answers. "Desleigh is a doctor. A friend of Cissa, Al and Audette's. Audette is on her way and asked Desleigh to check Tessa over as soon as possible. She said we couldn't wait with a head injury. Oh, and Felix will be here soon, too."

It was all too much information. I just couldn't comprehend any of it. All I knew was that we had rescued Tessa. Tessa was hurt. And I was never going to let her go. Everything else was just too much.

Then I was hit by two cannonballs embracing me and Tessa with wiry, deceptively strong arms. Peace started leaching into my brain and I realised Raph needed to see her. I sat on the couch, Tessa still fiercely clinging to me, and my little brother laid his hands on her head and closed his eyes. With one of Riah's hands still on me and the other on my wife, reason knocked on the door. "Thank you everyone for coming." I looked at Cissa and Al. "Aren't you away?"

Cissa laughed. "We were, we're back now. We dropped in to say hello on our way in and the twins told us what was happening."

The old woman said, "And as you know, Audette called me and asked me to look at the girl. I'm happy to help, but for that to happen,

I actually need to examine her." Desleigh had a stethoscope around her neck and a medical bag, neither of which I had seen before.

Raph sat up, stroked Tessa's hair and very quietly said to me, "She has no brain injury or bleed. I have done what I can to relieve her pain." At that point I could understand those times Tessa complained about not having enough arms.

The doctor stood over us all, so I gently encouraged Tessa to release her iron grip on my neck and, using my eyes, I asked Riah for some help. She pumped more peace, so much so it started filling the room.

I tried to reassure my wife. "It's okay, Tessa, you're safe. We're all here. No one can hurt you here."

Tessa sat up and the doctor changed places with Raph and started checking her vitals. I don't think Tessa noticed, instead she stared into nothing and declared, "Everything is ruined. I can't... I won't. Over, it's all over...." Then the sobbing started.

Desleigh tried to calm her. "Yes, Tessa, it's over. You can relax. You're safe. Everything is okay."

But her sobbing increased. "No. No, it's not." The only words I could discern after that were "ruined" and "failure".

"Calm down, girl, your blood pressure is climbing and that's not going to do your knock on the head any good." Despite Desleigh's bedside manner being as gentle as a brick, it didn't break through Tessa's grief.

But Cissa's declaration did. "I will mentor you." The room's focus swivelled one-eighty.

Was now really the time to be thinking about work? Seriously, what was the woman thinking. She had no idea what was going on here.

Tessa interrupted my silent rant with, "But, you can't sew."

"You don't know that. But that's not where you need mentoring. From what I see and hear, *you* can sew. What you need help with is"— Cissa threw her arms wide—"building an empire." She winked. "Despite the Guild."

Hope flickered up Tessa's spine, before she collapsed again. "But I failed. I didn't listen. I made a mess of everything." She started quietly rolling in on herself again.

Cissa glided over the couch and crouched to eye level. "I also know a thing or two about fighting. Like the rest of your family." A long, elegant finger gently raised Tessa's blotchy face. "You've got a lot to learn, Tessa. But, from what I've heard, you've already come so far. You *can* do this."

34

RAPHAEL: SOME KIND OF FAMILY

"What's wrong? We're cooking Italian. You love Italian."
Jimmy was almost angry at my lack of enthusiasm. But I
just could not make myself care.

"I do not want to learn here anymore." I kept wiping my clean
bench as the noise of everyone getting pots and dishes out of the
cupboards erupted around us.

"What do you mean, you don't want to study here? You love
cooking."

"I do love cooking. Almost more than anything. And I love cooking
for my family… families most of all."

"Then why do you want to stop?"

"I will not join a Guild." I could not evict Tessa's experience from
my head. This morning in our brief 4.00 am catch-up with Val, she
was furious. It was the first time she showed real frustration at being
locked up. But I am glad she was. I did not think it would be a good
thing for her to declare war on the Guilds in this city.

"Raph…?" Jimmy tapped me on the arm. "Did you hear me? You
don't have to."

"But what if they ask you, and you turn them down. Then they
trap you and hurt you."

"What? What's happened? Where did you hear that?" Jimmy's face had turned so white it was tinged with blue.

"My sister. Last night. She was part of an extension program here at TAVE, in textile design. And she was invited to go to a meeting in preparation for the big Spring Show that she has work in. But when she said she did not want to do what they were doing, they would not let her leave and they locked her in a dog cage."

"How did she get free?" Jimmy's voice was a whisper.

I did not know how much to tell him. He was a friend, and I trusted him. But I was not sure if Tessa was still in danger, or if she would want me telling her story. I should not have said anything. But I could not get what happened out of my mind. Seeing her last night. Hearing her and Dan's stories. But I did not think the desperation and fear on Jimmy's face was fuelled by the hunger for gossip. He seemed hungry for reassurance.

So I answered his question.

Please let this be the right thing to do. Protect Tessa and forgive me if I am wrong.

"Her Guard was there. And so was Dan, her husband… my brother. And the Light sent some more Guards to help her, and help Dan. Then my parents came and cleared a way so they could get out. Then, this morning, when we were speaking with Val, my other mum, she wanted to hunt them all down… the Guild that is. But she cannot, because she is in jail."

Jimmy was silent. A statue. His face was a mix of so many emotions I did not know what he was thinking. I wish, sometimes, I had Abbot's gift of knowing what people were feeling. But at least some colour had returned to his face. "There are so many things there I need to unpack. But… your brother is married to your sister? That's just wrong on every level."

"We are all adopted. We were the first, Dan was the last." I could not hide my smile. "He was very scary. And dirty and smelly. He had been living on the streets for years."

"Homeless? Why?"

"Are you two cooking today, or do I need to call out for coffee so you can continue your chat in comfort?" Neither Jimmy nor I had noticed our teacher's approach.

I smiled and remembered my manners. "Thank you, but no, we will catch up later. I love Italian, Chef."

Our teacher almost choked and Jimmy muffled a cough, and we both pulled out our equipment and ingredients.

* * *

"So, your older sister, Tessa, went to a Guild meeting at the Temple of Dionysus—"

"No, the Theatre."

"That's also the Temple of Dionysus. But when she turned them down, they took her captive?"

Once again I shot a petition to the Light to ensure it was safe to tell Tessa's story. I did not receive a clear answer, but I felt peace. So I said, "Yes."

"Then, your brother, her husband, with his Guards...?"

"Yes."

"Broke into the temple, found her, released her, and took her home...?"

"Yes."

We were sitting in the courtyard of our usual cafe. It was a beautiful day, but still not many people came and sat in the shade of the garden. Birds played in the central fountain and the big orange-and-white fish—carp, I had learned—lazed in and out of huge lily leaves. The usual combination of musky earth smells and coffee made me feel calm and relaxed. The dappled light kept most of the sun's warmth away. But that was okay. It meant that others did not usually come to the courtyard. And I always brought a coat to TAVE.

Jimmy slumped back against the back of his seat and stared at the fountain. Two sparrows darted in and out, drinking. "Your brother and sister must be really important to have Guards."

"Yes... and no."

Jimmy narrowed his eyes and tried to read my mind. I used to think this was his angry face. But I had learned, instead, it was his thinking face. It did not worry me anymore.

"Yes, we are all important to the Light. That is why we all have Guards." I smiled my genuine gratitude and affection at my Guard who stood ever-present. He nodded back. "But we are not important… as far as the world thinks." I took a deep breath and considered how much I should tell Jimmy. They were not really my stories to tell, but he was very interested, and if he wanted to meet the Light, it might help him to know. "Riah and I were sold as young children and have belonged to three different owner—"

"What?"

"My sister… twin sister, and I have abilities that are seen as commodities worth owning. And so, we were… sold, and bought. Until the Dark's minions bought us and…" I tried to be brave and swallow the memories. But I could feel the red haze coming in. I really wished I had Tiger with me. I breathed in deeply, and out. Counted. Breathed. In. Out.

I am safe. That was in the past. We are safe. Riah is safe. You have us. We are in You.

In. Out. Count.

I rasped out, "It was not good." In. Out. "But our parents came for us. And rescued us. And killed the enemy. And then trained us how to do the same. Except I do not kill… anything. But Riah does. She loves it. But then, she was hurt far more than I was." I looked up at Jimmy, I had almost forgotten he was there. "So, you see, we were not important, we were not seen, we were only valued for what we could do. But the Light sees us, rescued us, and loves us. That is where our value comes from."

"No one rescued me."

"Then how did you survive?"

He was quiet for a very long time. "I rescued myself. I take care of myself. I don't need anyone."

"Then why do you come to TAVE every day to learn how to cook for your family? If you do not need them, you would not care for them."

Again, Jimmy was like a statue until the hint of a smile warmed his face. Then he burst out in laughter. "You think your family's odd; you should see mine." His laughter subsided. "Nah, I reckon I'm beyond that kind of saving. Done too much."

Now it was my turn to laugh. "You should meet Dan. I do not think there is much he has not done. He ran with one of the most savage gangs in Gomorrah. He had to do a lot to survive and prove his loyalty and worth to their leader. But it was not too much for the Light."

I could not help scrunching up my nose at the memory of when he first came into our home. "He was the filthiest, stenchiest, scariest human I had ever met. But time and again he has rescued us, stood up for us, and given so much of himself for us. I love him so much." My heart swelled and forced tears to form as more memories flooded my head. "But I know the Light sees him, values, and loves him more. I think that if the Light can forgive Dan and ask him to be part of His family, He can forgive and welcome anyone." I looked at Jimmy from under my lashes and breathed, "Even you."

Again, I was under Jimmy's intense, squint-eye scrutiny.

Please help me. If You want Jimmy in Your family, please make sure I do not say the wrong thing.

"You really are not as bad as you think. Or as mean. I think you are tough. I know you are a survivor. But you cannot hide from the Light. He sees right through everything... all defences, all masks. As bad as you think you are, He is bigger. As far away as you think you are, He is closer. As messy as you think your life is, He is greater."

"And He gives out Guards, you say?"

I looked to the Guard I did not recognise standing nearby and smiled from my toes to my nose. "Yes. He gives out Guards, too."

"And what, I just need to...?"

"Speak to Him."

"How?"

I swivelled in my seat and faced Jimmy full-on and shrugged my shoulders. "Just like we are talking now."

"What about sacrifices. Do I need to kill something to do that?"

"I told you I do not... will not kill anything. He will listen and speak to you just as we are speaking now.

"No cost?"

"There is a cost... a sacrifice of sorts. But you do not have to pay Him any money, or kill anything, or do anything like that."

"So, how do I pay the fee? I don't have anything."

How do I make this make sense? Have I said the wrong thing?

"First thing I should say is, there was a debt that had to be paid for us to reconnect with the Light. But no one could pay it. So, even though it was... like a fine we owed, the Light paid the fee: made the sacrifice on our behalf. Now, we have access to reconnection. The cost to us comes when we stand with, or in the Light. The world does not like Him. That is why my other parent, Valarie, is in prison. She made a stand for the Light, and the Community did not like it and had her arrested. Twice. That is the sacrifice we make in return." I was torn in two at the memory of Val. I missed her so much, but I was so proud of her and how strong she was. "Val never backs down." Emotion stole my voice.

"You have a pretty cool family."

I swallowed and nodded. "You should meet them."

"I'd like that. And I'd love you to meet mine. I think you could cope with them. Not many can."

"That sounds a lot like my family."

We were sitting there grinning like fools when Riah came by and rolled her eyes, just like Jimmy did. She then burst into a flurry of hand movements, the whiteboard too cumbersome to share her news. She had done so well with her art classes, her teacher had lined up for her to meet with a famous artist to do a workshop with him.

35

CONTESSA: DON'T CALL ME
STUPID

I stormed into our room and slammed the door.

And locked it.

I did not want an audience or interference in what was about to happen.

I'd had enough.

Dan obviously wasn't ready for the attack and almost fell over with one leg through his jeans, the other out.

"Stop it!"

"Stop what?" He froze, his jeans pooled at his feet, shirtless, with his arms half raised as if he was about to step on a landmine. His eyes wild, he glanced around our room, looking for the risk or potential attack.

Little did he know, it was me. "Stop being so nice to me."

He stood up taller and jerked his head back. "You want me to stop being nice to you?"

"Yes. Stop tiptoeing around me like I'm a time bomb ready to go off. I just can't stand it anymore. I'm about to explode." I threw my arms in the air to demonstrate just how flopping frustrated and close to detonation I was.

"Okay."

"Okay? Is that all you've got to say right now?"

"Um... yes?"

"Well, just stop it. You should be angry. And yelling at me. And being really nasty."

"You want me to be nasty to you?" Now he was looking at me like I was some weirdo wearing last winter's stock in the middle of summer.

"No. I don't *want* you to be nasty to me, but you should be. And yelling. There should be yelling," I yelled.

"Oka—"

"Do not. Say. Okay." I screamed.

"Alright?"

I screamed again.

And then did it again because it helped.

Dan stood like a mannequin, but his saucer eyes darted around the room, obviously looking for escape routes or divine intervention. Both his Guard and mine chose that moment to look typically stoic... in the other direction. So, I exhaled a fraction of my supreme frustration and decided to try to help him understand. "I was wrong. You told me not to go. You told me it was dangerous, and you didn't like the situation. But I went anyway. And you were right."

Then, like someone cleared a blocked drain, all my fear and anger and stupid-head, idiot-me emotions exploded in tears, and snot, and sweat, and a whole lot of ugly. It was noisy and it was very messy. Through the dams releasing from my eyes I saw a wavery Dan standing with his hands up again, like he was being arrested. His eyes still like saucers, but this time totally focused on me.

I couldn't believe it. Was that the best he could do?

He took a half-step forward. "I... I love? You?"

Well, that was just great. To demonstrate how not-helpful that was, I screamed again.

Then, finally, he amped up and gave me something to rail against. He raised his voice. "Tessa. Stop it. I don't know what to say. We both know you were wrong. You made a stupid mistake. We both know I'd been worried and it turned out it was a valid concern."

"You think I'm stupid? I'm not stupid Dan, I'm just..." I collapsed on the edge of the bed and wept, just as messily, but not as noisily. "Completely stupid. You told me not to go and you were right." The bed dipped beside me and the weight and warmth of Dan's arm came around my shoulders and he drew me in. I imagined the scent he always carried: a hint of caffeine and the clean smell of soap and a hint of whatever laundry detergent we were using. After spending years on the street, Dan had a thing about being clean—not tidy, but clean. But I couldn't smell him because my nose was stuffed from stupid-head crying. "It's not just you who told me. I think the Light was telling me, too."

"Oh?"

"Yeah. Oh. I had asked for the Badge of good-judgyness. After mixing up Kari and Felix, I wanted a good radar. And I think the Light was giving me a head's up about Jolena, but I didn't recognise it. Or listen."

"Well, I can't speak for the Light. But the way I see it, you're human and you made a mistake. Full stop. Life goes on."

I lifted my head and stared at him. "How can you say that?"

"What?"

"It's not that simple."

"Actually... it is. What else do you want? Everyone makes mistakes. It's one of the unifying factors of humanity. You're not special because you got it wrong. What differentiates us is what we do next. Do we get up and get on? Or do we stay in a hole and mope."

I pulled further away from him and squinted. "You accusing me of staying in a hole and moping?" Dan's eyes did his darting around the room thing. Gah. I let the rest of my rage escape in a sigh. "You're right. And, I'm sorry."

His arm, which was still around my shoulders, stiffened. I watched him steel his face then look directly at me. "Tessa?"

I waited.

Then waited some more. "Yes?"

His Adam's apple was like a huge, rolling road-bump. This was not going to be good. "I am not upset with you for making a mistake."

I waited. Nothing happened.

So I responded, "Thank you."

Now I was really nervous. Something big was coming. I balled my fists and dug my nails into my palms to stop myself from exploding all over again.

"What I am upset about is…" He looked down at his lap.

Oh. My. Word.

If he did not spit this out soon, I was going to strangle him.

"You totally disregarded my concerns." He exhaled, still not looking at me, and his body slumped.

"Ah… okay?"

Now he looked, and when he saw my complete confusion, became animated. "Listen, I get that we're going to disagree."

"You got that right."

He didn't say it, he didn't have to, his face made it very clear it was time for me to shut up and let him finish. And, since it took him so. Flopping. Long to get started, I was inclined to agree. I made a zipping motion across my lips, swivelled to face him and plastered an "I am humbly listening to everything you have to say right now" look on my face.

He rolled his eyes, but thankfully kept going. "We are not always going to agree. But I was really… hurt? annoyed? that you didn't even seem to take my concerns on board. I felt like you totally disregarded my perspective without even a second thought. All that mattered to you was ticking this box and getting on to the next thing. It frightened the skrat out of me that, from where I was sitting, there may not have been a next thing."

He took my hands. "I love you. You mean the world to me. I do not want to lose you. I get that this life we live is dangerous. I get that we may be called to give up our lives for the Light at any time, in any place. I can't forget Mary and Travis and their sacrifice at Sanctuary. What I can't accept is throwing our lives away with…"—he was obviously chewing over which word to use that wasn't going to set the crazy woman off on a crazy-woman-rant again—"…actions that haven't been thought through properly."

I had to nod and give him credit. That worked.

He looked at me.

I looked at him.

He jutted his head forward and did this little nod thing.

So, I did the same back.

He rolled his eyes again. "Well?"

Um... "Okay?"

I could not hold in my laugh as he growled a very masculine version of my scream. He stood and, with his hands on his hips, he glared at me rolling on my back laughing. I managed to pull myself together enough to mimic, to the best of my ability, his, "I... I love? You?"

Then lost it completely when he roared and launched himself on the bed next to me. "You minx." He held me close and I snuggled into his chest, my ear pressed against and absorbing his racing heart rate.

I wrapped my arms around him and pulled him closer. "Dan, I hear you. You're right. I am sorry, I really am. I know that's my thing. I always just want to get to the next thing. Get through everything on my list. But I need to slow down and look. And listen. Thank you for being so gracious." I altered my voice a bit and went a little softer and higher. "And wise." And then put a fair amount of breath into it. "And so good looking... and superior." I tried to continue but my laughing and his growl finished everything.

After a while the tide of emotion bled from me and I lay spent, fresh, released. We lay on our backs side by side on the bed, studying the ceiling. I tried to figure out exactly what I was feeling. Peace? Joy? Calm? All of the above?

Dan raised my hand and kissed my knuckles. "I do love you, Tessa."

I rolled on top of him and tried to fathom the depths of his deep blue-grey eyes. They were like the ocean he loved so much. "And you are my home."

"Did you lock the door?"

I grinned, ran my fingers through his hair and slowly bent down and kissed my wonderful, and, yes, amazingly gorgeous, husband.

36

BALASHKA: EYE OPENER

W ho… what… on earth had Gabby and Aran brought into our midst? This woman? Who was having a very unexpected effect on at least two of our family. Kirra was butting her head along the woman's shoulders, purring and softly mewling. However, she kept running into Richard who had totally forgotten all of his personal space lessons and was currently hugging? lying over? petting? our new nurse, with the special chant he normally reserved for Harry's Jag: "Pretty. Pretty. Pretty."

One had to admit, the woman was quite attractive—thick dark hair pulled back in a ponytail, medium build, with some… well-placed… curves. But it was the green armour covering her that threw me for a six. Although, I was very impressed with how she handled her particularly unusual welcome.

The new nurse attempted to edge her way out of the welcome. "Well, bless me, it is a pleasure to meet you guys. And I am… touched by this very special welcome." By this stage, both Aran and Gabby had tried to disentangle her. Gabby's protruding belly was not helping and Kirra's hissing at being taken from her new favourite toy was not helping.

Jemmy came to the rescue by shaking the kibble container. Kirra was torn. The pull of this exceedingly rare treat, or to stay with the new nurse? Gabby, ever alert, offered: "Kait will be here again tomorrow. And the day after. You can spend some time with her later after others have a chance to meet her." Kirra relented and went to receive a few tiny pieces of kibble and a cup of water from Jem. The fruit platter was then placed on the table and she was drawn to the strawberries. Jem then raced to the leftover charity shop bags and put them on the main table in the Undercover Area. "Richard?" She held up the bag. The same pain was etched on his face. To leave the new attraction or dig through an old favourite? It worked.

Without batting an eyelid, the newcomer looked around our property and smiled, with a genuine warmth and joy pulsing from her whole body. Then she saw me and her eyes widened and her head jerked to the side. Her smile intensified. "And I am very pleased to meet you."

Not the usual response one received from strangers. Or anyone really. "Welcome to our home. I must admit, I've never seen anyone receive such a response. But I have to ask, what's with the armour?"

Now everyone, well, Gabby, Aran, Jemmy and the green nurse, was staring at me in open shock.

"What armour?" Jemmy's voice was the loudest of the chorus.

"What do you mean, what armour? Look at her? She's covered in it. Green. Ornate. Full-body."

Still the four stared at me. No comprehension on three faces, total shock on the fourth. "Maybe all the events from yesterday and other stresses are taking their toll." Aran moved toward me with his "placating nurse" face on.

"Don't play that card with me, mate. I am not ill; I am not overtly stressed. And I am jolly well not seeing things. Do not treat me like that." Frustration and fury spiked and my heels dug in as I realised I was being shunted to the other side of the line. I held up my hand and stopped his approach and, thankfully, shocked that plastic mask from his face. "Don't try to placate me. I know what I see."

"Um... excuse me." The new nurse... wearing green armour... spoke. "Would it be okay if we"—she dropped her chin and her gaze bored into me with unmistakable intent—"go somewhere to have a chat?" Her eyes roamed until they landed on my shed above the Common Area, both roller doors up, two camp chairs in the opening. "There, perhaps?"

We would be in the open, fully visible, but our conversation would be private. My initial intention for the layout was that I could see as much as possible from my vantage point. But as my family grew, it became a definite positive: people could see me, know where I was if they needed me, but we weren't living in each other's pockets.

With my rage still simmering away, I nodded in agreement, turned and hobble-marched up the slope using my cane as an exclamation mark with every stride. Behind me I heard, "Please excuse me. I am looking forward to meeting everyone and learning how I can help you all here. But this is very important, if I may have a few moments?"

Seriously, what were they going to say? Of course she had to come up and explain what on earth was going on.

"Balashka?" She paused and held out her hand.

"Bal," I corrected as I took it and was surprised. I felt warm, calloused skin. Not cold, hard steel. I held her hand, turned it over and studied the encasing. She didn't pull back or resist me in any way. "What is this?" I looked up at her and my eyes feasted on the intricacy of the pattern, the hues of green, the beauty of the design. Now that I was allowed to study it, and I was invited to believe what I saw was real, I was intrigued and totally absorbed. Her voice came as a shock and I dropped her hand when I realised I was staring at her chest.

"You are not mad, Bal. What you see is hidden from most, so the response of your friends is quite normal. In fact, there are not many who are gifted with the sight: to see the Unseen."

"How is this possible? And how are you the first I have met?"

She looked around her at the walls of shrubs and the sky-high wall of Sardis behind us. Her laugh was deep and warm. "I'm guessing you don't get out much?" She laughed again as I rolled my eyes. "There are not many with the Sight. But we can distinguish each other by our armour, both those in the Light and those who have thrown in their lot with the Dark."

"Listen, I will admit you have been better accepted than most by our regular members here. I am happy to hear that I am not mad, and at least one other person on the planet can see your armour, but I am not sure I can cope with this right now. Maybe you could help a bit later. When there is less going on. But… not right now. I can't do this right now." I eased my way out of my chair and limped into my room and shut the door.

The ocean was breaking through my defences. I needed to retreat to the solitude of my room. Tomorrow, Gerald was bringing a student "with promise" around to meet me and get some pointers. He said she was "an interesting soul" and would fit in well here with "my lot". I was looking forward to seeing her skill. However, dealing with unseen green, regardless of how exquisite it was, was *not* on one's agenda.

When I knew the green nurse had gone, I came out, rolled shut the doors to my shed and gave myself to my painting. Light flooded through the skylight and bounced off the pale concrete floor and silver walls. I was in a ball of light, in front of a blank canvas and, enveloped by the acrid smell of paint, I could breathe.

* * *

THE FLAGS WERE OUT and would most likely be there for most of the day. Gerald was coming by with his student, as was Harry, to chew the fat. Gabby and Aran insisted on coming back with the green nurse. But I didn't particularly want to deal with her or her greenness. I would let the two of them introduce her to everyone and the routine, just as long as I didn't have to engage.

Today was not a good day. Maybe it was the stress of it all, but my hip pained and gave me added grief. So much so I had to curtail my rounds. Once the snacks and water station were restocked in the Undercover Area, I took Sweetie for a slow walk down the garden path to check for any more unwanted parcels of torture? sacrifice? Debris from one or more of the temples. It was now part of my normal routine. I just couldn't afford to have someone... anyone else find the offensive waste.

The gardens were unfurling from winter, eager for spring's influence. The air was crisp and there was a slight mist rising off the pond at the bottom of the block. Last night's rain blended with the underground water, giving the waterways an extra skip. Dew and remnant rainfall under the morning sun made everything sparkle, like I was growing a crop of diamonds. A gentle breeze tickled the shrubs and a soft brushing among the bamboo accompanied the birds' song of joy welcoming the day. My garden was a haven, a paradise, and I had the privilege to offer it to others to partake of its peace. A place I was safe, cared for and had opportunity to make a living—legally, adequately, to provide for others.

Checking the boundaries were clear, Sweetie and I trekked our way back, she patiently adjusting her pace to accommodate my struggle. Obviously, I had taken longer than I had anticipated. A very swollen Gabby waddled over with Aran to meet me and intercede for the green nurse who was currently trying to disengage Richard. Thankfully, Kirra wasn't here yet.

"Bal." Gabby was panting, and her hands were laced under her stomach. A man I didn't know supported her by holding one elbow and Aran had the other. "I know you're not happy about this, but time's up. I have—" She took fast breaths, puffing them out from rounded lips. "...run out of time. I am on my—" She tensed, her face screwed up, and then the panting continued. "...way to hospital."

"What are you doing here? Go."

The man I suspected was her husband glared at me. "She wouldn't go until she had your approval of the new nurse." He looked to his wife. "Can we go now?"

"Everyone—" More panting and tensing. "...calm down. I'm still at... eight... seven minutes."

"Go! Aran, help her into the car and go!" I could not believe the stubbornness of this woman, my friend.

"You give me your word, Bal. They need someone, and she's perfect. I will not go until I know they're going to be cared for. I swear it, I'm not going until you give me..." Gabby froze, her eyes wide, her mouth forming an "oh". She looked down and there was an explosion of fluid. Everyone stopped and stared.

The green nurse came racing over. "Okay, time's up, let's get you to the car now, Gabby."

Gabby's husband almost lifted and carried her. But over her shoulder she still yelled, "Promise me, Bal!"

"Okay, okay. Just go."

The green nurse grabbed the towels Aran had retrieved from the washroom and very carefully and adeptly wiped Gabby down and helped her into the car. She manoeuvred the seat and did some other things I was totally unaware of. All I could think of was the huge sac of fluid that had exploded in front of me. Was that the warmup? Was the child making its way out now? I felt quite nauseous. I was not going to recover from this... ever.

The next thing I knew, Aran was being helped into a seat, and the green nurse was handing me a cup of coffee. Real coffee, from the machine in the food truck. I just looked at her. She smiled a small, nervous smile. "Gabby told me you liked coffee. I put a bit extra sugar in there to help with the shock. I'll leave you to it now and go and help..." she looked around and saw Kirra and Cheryl making their way in, "these lovely ladies." Her smile exploded and she quietly went to join them, and patiently stood and accepted Kirra's affection expressed via rubbing her face against the green nurse's shoulder.

Before I could take a sip of the coffee, another vehicle arrived. Gerald must have bought a new car, I didn't recognise the dark SUV. I knew Harry would faithfully bring his racing-green Jag for Richard. But you could have bowled me over when Jemmy stepped out of the back seat. I scorched my leg as I lurched to my feet. "Are you alright. What's wrong? Why are you in a car? Are you hurt?"

"Bal, calm down. I'm fine." Jem ran-walked her way to me, waving papers in her hand. "Bal, please, sit down. Let me explain."

"Who are these people you have brought into our home?" I searched her face. "Jem. How could you?" My heart crumpled in on itself at her betrayal.

"Bal. Stop." She thrust the papers under my nose. "I spoke to Gerald and asked him what kind of things were on the non-disclosure forms you make people sign, and I made them agree to it."

"Them? There is more than one?" I searched the car, but the tinted windows made it impossible to see through to the inside.

"Please, Bal. Listen to me." I heard her, but I couldn't drag my eyes from the intruding vehicle. Jem shook my arm to get my attention, but I just couldn't think. Searching the grounds, I tried to see how everyone else was reacting to the intruders. But, because the flags were out, there was hardly anyone here. And those who were, were too distracted by the green nurse.

Jem must have read my mind. "I knew the flags would be out." Her deflated, defeated voice snagged my attention. "I told them to wait in the car so I could explain. I wanted you to meet my friend. His brother has a car, and I really wanted to meet him—"

"Wait. Why?"

She pursed her lips. "Because he has been homeless. He lived on the streets and survived. In a city worse than ours. I wanted to learn from him. But he is here mainly because he has a car and was happy to drive me and Raph, and I really wanted you to meet my friend. He's really interesting and... I thought you... I wanted you..." She exhaled loudly though her nose, set her face like flint, then stalked back to the car, throwing over her shoulder, "Don't worry about it," as she went.

"Nicely played, my friend." I had forgotten Aran was there. And that I had burned my leg. It was now an odd combination of cold wet fabric over burning, tender skin.

I looked to the nurse—the normal, non-armour wearing nurse I could trust—bewildered. "What just happened?"

"I'd say," he looked around to check if we had an audience, "your daughter just brought a friend over to meet you, because you mean a lot to her—and obviously so does this friend—and you... completely overreacted." I considered him. Of course he would have known Jem was a girl. But for him to bring it up was a big deal. "But"—he inclined his head to the car—"they're still here. If you wanted to try that again." He bent down and picked up my fallen walking stick and handed it to me. He then went over to the green nurse and left me bewildered and hobbling toward the SUV.

I tapped on the window of the door I had seen Jem enter. The window rolled down three centimetres. "Jem, I'm sorry. I was a bit thrown. With the green nurse being here, and Gabby going into labour, I—"

I almost fell backwards as the door flew open and Jem burst out of the car. "Gabby, in labour? Is she okay?

I told her the story and then used my stick to point to the green nurse and Aran speaking with Kirra, Cheryl and Richard. At least Richard had stopped patting her. "Gabby really wanted to make sure our family was properly taken care of and was convinced I'd be too stubborn to let"—I tilted my head—"*her* help."

Jem snorted. "She's got you pegged."

I breathed deeply and tried to force the stress from my body. There had been too many shocks… and new people in the last twenty-four hours. But if Jem wanted me to meet her friends, then I would just have to put those feelings away and deal with it. "Would you like to invite your friends to join us in the shed? Might be best if we stay away from the Undercover Area and general use areas for now."

"Wait. I brought a few things for the guys to help distract them." She leaned back into the car and withdrew a bag. She'd obviously stopped at a charity shop on the way. Then she took off down the slope and just left the bag to be discovered when it was needed. With a smile I'd never seen grace her face, my beautiful daughter walked back up the hill, beaming, carrying an extra two chairs.

"Okay, guys, it should be safe now. You can get out of the car." Jem then went to my shed and positioned the seats and I almost fell over again as a violet boy and an indigo man vacated the car.

I yelled, for the second time in ten minutes. "Jem, what have you done?"

BALASHKA: NOT THIS AGAIN

The two intruders froze with their hands in the air, the car separating them, the man nearest to me. Their eyes were wide, bouncing between me and Jem as she raced back.

Jem shook her head and screwed up her face. "What are you talking about?"

"Them." I used my stick again as a pointer, indicating the clear and present problem. "The indigo man and the violet boy."

Again, Jem flicked her attention between me and her guests. "What? Raph does cooking with me, and his brother Dan is studying design and construction with their dad. Their whole family is studying at TAVE. Except Dan's wife—Raph's other sister—who has just been kicked out because she turned the Textiles Guild down." Jem grabbed my arm, her gaze boring holes through to my skull. "She turned the Guild down and survived. She escaped. Dan rescued her. They have Guards, and Raph is going to tell me how to get one. Then I'll be safe, Bal. I can be safe with a Guard, too."

The indigo man spoke. "I just work down the road, so it was no problem dropping these guys off." As if him coming out of his way was my problem.

It was all just far too much for me to digest. My head started spinning and I couldn't comprehend any of it. Before I knew it, or had the opportunity to completely reject it, I was being helped by the indigo man and the green nurse. The violet boy and Jem were leading the way so I could sit. Everything hurt. My head, my hip, and my pride. "I'm not often this lightheaded. Where's Aran, he'll tell you." I looked around and called out, "Aran? Tell them. Where are you?"

"Right here, my friend. Jem, great idea bringing the goodies from the charity shop. I've also checked there are enough tools out for sorting if things get out of hand." He stepped in and took over from the indigo man and helped me sit. I couldn't help but release a pained groan.

"Excuse me, sir, would you like me to help you with that?" I looked up into the gangly teen's earnest eyes, then down to my chair.

"Ahh, thank you, but I am already sitting."

"No, sir, I can see you are in pain. May I help you?"

"How?"

"I might be able to help you feel better. Relieve your pain."

"How?"

"If you do not mind. I will put my hand on—"

Before he could finish his sentence, Gerald pulled up. I'd totally forgotten he was bringing his pupil today. I should have called and cancelled when… I don't know when I would have had the chance. I didn't have time to consider anything else before my friend and a red girl got out of the car and made their way over. The girl raised her hand in greeting.

"Hey, Riah," Jem responded. "I didn't know it was you coming over today." Jem then looked to me. "How cool is this. Riah is Raph's twin sister."

"And I'm their mum," the green nurse added.

I could feel waves of panic rising. It was all too much. But all of a sudden, a brick wall fell on my anxiety, impeding its attempt at a full takeover bid, and fingers of peace massaged the tension away. I considered the rainbow surrounding me. A rainbow only I could see, apparently. After exhaling and extracting my shoulders from my ears, I looked to Gerald. "Welcome to the party."

"Bad time, Bal? I can come back later?"

"No, the more the merrier." Before hysteria could get a foothold, peace and calm sat on it. I mean, quite literally squashed it like an elephant was using it as a seat at our ridiculous rainbow party. All we needed now was the unicorn.

"Hey, Jem, how about you and I go and get some more chairs?" Aran led my girl away and left me with the human light show. Thankfully, Gerald was still with me.

The violet boy spoke again. "Sir? All I have to do, if you do not mind, is to put my hand on you and I might be able to help."

"Why not. What else could go wrong today?" The hysteria was still herding my words with a giggle.

"That's a question I've learned not to ask," the indigo man muttered.

The boy stepped forward and very gently laid his hand on my shoulder. Instantly I felt soothing warmth soaking into my bones. I relaxed deeper into my chair. The kid shut his eyes and his mouth moved slightly like he was trying to lock irrepressible words behind his lips. I could only focus on him for a moment. Soon the only thing I could feel was relief. My oppressive companion of nine years had been evicted. Like a shunt had drained the leaden, toxic suffering and I was now a helium balloon barely grounded with the relief.

Instead of floating away, however, I wept. It was beyond my control. I just could not fathom or put into words the depth of release, the intensity of the liberation from pain. A rag doll, I collapsed back into my chair. I could barely hold myself up. Another light hand on my shoulder sent waves of peace and calm pulsing through me. And I was so unimaginably grateful.

It was then it came back to me. The Man in prison said, in time, He would fully heal me. "I will send someone to you and they will remove the rest of your pain. When they come, you will know they are from me. Listen to what they will say."

I opened my eyes and saw the green nurse considering me with narrowed eyes and a calculating smile. "Feeling better?"

All I could do was laugh. I was not proud of how maniacal or hysterical it sounded, but at least I was no longer crying… much. I sat up straight. Stood up tall. Then walked. Without a limp, without grinding pain, without hindrance. And, through my laughter, agreed. "Yes, thank you very much. I am." I then looked at this rainbow family. I tried to take them in. Red and violet twins who had magical powers. A tall—not as tall as me—indigo brother who looked mean, but behaved like a respectful lamb. A green nurse-mother who was shorter than them all, yet clearly called the shots.

Jem and Aran came back up the hill, both agog. It was Jem who spoke first. "What just happened? Why… how are you walking without a limp?"

"It appears your friend, whom I am very glad to have met, has magical pow—"

"It is not magic."

I looked at the young man still standing behind my chair next to his sister. The two of them were stunning, even if one was to remove the elaborate yet bewildering armour. There was so much that I wanted to know. Needed to know. But I returned to Jem. "He wields the power of the gods and—"

"Just the One God. The Light. It was the Light who healed you, not me, not other gods, not magic. Just the Light."

"The Light?"

This time the green nurse spoke. "Indeed. The Light has called us to Sardis for the very purpose of meeting you. We have been looking throughout the city, but He told us we would find you through TAVE. So, we all have been attending, learning, meeting people, looking around, until now."

"Now?"

"Bingo. We have found you. Although, I did not expect that four of us would find you at once. I guess it was going to take the four of us to make sure you were found."

In a weird sense, I could see the logic in that. The nurse, the friend and the artist. "What about him?" I threw my thumb over my shoulder at the indigo guy.

"Oh, I'm here just in case you make trouble."

I blanched.

Aran took a backward step.

Jem froze.

"Nah, just kidding." He wiggled his keys. "I got the wheels." His grin was cheeky and infectious.

I noticed the red girl mirroring his grin, but her twin looked horrified. "Do not scare him, Dan. Also, you are much more than transport. Remember, Jem wanted to talk to you about your time on the streets."

"Yeah, that too." The indigo man threw his arm around the violet boy's shoulders and pulled him close. I'm not sure I was supposed to hear, "You did well, mate. Great job. So proud of you."

Then everyone's attention was stolen by the royal-green Jaguar cruising into the carpark—perfectly perpendicular to my shed, and the cries of, "Hello, hello, hello. Pretty. Pretty. Hello."

Seriously, could this day get any more complicated.

* * *

GERALD, Harry and I held extremely well-made coffees thanks to the efforts of Jem and the indigo man, Dan, while the red girl, Sariah, held a hot chocolate. The other three were going to wait until they'd finished their tour of the garden and "talk". Dan was a bit frightening. I was glad I had seen him with the violet boy, Raph, otherwise one would have felt a tad more than warned with his parting words to his red sister: "You have any trouble, you even feel like you're gonna have trouble, you call me. I'll stay close by, and Kait is just down the hill."

She gave the perfect imitation of Jem's eye roll, which he checked with a savage glare. "Riah, I mean it. I'm still not over Tessa's—" Clenched teeth arrested his speech. "So don't push my buttons." He then served that savage glare to the three of us whilst continuing to speak to his sister. "Any trouble, and I come running."

His hostility bounced off the girl as she stepped forward and enveloped him with spindly arms. His face softened. She nodded, then turned to us and smiled, dismissing him and his threat. It was time to relegate all craziness—threatening big brothers, infiltration of rainbow hued people into my safe haven, and out-of-this-world healing abilities of young men—into a box and slide it into a dark cupboard and escape into the safety of art. Sariah's hot chocolate sat abandoned as her whiteboard was filled, wiped and refilled with answers. Gerald, Harry and I pored over the work in her portfolio. She had an eye.

"How old are you again?"

14, she wrote on her board.

We considered her work. So unique. Untrained… no, that was the wrong word. Unrestrained. Her choice of colour, her ability to mimic texture and movement, to imply depth and dimension. "How long have you been painting?"

3 years. She wiped the board with her stained sleeve, then rushed on, *Used to only have chalks + pastels*. Another swipe. *On concrete walls and floors*. Swipe. *Sometimes paper*. Swipe. *Only had paper + paint 3 years*. Swipe. The frenzy stopped. With a clear board and hungry eyes, she waited, poised, ravenous. She was as intriguing as her art.

"So, you started on walls and floors?"

Yes. In our home. Swipe. *Kait*. Swipe. *Mum + Dad + Val let me chalk our house*. Swipe.

"Your house?" The three of us responded in unison.

Yes. We lived in concrete bunker kind of place. Swipe. *Very grey. Huge skylight*. She paused and pointed up to mine. *Like yours*. Swipe. *Lots of light, no colour*. Swipe. *Raph + me rescued + recovering*. Swipe. *They gave him cooking. I took art + gardening*. Swipe. Pause. Wait.

Rescued and recovering? Obviously not biological kids. Unless the father was very tall and very dark. Again, I was teased with the temptation to want to know more. But for now, I had to focus on the art.

I pointed to my canvases. The completed ones against one wall, the works in progress on another, and the blank one set on my easel. "How do you feel about working on larger canvases?"

She didn't have to write a word, longing exploded from her eyes. I couldn't help but laugh. I could also sense the excitement in Gerald, and literally felt the heat coming from Harry's hands as they rubbed together in anticipation of what he could make from commissions from this kid.

"Okay. Before I let you loose in my space…" No one actually said— or wrote—a word, but the shocked faces on the three halted me. "What? That's why Sariah is here, isn't it?"

She madly nodded her head until I thought she might do herself an injury. Harry just raised his eyebrows. It was Gerald who spoke. "That's a mighty generous offer, Bal."

I rebuffed his concern with a wave of my hand. "First, however, I want to get your impressions of my work. I want you to be honest. Can you do that for me?"

The kid put her hands on her hips, raised one eyebrow and did this weird head wobble. I took that as a yes, she could, thank you very much. And again, I couldn't hold in my laugh. I wanted to know her story; the kid had spunk and confidence in spades. Yet, she had been "rescued". And the green nurse was part of her recovery team, and now her mother? It painted its own picture of what kind of woman Gabby and Aran had found. And I was beginning to see she was a good fit.

I led the tour of my works against the walls of my shed— completed and in progress—and was treated to a stilted commentary, via a whiteboard. She had come across as confident… overconfident. As soon as we began, the truth was laid bare. She was nervous and, to be perfectly honest, I was gratified by her responses.

It was Harry who broke the spell. "Okay, enough of Miss Nice, now it's time to be honest." It was my agent's turn to laugh at the fear and shock on her face. "It's okay, kid. The guy's good, but he's not perfect." He tilted his head and considered her. "I'll do you a deal. Be honest in your appraisal, and, if I buy it, I'll consider taking you on. Deal?"

The girl's dark skin paled. I almost choked and Gerald once again said, "That's a mighty generous offer, Harry."

"If they sell, I get commission, what have I got to lose? But you, my dear"—he levelled his eyes at Sariah—"have the world to gain."

The girl looked at me, squinted, and inspected my soul. It was unnerving. But eventually she turned back to Harry and nodded, set her face, lifted her whiteboard and wrote, *deal*.

The critique was circumspect, yet candid. The kid had some insight. She was still inexperienced and immature, still lacked confidence, but her natural eye shone with potential.

At the end of the morning, we sat around and Sariah finished her cold hot chocolate. Harry, once again, seemed unconcerned about Richard and Eric petting his car.

Gerald broke the communal musing. "You know, Bal, the main reason I wanted you to meet Sariah was because, even though you are very different artists, with different styles, and different eyes, there is something similar about your work. I can't put my finger on it. Side by side, they look nothing alike. But there is something…"

"I agree," Harry said.

I hadn't seen or thought about it. I looked over at Sariah, who was grinning and scribbling on her whiteboard. *We drink from the same source.* Swipe. *The Light.*

CONTESSA: A SPOONFUL OF SUGAR

"Right, everyone except Tessa and Felix, out." Val's edict had everyone scared. But I'd bet my buttooshie, no one was as scared as Felix and me.

"This is gonna hurt," Marcus mumbled as he stood. He leaned over and kissed the top of my head. "Tessa, me girl." He slapped Felix on the shoulder. "Me friend. Know that I love the both of you and remember, whatever she serves you, she actually does like you."

"Tessa, honey, my sweet girl, I'll be right outside. I love you and... well... good luck." Kait also kissed my head and squeezed my shoulder before she left.

My husband and the rest of my family filed out of our apartment to have coffee with Cissa and Al at their place. We'd only just started our 4.00 am check-in with Val and, before anyone could get a word in, she'd laid down the law. And along with everyone else, I had the feeling this was going to end in tears. Without saying a word, Felix's focus on everyone's feet leaving the room kind of gave the impression he agreed.

"We don't have a lot of time, so let's get to it." Val stared her laser beams at me. "Tessa, time to move on."

"What? What do you mean?" Oh my goodness! Did she want me to leave?

"You had an incident, it turned ugly, you survived, now move on."

Oh, thank the Light. "Val, I'm just so angry... and disappointed... and frustrated at myself. Why do I have to keep being saved? Why can't I ever be my own hero?"

She just looked at me. I mean, like, seriously, Val didn't ever roll her eyes, but she kind of did without having to. Truth was, she kind of made me feel like an idiot.

"I mean, I always need help. Like, all. The. Time." My shame and guilt literally bubbled out of me like a burst pipe.

"So? We all do. It's called being human, Tessa."

"You don't."

Val snorted. Yep. Full-on ugly-features snort. "Don't I? Not even when I'm stuck full of knives? When we don't have a place to stay? When we don't have fixed or secure income? When we land in a city with nothing, and yet are responsible for caring for six people? I always need help, Tessa."

"Not in a battle you don't. In Philadelphia you were hard-core berserker. Nothing could touch you."

Oh. My. Word. I was so happy I was talking to a hologram right now and not dealing with Val face to face. She looked to the ceiling and exhaled. Then, very slowly, looked back to me. "I know you are neither blind nor ignorant, Tessa. So, could you please tell me when was the last time you saw me engage the enemy—Seen or Unseen—without help? One." She ran her hand down her body, indicating her kick-butt armour. "I am encased, inside and out, by the Light." She held her second finger up. "Two. Who is always by my side? The only reason I can fight like that is because I always have Marcus and Kait watching my back. If they can't be there, I have someone else. Who do you always have by your side in battle?"

I kind of felt I didn't need to answer that.

"You are always going to need help, Tessa. That is the way we are made. We are made for family, and we are mortal. We need help and we need each other, in battle and in life." Val turned to face a fidgeting

234

Felix. "Which brings me to you. Why are you still in Sardis? It has been five months, and you are still here? Why?"

"Well, Valarie, I am very... concerned about you."

I had to see it to believe it, but Val's steel softened to something closer to lead. "I appreciate that, Felix. I appreciate all that you do for us and your concern for us. But realistically, there is nothing you can do here in Sardis. And *you* are the administrator of the Community of Light in Laodicea. *You* are the spearhead of the Alliance of the Community in the Seven Cities. *You* are needed in *your* job."

"I understand that, Valarie, and I have been working from here... I have a nice apartment, and I communicate with my team daily via the web."

Val sighed. "Felix, who else can do your job?"

That made him sit up. "I am not sure I understand what you mean."

"Who else, can do, your job?"

"I heard what you said the first time. However, I am... still... confused by your inclination and implication."

"You are a one-off, Felix. At this time in history... ever... anywhere, there is no one like you. No one can do your job like you do." Felix went to interrupt but Val held up a hand and kept going. "Yes, you are replaceable. We all are. But no one has the skills, the intellect, the ability to hold all the information, possibilities, constructs and plans in their head like you do. No one can do the job, in Laodicea, right now, like you can."

"Marlene helps me. I do not achieve any... objectives without help."

Val looked at me with a pointed glare. "Did you hear that, Tessa?" Then continued her gentle debate with Felix. "And what about Marlene. Is she based in Sardis with you or in Laodicea?"

"Both."

"So, in order for you to fulfil your desire to be nearby, not only is your team going without you, the hospital board going without you, the other Communities in the Alliance going without you, Marlene is forced to travel back and forth between cities to accommodate you. What about Gem?"

Felix sat up straighter, gobsmacked. Val patiently waited for him to find his words. "Valarie, I do not think you quite understand. You are very special to me." Felix became intensely focused on his knotting fingers. "All my life, people have made excuses for me or shunned me. Marlene is my right hand and enables me to do my job. I would be useless without her. But you..." Felix swallowed and breathed in and out slowly. "You saw me. Me. Broken, awkward, odd, me. You took the time to get to know, me. Not the me you wanted me to be, the me I am." He stopped again, coughed and got his voice back under control. "You then gave me the keys to discover the Light, and all I could be, in the Light."

"No, Felix. I showed you the door. The Light gave you the keys, the Light enabled you, the Light transformed you. Not me." Val's voice was soft and compassion coated every word. I almost felt like I was intruding on an intensely private moment and that I should leave. But I dared not move in case I became the victim of Val's focus. I also didn't want to interrupt this very delicate conversation. So, I sat perfectly still and thought invisible thoughts as Val continued. "Felix, your hope, confidence and foundation is in the Light. Not me. One day I will die, hopefully in battle, but I will be taken from you. What then? Will you cease to be? Will you stop your work? Let your purpose go unfulfilled?"

Very quickly, Felix wiped his eyes, then lifted his chin, his face a mask.

"Felix, you are very dear to me. A friend like I have never had. A friend I will work to keep for the rest of my days. I am so very grateful for your concern and care. I have never met anyone who has shown me such attention." She went on, but that kind of floored me. Seriously, we all thought of Val as a machine. Well, everyone except Felix, obviously. I missed some of what she said but caught the tail end. "... always be my true and genuine friend."

Just so you know, when she said friend, I got the impression she wasn't saying it like Dan and I use the word "friend", like "special-one-

and-only-lifelong-married friend". It was more like normal-people "friend".

She continued, "I cannot even think of how hard this would have been for everyone... and me, if you hadn't have gifted me with the ShellCom. Or, how hard it would have been for us to continue to use Old Faithful, that dinosaur of a truck. Your gift of an electric car to Tessa and Da—"

"It was an engagement gift."

Now it was my turn to snort. "Sorry, Felix. But we all kind of know it was so much more. Especially as how it is far more comfortable for Val to get around in. But seriously, I cannot tell you how grateful we are to have it, and you, in our lives."

Val smiled at me, then sunk the boot in. "So, Tessa, time for you to stop being a victim. You're not. You are a child of the Light and we are at war. No situation is unsalvageable or beyond the use of the Light. I am here, stuck in jail. I am not a victim; this is an opportunity. I might have come here with my hands bound, but my mouth is free, and the Light is greater than these walls and restrictions. He has seen to it that I have permission to teach. Do you know how many ladies I have brought into the Light? How many women I am teaching how to defend themselves? How many girls I am able to reach and empower? Regardless of what the world does to me, I am not a victim. I am a soldier following the lead of my commander. Time for you to woman up and do the same."

"But, Val, I wanted to go to the Spring Festival. It's going to be huge, and my work is going to be displayed. I really wanted you all to see my creation. I had been keeping it as a surprise. It was going to be my big reveal." I kind of felt like a sulky brat looking for attention and pats on the back. And I had to kind of admit it was true. I was.

"Well then, go."

"But they'll recognise me."

"Wear a hat. Wear a coat."

"They took my coat."

"Get another one. Tessa, stop making excuses. If you want it, go get it."

I felt like I was in a certain fairytale I grew up listening to. But instead of a nice fairy godmother making it all happen for me, mine was giving me a kick up the buttooshie, telling me to go source my own gown and carriage and make my own way to the ball. "I wish you could see it, Val."

She just glared at me, then her face softened. "I would do anything to be there, Tessa. I am really sorry I can't be with you. I know it will be amazing. Perhaps you could film it with your fancy phone, and show me when I get out?"

"That's a brilliant idea, Val. I will."

She turned to Felix and smiled. "And time for you to get back to work—"

"But Achan is here in Sardis."

"I know."

"He is out to get you."

Val made a point of looking around her. "I know."

"I need to—"

"You need... *we* need you where the Light planted you. You are too valuable to be wasting time here. I have already been caught by Achan. And truth be told, I'm probably safer here than out there with you lot. He thinks he's won. I'm out of the picture. What he doesn't know is that he's played right into the Light's plans.

"In fact, you, Felix, are in more danger here from that man than I am. Go back to Laodicea and get back to work. I will be in touch. I will keep you updated." We both nodded and she continued, "Now, quickly, call the others back before I have to go. I want to hear how Raph and Riah are doing and how Dan and Marcus are going with building..."

39

CONTESSA: LESSON ONE

"Tessa, the first thing you need to know if you're going to make it on your own, without the support of the Textile Guild, is that you need to go to a new audience. You need to pull from different inspiration so that you are offering something original. You need to find your niche, plant your flag and claim the territory. Start small and build your brand, creating something that no one else can. And you've already done that. So, well done."

We were in a small meeting room on one of the upper floors of Black & Light Tower and Cissa paced back and forth in front of the wall of windows overlooking the city. She wasn't reading from notes, and she was dressed in the most classic of pant suits. Dark burgundy to match her armour. It was just the two of us, and I madly wrote down everything that came out of her mouth but stopped when I read the last words on my tablet: "well done". I couldn't help… or hide, my blush.

She turned to face me and caught the tail end of the red comet consuming my paper-white complexion and tilted her head. I responded to her unspoken question. "I am not sure how I am doing that." All I could think about was my latest creation—that had been stolen from me—which had been inspired by a reel of vintage icons Jolena showed us. But, of course, Cissa hadn't seen that.

"Your website. Your line of products made from offcuts. Your line of clothing remade from charity shop items. Those shirts you made for Val. You are creating something new, because your sources are used-and-discarded items. More impressively, you produce functional clothing produced with quality craftsmanship, unique style, thoughtful fabric choice, and classic, understated chic."

What could a girl say, apart from, "Oh. I'd forgotten about that."

"And that is what will happen if you keep swimming in the pool with all the others. If you keep going back to the same source as everyone else for your inspiration." I was about to challenge her about that, but she held up her hand and overruled me. "It is important to acknowledge and respect those greats who have gone before us. I suspect fashion is a lot like architecture. The bones have to be good or everything falls down, but how you dress those bones is the art. Be inspired and learn from the giants on whose shoulders we stand, but don't be limited by them. They were building for their time, their cultures, their environment. Always think: what is *my* time, *my* culture, *my* environment? Then go one step further: what will *my* audience need one step further in time, culture and environment? And that is your first assignment." She grinned at me.

I shrank back. "Assignment?"

"Well, of course. I would like you to explore this city and find an audience not already catered to. I would like you to then outline their needs, their culture and their environment. Then, detail how you can meet their needs, in a way they can afford, drawing from your... *our* unique source"—she ran a hand down the length of her armoured arm —"to create function-required clothing, produced with quality crafts-manship, unique style, thoughtful fabric choice, and classic, under-stated chic."

Oh. My. Goodness.

Intimidating, much.

But there was a small bubble of excitement that was trying with all its might to fight through the overwhelming immensity of the task. "Um… how long do I have to complete my assignment?"

Cissa turned back to the window and tapped her elegant, long, lacquered finger-nailed finger on her chin. "One month."

Internally I was gasping for breath. Outwardly I suspect I looked like a stunned mullet. Thankfully, she was still looking out the window. "With weekly check-ins. I will get Frayer to set up a half hour meeting…"—she continued with the chin tapping, then looked at her watch—"Wednesdays, 12:30. We'll do lunch." She turned back to face me and I'd still not managed to wipe the mullet from my face. "Suit you?"

I dropped my eyes to my tablet and brought up my schedule. It was silly, really—like I had to consult my calendar. At the beginning of the week I had received notification that my enrolment at TAVE had been cancelled and my schedule had been wiped clean. I didn't know if I was a "wanted woman" still being hunted, or "discarded goods". I tried very hard to channel Val: cool, calm and brave. I looked up to Cissa and said, "Yes. Thank you." And hoped like crazy she didn't notice the tremor in my voice.

40

JEMIMAH: BURNING DOWN THE HOUSE

"What the hell are you doing?" I was on my way home from TAVE when I passed The Wreckage across the road from Bal's place. Bulldozers, dump trucks and a whole lotta guys standing around in hard hats and high-vis were watching the destruction of my family's home. Well, their night homes. I launched myself in front of the machines and waved my arms, turning the air blue with trash talk.

Raph's big brother, Dan—standing there with a sheaf of papers—just looked at me. I turned on him and screamed, "I thought you were on our side? What are you doing?" Rage consumed me, and everything I saw was tainted with a red filter.

He spoke into a handset and the engines died, and slowly the message seemed to do the rounds. It took a while to get through to the guys on the other machines, but by way of using an old fashioned two-way and a lot of yelling, the site stilled. Eventually, silence hit us all like a sledgehammer and the stand-off began. Thankfully, the delay gave me time to breathe and try to get some words sorted out in my head. Dan marched over to me, confusion clouding his eyes. "Hi Jimmy." I think he was grinding his teeth. "What seems to be the problem?"

I tried to follow his lead and speak calmly. Keeping my voice low.

"The problem is you are destroying the homes of a number of people here, without permission."

He tilted his head like a confused dog. "For the past two months we've done nothing but canvass this whole area, we've paid the owners money for their houses, we've built them temporary accommodation, we have permission from Council, plans have been approved and, as we now own the area, we're in the process of demolishing these unsafe dwellings so that we can rebuild suitable housing." Like a coffee machine, his frustration started infusing and heating his calm, and his volume and colour rose.

Raph's dad walked over and slapped him on the shoulder. "If there's a problem with some of the residents, we're sorry kid, but we were told, and after thorough inspection, found these places were uninhabited. Could you tell us where your friends are so we can sort this out?"

How could I possibly make them understand? I felt a bit of the espresso infusing my own brain. But sadly, for me, it only stole what little sense I had when it came to arguing against my superiors. "Listen, you've been to Bal's place." I pointed to his home across the main road. "You"—I pointed to Dan—"know who our people are. They live here. At night. I keep an eye on them. Make sure they're safe from the Catchers. If you take these shelters away, they will have nowhere to go." I hated that my frustration had turned to tears. I brushed my face madly. Boys weren't supposed to cry. Or have a high-pitched voice when they were distressed.

Back to the confused-dog act, Dan asked, "Don't they live onsite? Or in the garden?"

"No. They live here." It was beginning to be all a bit too much. How could I explain? It was hard enough trying to make Bal understand and I'd known him for almost two years now.

Raph's dad—who I wasn't supposed to know was Raph's dad because I wasn't supposed to have been following them for four months now—spoke into his two-way. "Time for a break, boys. We'll be back in a jiffy when we've learned what's going on." The man looked to me and smiled. I was surprised to see genuine warmth in his crinkled eyes. "Now, why don't we have a chat and you can shed some light and lead the way out of this maze."

I tried to hide the fact that I was wiping my tears on my shoulders, and nodded. The knot in my throat was making it too hard to speak. I led them to the first house, the one facing off against the angry jaws of the destructo-machine. Knowing the door would be locked—because I kept it that way—I led the men through the window. I thought the older guy would have trouble climbing through, but he slipped in, easy as.

Even in the middle of the day, the interior was dark. I kept most windows and curtains closed, so if anyone was slow to get up, or needed hiding through the day, they were safe. First, I showed them the space where Richard slept. Directly under the gaping hole in the roof, his green sleeping bag was laid out with his green pillow. Then I took them to the laundry where there was a huge closet. At the bottom was a nest of old doonas where Kirra had her space. After showing them Eric's hideout, I took them next door to where the others lived. "They feel safe here. They *are* safe here. I make sure of it." The emotion still worked its way through my words, but I think they were too focused on what I was showing them to notice.

The two men didn't say a word. Raph's dad was taking everything in. Dan was looking but not seeing: his eyes were miles away. "Right then." Raph's dad broke the silence. "Are there any more we need to know about?"

I nodded to the hovel next door. "Just the one." We both looked to Dan who was still communing with the fairies.

I jumped when he blurted out, "Why don't they live at Bal's place?" It wasn't an accusation, just a blunt question.

"At first, it was because they didn't know him. They... I... didn't trust him. Then, it was because they don't cope with change. So, they needed a place to be safe while they were getting used to all the adjustments there, all the new people coming and going." I looked to Dan. "Some still struggle, which is why we use the flags." I looked to Raph's dad. "That's how we let them know there's new stuff going on, new people, and the ones who are scared, stay away. But I guess, now, the main reason is, it's how it is. Because… it works. It had worked… until now."

"Would Bal allow you all to move onsite?" Again, Dan made with the blurt.

"He's been hounding me for ages to join him, but I can't leave these guys. And they won't move to a place that isn't safe."

Both of them looked at me like I was a compete weirdo. "And this is safe, is it now? This dump of condemnation? Well, that's one for the books." The older man looked to his son.

His arrogance had me burring up. "There are other things to be worried about than just your house falling in, you know. These guys think if there was another quake, they would be able to get out of a semi stable house—less to fight through—and that's why Richard has an opening above his head. But then there are the Catchers, too."

Raph's dad was still confused. "Your friends are scared of animal catchers?"

He had no idea. "Temple Catchers hunt for strays to supply some of the temples with animals to sacrifice and humans to"—I tried not to gag—"do stuff to. It's all whacked and wrong and they're all sick in the head. Doesn't mean it isn't real. And there's no way I'm gonna let any of my friends get caught up in that skrat."

Again, there was silence… thoughtful silence. I could almost hear the wheels in Dan's head whirring. "Right. Can you race over and ask Bal for a meeting? It's pretty important and needs to happen asap. As in, can you tell him we're heading over in two minutes? We'll be on your heels."

For some reason—actually, for the specific reasons: one, I had been trailing these guys for four months; two, I had met their family; and three, I had got to know Raph—I knew I could trust Dan. I believed he would do his best to help our people. So I didn't waste any time. Bolting like a scalded cat, I exited the building, The Wreckage and fled into Bal's Garden. "Bal! Bal, where are you?"

True to their word, within five minutes the two visitors were sitting with Bal in the doorway of his shed, whilst Kait was helping me carry four cups of coffee. When we climbed the hill, the three of them were leaning over a sketch pad of Bal's, as Dan's hand flew across the page with one of Bal's pencils.

"What do you think?" Dan asked.

They all sat up and were lost in thought as we handed out the coffee. Kait gave me a one-armed hug and a wink, kissed her husband's cheek, and walked back down the hill to continue working with Aran.

I was desperate to see what Dan'd come up with. Bal shifted the sketch pad so I could see. Once again, tears came to my eyes. It was perfect. Perfect. I looked to Bal and he raised an eyebrow in silent question, *Will this work, my dear girl? Will they be happy with this... will you?*

I gave a hint of a nod and was struggling to keep my emotions in check. Bal understood. "Jimmy, how about you pop these away for me"—he indicated the art supplies—"then join us on a tour of the garden so Dan and Marcus can explain what they're thinking?"

Bal distracted our two visitors as I raced to follow his instructions and ducked into his bathroom to wash my face and blow my nose. I then joined them on the tour. Which had come to a standstill at the garden path.

Bal was waving his hand around, indicating the area between the food truck and the washrooms. "Why can't you put them up here?"

"One, because, whilst there's space here, there isn't enough space. And two"—he looked to me as I joined them—"I thought you said your people were skittish. Didn't like change?" He looked back to Bal. "And you said you need to put flags up to warn them if people are coming over, or there's something going on... a visitor? Surely setting up accommodation down in the garden would solve those issues." Dan indicated the path. "Put flags across here, they know to stay down the back till it's all clear. They can wander the garden, they can be free to leave their cabins, live uninterrupted until they feel safe. And, all the while, they're out of the Catcher's?"—he looked to me and I nodded—"eyes."

He was making a lot of sense and I couldn't understand Bal's reluctance.

"But it's not safe."

Here's a life lesson I've learned to respect: don't ignore my gut. "Bal?" He looked at me. "What's going on? What aren't you telling us?" He made like a gaping fish but I soon lost patience. "What are you hiding?"

My friend, and to be honest, the guy I had adopted as a father-figure was turning himself inside out in what looked to be a huge effort to both speak and not speak.

Raph's dad grew impatient. "Don't want to be rude, can see a cat's stuck in your craw, but the clock's ticking and we're paying people to sit on their buttooshies across the road. Could we get a move on and sort this out? Please?"

Dan took over from Marcus. "We want to help. We really do. And I believe we can. Do you not want these people living on your property?"

"Of course I do. It would be my utter delight."

"Then what's wrong with the garden? Don't you want them messing it up?"

"Of course not. I mean, they won't be messing it up. It's what I had always hoped would happen."

Marcus's frustration came out in a bit of a growl. "Then for bleeding sakes, man, what's the problem?"

"They haven't stopped!" Bal's yell had us all taking a step back.

I jumped in with the obvious. "Stopped what?"

I swear tears were in Bal's eyes when he looked at me. "Dumping waste. Bloody sheets. Body parts. Every two or three days another bag is thrown over the wall. I collect it before dawn and take it inside the city gate where the police pick it up and do something about it." He stooped to look me in the eye and took my hands. "I didn't want you to know. To be scared."

All I could do was focus on breathing slowly. In and out. Slowly. And try not to fall over.

Marcus whispered, "Body parts, you say?"

"The police know about it. I've spoken to them. They know it's being thrown over the wall. They've been through here with a fine-tooth comb. It's obviously not happening here."

"What are they doing about it? Are they angry you're moving the evidence?" I was aware of Dan speaking. I was kind of thinking the same thing through the fog of fear threatening to overwhelm me.

Bal answered, "They don't seem to care. About me moving the bags that is. I am not sure what they're doing about the... incidents. Not like they're going to tell me. I just said my people can't be allowed to see it. Once I was ruled out of the equation, they really didn't seem to mind. I just call and tell them there is a new bag and send them a photo of where and how I found it, on my new phone." A weight caused his shoulders to slump. "I am so sorry, Jimmy, I know I should have told you. But... I didn't know how. I didn't want to scare you."

Dan interrupted. "Listen, I can see you've got a lot to sort out here. We should leave you to it and get back across the road. This situation is totally whacked and wrong on so many levels. So we'll leave you to work out what you want to do."

That was enough to bring me back to the bigger problem. "No. Please." I spoke to Bal, "We can figure this out. But please, Bal, can we talk about it later? Our family needs a place to stay and tonight their houses will be gone."

Bal nodded and said to Dan, "Thank you for your time. Please tell us what you had in mind... for in the garden."

Dan started talking as soon as we turned down the path to the back. "You have heaps of space here. We could put up a couple of cabins, same sleeping arrangements as they have across the road, in lightweight, durable materials." He looked to Marcus. "We could call Craig and Kelly over with some of the Sanctuary crew to work on this, while we focus on the other side of the road. Maybe Josh and Tim could divide their time between the two projects? That way it would be done super-quick. In the meantime"—he looked back at me —"would your guys be happy sleeping in a canvas shelter? Like big tents? I know Sanctuary still have all the tents we lived in. That way, if they moved onsite, I'm assuming they'd be safe from those... Catchers? You've been speaking of?"

I nodded.

"Right, and then, by tonight we could have temporary accommodation set up here. You could let them know today. Maybe with Kait, Aran and you two? You could help them adjust? While we continue to fix up across the road." He started to look around then nodded and spoke again. "Are there any other people we need to be aware of?"

I shook my head, again worried the action would make my tears fall.

"Yes." Bal interrupted the negotiations. We all looked at him. "Jimmy needs somewhere to stay."

I rolled my eyes. "I'm fine, I just keep using the food va—" *Skrat.* We hadn't ever acknowledged I was doing that... out loud, that was. I looked to Bal.

He dropped his chin and raised his eyebrows. "What was that?"

This was not the time or the place to have this discussion. But it was kind of taken out of my hands when Marcus spoke up. "Right, then, we add another cabin. That work for you, Jimmy?"

Bal clapped his hands. "Perfect."

Before I had an opportunity to speak, we were all walking back up the hill. Kait met us at the head of the path. "Any luck?"

Bal declared on everyone's behalf, "Perfect, dear woman. It is going to be perfect."

Marcus said, "Right then. You get back to work, lad. I'll get on to Sanctuary and see if Craig and Kelly can't bring the midnight oil and their old gear. And some photos of what we've done at Sanctuary. They can help set up and check things over here. I'll be over in a jiffy." He looked at Bal and me. "If you're free we can walk and talk and bring the drawing board to life. Does that work for everyone?"

Like me, Bal was shocked into silence. We looked at each other, nodded and then laughed at the sheer joy of being offered help. Big help. Right how we needed it. "I'll come and get their stuff." Then it hit me. Introducing such a huge change was going to be one hell of an ordeal. But it was going to be worth it.

41

ALARIO: CROSSHATCH

I tapped the table twice. Noodle-laden chopsticks stopped mid-journey to my wife's opened mouth. She looked to my finger on the table, then back to me. Mouth still open, chopsticks still halted mid-flight.

We were sitting at our little table pulled up to the wall of windows overlooking the city below. Our favourite jazz album played quietly on shuffle, and I sat across from my stunning wife considering just how much she had grown into her beauty. We'd just finished our weekly debrief about our marriage and how things were going with our newly improved communication. Which, I was happy to report, was going well. We still had a long way to go, but we were a lot further along the "happy marriage trail" than we were when we started the process.

Each week we gave the other a free pass to ask a question that required an honest answer, with no repercussions. It was an idea we had brought home from a work practice Cissa had instigated, unintentionally.

When Cissa had been making her point to the staff that she wanted honesty and was prepared to give it, she slammed her fist on the table. Twice. Just to be sure she had our attention. In a well-received parody of her vehemence, we now tapped on the table twice when we wanted to hear the truth from a staff member on any given matter.

It had worked well at Black & Light Designs, so we decided to bring it home. Cissa and I both wanted to make this marriage work and we acknowledged, at forty-four, we were just too old to tiptoe around the edges. So, with a spoonful of cement, we served up some home truths. I hadn't used my double tap during our debrief, I had reserved it for now.

With her full and undivided attention, I dived straight in. "So, do you want to have kids?"

Thank goodness she hadn't put those noodles into her mouth. I would have been wearing them. "What?"

I reached over and mopped up the chopsticks malfunction with my napkin. And, without looking her in the eye this time, pretending to be very busy "cleaning", I repeated myself. "Kids. I want to know, honestly, what you think... have thought... about trying to have them."

"Is this because of what Mother said about making babies with limited fertility and old wombs?"

"Please don't... ever... refer to your mother and making babies in the same sentence. Ever. Again. My cojones are currently hiding up above my stomach disguising themselves as gallstones."

Cissa's roar of laughter helped dilute the image of her mother plaguing my visuals. Eventually she calmed down, wiped her eyes and tilted her head. "Do you want kids?"

"Uh-ah! I double tapped and asked you."

She turned to study the city below us. It was giving off its usual light show of flashing gaudiness. The demons still crawled over, swam through and dwelled within most things down there. I really didn't like Sardis. Cissa took a sip of her sparkling water and looked back at me. "You know, I think I might be too old."

"Actually, I've looked into it and you're not. I believe you have a few years left to try, but that isn't answering the question. Do you *want* kids?"

"What about our business and all we've worked for? It would mean taking a step back, handing over the reins."

"Irrelevant to the bigger issue. And you're still evading the question."

"We're just starting to get to know each other again. To reconstruct our relationship. Would we throw everything away by introducing kids? I mean, what kind of parents would we be when we don't even yet know what kind of marriage partners we are?"

"Well, I figure we've got a pretty good example of what not to be like: your mothe—"

"I thought we weren't mentioning my mother in reference to making babies." She laughed.

"We're not talking about making babies. We're talking about parenting, and, as I was about to say, your mother is the perfect example of what not to do... or be like.... My folks weren't too bad, I guess. We could make it up as we went along. Ask others for advice." No way was I going to mention Jonathan's name in this fragile conversation. But he was the one I'd be learning from the most. "But still, that doesn't answer my question." I double tapped the table again, to remind her of her duty to share the honest truth.

She looked back out the window and was lost to me for a while. "What about the battle?" She twitched her head, indicating the Dark drowning the city. The glossy curtains of her hair shimmered in the dim lighting of the room. "It's a dangerous world to bring kids into."

We both fell into silence, possibly both lost reminiscing the Battle of Philadelphia and watching those kids... babies... threatened by the Gerent. He would have killed them. I can guarantee that was the honest truth, right there. And *that* would have killed their parents. It almost killed me, and I hardly knew them. But thinking Ruby, Jonathan's daughter, was at risk... I had to physically shake my head to get rid of the memory... the anger... the soul crushing fear that the Gerent would hurt her. The kid had really grown on me.

I thought of Marcus and Kait and how they had been helpless

when their kids were fighting in the Battle of Laodicea. I'd seen the footage. It was insane. Crazy. Brave. Intense. But how would they have felt, unable to get in there to save their kids? I had no idea. And quite frankly, didn't want to know. "It would be something we would have to trust the Light with. And still, she evades the question." I smiled.

She smiled back, then looked at my hand again. "Honest truth? I don't know. I thought about it a lot, earlier on. But just buried myself in work. Now? It's not even on my radar."

"All I'm saying is, when we first got married, we were kids ourselves. Then we were students, then we were working flat out to build our business, then we were not talking, then we lived in different cities. But now...?"

"But now..." She smiled again and laid her hand over mine. "Honest truth? I'll think about it. And thank you for asking, for putting it on the table. And for researching information about my limited fertility and ancient womb."

"Actually, I think you'll find your mother said"—I used a very bad imitation of Babel's husky, smoke-and-alcohol scarred voice box— "blah, blah, blah, new fertility programs blah, blah, Laodicea. Blah, you don't require a young womb or a man. Since you have neither..."

Again, Cissa laughed. "But now I have a man *and* non-unrepairable, shrivelled womb, it is something I need to consider. And I will. Honest truth."

That was all I was asking. To be fair, I didn't know how I felt about it. Well, that wasn't the honest truth. The idea scared the living daylights out of me. I just felt it was something I didn't want her... or me, to regret because we had been too messed up to figure our marriage out earlier. Would it be fair to the kids? Who knew? Would it be fair to us? Same. I was so used to living my life the way I wanted. This new arrangement took an awful lot of give and a little bit of take, but, it was wort—

"Al?" Cissa squeezed my hand. "Did you hear me?"

"Sorry, what?"

"I'm speaking at a three-day conference in Ephesus in a couple of days. Do you want to join me? We could visit the office there and touch base in person, then take a day or two and cool our heels by the sea."

I grasped Cissa's hand and leaned back, forcing her out of her chair. I stood and embraced her and together we swayed in a relaxed version of dancing to one of my favourite songs. "Sounds good."

42

CONTESSA: TAKE 2

Inspiration. Inspiration. Inspiration.

So, You know how You helped with my assignment for TAVE? I was kind of wondering if You could please help me again for my assignment for Cissa?

I left the work crew behind and strolled through the war zone of The Wreckage. It was actually really hard to focus on figuring out what I could do for Cissa, because the devastation was so widespread. I mean, seriously, the city above the wall had been repaired and restored fast as a... very fast thing.

But it looked like these guys had not received one jot of help. For the most part, buildings still leaned against each other. Trees and gardens still lay in chaos, but the weeds had started taking over the space where help had turned a blind eye. And a deaf ear by the sounds of it.

From what I could see, there was very little life left here—human, that was. The wildlife was definitely doing okay for itself. There weren't many residents in the first few blocks of the estate, and they'd all taken the money Black & Light had offered them. They were now living in temporary housing somewhere, because now, where their houses had been, was cleared land.

Seriously, I could see why they called it The Wreckage. There was nothing whole and unharmed by The Quake. But once it had all been cleared, the next problem had been fixing all the broken drainage and redirecting the underground springs that bubbled up through the soil and trickled over the worksite. Not to mention the huge stormwater drains that channelled excess water from the city through the estate. The people at TAVE had suggested the engineering, horticulture, and landscaping students come and do a project to deal with all that.

So, yay. Now there were lovely little water canals and bridges already in place around the sites where the new houses were going to go. They'd even worked in a community space that was going to host a vegetable garden and fruit orchard, a playground and a mini sports-ground. Once the little houses were finished, the same horticultural team were going to come in and design gardens for the houses and streets, and plant trees as soon as possible to create shade, and cooling from the baking heat of the huge wall behind it all.

I think talks were going on about what other groups at TAVE could come and use this as a space to practise "real-world application". I was just super grateful that the textile and design faculty would have no need to come down here. I did not want to run into Jolena or any of my old classmates again. Ever. But that brought me back to my dilemma. I continued through the heart of The Wreckage.

Inspiration. Inspiration. Inspiration.

I had been tasked to explore the city and find an audience not already catered to.

Check.

I then had to outline their needs, their culture and their environment.

Well, the people here had no money.

No electricity.

And no source of income.

So their needs were great.

Their culture was.... I stopped and did a three-sixty. The first word that came to mind was "desperate". But then I slowed down and turned again. I saw a few heads disappear behind curtains. A few broken toys in a yard not covered in weeds. I saw a football in an open grassy area. I saw an ice cream container and several old plastic milk bottles sitting neatly next to a dripping tap. I saw a few flowering plants in weeded gardens. And I saw a couple of perfectly functioning bicycles lying in the shade of a tree, just underneath some bare feet dangling from the branches. I pretended not to see and continued my surveillance.

The culture here was not desperate.

It was survival.

Finding a way.

Defiance.

Strength.

My heartbeat picked up. The kernel of an idea was forming. The environment beyond the wall was tough, but the people who survived here were tougher. They had great need, but they also had great resilience. The situation reminded me a lot of Sanctuary in Philadelphia. I had learned how I could help the people there, and I began to grow in confidence that I would learn how I could support and serve the people here.

Next step would be getting someone to talk to me. To let me in so I could learn more. For now, however, I had a start. I stealthily took some photos, not of the houses where I suspected people lived… or of the bare feet, and quietly dictated some notes through my earpiece to fill out later and share with Cissa. We were supposed to be meeting tomorrow, but she was in Ephesus again and I had been asked if we could move our appointment back a couple of days.

Kait was across the road at the place she worked at most days. The twins were tied up with studies at TAVE, and Dan and Marcus, who I got a ride with, were busy with fixing the world.

I knew I had a long wait in front of me, so, with the initial work done, I spent more time wandering and pondering: how could I meet their needs—whatever they were found to be—in a way they could afford? How could I create clothing that was functional, produced with quality craftsmanship, a unique style, thoughtful fabric choice and classic, understated chic when I had no resources? Just as well I had the starting block, because the rest of the project was beyond me.

Dan interrupted my musing. "Tessa, we need some help."

"I am not climbing in a ditch or over a roof."

Dan laughed and Marcus scoffed. "Thought I raised you better than that, me girl."

Dan intervened before I could relieve some of my boredom with a good argument with Marcus. "No need for that. It's just that the twins have a half day today and they'll be finished soon. We're in the middle of something here and can't leave, and we need someone to go get them."

I looked between the two of them. "But I can't drive."

"High time we painted that dragon green to go," Marcus said.

Both Dan and I looked at him, then Dan continued, "I know. But the Pods run from the gate to the ring road. From there you catch another Pod to the TAVE stop; the twins will meet you there. Can you bring them back here? Then, once we're done, we'll go grab something for dinner."

"Um..." It sounded simple. I looked around at the busy site with everyone hot, sweaty and filthy, dirty up to their armpits in work. I then looked across the main road to the side lane that led to the Old Tip. Then back to Dan. "I guess I could give it a go."

"You've got your phone. Contact a grown-up if you need help." There was a gleam in Marcus's eye. "And someone will come rescue you."

I inhaled deeply at the insult and, once again, before I could unleash my fury at Marcus's dig, Dan kissed me on the lips. "Thanks, knew you wouldn't let them down."

I stared at the both of them. Furious that their psychological warfare was brutal and effective. I tapped my hip pocket and waited till I received notification Marcus had transferred enough cash into my account to pay for something nice for afternoon tea. I spun on my sensibly heeled, gorgeous faux-leather ankle-booted foot and marched to the city gate to wait for the next Pod.

* * *

ONE THING I didn't think I'd ever get over, used to, or ever take for granted was apple turnover with fresh cream. I hadn't had one for years. "Can you make these?" I asked Raph as the three of us—four if you counted Tiger in his travel basket—sat at the stop waiting for the return Pod that would take us back to the worksite. I had also grabbed something for Dan and Marcus.

"I think desserts are next term. But I will ask for you."

Thankfully, the Pod arrived and not long afterwards, we were deposited at the side gates to the city. I had followed the map on my phone and managed to get to TAVE and back, including a side trip to collect Tiger, without too many wrong turns.

The twins stowed their bags in our car. Without decent wi-fi reception in the shadow of the wall, they couldn't do homework for school. Neither could they set up and do work for TAVE, and I didn't have any pressing work to do... except trying to talk to people who didn't want to meet me.

We did a bit of sword practice, but we were all tired and not in the mood.

We tried kicking an abandoned ball around for a while, but none of us had ever really done it before, and we kind of sucked at it.

We went for a walk, but after a while that was just really depressing.

We sat and played word games, but... I'm not wordy, and Riah's offerings were getting a bit rude with her boredom. She picked up a stick and threw it at an old metal garbage bin and it made a good sound. All of our ears pricked up.

She collected the stick and grabbed the bin and brought them back. Then Raph and I were on the hunt. Raph found an old polystyrene food box that didn't have a lid, and I found an old plastic drink container that did. We put some sand in the bottle and found another stick for Riah's bin. And, with Raph tapping the box like a bongo, the fun began.

We started with an old favourite. Raph and I sang, Riah and Raph kept the beat, and I added rhythm with my shaker. Before we knew it, time was being consumed by our joy. And when we stopped for a breather, we had an audience. Not a big one. But considering we'd not seen hide nor hair of anyone before, the seven kids who were watching was a serious crowd.

"Hey." Raph kicked off the conversation. "Would any of you be interested in joining us? You just need something to hit that makes a good sound."

43

CONTESSA: CINDERELLA

I had followed Val's advice and determined to go to the Spring Festival. And because no one from my class had met any of my family, they didn't have to worry about disguises. But because I didn't know how Jolena felt about me, I did. I was so grateful the kick-off event was not at the Theatre. Rather, it was set at the most amazingly gorgeous public pools located in the Cultural District.

Natural rock walls from the mountain were exposed and featured as part of the landscaping. Lavish gardens bursting with life were the backdrop to a spectacular light show, courtesy of the overhead drones. The huge stone pillars of the grand entry colonnade were illuminated, drawing us along and into the venue. Upbeat music with an edgy vibe pumped out from somewhere overhead.

There was a light breeze blowing which made it perfectly acceptable to wear my disguise. I'd found a gorgeous silk scarf, large dark sunglasses, and a flowy new coat, all from a classic little charity shop not far from our apartment. Sadly, I had to ditch the glasses, they'd made me as blind as a bat. But they went straight into my new little clutch. There was no way I was letting go of those treasures.

Waiters threaded their way through the crowd, carrying trays of tall, thin glasses full of golden bubbles. Trays of finger food were also made freely available. I'm so glad we'd fed Dan, Marcus and Raph... and Riah sufficiently before we left. They'd only have eyes for the food if we hadn't.

I was torn between wanting to be up the front so as not to miss a thing and needing to be buried in the shadows at the back. So, we settled for finding a space in the middle, and with Dan on my left, Marcus on my right, Kait and Riah sort of in front—they were both taller than me—and Raph at my back, I felt safe. I also knew we had our normal Guards, plus an extra few for the event.

I guess, as the kick-off—featuring students' work and no big names—this was a low-key function. And that was understandable. But for me it was one of the biggest experiences of my life—apart from my wedding and my first big battle in Sodom, that was.

When all the lights turned blue-white and flashed three times, the whole crowd quieted. Waiters withdrew and the music swelled as a figure, captivating a spotlight and the audience, strutted down the catwalk. Jolena, in another figure-hugging, unimaginative black body-glove welcomed us all and started the show by filling everyone in on the extension program and the exceptional talent of this year's cohort.

Gag.

Thankfully she didn't take too long before the normal students' designs were on show. I was impressed. I had seen most of the work from the classroom of my day classes. Everyone had done really well.

Then came the big event and I had to keep reminding myself to breathe and act normal.

Cool as a cucumber.

A bright yellow, crazy-haired, cucumber.

In a classy new coat.

I could do this.

I knew my classmates would all be here—the day class and the extension class. And, of course, Xavier would be here. The pig. I caught sight of Wallace, Travis and Oscar. They were standing with Emma, but not Kayleigh. Instead of watching the show, I was desperately trying to locate the others. I didn't want to be caught out. My family didn't know what everyone looked like, except Dan who could identify Xavier at one hundred paces, I'm sure.

Then I saw them. My arch nemesis was standing next to some of the people I recognised from the horror night at the Temple: Jolena's henchmen.

And, eventually, after scouring the shadows and groups, I found Kayleigh standing by herself, to the side. Very much out of the lime-light, with her arms wrapped around her middle. And, just like my attention tapped her on the shoulder, her head spun, and her eyes locked on me for the total of one second. Then, everything went black. A communal gasp was drowned out by the start of really loud music, explosions of light, colour and sound. The finale was underway.

When the lights came back on, she'd moved. And I couldn't find her anywhere. What was she going to do? Tell Jolena? Xavier? Despite it being a small show, there was still a large crowd. I didn't want to draw attention to myself by moving our group. So, for the time being, I didn't tell the others. I had no eyes for the show, only for the crowd and potential attack.

Dan pumped my hand twice and leant over and kissed the top of my head… scarf. "We've got you covered." He tilted his head toward the Guards standing among the crowd and our own personal Guard standing around us. "Now, try to relax and watch the show."

I was very grateful that Sariah had been videoing the action for Val, Cissa and Al. We all knew that Val would not be the slightest bit interested in anything this show had to offer, except my piece. But Cissa had said it wouldn't be wise for her to rock up, especially since she had a really bad relationship with the Guild as well. I had an idea she and Jolena went way back, and none of that history was pretty. But she was keen to see the show, so Riah insisted on videoing the lot.

Come to think of it, the only person who was genuinely interested in the whole thing, apart from me, was Kait. Marcus had made a good attempt at a fake enthusiasm but was hoping there was going to be some fight action before getting home. Considering this, and that Dan was also keen on releasing some pent-up frustration, angst and stress from work, I made an effort to exhale and watch the show... with at least one eye. I couldn't help a continual scan for Kayleigh, and making sure I knew where the other five were at all times.

But then my phone buzzed.

Kayleigh: Are you okay?

Madly I typed back.

Tessa: Yes. Are you? What happened? You're still at TAVE?

Kayleigh: Yeah. I'm okay. Just got to get through tonight, then I'm outta here. There was a bit of blow up after you escaped. But you're old news now. Crowning Xavier and the new batch is all she cares about. If you lay low, you should be fine.

Tessa: You sure you're okay?

Kayleigh: Yeah. Stay safe.

Tessa: You too. If you ever need me for anything, you have my number.

Kayleigh: <3

I still didn't know where she was, but I was relieved to know she was okay. And that I was off Jolena's "wanted" list. Now I only had eyes for the horrid woman as she stepped up to the mic. "And now for our finale. Our top six students have been slaving away nights as well as days in extra classes to push their boundaries. It was my intent to squeeze every last drop of genius from them. And I can tell you, they did not disappoint. I am here to introduce Sardis's... the Seven Cities'... the Continent's future in fashion." With a flurry of her hands, she withdrew as the lights dimmed, and once again the spotlight hit the curtains as the music swelled.

Oscar's contribution of a pale blue pant suit was first out. It was beautifully tailored, no doubt about it. At the end of the runway, his model took off the jacket to reveal a finely crafted, sleeveless, back-buttoned linen shirt. Wallace's work came next. His model wore a flowing floral dress and a bolero jacket. His third piece was an attempt at a hat. I'd been impressed when I'd seen it in class, but under the lights with the complete outfit on his gorgeous model, it was amazing.

Emma's contribution was next and out of everyone's, it was my least favourite, but the lack of fabric and excessive flesh drew an extra round of applause from the audience. Kayleigh's flared, wrap skirt that somehow seamlessly went from short to long with a flick of the model's wrist was, in my opinion, a showstopper. There was so much colour, movement and fabric in the skirt. The simple, elegant top was the perfect complement.

Travis's entry was the only men's outfit. His traditional three-piece suit with an interesting twist to the dimensions and cut was truly innovative. Xavier's work was revealed next and with his evening gown combining similar ideas to Kayleigh's skirt and Oscar's twisting of traditional dimensions, and Emma's idea of less fabric being more, he also drew a lot of appreciation from the crowd. But in truth, I think the greatest demonstration of genius was how he made the barely-there fabric stay up on his model. Perhaps his third element was body tape?

I couldn't believe mine was the last piece. The finale. Each model waited on the wings of the stage so each student's work remained on display throughout. As JJ stepped onto the runway, all the light's dimmed again and her gorgeous dark skin glowed. Her wild madness of hair was teased up and out. Gold sparkly eyeshadow, the same hue as the lining of my jacket, adorned her eyes and cheek bones. She strutted out into the spotlight her head held high and her hands on her hips like an Amazonian warrior—in classic chic—and I loved her for it.

Then she took off prowling along the runway. When she got to the end, she turned, undid the jacket and dropped it to the floor. Then, she picked a spot in the audience and winked as she undid the little top. The sparkle, colour, and ease with which it came off had the crowd gasping and me jumping up and down, clapping and crying and cheering. At the sound of my response, JJ turned, put her fist on her heart and bowed her head.

Heads turned between the two of us, but before anything happened or people thought too much, JJ dropped in a graceful squat, collected the jacket, spun and was strutting back down the runway to stand at the front of the arrowhead of my class's contribution to the opening of the Spring Festival. I was so proud.

I was also burning with rage as each student was invited up onto the stage to stand next to their model. And Xavier stood next to JJ. He had one arm linked through the arm of his model and tried to link his other arm through JJ's, but she wouldn't let him. It was noticed. Jolena was not impressed and made sure JJ understood.

Xavier tried again.

And again, JJ refused.

Murmuring grew among the crowd. But as music started for the final parade, JJ still refused to acknowledge Xavier. There were flickers from the curtains on the stage and JJ took off down the runway. Xavier followed with his model, the others lining up behind like good, obedient ducklings. Once again, when she came to the end, JJ planted her feet, looked to the general area I was standing and saluted.

Someone in the stage crew had cottoned on, and not obeying the runsheet, flicked a spotlight till it landed on me. JJ then started clapping until Jolena herself came and escorted my beautiful, loyal model off the runway, and out of a career.

I would never be able to thank her enough, but for now, we had other problems. Not only had the guy with the spotlight found me, so too had Xavier, Jolena, all her henchmen and the drones. Midnight had struck for this fairytale princess, and it was time for me and my crew to hit the road. The crowd moved in to get a better look, but when they realised there was trouble, they moved away. This enabled us to get out of there, quick smart. But, of course, that was never going to happen.

Marcus took the lead, and, like an icebreaker, he used his mass, height and intimidating fight-face to clear a path. This sent the initial people-barrier skittering, and we managed to make progress again. However, when we hit a roadblock of confused bystanders who'd not been aware of anything going on around them, Marcus used his voice. He dropped it an octave and growled, which transformed confusion to fear and freeze into flight. I often wondered if intimidation was a Badge.

Just behind his right shoulder was Kait, who wore what Dan called her "Mamma Bear face" and carried her sword. Not that anyone could see it, but I think it made her feel better, like a security blanket... or chew toy. I pulled Raph along with me and, somehow, we ended up with Dan and Riah bringing up the rear. I was not happy about this arrangement. As our progress slowed to overcome another roadblock, I turned to voice my complaint. My eyes flicked to the stage where Jolena still stood, her eyes narrowed and calculating. The most worrisome thing of all, however, was that she was no longer surrounded by her apes and Xavier.

I totally forgot to complain about being designated to protection detail and passed on my concerns to Marcus. "They're coming. Hurry!" I was completely unsuccessful at keeping the fear from my voice. All I could think about was the animal crate awaiting me back at the Theatre.

Over his shoulder he growled back, "Those dog-faced drones are tying us up like rats in a honey trap."

Thankfully, the crowd was neither enthusiastic nor passionate. So, with ample intimidation from Marcus and Kait, I'm happy to report minimal damage to the innocent bystanders. Eventually we made our way to the colonnade and started to get some relief from the floppingly annoying drone lights.

But, of course, the shadows are home to the Dark. And they were, like, heaving with the enemy. I was so grateful Kait had her sword drawn... and we still had our filled-out Guard. Immediately, we took up formation. Kait and Marcus faced one side of the main colonnade, Dan, Riah and I, the other. Raph stood in the middle, keeping an eye on the entrance and exit. Our Guards, once again, were amazing at covering the brunt of the attack, allowing us to deal with the ones who broke through. But it was enough to slow us down and give Jolena's crew time to catch up.

And the enemy knew it.

They were just playing with us.

Delaying us.

Raph yelled, "We have to leave now. Right now. They are coming." I almost didn't hear him over the snarling and spitting of the demons that surrounded us. He knew better than to get too close to Kait and Marcus, so he used his broken sword to tap them on the shoulders and yelled when there was a gap in their attention, "Follow me."

Riah was so attuned to her brother she was on his heels. I grabbed Dan's elbow and yanked. Within moments our Guard had stepped in and covered our retreat. I had no idea where we were going, but I followed the rest as we skirted the edges of the pools, ran around and jumped over gardens, until we were running through dark passages cut within the rock wall.

The drones had lost us, but in the dark crevice we were blind. Marcus cursed and sent a message back, "Keep your head down." Then his voice projected... in a very hoarse whisper, "For bleeding heck, slow down."

An unfamiliar voice whispered back, "Sorry."

44

CONTESSA: NEW DISCOVERIES

The silence almost hurt. I was desperately straining to hear if there was anyone still chasing us. If anyone was sneaking up on us. But all I could hear was the ringing in my ears, my heartbeat bashing a rubbish-can drum in my head, and my family catching their breath. We had come to a stop, all spread out in a line along the narrow tunnel. I leaned against the rough rock wall at my back, and when I stretched my hand out in front of me, I could feel more cold rock. Dan fumbled for my right hand and I found Riah's with my left.

Nothing.

No one was coming.

No one I could hear, at least.

Seen or Unseen.

The only reason I knew there was the hope of a way out was a lightening of the pitch black further along the path. Now that I knew we were relatively safe, I allowed myself to think of who it was that had led us. I could make out the start of a soft, whispered conversation up the front, but the echo made discerning the words and speakers impossible.

Then I heard Raph's voice directed toward us. "This path will take us out to the top side of the dividing road. We will be hidden all the way. We can wait in the mouth of the cave until we see a Pod approaching. Jimmy says we should be safe if we catch one heading away from the pools. Then, later on tonight, we can go back to our home on another one."

Dan whisper-yelled over my shoulder, "Thanks, Jimmy, we owe you."

I had heard Raph speak of this kid. But to be honest, I had been so caught up in my deadlines and projects, I hadn't really paid much attention.

And, just as Raph's friend had described it, so it was. Spread out and sprawled over the lounge chairs in our apartment, changed out of our "ball gowns" and back in casual gear, we started a debrief of the night. We'd insisted Raph's friend join us.

She was an interesting character with beautiful eyes and a gorgeous face to match. Why she chose to wear baggy boys' clothes I had no idea. Here and now, however, she sat quietly, wide-eyed, staring at all of us, sipping a coffee Raph had made her. Maybe she'd never been in such a flash home before? Or maybe she wasn't used to such a weird family? Whatever it was, she just kept staring. And sipping.

Kait was the first to turn the conversation. "Jim, thank you so much for rescuing us."

She almost spat her drink when she realised we were all considering her and agreeing with Kait. "You're welcome," she stuttered.

"I did not know you were planning on coming tonight," Raph said.

"I... I wanted to see the one..."—she flicked her eyes to me—"who had escaped the Guild."

Then a few pennies dropped into place for me. "Oh, sweetheart, were you captured by them too? Is that why you're hiding in that disguise?"

Now it was everyone else's turn to spit their drinks.

"Sweetheart?"

"Captured?"

"Disguise?"

I was completely taken aback. Surely they could see it. Underneath the layers. Jim was the first to move. "I… I have to go. Thank you for the drink—"

Raph lurched to his feet. "Do not go, Jimmy." It wasn't an order but a heartfelt plea. And it worked. Or at least slowed Jimmy's escape from our home. "You are safe. We will not tell. We will help."

Jimmy's frightened-rabbit eyes ghosted over everyone again, slowing when she got to Dan, and stopping when she got to me. I smiled. "The Guild is seriously horrible, and the temples are"—I couldn't restrain my shudder when I thought of what went on there— "sickening, aren't they? Disgusting."

Slowly, she nodded.

"Were you captured too?"

She nodded again.

"That must have been absolutely awful."

Tears made her eyes glisten, and one fell as she nodded for the third time.

I could feel Kait's mother-hen feathers ruffle. She was desperate to hug the kid, and I kind of felt the same way. But, not wanting to spook her, neither of us moved, and I tried to encourage her with my words instead. "I think you are very brave. I had lots of help to escape. There is no way I could have done it without Dan and"—I looked to Kait and Marcus—"my family"—I smiled at my Guard—"and the Light's provision."

Jimmy hadn't moved. Like a rabbit caught in the headlights, she stood locked halfway between the lounge and the door.

"Tonight, when they… Jolena"—I couldn't stop my face screwing up—"spotted me, I was so scared she was going to capture me again. I know I had my family and Guard around me, but I don't know if I would have made it out of there… that any of us would have made it out of there, without your help. So, please hear me when I say, from the bottom of my heart, thank you. If there is anything I can ever do to repay the favour, please let me know."

With a final look around the room, Jimmy nodded then quietly slipped through the door.

45

JEMIMAH: EYE OPENER

S o... *Raph says I can just... like... speak to You and... and You will hear. That I don't have to pay a fee or go to a temple to "commune" with You?*
I waited. Nothing happened. No voice. No answer. No response.

No god. Just another hot-air, empty-promised myth.

Right. You're just like all the rest. A useless, faceless, pointless exercise in stupidity.

But I had seen it.

I had seen their armour.

I had seen those... hideous... sickening... frightening beasts attack them. I had seen those amazing Warriors stand around them and hold back the swarm trying to get them. I had seen how they each had one Protector stand at their shoulder and fight for them.

The Guards.

What? Aren't I good enough for You? Raph said You rescued his brother, Dan. He said You loved him. Loved them all. I'm too filthy for You, aren't I? Too used, hopeless? Yeah, well, sorry about that.

I wasn't sorry at all. I'd fought to survive. And I'd done it all by myself. I hadn't had any help from anyone. I didn't need anyone. And I didn't need another useless god clogging up my life demanding more things from me.

I sank deeper into the covers of my new bed, in my new hut. I hadn't had to do the rounds tonight. I knew perfectly well where my mother was. I had seen her attack Tessa and send her minions after Raph's family. I didn't have to check on my family as they were safe within the walls of Bal's garden.

The moon was full and I stared out the window. The light blanketed the garden in a soft blueish tint. It reminded me of the night I escaped the temple. And my mother.

And then I wept.

I'd lied.

I hadn't rescued myself.

For years I had blanked it out.

Refused to remember, refused to think about the night I'd lost both parents, and my life—as I'd known it.

Memories of escaping the Catchers, the boys hunting me on the street. The first night I was stupid enough to go back to Artemis's temple in the middle of a crowd. Memories of first meeting Bal, of his provision and acceptance. Of his generosity. Not just to me, but to us all. Then I was convicted of such guilt. Here I was in my own hut, safe in Bal's garden. All the people I cared about were safe, provided for, sheltered.

I was bombarded by memories of how I had never been alone. I'd always had help. I'd always been watched. Then the tears came. I felt pinned to my mattress by guilt. I had taken credit and run. I had lied to my family. I had stolen from the one who had given me the most: Bal. The shame was so heavy. But the oppression of my guilt and the filth of my actions against this One I didn't know knotted my heart. My head was spinning as my body was taken by full-forced sobs.

I am so sorry. I can see I need You. I can see You have been there for me. And I have been running. But how do I stop? How do I... I don't know what I'm supposed to do! Help me figure this out.

A calm settled over me. Peace. Quiet. Then I remembered Raph saying something about a cost. Not one I had to pay. But one that'd already been paid for me. A debt. A sacrifice on my behalf. And now it was paid, I could have… connection? A fresh start? A clean slate?

Is that true? He said You were close. Big. Bigger than the bad guys. Bigger than the mess of my life? If it is, then, that's what I want. If You've paid the debt so I can have that, then... thank You. Thank You. Show me how I get that connection. Show me how I get to be in Your... family? A real follower, not like the freaks at the temples. Not like my mother. Show me how I can be like them... Raph's family, who stand up against the Guild. Who stand up against the other gods. I really want what they have. I want You. If making a stand is the cost. Show me how to do that. Please. I don't want to be lost anymore. I don't want to run anymore. I don't want to be scared and untethered anymore.

I waited for a response. An answer. But there was nothing. Nothing at all. My mind was still. Empty. I strained to hear. To see. To feel. But there was nothing but a sigh of peace that breathed through my soul. My body was heavy and limp and relaxed. Warmth encased me and my eyes grew heavy and my heart beat slow and steady. No longer fighting and tearing its way out of my chest. Peace was the last thing I was aware of before I drifted off into a dreamless sleep. That and the words: *Rest well my child. You are seen and You are loved. You are Mine.*

46

KAITLYN: YOU CAN RUN, BUT YOU CAN'T HIDE

"Balashka, we need to talk." I tell you what, this man could run and hide like a fox down a rabbit hole. He was just as wily and cunning as well. It had been six weeks since Raph had healed his hip and fourteen years since the Light had met him in prison. He'd been allowed to get away, hiding from everything and everyone in jail, and now he was doing the same thing in his little Fort Knox. He'd sweet-talked everyone into covering his buttooshie and doing his dirty work. Well, his time was up.

"Ahh, sorry, Kait, is that the time?" He vaguely waved his wrist—sans-watch—in front of his face. "I really have to work on my piece for Harry. He's coming by later... today."

Before I could call him out on his bald-faced lie, he'd hightailed it up into his shed and pulled down the doors. If it wasn't his art, or the supplies coming, or being needed for some fanciful thing he'd created, he was too tired, too sick, or too distracted. Another favourite excuse was needing to assist Aran, or Jimmy... Jemmy—I was still adjusting to the fact he was a girl and we'd been granted permission to use her real name. Jem, short for Jemimah.

Today, I had had my fill of Balashka's pathetic excuses and we were going to talk.

I waved farewell to Aran and went into the food truck to help Jemmy prep dinner. Because Balashka thought it was safe to come out, the roller door slowly opened. I stopped chopping carrots and, through the open service window, I watched and waited. He stood at the top of the hill, just outside his shed, Sweetie at his heels, and smiled. His chest swelled and his grin grew. He reached down and petted his dog, and then with a skip in his step—made possible by the Light and my son—he made his way down to the Undercover Area. He even began to whistle... poorly. The man was so happy. I almost felt bad. But then I looked to Jemmy whose sneaky grin matched mine.

The sweet girl had come to me and we had talked about the Light. Her beautiful baby-pink armour was coming along very nicely. Every meal break at TAVE, Raph and Riah had been leading her through The Way. And the Light was growing in her. Just as she was growing in the Light.

But as far as Balashka was concerned, our Seeing Blind Man had no idea he was about to have his comeuppance.

"Your time is up; it is time for you to confront your demons. And your fears. Between the two, you are being held hostage." He had no idea, still partially blind to the Unseen, literally. The demons hounded this man, shackling him to his past.

He froze, looking around madly to find the source of my voice. Before he could run, I left the food truck and continued, "It is time for you to step up. You are a leader here, a model, a provider, a father." The more I thought about all that he had been given, and how he was refusing to take the bull by the horns, the more my anger stewed.

At least I had his attention, his shock stopping him from running. But then his face transformed and he turned on me. "I know that." His roar equalled mine. "Don't you think I don't know that?" He ripped his hands through his hair. Fear and fatigue and frustration flushed his face. "But you don't know what it's like. What's waiting for me out there. I've tried." Rage had fuelled his response and I did not take it personally.

I tried to quietly bring him down. "How about you tell me what it was like. You tell me what it's like out there." I pointed to the gates that he hid behind permanently.

He sighed and fell into a seat near the table. With his elbows on his knees, his hands caught his head. I turned to Jemmy and asked her to make us all a coffee. It was going to be a long night. My family knew the plan. Tonight, we were all meeting at the worksite. If I hadn't shown up by the time they'd downed tools for the day, they'd meet me here. All the while, they were to be petitioning the Light for this conversation.

"I tried. From the moment The Man came to me and showed me the way forward, out of the hell I'd created, I've tried to give back, to apologise, to make amends. I have returned everything I took with interest. Yet, it wasn't enough. I wrote letters, I tried to visit... never, never was it enough." Tears of defeat washed his face.

My heart broke. Quietly I pulled a chair alongside him. "That is a lie you have been carrying and being held hostage by for fourteen years. It was enough. It is enough."

Balashka turned his head to look at me, his brow furrowed. "How can you say that? The hatred, the lack of mercy, the denial of forgiveness, the vitriol..."

"I wish you would allow the Light in, Bal. If you would, then you could see, in the big picture, it was Him you had wronged. It was His laws you broke. But The Man who visited you showed you what you had to do, and you did it. He does not hate you; He loves you. He knows your heart, and He forgives you. He only has grace, mercy and encouragement for you. But if you keep running and hiding from Him, you are missing all that He has to give you. Not just all of that, but so much more. You are living a fraction of the life he has for you."

"But, Kait, I can't go out there. You don't know what they did. What they want to do."

Please help me find the way to break this cycle, to bring him home.

Jemmy chose that moment of silence to step out of the shadows to place two cups on the table next to us. And then it hit me: Truth given in a Word from the Light. And it rocked me to my core. That precious, brave girl.

"Bal, every day, this beautiful girl of yours confronts her fears. Every day she goes back into the lion's den where the one who hurt her—her mother—the one who hunts her, lives... works..." I turned to look at Jemimah: a deer spooked by an unknown noise. "Every day she has to choose between learning the skill that helps her family here and being discovered by her huntress." Tears sprang to Jemmy's eyes and her hands started shaking.

Bal sat up and stared at her. "Is that true?"

With mouth wide like her eyes, she looked from me to Bal then back to me. A groan escaped her lungs. Shaking started taking over her body. I stood and edged my way to her and gently led her to a chair and tested whether she would allow me to place my arm around her shoulders. She hadn't noticed, so I kept it there. Bal shuffled his seat forward and took her hands in his. Behind them, I saw our family car's lights creep into the car park.

Bal brought my attention back to the situation unravelling before me. "You never said. I wouldn't have made you go, you know. We could have done it another way."

"I wanted to learn. I wanted to contribute. I was... am careful. She doesn't expect me there. I dye my hair"—she pulled a hand free and ran it over her scarred scalp—"I wear baggy clothes like she would hate. I stay away from her faculty. I figured I was invisible." She put her hand back in Bal's, but I don't think she was aware. "It's worked so far." An audible gulp interrupted her sharing. "But I think she's found me."

Both Bal and I sat up at that. She came back to us, then, and looked between us. She rolled her lips as if she was trying to take the words back. She tried to withdraw her hands, but Bal hung on. "What do you mean? Tell me, Jem, please, let me help."

"The bags of bloody sheets. It's her."

Steel filled Bal's spine and fire sparked in his eyes. "I will protect you."

Jem pulled back then. "How can you? You don't understand. You haven't been there. You haven't experienced what she can do. Not like Tessa. Not like Dan. They survived. They have Guards. And Raph told me all I had to do was ask and The Light would give me a Guard too. And He did." The sheer force of her scream stilled the night. She took a ragged breath. "You don't understand, Bal. She is too powerful, but the Light can help me. He can protect me. You can't."

And with her fervent declaration of the Light's power from her uninitiated mouth, like moths to a flame, the Darkness came. They had already been lurking in the background for this talk Balashka had been evading for weeks. They had been circling like vultures, throwing blocks at him which he had been grabbing onto like life-lines. But now that I had pinned his wings, and Jem had declared her faith, they came a-running.

Bal hardly noticed my family had not only arrived, they had moved to surround us. Our Guards, with a few more to bulk out their number, joined us. Jem looked up and startled at the sight. It was a good sign her growth and heart were genuine.

Cissa strolled over, dispatching some demons along the way, and introduced herself. "Hope you don't mind some company, but by the looks of it"—she twitched her head over her shoulder to the growing horde—"you could use some help." She shook hands with a dumb-founded Bal and an awestruck Jem. Before either of them could respond, she was back out there.

It had given me the opportunity to draw my sword and scout the surroundings. Marcus stood to Cissa's left and fought as a tripod with Al and her, facing the driveway. Tessa, Dan and Riah formed their normal formation in the space heading to the back garden and Raph came over to join us, facing outwards, as last line of defence.

"What's going on? Who are these people and... what's going on? I know something is happening, but I can't see." Frustration caused Bal's voice to crack. He looked to Jem, but she only had goggle eyes for the battle unfolding around her. Obviously awed by what he couldn't see.

She seemed totally unaware he'd spoken. "Their armour is so bright. So pure. So beautiful. I could never have something so precious, so... amazing." She dropped her head into her hands and started weeping. Her body shook and she was totally unaware of Bal and his attempt to discern what was going on. Raph stepped in and squatted down next to Jem and laid a hand on her knee. "Look, Jem. Look at your armour. You are in the Light. The Light loves you and the Light is protecting you. Not only has He sent His Guards and us, your new family, He has encased you. Look at your armour."

Jem's gasp drew Bal's attention back to his immediate surroundings. I knew he could see in some part. He knew we wore armour and he knew our colours. But now there was no denying Jem's beautiful pink, blasting like a flare in the night.

As Raph continued quietly talking to her, murmuring reassuringly, reminding her of what he had shown her in The Way, he had her draw the sword from her back brace. As the battled raged, metal rang and minions roared, her crying turned to awe.

I left Jem in my beautiful boy's care, and turned to the vexing man who was stuck in the mud. "Bal? What can you see?"

Tearing his eyes from Jem, he looked at me, wild-eyed. "What?" His head shook in confusion. "What can I see? I can see you in green armour, the boy there in violet and the others... all of them in a halo of colour. And my Jem is now in radiant pink."

"Can you see anything else?"

"Yes, I can see that all these people you have brought here are dancing around waving swords at nothing and acting out some ridiculous pantomime. If this is something you've organised to shock me into some... some... I don't know what.... Well, I'm not buying it—"

Jem sat up, her face swollen, her eyes red and glassy. "Open your eyes, Bal. They are defending us. While we sit here and talk, they"— she jabbed her finger toward Tessa, Dan and Riah—"are defending us. The horrors painted on the inner walls of the Temple have come to life and they are trying to get to us. But these are defending us. And so are the Guards. Why can't you see it? Why will you not see it."

Bal launched to his feet and stormed off toward the three Jem had just indicated. He turned and yelled at us, waving his arms around like wild windmills, "There is nothing here! Nothing."

His declaration and proximity to the enemy's line caused a mad flurry. Demons lurched to grab him. The fool had caused my three children to be in danger as the swarm came to grab him. My chair flew out from behind me as I raced to intercede for him. I tackled him to the ground, bounded to my feet and started swinging away above him to protect his sorry butt.

Raph came flying in and slid in next to Bal's prone body. He held his hands up, ready to defend Bal against any who got past me.

"What's going on?" Bal, thank the Light, was still partially winded from my tackle.

I growled at him, "Stay down."

More Guards appeared around us and helped reduce the heat of the attack. Dan disengaged when it was safe to do so, helped Bal stand and almost dragged him back to the table. Now it was his turn to growl, "Stay." He pushed Bal into a chair and got in his face. "You wanna play with us? You get yourself equipped. Do not"—Dan looked away and forcibly took a breath before looking back—"step into battle like that again and endanger my wife, my sister, my mum and my brother."

Then he got up close and real personal in Bal's blanched face. "If you do, I will personally deal with you, you have my word." With a gravelly growl that I could barely hear, he finished his instructions. "Now park your sorry butt until I say you can move." With that, he prowled back to the line, swinging his blade and rolling his shoulders.

Bal was visibly shaken. Jem looked at him and just shook her head, her body language oozing disappointment. "These people just saved your life. You were so close. And they saved you. Not just them"—again she pointed to my beautiful kids—"but them too." Now she pointed to the Guards who had stepped in. "There is so much going on and you are still choosing to hide."

"It's not that easy, Jem. I want to see, but I... just can't."

I jumped into the conversation at that point. "Do you? Because right now, you've got to make a choice. You can either continue in the Dark, hiding, defenceless. Or, you can come into the Light, have your eyes opened and discover all that is around you, in store for you, what the Light—The Man—has planned for you." I pinned the aggravating man with my eyes. "There is a big battle coming and you are part of it. You can either sign up to the Light and fight, or you will lose everyone. You can keep this home"—I waved my arm to encompass his beautiful surroundings that were still the battle ground of Unseen warfare—"but you will be here alone. Because everyone else will be gone." Gone somewhere else, or dead, hadn't been revealed to me. So I left the interpretation hanging for him to decipher.

"But out there"—he pointed in the general direction of the main gate—"is dangerous. They want to hurt me. Kill me."

"All around you, in here, are things that are extraordinarily dangerous, that want to, and can, hurt you. That want to, and can, kill you. That want to, and can, devour your immortal soul. Would you rather stumble through this minefield blindfolded, uninformed, unprotected, unaware? Or would you rather see what faces you, and learn how to protect yourself"—I looked to Jem—"and others." I gave him my best Mamma Bear glare. "You've had three years to hide. Now it is time to choose: blindness and death, or Light and life. Your time is up." The shock of what he'd just put my kids through was starting to hit home. The frustration at his indecision was wearing my grace thin. "And if you ever..."—it was a growl, no denying it—"endanger my kids again, you can add me to the list of dangerous things that can and will harm you."

Raph stood at Jem's shoulder, both their eyes constantly scoping the periphery. My darling boy cloaked in violet, Jem in a beautiful pink. A Guard stood behind each of them, also at attention, swords drawn, ready to defend.

From the depths of Jem's eyes, awash with tears of joy, a glow of peace encased her form. "Please, Bal. Please say yes to Him."

47

BALASHKA: A NEW LOOK

*Y*es, well, here we are. Apparently, my time is up. Or so that horrid woman suggests. My goodness, what an obstinate family. Even if one was feeling charitable, one could not find many redeeming characteristics about them. They are pushy, invasive, aggressive and... well, alright, generous. They have supplied us with much help and not asked for anything in return. I will grant them that.

Everyone had gone home and the residents of my garden were all safely tucked up in their cabins sheltered behind my walls. But I couldn't quite put to rest what had happened this evening. I sat in the open doorway of my shed, overlooking my haven. I could just make out some lights dotted on the plain below. And, of course, I had a front row seat to the starry host above.

There is no doubt about the change this whole business has brought about in Jem. And that is encouraging. She obviously trusts them enough to share her identity with them. And I will admit, to see her in that spectacular armour is impressive. And... encouraging? Yes. Encouraging. If there is something out there, I want her safe. Yet, one feels one is being left behind. She is moving on without me. And this makes me feel... lonely and isolated again.

But... is it true? Are there things I can't see more dangerous than those I can? Surely I have done my bit. I have built this place, and offered it to any who want to partake of its offerings. I have paid back. I supply and protect and provide. What more is there to do? What more could you possibly want?

"I want you safe, Balashka." The Man walked out of the shadows and joined me in the vacant camp chair. He looked to the heavens and smiled. Then looked back to me. "As you are, you are neither in nor out. You stand in the doorway. You can see partially, but not in whole. You have received some part of the gift"—He pointed to my hip—"but not the whole. You have part protection"—He looked over my shoulder and nodded at my Guard—"but not the whole." He leaned on His elbow bringing His face a tad closer to mine. "And I will answer you this, Balashka. There are things you cannot see that are far more dangerous than those you can. The Darkness prowls, longing to devour you. But I have stayed his hand. And you must make your choice."

We both looked over the scene set before us. The expanse, the endless night, the pinpricks of light in the night sky mirrored by lights sparkling on the plain. And all of a sudden, I felt very small and vulnerable. One was feeling the depth of one's mortality and frailty.

I turned back to The Man and asked, "What must I do?"

The warmth of His smile lit my soul like a cheery fire: warm, jolly and comforting. He simply said, "Say yes."

And yet, I knew it was not simple, I didn't know what I was signing "yes" too. I wanted to see the contract, to have my lawyers go over the fine print and discern the loopholes, to be guaranteed a cooling-off period.

Again The Man leaned in close. "Balashka, do you trust me?"

With no control, a stream of images and memories flickered through my mind like an old fashioned movie reel. I was recalling His presence and His presents. I was recalling His visits, His patience. His encouragement, His healing, His peace. He had offered me healing and peace for all the wrongs I had done. The ability to be free from the guilt. What could I say but, "Yes."

"Balashka"—His eyes burned to my inner depths: to my secret places—"Do you love me?"

Tears came to my eyes unbidden. I had nowhere to hide. I had wronged Him, yet He had forgiven me: a wretch; a thief; a liar. He knew my truth and still He loved me. "Yes."

"Balashka, will you follow Me?"

A lump in my throat had made it literally impossible to speak. I was having a hard enough time breathing. I could hardly see a thing through the tears, so I nodded. *Yes.*

"So be it." Light flashed as He stood. He leaned over and kissed the top of my head. "Be at peace, My son. You are loved."

And then He left me. Disappeared. Not that I really noticed. The lilac armour encasing my body had my full and undivided attention.

48

KAITLYN: POINTY END

Val's voice still held authority despite the whisper-growl. "Listen up, everyone, and calm down. Yes, the Gerent is coming, and yes, you guys have trackers. But no one has done anything worthy of being on his, or anyone's, radar. You have been working to help those people the city ignored… outside the wall. They may be his citizens, but they aren't officially citizens of Sardis."

She looked at Tessa. "You had one run-in with the Guild. But there is no proof that you did anything wrong. They're not going to complain that a slip of a girl escaped from a dog crate in the heart of the building, whilst a feast was going on. It will only make them look more stupid."

We all sat at one of the tables of the Undercover Area at Bal's place, sipping coffee. We'd finished our morning sets and Val had snuck away from her routine for an emergency meeting. We didn't have time for niceties. She'd placed herself in great danger to meet with us and deal with the very real threat that was bearing down on us like a herd of stampeding buffalo. I figured we were all on edge because none of us could forget what the man had done. Or his reach throughout the Seven Cities. Or his utter insanity. Or the fact that three of our kids were on his radar.

"All you can do is"—the signal became blotchy for a moment before coming back online—"keep petitioning the Light, keep your heads down and noses clean. Be 'good citizens'. Basically, do what we're called to do, help those who need it, teach those who will hear it, and love everyone." With her hands on her hips, Val grinned to the lot of us. "Easy."

"How are you going, dear heart? Are you okay? Any word on your release date yet?" My arm was linked through Marcus's and I pulled him a bit closer. I still hadn't got over, or used to, my sister being in prison. I knew it could be a lot worse. She was treated well. She was given a lot of liberties—even allowed to teach others self-defence. As was the only way she knew, Val had also been sharing the truth about the Light and as a result had been bringing those ladies into relationship with Him. She had a group of women she was mentoring and over the past eight months they had been growing in the Light.

She was fit, healthy, fed and safe. I had nothing to be worried about, but I missed her, and it still stuck in my craw that Achan had set the trap and encouraged the Community of Light to betray her. Then scarpered before I could get my hands on him. I couldn't afford to think about that too much, however. It tended to get me overly riled, and that was not good for anyone. The Light had her, the Light knew what was going on, and the Light had a plan.

"Kait." Val called me back from my musing.

I looked up at the flickering image projected by the ShellCom. "Yes?"

She gave me one of her looks, the one eyebrow raised, eyes boring into me. I couldn't help but laugh. She responded, "I said, my release date has been brought forward to two weeks' time." Unbidden tears flooded my eyes and emotion stole my voice. Thankfully I wasn't required to speak as she continued, "Nothing concrete yet, but it's looking good. I will be out just in time for the Gerent's visit." A nasty gleam shadowed her eyes.

"What? What are you planning, Val? Please don't take him on. Please don't start something with him just when you're out." I knew it was the wrong response. It was more likely to get her back up than anything else.

Her face softened, but just as she went to speak, the image gave out altogether. I gasped and a few others cried out. "Is it the battery?" It was a question aimed at no one in particular.

Al was the only one who offered an answer. "I guess we'll just have to wait and see if she can get back in touch later."

We spent time petitioning the Light about what lay ahead of us, His plans, opportunities and priorities for us. We petitioned Him for Val's safety and that the ShellCom could hang on for a little bit longer. And above all, that we might be aligned and prepared for what was in store. In my head and heart, I was mostly preoccupied with what He wanted for us for this upcoming visit. What part, if any, we would play. And... *oh, Lord, please let my babies be okay.*

* * *

WHILST THE CONFERENCE room at Black & Light Tower was still suitable for Gatherings of the True Community of Light, it was not ideal for morning sets. On the other hand, the garden Molly had created in Bal's Haven was simply stunning and the perfect place for us to start the day. Thankfully, since we weren't reliant on Pods, it didn't take us long to drive here along empty streets.

And as was His gracious and perfect way, we were outside the eastern wall of the city. We were gifted with the most amazing sight as the sun rose over the plain below. So, surrounded by stunning scenery, we soaked up serenity via the sound of the waterways and the scent of the dew-laden flowers, as we witnessed the Light display his wonder again for us this morning.

As the day brightened, and colour emerged from the predawn light, Raph broke into the post-set peace. "What is that in the bushes over there?"

We all turned and looked at the stark white fabric exposed through the burst garbage bag. Both Jem and Bal froze, then looked to each other. Bal was the first to break the silence. "If you will excuse me, I will be back shortly. Please begin the next phase of the morning's program without me. I won't be long."

He marched over to the bag, took photos with his phone, then pulled a fresh garbage bag and disposable gloves from his pocket and proceeded to collect the offending material.

We all just looked at each other, before most of our group broke off to join him. I stayed with the twins and Jem. From where we stood, I couldn't hear the conversation, but the body language spoke volumes. Marcus and Dan started helping Bal, while the other three were appalled. It was Dan who stopped, explained, then finished helping. Shortly after, Tessa came back as the other four helped Bal carry the bags up through the garden.

Tessa spoke to Jem. "So this happens often, then?"

Jem's eyes were still focused on the path joining the garden to the main area. She nodded.

"Well, that is… just… all kinds of… wrong."

Jem nodded again as a brokenness claimed her body.

Even though summer was officially upon us, the mornings were still fresh. Bal kindly let all of us from Black & Light Tower meet in his shed for morning coffee after sets… and the clean-up detail had returned. With the comfort of the known—family, routine, hot drinks —the discomfort started to thaw.

Bal reached over to pat Jem's hand.

She looked at him. "She knows I'm here. She's found me."

Alarm bells rang in my head. She had said this before, and I hadn't the time or space to inquire what she had meant. I knew this child had been hunted for a while now, and this had been her hideout, her safe place. She had been so brave, but now her walls, facade and bravado crumpled like wet tissue paper.

"She's getting ready for the High Feast." I was confident Jemmy knew she was surrounded by a wall of armour, both ours and the Guards. But her journey had brought her to a place of trust, or maybe the weariness of the chase had worn her defences down. We all sat enthralled, rapt, held captive by her tale.

However, I suspect she was only really aware of Balashka, who had positioned himself in front of her, faithful Sweetie at his feet. "My mother did something to offend Artemis. I don't know what. But, knowing my mother, she probably declared she was a better hunter than the goddess." Jemmy stopped, looked around her at the Guard, her brow furrowed, and she looked to me. "Are there other gods?"

"No, sweetheart, there is the Light and then there is the imitator: the Dark Lord. He comes in many guises and imitates whomever he must, to bait his hook with honey and draw his victims away from the Light."

"An oracle told Mother that she had offended Artemis, and she would have no victories in her pursuit of success because she had angered the goddess. Mother was broken and begged Artemis for forgiveness. The oracle came back and said there was only one thing she would accept, and that was the sacrifice of her daughter.

"Dad would never have allowed it. But Mum tricked him. She had me bound, drugged and was preparing me"—she indicated the scars on her upper arms—"for sacrifice in the medical room. The only thing that saved me was she was still recovering from a frenzied worship session of Dionysus and was still partly out of her tree. I wasn't properly tied up and, as I came back to my senses, I had an idea of what was going on. She'd already started bleeding me. Draining my energy. The blood was an offering to one god, my life was to be an offering to another. I'm sure if she could have figured out how to use some other part of me to gain favour with any other god, she would have done that too.

"Dad found out and barged in. He was furious. Even in my drugged state, I was aware of his rage. He started undoing my straps. But he didn't think about the crowd. Or Mum. Maybe he wasn't thinking at all." Jem was quiet again for a while. No one breathed or moved, waiting for her to continue.

"Someone grabbed him from behind. There was a fight, and... yelling. Mum was there. I remember them having an all-in row in the midst of an Artemis orgy." She looked up to Bal. "They just went from one bender to the next. A madness crawl. He'd never liked the scene. Stayed well away. But then, even in their crazed state, the crowd became aware something was happening. And that's when they came for him." Huge tears rolled down her face and her voice dropped to a whisper as she continued, "They dragged him away. All I can remember is him disappearing into a heightened crowd that were salivating and baying for blood.

"I can remember the struggle within my head. The fog made everything so hard. I had to get away. I had to save my dad. But the most important thing... I had to get free." Jem's fingers traced the raised scars on the inside of her upper arms. "I finished what he started and dragged my wounded, weakened body out of there and hid in the shadows. I had enough awareness to bind my wounds well enough not to bleed out. First thing I did was make my way to the outer wall. I found an abandoned home and crashed. From there, I wove my way up to the Shelter, got cleaned up and started my new life.

"She's been looking for me ever since. I never saw my father again and suspect she offered him in my place. But I don't think Artemis was impressed. I keep a watch on the Guild Hall and temples. Over the years I have found places to hide in the eaves and in the wings. When they are in the madness, I listen. I watch. And now I know. Each year, girls go missing. And it'll continue. Artemis rejects the offering, because it is not me.

"My mother is convinced she will never have success in anything until she finds me and gives me up to the goddess. That's what she's doing. She's bleeding her hostage. Preparing them for the sacrifice. Someone else's daughter will be taken and killed in my place. I hate it, but I just can't make myself step in to save them."

Her desperation grew and the bile in my stomach bubbled over. How could this woman do such a thing. How could she put her success, her pride, her dreams above her child.

Then an arrow pierced my heart, because I knew I was guilty of the same thing. I had allowed my kids to suffer when I had chased my dreams of being a mother. Of having a baby. The Light had been gracious in showing me the error of my ways and allowing me a second chance. So too had my kids and husband. And yet, even though I could admit guilt, I could not relate to this woman's crime.

Now that Jem had released her truth like lancing a boil, Bal looked to the girl, his face a checkerboard of emotion. "Well, my dear girl, I am grateful that you have finally trusted me... us... with your story. You are an extraordinary human being. But we already knew that." He smiled at her and she dropped her head. "But I am not sure you have been discovered. We've known for years that people are too lazy to make their way to the new dump site. And, like human beings the world over, people do like dropping things from a great height."

He paused until she looked at him. "I don't think she's found you. I think they know they can get away with it. This has been happening for months. The police know, and nothing has been done about it." He then looked to his cold cup. "I do believe that it is a case of, 'if it ain't broke, don't fix it'. Whomever is doing this has the perfect system. They drop their garbage into our garden. I take it to the drop-off point for the police. They sweep it under the carpet."

Bal lifted his eyes, addressing us all, his drink still now that his hands had stopped shaking. "We each do our bit to pretend it isn't happening. That no one is getting hurt. That people aren't getting hurt or dying. That the depravity of religion is perfectly acceptable." His new lilac armour glowed despite his pallid face. "And I'm one link in their chain." These last words were a tear-laden whisper.

"It has to stop. I have been trying to protect my family"—he gulped —"my safety. But the cost is unacceptable. I have been trying to change. To turn my life around. To pay back. But, in truth, I am doing exactly the same thing I was convicted of years ago." A heavy, pregnant void overtook the conversation. No one breathed or moved.

Please help this man. Please show us what we can do here.

"I have to... I need to... I..." He looked around the group, totally lost. "I don't know what to do. I just know I have to do something. But..."

It was Al who broke the silence. "You're not alone, Bal. That's what this whole Light adventure is about."

Cissa continued, "We're here, and so too is the Light and His

Warriors. You're His now and you are never alone. You are one of many and, thankfully, He calls the shots. Not us." A huge grin I was coming to expect from this beautiful woman turned our focus back where it should be. Not on defeat, but on how to fight our way through this next challenge.

I looked to my husband, our new friends and my children. "Bal, first thing we do is petition the Light. I cannot imagine He would not have something for us to do in this situation, but first we must seek His protection for us and the victims of this ritual, wisdom for what to do, and guidance on how to go about it."

49

CONTESSA: OWNING THE BRAND

S o I was on babysitting detail again.

But not.

The procedure was to meet the twins at TAVE, call at home to collect Tiger, then catch another Pod to The Wreckage.

I mean to say, the twins were completely capable of doing that by themselves. But to be honest, I spent most of my time wandering around that place searching for inspiration. And, when I looked at the people I wanted to serve, all I could come up with was more of the same as what I was doing in Philadelphia.

But at The Wreckage, no one was earning money. I mean, I had some money from what I'd sold online, but with no income to buy new stuff, I had nothing to sell. So my next problem... after digging inspiration out of thin air, was to figure out how I was going to finance the flopping thing.

So, taking a break from bashing my head against a brick wall, I had volunteered to meet Raph and Riah and travel back with them outside the wall, where the contrast was all kinds of wrong. The wealth and beauty of this city was seriously crazy. It may even have outshone Laodicea. Actually, I totally felt it outshone Laodicea. Everything was beautiful, well-designed, golden.

Except the people.

They were seriously freaky.

I couldn't escape the memory of that horrible night with the Guild. It was jumping all over this beautiful day with its nasty fingers, trapping me back in my regular self-loathing spiral, when I was crash-tackled by my sister. Seriously, for a kid who was so graceful and light on her feet, she could be such an oaf—I hugged her—and tall. "When did you get so tall?" I pulled out of our embrace and really looked at her. "And gorgeous?" And... Oh. My. Word... Womanly. It just occurred to me, Sariah had more curves than I did. And I was twice as old as her.

Talk about an extra shove down the self-loathing spiral.

But then a sprinkling of golden stardust peaked out of a paper shopping bag. "What are they?"

Jem, who more often than not hung out with the twins, froze mid-stride, like I had shot her with a stun gun. "What? Nothing? Why?"

I couldn't hide the tremor of excitement as I drew closer to the bags.

"They're nothing." Jem spoke over my shoulder, I'm assuming to Raph. "What's wrong with her. Make her stop." She thrust the bags behind her back and stood tall, stopping me short of my goal. "Are you judging me... us? So what if we shop at charity shops?"

Out of the corner of my eye I noticed Riah shaking with laughter as Raph came running over to explain. "Tessa, you cannot have those. They are for the people at Bal's." As the cold water of disappointment rained on my parade, Raph explained to Jem, "Tessa is not judging you. She just has not had the chance to go charity shopping for a long time. It is what she loves the most."

He went on to explain, but I wasn't listening. I was trying to get a look at what treasure she had in those bags. "So, um, do you use all of them?" I tried to sound professional—in my head I was imitating Cissa—and not behave like an obsessed addict. "And, if not, what do you do with the ones you don't use?"

Jem had calmed down and dropped her defences. "After I let the guys pick through and take what they want, I just take the leftovers back."

"Do they return your money?"

"What? No! It's a charity shop. We donate it back. It's not like it cost us... Bal, much in the first place."

"So do you think that I might be able to look through your leftovers? Before you return them? I would be so grateful." She looked at me like I was every inch the obsessed tripper I was. Begging for second—third-hand clothing.

When Jem looked to be sizing me up, Riah rolled her eyes and gave the girl a bit of a shove. Jem grinned and held out her hand. "Deal."

I tried to cling to the wafer-thin facade of cool, calm cucumber for the ride back to the worksite and not overwhelm the girl with questions such as, "Where do you buy your stock? How often do you go? What's your selection criteria? What's your budget?" And most importantly, "Can I come with you?"

* * *

So it turns out there are certain things all people need to survive: food, water, warmth, safety and security. My wonderful husband and dad, with their humongous team, were working on that. But once those things were taken care of, I read that people also needed to feel like they belonged, that they were part of something and have something to contribute to the group. They needed friends and to feel valued.

I had been doing study and research for my assignment for Cissa. Now I had access to clothing I could alter, I'd moved my sewing machine and equipment to Bal's. Using one of the short-term, vacated shelters brought over from Sanctuary, I was making uniforms.

Yes, uniforms.

But not boring ones.

And not ones that all looked the same.

I mean, you could identify they all belonged to the same group.

But everyone's was different.

Each afternoon, after TAVE, Raph, Riah and I had been meeting up with the kids from The Wreckage and we'd been working on a "beat band", I guess you'd call it. To be part of the band, you had to bring some object to hit that made a good sound and didn't previously belong to someone else. And, you had to sign up to having a uniform made.

Glee.

Utter glee.

I only made tops.

But everyone loved them.

Even the kids who pretended they didn't want to belong at the beginning.

Since I had to start with cast-offs from Jem's shopping, one of the main colours available was green. After that there was a lot of fluoro and florals. I had never been a fan of fluoro, and I didn't even want to ask these boys in the group to wear floral.

So, we had a vote.

And fluoro it was.

Every member was offered a shirt—long or short-sleeved—or a vest. The greens were different but I only picked matching hues of beautiful forests or jades. Then, each item had our icon of three sets of crossed drumsticks sewn into the garment, with the client's choice of fluoro colour and placement: front or back.

Raph, Riah and I also wore them. Now when everyone showed up for practice, they wore their tops. As we sat in a circle—fourteen of them and the three of us—we could all see that we belonged. And, as we each hit our "drum", and some of us sang, we could see we were part of something bigger and each of us played a part. Added to this, when we started to sound good, the kids noticed and the smiles grew, and chests puffed.

Yay.

Just... yay.

I was so happy.

I had taken photos and video of our Beat Band to show Cissa at our next meeting. I think she was going to be as stoked as I was.

Brief met.

Check.

And what was even better, each kid loved their uniform and treated it really well. So, when Jem offered to take them back to Bal's to wash, I almost cried with gratitude. So did some of the kids, even though they tried to hide it. I knew from a lifetime of experience, I couldn't even attempt to hide my emotions. But that was okay. It took the focus off those other kids who didn't feel safe enough to cry in public. Even happy tears.

Like Jem.

Her complexion helped her hide tears, which she didn't do well when she was voted in as an honorary member. She wouldn't sing or beat a drum, but she brought fruit and raw veggie snacks over for afternoon tea every day... with some of her friends—the residents from Bal's. Turns out that some of them also wanted to be in our band. Which was the coolest thing ever.

So, not only did I make them uniforms, I made Jem one too. A beautiful, fitted, classically styled top, with bright sapphire-blue details of our logo—which sat on her left shoulder blade—to bring out the blue in her eyes, and the tint in her hair, and which really set off the most gorgeous baby-pink of her armour. This girl really was a stunner.

And also, a very curvy teen.

But that was okay.

My husband loved my figure.

And me.

He even loved my hair!

And, the world needed sveltes as well as curvy women.

Because no one could wear a shift dress like a svelte.

ALARIO: HOPE IN HELL

I t was almost Festival of Feasts and, as was the same the world over, everyone took a week's holiday for the opportunity to drink deep and swim without conscience in the ocean of salaciousness that was world religion. Here in Sardis, there would be a temple crawl, a full day attending to each of the local gods at their "home base". All that was required of the fickle worshippers was to put off their sense of decency and indulge fully in whichever depravity the deity deemed suitable for their worship. As was the tradition, the Procession of Festivals started off with the tamest of the lot, Artemis. Then worked their way around to the most obscene, Dionysus.

Not only did the Gerent fully endorse this holiday season, he funded it. Each year he would visit one of the Seven Cities and lavish his minions with illicit treats and excessive amounts of food and alcohol. All in the name of "public wellbeing". Or in other words, "purchasing popularity". And lucky us, this was Sardis's year.

Naturally, this had the city in an uproar. Those in favour of our Overlord's visit were salivating at the bit, ready to sacrifice more of their decency. Those not in favour, i.e., our lot, were turning themselves inside out with concern. Because, obviously, not only did we have to deal with the heightened demonic activity during the weeks leading up to and following the event—and the event itself—we also had to be on guard against the Dark's greatest puppet of this era: the Gerent.

Cissa and I were home from our latest visit to Ephesus, and were in the process of pausing and/or closing out accounts for the holiday. I had been surprised how much I'd missed the early morning meetings with our Philly friends whilst we were away. So much so, Cissa and I talked of getting our own ShellCom, and asking if we could join in when we couldn't be here in person. Even though we could write it off as a work expense, it would still cost a fair bit. And this year our "business expenses" had taken a beating. And now we were persona non grata due to our public allegiance to the Light. It was turning into a very tight season.

A sharp pinch to my thigh had me coming back to the early morning meeting at that interesting fellow, Balashka's, place. I didn't have to look to my wife to know she was glaring at me. I could feel the weight of it like it was her sword tip pressing into my temple. I patted her leg. I knew it came across as patronising. But I feigned nonchalance for two reasons: one, not to draw attention to the fact I'd slipped out of the conversation; and two, the response it garnered was a gift that just kept on giving. Regardless of how good our marriage was, and how far we'd come, some things, like getting under my wife's skin, never grew old.

I smirked, she growled, and Dan continued. "Jem, did you say that your mum would offer a girl? During the Festival?" The child nodded. Dan looked to my wife and me, then continued, "And you say, typically, the Community of Light is too blind to realise how warped that is and agrees to participate?" I assumed there had been some discussion about the whole festival and not just human sacrifice, so I gave a wry smile and nodded. He continued, "Has our True Community of Light received an invitation to participate yet?"

Cissa said, "Not yet. I believe we have been labelled 'does not play well with others.'"

"Can we get an invitation?" At the look of disgust on everyone's face, Dan ploughed on. "We need a reason to be there, and we need a cover." He looked around the group. "If we can think of something we could contribute to the festival's performances, everyone will see us in the crowd, on stage, working around the edges. It will appear we are trying to 'get along.'"

Cissa looked to me, I shrugged. I had no idea. She answered Dan, "I believe there are standing invitations to all religious codes. There are two main events for the week: the opening and the grand finale at the Theatre. I can check with Albert and confirm our invitation if that would help? And since we're such late entries, it's likely we could get a spot at the beginning of the week. They're less coveted."

Jem piped up, "How will that help us stop my mother and save the girl? If she's still alive."

Balashka had been doing a good job of keeping Jem not completely aware of the situation. From what we'd seen in those garbage bags, the mission wasn't to keep people alive, it was to stop more being killed.

Dan's face was obliterated by a smile. "Because we will not all be performing, schmoozing and being pleasant little decoys. A few of us will be behind the scenes, getting the job done."

Silence stole the conversation. I assumed everyone was doing the same as me, which was, imagining that situation. What it would look like. How we would carry it off and... how absolutely, ridiculously dangerous it would be. Especially for those behind the scenes. They wouldn't have the whole team to help.

Kait's sigh slipped into the silence. "If only Val was here. I would feel one hundred percent better if she could be part of it."

Tessa spoke up. "But she will be. Don't you remember? Her time is almost up. She gets out next Sunday."

We all just stared at her and I could not hold back the obvious fly in that lovely ointment. "But the Festival begins next Saturday."

Tessa shook her head. "But it goes for a whole week. We don't have to go in there all kinds of commando on day one. Maybe we could ask for a spot at the closing celebration."

The girl was right and Cissa, as was her way, spoke my thoughts. "If we spend the week playing along, but not too politely—we don't want to draw suspicion by having a complete change of heart—then we could build up a false sense of security."

The group was silent and heads were nodding. We were on to something and I could feel a plan permeating between the great minds in the garden.

"But my mother's debt is to Artemis. Her celebration kicks the whole thing off at the beginning of the week. Your friend won't be in time for that."

There may have been a few whispered curse words. Or it could just have been the yell of mine bouncing around inside my head.

"Truth be, like paddles in a canoe, Val's a preferred addition to the adventure. But we'll just have to go ahead without her. 'Cause you can bet your bippy, the Light'll be with us if this is where He wants us."

We spent the next hour petitioning the Light, discussing possibilities and drinking coffee. A completed plan had not been nailed down by the end of our time. But there was a confidence that this was one of the main purposes the Light had been preparing us for.

What if we could not only stop the hideous practice of human sacrifice for the Festival, but put an end to it permanently? With or without Val, we had the Light. He was the key to this mess, and the answer.

51

ALARIO: CLASH OF TITANS

W e'd been told the dress code was smart casual, whatever that meant, but I had showered and changed after work and driven Cissa down to Balashka's garden. Marcus and Kait came with us. Dan and Tessa drove Sariah. Her twin was already there helping with the food.

When we arrived at the gates, we were met by some of the local characters and some waifs. All of whom were clean, dressed in button downs or dresses. And had shoes on. A teen with tied-back sandy hair and a green shirt with some kind of design over the top of his left shoulder approached my open window. "Good evening. Welcome to our Garden Gala. Could I please see your tickets?"

Tickets? I didn't have tickets. I was about to share this awkward bombshell when Kait leaned forward and offered me four slips of paper. In the light of the kid's torch, I could see each was decorated with crazy colours and designs, nothing matched or made sense. The boy reached in, took the "tickets" and said, "Please park to the left by the washrooms. We hope you enjoy the evening."

I muttered my thanks, then followed the fairy lights around to the carpark. The place had been transformed. The main area was decorated with lights, flowers, and paper chains. Flood lights from the

Undercover Area and the food truck lit up the place to reveal a makeshift stage. The bank leading up to Bal's shed was populated with blankets and towels placed in shallow arcs.

Another kid, also wearing a green shirt, approached as we walked to the Undercover Area. The same logo decorated the bottom right side of her hem. I noticed Cissa nodding. "Clever girl. Nice work." I thought she was talking to the teen, but then she dropped my arm and waited for Tessa to catch up. "I am impressed."

Tessa didn't say a word, but the beaming of her eyes said it all. She'd won Cissa's approval and that meant something.

The kid waited till the seven of us had come together, then offered us some food and drinks laid out on a table. "One of our ushers will show you to your places. The show will begin soon." She squealed, did a bit of a jig, hugged Tessa, then ran away.

"At the risk of sounding like a complete fool"—it was inevitable—"I was wondering if someone could please explain what this is all about?"

Before anyone could answer me, a man in his mid-thirties approached, accompanied by a woman dressed in a clash of layered fluorescent Lycra. The woman was waving a piece of fabric like a flag. It often obscured her face, and when it did we were able to see glimpses of a green fabric sash sitting across her left shoulder and wrapping around her right hip. Where it crossed her chest, the same logo in multi-coloured fluoro was revealed.

The man spoke. "Good evening. My name is Aran, and this is Cheryl. We will show you to your places."

Drinks in hand, we followed the frolicking rainbow woman who was tethered to our usher, Aran.

Kait explained, "As you know, a few kids in the Beat Band will be filling one of our allocated spots for the Festival of Feasts' opening concert. It has been hard to explain to the residents here that it is too dangerous for them to join us. They would be too vulnerable and overwhelmed by it all. So, tonight is their night to perform and have their time in the spotlight in a safe space."

In the distance, Balashka was speed-walking between groups

milling in the Undercover Area, flitting from one hub to the next. Sweetie valiantly trying to keep up.

Raphael came jogging up the hill, hugged everyone, and took Dan, Tessa and Sariah away. Once they'd left, Kait continued, "It's also an opportunity for the kids from The Wreckage to have a dress rehearsal in front of an audience."

I looked around at the number of people sitting on the hill. I was surprised there were so many who knew about this place. Then, I was stopped in my tracks before leaning over to Cissa to say, "Is that Harry?" I didn't know anyone else who drove a green Jag.

Before she could answer, there was a call of "Pretty. Pretty. Pretty." from somewhere in the garden. A man dressed completely in green flew to the car, draped himself over the boot and started stroking it. I didn't know which was more surprising: seeing Cissa's brother here, the green man's behaviour, or the way Harry ignored the fellow stroking his car.

Harry's mosey and mingle through the residents and up the slope indicated that, not only was he known here, he was well-known. Fluorescent Woman gushed over him and Cat Woman head-butted his arm. He took it all in his stride, until he saw us.

"Didn't think this'd be big enough for one of your crusades, Cissy?"

"Didn't think there was enough cash here to draw your interest, Harry?"

He leaned down and kissed her cheek. "Darling, what on earth are you doing here?"

She clung to him and simply said, "Ditto."

Balashka interrupted their reunion. "Do you know each other?" Irrelevant question, really. When they stood side-by-side it was hard to conceive they weren't twins. When they didn't respond, but both looked at him with the same "what do you think?" expression, Balashka laughed and relaxed. But then looked at the siblings again. "Why don't you have armour?"

Harry pursed his lips and shook his head. "You've not joined the nutters, have you, Bal? Here I was, thinking, despite it all, you had a modicum of sense."

Our host was confused, his doubt bouncing between Cissa, me, Kait and Marcus—who remained seated behind us—and Harry. He looked down at his own lilac armour. "Nutter?"

Harry flopped to the ground, swivelled and stuck his hand out for a brief introduction to Kait and Marcus, then looked up at Balashka. "You know, those folk like my darling sister who get their knickers in a knot about... religion."

"Religions, Harry. All of the religions that hurt people."

"See? She's both relentless and intolerable." Harry winked at my wife and she shook her head. It was a lifelong argument.

"But, Harry, she's righ—"

"We'd like to welcome you all to tonight's performance, the inaugural Balashka's Garden Gala." Dan's voice through the portable speakers interrupted their conversation.

A round of applause and cheers broke out from the gathering around us. There were parents and young children dressed in very simple, ragged clothes. But before Dan could continue, Sariah stepped forward from where she and a group of kids were waiting on the edge of the "stage" and tapped Dan's shoulder. She tilted her head to indicate the car that had just arrived.

A man raced from the car, high-fived Sariah, and made his way up the slope, post-haste. He shook Bal and Harry's hands and whispered to the group we were with, "Sorry I'm late. What have I missed?"

"Nothing so far, my friend." With a vague wave in our general direction, Balashka made the introductions. "Everyone this is Gerald. Gerald this is everyone."

After that, there were no more interruptions, and we were treated to a most entertaining evening of music. To begin with, Dan, Tessa, Sariah and Raph performed a few songs with guitars and drums. Then some of the older kids joined them with home-made maracas, tambourines and boxes.

Perhaps the most entertaining act followed. The stage was cleared and all the kids who'd been sitting on the hill with us, and a number of residents from Bal's garden, raced to the stage, picked up all manner of boxes and formed a two-rowed semicircle. All ages, all sizes, all of them wearing some form of green tops with the same drumstick logo, somewhere. I had to admit, they looked great.

Then Raphael came out the front and faced the group. Sitting on a stool, he placed a bongo drum between his knees and led and controlled the whole group like a conductor. Some of the performers had no idea what they were doing. Some wore smiles, some were stern, but all of them, good or bad, were one hundred percent focused on Raph and what they were supposed to be doing.

The group performed three renditions of cacophonous noise, at the end of which, they received a standing ovation accompanied by cries and cheers and whistles. It was brilliant. Amazing. Definitely not perfect, but the look on the faces of the residents and kids was priceless.

With beaming smiles and quite a few tears, the bulk of the group were ushered off the stage and came back to join parents, carers, and guests on the hill. Then the five teenagers who would be performing at the Festival stayed on stage and arranged themselves with Dan, Tessa, Raphael and Sariah into one semicircle. Each could see the other, and we could see them all. Dan sat on one end, and quietly mumbled some words to the kids we couldn't hear. Then, after silence and a count of three, he led them.

They then proceeded to awe and amaze us with the rhythm and syncopation of their beating of old bins, boxes and bottles. They were in complete unison whilst beating complementary patterns. The different sounds they produced defied understanding. How could they achieve that sound with junk?

When they finished their set, there was silence. Stunned silence. The crew on the stage looked up, confused and, bit by bit, demoralised. Then cheering erupted. Most on the hill rushed the stage and embraced and backslapped the performers.

My jaw literally dropped. I couldn't believe it. They were amazing. I leaned over to Marcus. "How long did you say they'd been at this?"

Marcus had to clear his throat. "My lot, for a few years now. These new kids, only two months." He shook his head and wiped his eyes.

Kait took over, emotion making her voice a bit rough. "They practise hours every day. They have no school. They have no work. But now, they have this, and they have given it everything."

Marcus took over again, a bit more composed. "Once we're finished the first lot of huts, we're going to build a school space... with a music room."

"Are you lot responsible for what's happening across the road?" Harry couldn't keep out of the conversation any longer.

"Aye, me and the lad"—Marcus dipped his head to indicate Dan— "are building them homes. Me kids are teaching them music. Me daughter, Tessa, is making them clothes. And these two"—he dipped his head to me and Cissa—"are funding and inspiring the lot."

"Well, I wouldn't go that far," I interjected. "Cissa is mentoring Tessa since she was expelled from the Guild. And we're backing the project. But it's all these guys, really. They're the driving force."

Harry was silent then. Wheels visibly turning in his head. He turned to Balashka. "You're not suggesting this lot go to the Festival? They can't." He didn't say the words, but the implication hung in the air: *I won't let you.* In all the years I'd known Harry, I'd never seen him express so much... emotion, be so... agitated.

"My goodness, Harry. Are trying to tell me you care?" Balashka's voice was filled with laughter. I wondered if he understood just how important this was. "Of course we're not letting our family go to the Festival. This is what tonight is all about. They have been working so hard, and they don't understand why they can't go. So, we made tonight their big night."

"But those kids"—he looked to the stage where the performers still mingled—"you can't send them."

Our attention was drawn to the happy crowd. Jem and Raph had put all the food out, the girl walking through the group, embracing the residents, wearing her own version of their uniform.

"We have to, my friend." Balashka's voice was heavy and quiet. "All the parents and kids know the risks."

Harry turned on his sister with a fire I'd never seen. "This is all you, isn't it. You and your crusades... your fights... your bloody martyrdom, death wish." I was standing and ready to take him down with extreme force if needed. I was trying to get my blood to cool when Cissa took my hand and let Harry continue. "Well, it's all very well when it's just you who wants to go off and die on some bloody hill and abandon the rest of us alone to suffer. But this is too much. Even for you, Cissa. You can't endanger these kids like this."

"What do you know, Harry?" Cissa's reaction was like cold water over my head. Everyone else stilled, poised for the eruption that was certainly coming. I was grateful everyone was down the hill, celebrating. There was no way this wasn't going to be messy.

Please help us here.

Cissa pushed her brother a bit more. "What aren't you telling us, Harry? We know the Festival is disgusting, obscene and abhorrent. But why are you so angry?"

"Because you've been living in the dark for so long, you have no idea what's really going on. You go in there on your high and mighty horse, Cissa, people are going to get hurt."

"What if I do know what's going on? What if that's why we're doing this?"

The silence was suffocating. Harry was obviously aware of the situation. A nasty feeling pervaded my gut. "You haven't started worshipping at the temples, have you, Harry?" I didn't mean it to sound as threatening and ominous as it did. But if he was involved in what was being thrown over the walls here, he was going to pay.

"What? Are you insane? Of course I bloody haven't. But I have been helping Bal clean up the mess. I know who runs the show up there." He pointed to the top of the wall behind us. "And I know just how dangerous they are." I could finally breathe again. I didn't want to fight with him. But I would have. "I cannot let you do this." He spun to face Bal. "I won't let you do this. I will resign. Leave you to deal with all your skrat yourself."

Bal was a broken man. "I understand, Harry. I do. Thank you for all you've done for me. I couldn't have done it... I wouldn't be here without you."

"So you're really going to do this. Put these kid's lives in danger."

"I am ashamed to say that I *would* sacrifice the security of others.

That I would willingly… *knowingly* let them be in danger"—he inhaled deeply and exhaled raggedly—"because it's for Jem. It's to ensure her safety."

Again, the clear night seemed to intensify the silence, finally broken by Harry's declaration: "How can I help?"

52

RAPHAEL: FALSE START

I was walking a tightrope of nerves with a herd of cats pouncing in my belly. Even though Dan and Tessa were trying very hard to hide it, I could tell—the constant glances, slight nods and occasional grim smiles—they were feeling the same. Our new friends from The Wreckage either were not trying or could not hide it. It was their first real performance.

We were all very proud to be wearing the uniforms Tessa had made us. It helped us... me feel I was a small piece in a big jigsaw puzzle. They needed my tabs. Just like I needed their slots. I loved that our band was different, and I was proud that we made great music with our bins, boxes, lids, shakers and sticks.

Because we had only been able to get the one spot for the opening and another at the finale, we decided it would be safest to have the Beat Band perform tonight. Dan, Tessa, Riah and I alone would perform at the finale. It was just too dangerous to have Unseeing family around Dionysus celebrations.

My new friends made all the horrible things that had happened in Sardis less horrible. Not only did I really like them, I felt, in a small way, I was helping. Tessa, Riah and I had been able to be extra struts in the bridge between the two wonderful rivers of survivors at Bal's garden and The Wreckage. It made my heart sing. Together, they had become a raging river of possibilities.

I do not know what the outcome of tonight would be for them. I hoped it would be good. I mean, I knew the performance would be excellent. But how it impacted them afterwards…?

I felt my hand pumped twice and I looked to my sister. *Are you okay? You worried?*

I leaned in close and spoke quietly. "I am thinking about them." I tilted my head to our five new friends behind us. She already knew and understood my concerns.

She also understood how I was more concerned for what was going to be happening behind the scenes. We did not have a very long timeslot on stage. Would our family be safe? Would they find the sacrifices? Would they be able to save them and stop this happening again?

The walk around the outside of the bottom wall of Sardis, from the eastern gate to the Temple of Artemis, was good for our band members. It helped use up all their nervous energy. But it was not good for me. It just gave the red haze more time to get its claws into me.

I felt a double pump in my other hand and looked down to see Tessa smiling at me. She leaned up and kissed my cheek and fake-gravelled, "Love ya, kiddo," in a very bad imitation of Dad's voice. It broke some of the haze's hold. I wrapped my arm around her shoulders and drawled, "I love you too, dear heart." It was an even worse imitation of Mum. But it made everyone laugh and it helped break the hold even more.

And there it was. Lit up like a satellite, Artemis's temple and all its surrounding buildings. It was the biggest temple in… around Sardis, and even though it was not completely finished, it was the most spectacular. We had been here during the day, once. The day that changed our lives. When the Community of Light caused Val to be arrested. The memory made the cats in my stomach pounce harder. I knew there would be people from that morning, eight months ago, among the crowd. Would they recognise us? Would they have us arrested?

But then I remembered we were here to perform. We were not challenging anyone about the truth, we were here to save someone. Then a wave of rage started building. How dared they? How dared they masquerade as children of Light? How dared people of this city think they could take "strays" and use them for entertainment and as an offering to the Dark. Their arrogance and abuse reminded me of our beginning. All of it. Being sold, used, treated as possessions, and abused. My fury melted the fear icicles.

Please help us find those responsible so You can deal with them and stop this happening.

Once our lanyards had been approved by the attendant, he sent information and directions to our phones. We guided our friends to the "backstage" area in the grounds of the Temple. The building itself was too small to contain the crowd. A platform had been built, with huge curtains hung from scaffolding. Spotlights rotated in different colours, and drones flew overhead emitting upbeat music. There were big tents to the side and back of the stage with tables, chairs, lounges and portable bathrooms. There was a long wooden table stretched across the first tent with five people stationed behind computers.

Dan approached the lady who signalled us, and gave our name and act. We were sent a message on our phones that indicated we were permitted to be there. It was accompanied by a schedule for the night: the acts and the times. Across the top of the message, in flashing red, was a warning: "Do not be late. We will not wait." Then underneath: "Thank you for your participation. Enjoy the evening."

The lady pointed to a crowded area and said we were to wait with all the other acts, with another warning, "Don't wander. We won't come looking for you if you're not here."

Because our friends from The Wreckage did not have phones, Dan gave them a polite version of the instructions and told them we had about two hours before we went on. We were very close to the end of the concert. I heard through my earpiece, in our family chat, that Tessa had let Mum and Dad know when we were going on. She also sent them the program for the evening.

Now it was a matter of sitting in a crowd of made-up performers who were not interested in speaking to us. I was very glad we were wearing Tessa's uniforms: it made us look like we had a right to be there. Even though all the other people made it clear they did not agree. As did the swarm of demons who paraded around the crowd: backstage and out front. We were on their territory, and I hoped we did not have to battle before we went on. I did not think the organisers would like that.

Just as I thought it, an extra group of Warriors appeared and arranged themselves around us. It seemed the Light agreed.

Thank You.

53

JEMIMAH: RUG PULL

It was no coincidence that there was a full moon: The Festival of
Feasts was scheduled by it. The cloudless night was bright enough
that we wouldn't need torches. We'd be easy pickings for the moni-
toring drones otherwise. Most of the city was gathering in and
around the temple. Except us. We were attempting to sneak in
through the back door.

Cissa and Al—Harry's sister and brother-in-law. I still couldn't get
my head around that—dropped us off in Dan and Tessa's flash-as SUV
on their way down the mountain. It was like a super-cool movie.
There wasn't heaps of traffic using the outside road. Most people rode
Pods to the main gate then the buses round the outside of the wall to
the temple. Or rode the Sky-Rail from the Acropolis down the mountain. Its route followed the road we were on.

Acting like psyched-out tourists, Cissa and Al pulled over and
started taking photos as the Sky-Rail passed. Then they leaned on the
car and embraced as we—Raph's mum and dad, Bal and me—
scarpered out the other side of the car into the bush. All of us were in
black, but we weren't OTT. If we were caught in the wrong place, we
didn't want to look like spies, just misguided guests.

We hunkered low and waited till the car took off. The sound of

315

the crowds partying at the temple travelled up the side of the mountain. I didn't know about the others, but I was straining hard-as to hear anything close by. After about ten minutes, when there were no cars, no carriages overhead and no movement and no new sounds, I showed my crew a side track. It didn't take too long, maybe twenty minutes, and we were on the outer limits of the temple complex.

There was no public access here. I mean, you could walk around the back, but you had to pass all the "Private" signs and all, so it was obvious you weren't supposed to be here. Again, worked for and against us: less chance of getting caught, more chance of sticking out like sore thumbs.

Bal had bought me a phone and paired earpiece so I could be in touch with the others silently. I used to have a set, so it wasn't too hard to learn the updates and new features created in the last two years. But the "thought to voice message" function was mind blowing. And just a little bit freaky.

Jem: The first building is the acolyte dorm. Next is the kitchen, common room, medical room.

We sat in the shadows near the dumpsters that had given me cover on countless occasions. Kait and Marcus squatted side-by-side, Bal and I sat behind their shoulders. We tried to make ourselves comfortable 'cause it was too early to move yet. Might give Bal a chance to settle and stop shaking.

Kait: I've just received the schedule from Tessa. They're not on till near the end. Best we wait here until it gets well underway.

I knew they knew this already but was kind of compelled to remind them.

Jem: But the worship and sacrifice will be at the end. The grand finale, kind of thing. Not everyone will go, maybe just those in the know, but we got to be in and out before the end. Well before the end so we don't get caught by those doing the prep.

Marcus: Okay, kiddo. As soon as the oil has settled on the water, I'll scout about and check the lay of the land.

Jem: No, I'll do it.

Bal flicked his head around to me so fast, I'm surprised he didn't lose his earpiece.

It made me sick to say it, and I kind of wished I'd kept my fingers still. But the words were typed before I'd thought them through. They all stared at me.

Jem: I know this place really well. I know all the places they may have someone held captive. I will know what is different, if anything, and can then —I tapped my earpiece—*let you know.*

It was kind of nice the way they all started to protest at the same time. The three knew I was right, but I reckoned they were trying to protect me. Just made me like them even more. But theirs was a stupid idea.

Bal: No. No. No. No. Just... no.

Jem: I know this place better than you, don't I?

Bal glared at me. He hadn't stopped shaking, but I think it had transferred to fear for *me*... with a hint of anger.

But in the end, they couldn't argue with the truth, so we settled in for the wait.

Here's a life lesson I've learned to respect: when you're in the company of pros, watch and learn. I noticed, every so often, Marcus and Kait did this slow stretch thing. It was only noticeable because I was pretty much sitting in their laps. But I figured, if I wasn't so close, I wouldn't have seen it. Somehow, they managed to stay loose whilst they waited in hiding. Something I'd never mastered. So, I tried it myself. When Marcus saw my attempt, he sent me a few tips via text and explained the process. Good to know.

The crowd were singing along with one of the favourite local bands and the music was thumping and thrumming through my veins even from this side of the temple. I had my back against the acolyte dorm and was keeping to the shadows as I took the long way round the outside of the complex.

After a quick check of the medical rooms—where they, for some unknown reason, still kept tie-downs attached to the examination bed —I made my way to the heart of Artemis's temple. I reckoned they weren't going to keep a hostage in the common room, or the dormitories: priestesses' or acolytes'. The hard part was going to be keeping to the shadows once I was inside. The temple had few places to hide. But the gift horse in this scenario was the fact they had never got round to finishing the building. There were enough places—equipment, stone blocks, broken lines—to blend into.

A prisoner could be held anywhere, especially if they were drugged. But my guess was they'd be stashed somewhere close to the altar. And, lucky me, the altar was under the spotlight in the centre of the sandstone floor at the heart of the temple. It was so large you could hold a school dance in the space and not hit anything. It was going to take an act of God for me to get across there unseen.

Jem: So far, no sign. I'm in the temple. I need to get to the altar to check it out.

Both Marcus and Kait's messages came in at the same time.

Marcus: Do not proceed. Stop. We're on our way.

Kait: Sit tight, sweetheart. We'll be there soon. Please wait.

I don't think Marcus meant to transmit, but his whisper-bark at Bal came through anyway.

Marcus: Park your buttooshie. Now. You go in there all guns blazing, you'll compromise her safety. You are here as a lookout. Only. Understood?

There was silence, so I guessed it was understood.

Bal: Please be careful, my girl. Please.

Jem: Not going in with a song and a dance, now, am I?

Felt a bit bad after that. So added…

Jem: Will do, Bal. Thanks for coming. I know it was hard. I promise to be careful.

I looked over my shoulder and checked my Guard was still with me. I sat behind the last huge pillar before the expanse between me and the altar. I took a moment to revel in my armour. Not that I would confess this to anyone, but I super loved the baby pink.

Thanks. Also, any chance You could kind of help me across the floor? I really want to be brave. I really want to make sure no one is going to be hurt tonight.

I was mid-breath, readying myself for the dash, when ice froze my blood.

"Well, aren't you an interesting fellow." Mother.

My body started trembling.

"Hello. Hello. Hello." Frack! Richard.

"That's an interesting shirt you're wearing. It reminds me of... let me think."

"Hello. Hello. Hello. Pretty."

"Why, thank you."

Here's a life lesson I've learned to respect: Panic will give you away faster than you could play *Viva La Sardis* on the kazoo. I'd been in this boat before. It was time to chew on some home truths: I hadn't been discovered yet; I had time to think; not much, but enough.

I tried to slow my breathing down.

Curling my body around the pillar, I fought to hold the bile back. Mother was wearing a green gown in honour of the great huntress. To Richard, it was honey to his green bee. "Pretty. Pretty. Pretty."

I snapped back behind the pillar and managed to fire off a message before I slid to the floor.

Jem: Richard is here! So is Mother. They're both in the temple.

Mother's voice took on an ugly air. "Ahh, there, there, dear fellow. You can look, but you can't touch." From years of experience, I knew this tone was the indicator of imminent punishment.

"Pretty. Pretty. Pretty."

I could see it in my mind's eye. Richard reaching out to my mother. Mother thinking he was trying to grope her. This was an absolute disaster. My friend was in danger and I was consumed by absolute fear. The previous two years, I'd been in denial. Pretending I was brave. I was not brave. One close and very real encounter with Mother had me transformed into a puddle of water.

"Richard, there you are. We have been looking everywhere for you." Kait's voice echoed from the entrance to the temple.

"Pretty. Pretty. Pretty."

"Yes, it is a lovely gown. But come along now. Let's go and see the band. They're about to perform."

Thank You. I would wait this out, then run. Run and never come back under any circumstance. Ever.

That had his attention. I could hear his imitation of the beat band, "Bang. Bang. Bang," heading toward the entrance.

I relaxed. They were going to be safe, and I could stay hidden. Everything was going to be fine and, once they were gone, I could quickly check the altar. But then my heart stopped.

"Jemmy, Jemmy, Jemmy."

Marcus: Do not come out.

Kait: Stay put darlin', we'll handle this.

Bal: What's going on?

Marcus: STAY PUT!

"Jemmy? Jemimah?" Mother's voice took on a delighted edge. "Is she here?"

The trembling intensified. All I could see was her ordering her minions to tie me to the examination bed.

"Jemmy, Jemmy, Jemmy. Hello. Hello." Richard was getting agitated and confused.

Frack. Frack... Frack. Nausea swam in my gut. I could barely stand up, but I knew what I had to do. Kait and Marcus were there. It was a public place. Lots of openings. I knew the escape routes. I could run. Fast. I wasn't alone. I checked my armour and my Guard.

I edged my way up and stepped out from behind the pillar like the terrified, whipped dog I was. Beaten. Richard came running to hug me, dragging Kait and Marcus in his wake. For once, I was grateful for Richard's bear-like embrace. Whether it was because he was out of his comfort zone, or because I hadn't stepped away, he held on and didn't let go. It helped hide my full-body shakes.

"Oh, my dear girl, so lovely to see you again. You must have been busy this week? On other campaigns? I've not seen you around."

Kait went to speak, but Mother looked down her nose and spoke over the top of her.

"Whatever you're looking for, you won't find it here." My mother strolled closer to our group and looked my companions over. "I'm afraid she's wasted your time. Led you on a wild goose chase." She leaned over and pretended to speak conspiratorially to Kait and Marcus. "She does that you know. Goes off on wild adventures, pretends she's a... what is it, dear? A hero? A saviour? She has her little tribe she watches over." She nodded in Richard's direction. With the approach of Mother's green dress, Richard had released me and started edging his way toward her. "Keeping all the little freaks safe and sound in their little broken homes."

I couldn't hold in my gasp. The shock was enough to shake me out of my panic attack.

"Oh you silly, silly girl. Did you think I didn't know? That I wasn't watching your pathetic efforts over these past two years? I watch you at TAVE, at the temples, outside my home." She sneered and brushed me off like I was lint daring to pollute her transparent gown. "Of course I saw you."

"But I thought you were hunting me? You wanted to kill me?"

"Why on earth would I do that?"

"Artemis."

"Oh, that. Artemis was happy to accept your father's life in your place. Couldn't you see me rise? My climb continued once I'd made my peace with the Goddess." She ran her hands down her curved hips. "In fact, she was so impressed with my offering, she gifted me with youthful looks as well as success in the hunt. Hence why you could never hide from me."

"In my place?" My brain stopped functioning.

"Why, of course. She didn't really care who it was in particular, just someone who was close to me. When he came blustering in ready to avenge you, I simply accepted his offer."

My dad. My world. The sun I orbited... "He offered to die in my place?"

"Well, not in so many words. But he did carry on and he was quite upset. And he did say, 'over my dead body'. So..." She hitched her shoulders. "I agreed. When we came back you were gone. But it was irrelevant. The Goddess was appeased, and I was free of the both of you."

The earth shifted under my feet. I was rocked to the core. I had known my father was gone. If he were alive, I would have known. If there was life in his bones he would have found me. But that he had stood in my place? That he'd stepped into the fire... the ravenous chaos... and suffered... and died... for me? I didn't know what to do with the weight of it. What was I supposed to do... with that knowledge? How could I live... with that truth? And all this time...."Why didn't you let me know?"

"Because I was having so much fun watching you, thinking you were watching... hunting *me?*" Her scream of laughter brought acolytes running. She didn't notice or care, she just kept up her rant. "Everything worked out perfectly. You see, darling, not only did you have the impudence to be born a girl—your father's fault. That man couldn't do anything right—you had the audacity to rival my looks." Hatred oozed through her glare. "You would have threatened my position. My hold. My power."

Dismissing me with a flick of her wrist, she continued, "Watching you try to turn yourself into a boy... How ironic. Choosing to hide those amazing curves, the weapon I blessed you with." She burst out laughing. "The peroxide stubble was the best look ever. This blue tint, however... that could actually work for you." She was thoughtful and looked me over like I was one of her models, like she was actually seeing me. "Who's dressing you?" Her finger waved up and down, indicating the clothing Tessa had insisted I wear.

Before she could continue, a priestess interrupted. "Excuse me. This is currently out of bounds. We need to prepare for our worship, you may return... Oh, Jolena. You're here already. Come along, the other guests are gathering out the back." The priestess turned and left, a reluctant Mother in her wake.

"Pretty. Pretty. Pretty."

"That ain't pretty, me man. That there is toxic waste in a chocolate wrapper."

Actually couldn't disagree with Marcus's definition of the woman who birthed me. His summary helped me find my bearings after she'd just pulled the rug of my existence for the past two years out from under my feet.

She knew.

I was... lost, confused.

She knew.

Memories: all the hardships, the suffering, the victories.

She knew!

I'd lost so much. Gone without. Fought so hard.

And she'd known all along.

Fury started building, and blinding me to where we were and what we were supposed to be doing. I was so fracking angry at the way she had manipulated, humiliated and ridiculed me. Hate so powerful started consuming every part of me.

Hands shook my shoulders, eventually breaking the hold of my wrath. "Whatever you're thinking right now, you let it go." Kait gripped me extra hard when I hissed. "Do you hear me? You let it go."

"What? Let it go? Did you not hear what she said... what she's done?"

"Look to your armour. This is the battle. This is what the Dark wants. You cannot afford to be vulnerable right now."

"What?"

"Look."

I did what she said and gasped. My beautiful pink armour had faded. Desperately, I swung out of Kait's hold and tried to find my Guard.

"He is still there," she said. "But we are in a battle and the Dark has placed your mother in your way to weaken you." Kait wrapped me in a fierce hold and hugged the stiffness out of me. I do not know how that woman did it. But being held by Kait was like coming home. "Sweetheart, you are loved. You are skilled, talented, and very, very smart. You have a family. You are needed, and you are absolutely treasured. Do not let this woman have a victory over you."

Then Marcus spoke. "You know, you should be thanking that viper of yours."

"What?" Again, my vocabulary had become dumb-as.

"Well, would you have found Bal and this fine gentleman?" He nodded to Richard, whom he held in a firm grip to stop him chasing after my mother's green skirt. "Would you have learned the ins and outs of this fine city without the actions of that malignant she-dog?

Would you have the life skills, be studying at TAVE, would you be in the Light, if it weren't for the path that woman kicked you to?"

Once again, I relaxed into Kait's embrace. He was right. But it didn't mean I didn't hate the twik. "We still need to find out if they've kidnapped someone for their sacrifice."

A quiet voice stepped out from behind a pillar on the other side of the temple. I guess two—more than two, considering all the pillars—could play that game. "You won't find anyone held prisoner here." A priestess quickly checked over each shoulder then shuffle-ran over to us.

"You." It was the angel of mercy who'd helped me when I first tried to come back here.

She smiled. "I figured you must be Jemimah." She leaned in and whispered, "I never really liked your mother. But she is not here very often anymore."

Kait asked, "Do you know if they're planning a human sacrifice tonight?"

The woman recoiled. "We would never keep prisoners, or even think of sacrificing someone. Or an animal." She shook her head as if trying to get rid of the image. But then stopped and looked to me. "I don't understand what happened. Why the goddess asked for your life." Again, she shook her head. "It was unheard of. But the oracle checked multiple times." She darted a look over her shoulders and continued in a quieter whisper, "I never agreed. It's why I helped you when I figured out who you were."

She took my hands and tears made her eyes sparkle. "I am so sorry. It was wrong. We worship our goddess by the celebration of love, freely expressed to all who wish to celebrate. The one who demands sacrifice of life is Dionysus. Not Artemis. She loves women." Again, she shook her head and screwed up her face.

I was so taken by her confession, I embraced her. "Thank you. Thank you for then and thank you for now."

Wiping her eyes, she nodded. "I have to run. But... I am so happy you found your home. Your family." With a watery smile, she turned and ran to the exit at the rear of the building.

"I think that'd be our cue to make like a flock and leave." Marcus took Richard and turned to the exit. "Let's go and enjoy the show, then come up with Plan B."

Richard swung his arms, mimicking drumming. "Bang. Bang. Bang."

"Couldn't agree more, me man. Couldn't agree more."

54

BALASHKA: DEATH WISH

"I almost died. Could have killed the man. But almost died first." Everyone had come round to debrief over breakfast and to discuss the debacle that was last night. I'd wanted to give Jem the morning off and so, since Harry was so keen to help, had asked him to bring pastries and coffee for everyone. "What an absolute horror. Ghastly failure is what it was," I declared to the group who had not been present in the temple. Not that I was, but I had snuck over and listened from the shadows.

The little woman in the ShellCom's image challenged me. "How so?"

Her stupidity brought me up short. "Dear woman, how could any of that be considered a success. They almost caught Jem." Nausea blindsided me. I put my coffee down and continued pacing.

"On the contrary. She wasn't almost caught because no one is hunting her. In fact, an added bonus is that she now knows and doesn't have to hide anymore."

It made me even sicker. Of course I understood that. But... what if she left because she didn't need my help anymore. Or protection. Or provision. I had to sit down.

But the wretched woman just kept speaking. "You learned that the sacrifices are happening at the Theatre. The band had some exposure and were so successful, they were invited to come back to the finale. So now, we have two acts in the show that we can work through."

She did have the decency to stop then and consider the absolute disaster *that* was. "Granted, not the ideal situation to have those kids in that place... ever. It wasn't our original plan, we'll have to be extra careful. Although, just because we have the invitation, doesn't mean we have to accept." But then she was back at the "positive" lecture. I do believe I began to hate her and wished the wretched battery would give out altogether and we never had to hear from her again. "And of course, the best thing of all"—a hideous grin broke out across her face —"I'll be there to join you. It's been approved. I'm out, day after tomorrow."

All sense and reason evaporated as everyone started cheering and embracing. For goodness' sake, it was like she was some kind of rock star. Thank the heavens, Harry, Al and Cissa weren't behaving like loons. But Al and Cissa were looking exceedingly relieved. "Do you actually know this woman?" Not that I knew them, but since I knew Harry and Harry knew them, I felt a sense of connection.

Cissa answered, "Know her? Not really. Have I met her? Been blown away by her? Saved by her? Inspired by her?" A serene smile graced her face. "Yes."

"She really is quite remarkable. And I... both of us, feel a lot better knowing she will be with us," Al finished by speaking on his wife's behalf.

"Intriguing." Harry threw his two cents' worth in after studying his sister's response. "Looking forward to meeting her."

The Blue man, the father of the lot of them, it seemed, shared his convoluted, confusing opinion. "Right it is, and no two ways about it. The Light had this card up His sleeve the whole time. Now, let's not be wasting any more time and get our heads into the planning of it. With all our horses in the stable, let's nut out a winning formula."

I was quite positive I would never understand that man. But I was grateful for what he and his son had done for my family and the folk across the road, so I would humour him. One was also a bit impressed with his wife. And his daughter. And her twin. Oh, okay, so the whole family was impressive. Intrusive, disruptive, but impressive none-theless.

Just don't let them or anyone take Jem from me. Please.

Why did they need her... and my help, anyway? If they were so good? "I've changed my mind." I was aware that the conversation had been going on without me. Right now, however, I had everyone's attention. "I don't want to help anymore." A few jaws dropped and some eyes widened. "You don't need us. We'll just get in the way." I felt so much better I had clarified that. But just to be sure, I said it again, "You don't need my or Jem's help. You can do it without us."

"Okay, Bal." Kait was the first to respond. "We respect that. You don't have to participate. We appreciate your help at Artemis's temple. We can take it from here."

Great. Now they were all looking at me like I was some "special needs" person. "Stop it."

They looked to each other. Kait was spokeswoman again. "Stop what?"

"Treating me like I'm... I'm like..." Now they had me. How could I say like my family without insulting my family? "Like I have issues. Like I'm not normal."

Harry burst out laughing. "Good one, Bal."

There was a general unease from the group at his eruption and a burn of embarrassment from me. "What do you mean?"

"Look around you, Bal. The fortress you've built. The fortune you spend to not have to deal with the world outside. You *do* have issues. But whether or not you're normal is up to you." Before I could inter-ject, he continued, "What is it you're always preaching, Bal? 'Normal is feeling like you fit in. Like you're acceptable. Even if... when... you're radically different.' So, what is it to be?" He leaned in close. "Right now, Bal. Do you feel acceptable? Because even you would have to agree, you're radically different, my friend." The last bit dimmed the sting of his accusation.

"Harry, stop it. Leave him alone." My beautiful girl jumped to my defence. Even though I didn't need it, I was gratified. "If he's not up to going out again, we'll leave him here. You don't have to make him feel bad about being scared."

"Ow. That's gotta hurt. Don't hold back, kid." Dan pretty much took the words out of my mouth. The young man was sitting directly opposite me with his back to the morning sun.

I looked around the group occupying my shed. My shed. They were my guests. And here they were, attacking me and accusing me of being scared. Of being a freak. Of having issues.

Anger. Frustration. Humiliation. I couldn't identify the most prominent. I was a boiling soup of hostile sensations all fighting for supremacy. The worst thing was, though, I couldn't leave. It was my house. And if I demanded they leave, they would. But they'd take Jem with them. And that was not acceptable. At all. "You can't go, Jem." The whole group looked at me like I was an exhibit at a freak show.

"You said what?" At Jem's rebuttal, my awareness narrowed to just her and me.

"I said, you can't go. You don't need to go. Your mother is not hunting you. You are safe. You don't need to prove anything to anyone. These people can take care of the situation and save the day without you. And anyway, we're not even citizens of this city. After all they've done to us, why should we help them anyway?"

She was speechless. Motionless. "Maybe because I'm a decent human being. Because I know what it's like to be trapped. And at the mercy of savage beasts—"

"So do I!" I didn't mean to yell. But I was up and pacing—momentarily grateful that my hip no longer held me hostage—ripping my hair out. "I know what they can do. I know what they *will* do." I turned to face her. Her stupidity was going to get her killed. Why couldn't she see that. "And no matter what we, you, or they"—I stabbed my finger in the general direction of our guests—"do, people are still going to keep hurting and abusing others. There is nothing we can do to stop it."

"So we shouldn't even try?"

"To what end? To save one person? What difference does that make?"

Time froze and Jem just stared at me. "I was one person, Bal. And it made a hell of a lot of difference to me."

"And now? And now you're planning to throw yourself in their sights, again. And they're going to hurt you. Again. Why on earth can't you understand? Do you have a death wish? Are you... what? Too safe now? You have your little home here behind *my* walls. Our family are now finally safe, you have no reason to throw yourself in harm's way anymore. Are you addicted to the high of the danger, Jem? Or do you just want to hurt me?"

The silence stretched for eternity and allowed me to hear the trembling of my heart... my brain... my soul.

Very quietly, Jem replied, "I will always be grateful for what you've done for me and my family, Bal." Her emphasis of the word "my" didn't escape me. Tears streamed down her face, but her voice took on a formal, distant edge. "But I can see we are heading along different paths." She wouldn't let me speak. "I know I might be in danger by helping these people—people I don't know, innocent victims like me. In helping one, I'm repaying the gift that was given to me. By helping two or more, I'm making a difference to a number of lives, not only the victims', but their families, friends, their kids. But if I can help play my part in shutting this warped practice down, and stop it happening again, I can help impact this city. Which I don't owe anything to, but I still call my home."

She stood tall and, even though she was carving my heart out with her words, I couldn't help but be proud of this young woman and how far she had come. "I choose to trust the Light to do what He says He will do. I trust this armour He has put me in and the Guard He protects me with." For a moment, her eyes sparked and the old Jem came out from behind the mask. "Imagine, Bal. Imagine if everyone could have the chance to get this armour. Have a Guard. Can you imagine just how amazing that would be? Everyone could feel safe. Everyone would be safe. But they can't see. And they won't if they don't know. And they can't know if they're dead.

"I don't need your permission." She smirked at me then. "You should know that by now. But I'd really like your blessing."

I slumped back in my chair. My body ached. My head thumped. And every ounce of fight was gone. I knew she'd go. Trying to stop her had merely pushed her out the door. But woven through every fibre of my being, I knew… I knew I would lose her. I couldn't stop her. And I couldn't stop the tears.

Why did You bring her into my life just to take her away again?

I pulled myself to my feet, dragged my sack of a body to my bedroom and quietly shut the door. I was aware of scraping chairs, clinking cups and soft mumbling. I didn't care. I knew Harry would shut the door… and there it was. The familiar screech of the roller door sliding back into place. Finally, I was alone.

Take me. Please. Just let me die. After everything, it has come to this. I no longer want to live. Joy has abandoned me. Please. Can You just end me. Just let me go to sleep and never wake up. It's all too hard. Why did You bother stopping me, in prison.

I tried to ignore the scratching at my door. When the whining started, I slammed a pillow over my head. But the incessant howling had me. Rage spiked and pushed me out of bed. "What?" Sweetie cowered at my feet. Then the tears came.

I scooped her up, kissed her wiry hair and held her so very close. "I'm sorry. I'm sorry. Sorry, my sweet girl. I didn't mean to yell. I didn't mean to upset you. My dear girl, please forgive me." A little warm, wet tongue started mopping up my tears.

Back in bed, wrapped in a ball around my faithful little friend, I sobbed myself to sleep and petitioned the Light that it would be endless.

55

ALARIO: HONEST TRUTH

We sat at our table by the windows for dinner, like we normally did. Cissa exuded innate class and subtle beauty, like she usually did. And the Dark pulsed through the city below us, as it was wont to do. "Happy anniversary." I laid the gift beside Cissa's cleaned plate. Her face froze, her eyes locked on the exquisite package. "Obviously, I didn't wrap it." She was yet to lift her face. I laughed. "Did you forget the date?"

Slowly, her eyes found mine, light from the candle refracted in her tears. A slight shake of her head dislodged one. I watched it until it disappeared behind the hand covering her mouth. And still, she didn't say a word.

"You're going to make me work for this aren't you?"

She looked to the little parcel that had stolen her voice and back to me, a hint of her humour returning in a slight nod. Watching like a hawk as I carefully peeled back the ribbon and released the paper. Taking the velvet box inside, I went round to my wife, got down on one knee, and popped the lid. "Cissa, my love, my life. Nine months ago, I landed back on your doorstep. Five months ago, we jumped into the unknown for the Light. Three months ago, we took time out to be... just the two of us, for the first time in twenty-six years. Tomorrow, we take on the horrors of hell. And you would do me the greatest honour if you'd join me as my wife… for the second time round. Cissa, will you marry me… again?"

Twin trails of tears tracked down her face, both hands covered her mouth and, as she nodded her head, a quiet sob broke her silence. Placing the ring-box on the table, I stood and embraced my wife. She leaned into me and I waited till the storm of emotion had stilled. Breaking from my hold, Cissa raced to the kitchen, grabbed a handful of tissues, gave me one then dived back into my arms as she wiped her face and exhaled.

Before she could speak, "our song" serenaded us from the sound system. And yes, I'd loosely planned it that way and was incredibly grateful it had come off.

Thank You.

We swayed to the music in each other's arms, allowing the lyrics to sink deep. As the song came to an end, we stilled. Cissa pulled back from me. Her hand traced my rough cheek. I'd not shaved for dinner: she preferred I didn't. Her lips rested on mine for an eternity, then she said, "Yes." But then followed it with a hint of a smile and a whole lot of tease. "And, no, to your earlier question."

The woman had me in a bind. Yes, to marriage… again, and no to…? My brain was turning somersaults desperately trying to figure out what on earth I was stupid enough to ask her and not remember. No, to going tomorrow? I knew her parents would be there and that was going to be a skrat-load of hell right there.

No, to going to Ephesus to celebrate closing the Sanders deal? It had been a huge relief. It meant we didn't have to put off staff yet. The contract would tide us over for another six months. We trusted the Light to come through with something else after that.

No to…

"Al." Both my hands throbbed from her enthusiastic grip.

"What?" I was panicked, I hadn't meant to bark, so quickly amended it to: "Pardon?"

Trouble, Cissa's particular flavour, coloured her eyes. Her smile was sly. This particular cat was enjoying a dessert of cream. "No." My heart was on hold as were all thoughts and function. "I don't want to have kids. But thank you for asking."

The relief was instant. Not that she didn't want kids. I'd forgotten it was still on the table. I was just so grateful it wasn't something I couldn't live with. Or without.

She was talking again. I could tell by the increasingly firm grip on my hand, she expected me to stay with her for this next bit. "Our future is uncertain, but our goal and purpose are not. I am too old"— she raced on at my protest—"I do not want to be going through that process at this point in my life. I understand others do, and I respect that. But... it's not for me. Honest truth." Peace settled around her like a cloak. It embraced me as well.

"And I was thinking"—my nerves went on high alert again—"Kait has the right of it." She laughed at my shock. "A woman doesn't have to physically bear children to be a mother. I'm thinking Jemimah might be in want of some parental influence. A mother-figure who doesn't want to throw her to the dogs, and a father-figure who can step out from his castle walls."

I was nodding before I realised it, and I couldn't fight the words "honest truth" as they took root in my heart.

"Now, are you going to put that thing on my finger, or am I going to have to do it myself?"

MARCUS: EAGLE EYE

T hings were as subdued as a faster's snack after Bal's meltdown. Apart from Val's welcome home, that was. Our celebration was short-lived, however. Since Bal's place was now a no-go zone, and the whole city had downed tools and poured out onto the streets for the week's celebration, we thought it best if Val stayed at Sanctuary. It broke our collective heart we couldn't have her stay with us.

Me sister was our main weapon and spearhead for the secret assault on the temple, so we were determined to keep her under wraps. We'd not want any to identify her as the troublemaker she'd been painted. She would stay in her own cabin there and come over daily with Jonathan and Daisy. Our meet up was the recently finished green space at the heart of The Wreckage, tucked out of view beside new homes and the behemoth wall.

Some thought we were building molehills into mountains. But we never knew which strings Achan was twitching. It wasn't a far toss to believe he was in the Gerent's pocket, but truth be, we didn't know. So, we were taping our cards to our chest.

On holiday with the rest of the city, our little mouse in pink armour led groups of us through every escape route from the Theatre. Others from the True Community wanted to lend a hand. But considering the danger involved, they were planted behind the scenes, petitioning the Light and on transport detail.

We'd also been offered help from February and October, our tech gurus in Philadelphia, to cover what they could with their higher than high-tech drones. They'd told us the Gerent would certainly have access to fandangled technology that intercepted text messages and would access our GPS. But again, the Light had laid the stepping stones prior to the big event. Those of us behind the scenes had side-stepped that snare by borrowing old fashioned two-ways and headsets we'd been using on the worksite. Of course, once word got out of what we were planning, Indy and Amina from Laodicea had demanded to help, as had Felix, Marlene and Fleur.

The closer we got to planning the actual assault, however, the fainter the details became. All we had to go on was Tessa's night of terrors. And what Jem had up her sleeve from local knowledge, and forays around the doorways of the Theatre's dark heart. Our mouse was a quick whip: she'd brains enough not to dance too deeply in that particular lair of the devil. Even before she had the Sight.

So it was with many hands and minor plans we'd petitioned the Light. We'd been in training. We'd checked our armour and escape routes. We'd gone over our attack, time and again, trying to come up with every conceivable scenario and create strategies to match them. But in the end, our plan was as holey as a string vest. We trusted we were on the Light's path, and, by the large number of extra Guards, we figured we were in for a wild ride whichever way the pear crumpled.

And now it was time. In the audience were significant members of the True Community: Al, Cissa, Albert and a few others. Harry had decided to throw in his lot with them, even though he didn't yet have the Sight. Other members were parked around the city, ready to whisk away any of ours and the escaped prisoner, if we were successful. Desleigh and Audette, our doctors, were on hand at The Wreckage to mop up emergencies and any injuries from the battle.

Jonathan refused to stay safe at Sanctuary, but conceded he couldn't afford to be caught or identified as having any part in this.

So, he and Daisy sat in Old Faithful at the city's gate next to The Wreckage. February and October's base of operations was in the back of the old truck.

As always, there were two sides of this coin. It was all very well trying to be stealthy and consider all possible human errors, but we were very aware that the main issue was the Unseen enemy. We couldn't hide anything from him or his minions. If he decided to pass on information, we were done in. That's where the armour and the petitioning came in. The Dark was powerful and sneaky and remorseless. But the Light was all powerful and set the Dark's limits.

In the eyes of the world, we were small in number and shy on might. And truth be, on our own, each of us could only be an irritation: a fractured splinter under the quick. But fused together, in the Light, our little barbs had the power to break the neck of the Dark's hold on Sardis.

So, leaving all things in the Light's lap, it was game time. Within the Theatre, Cissa, Al and Harry had seats on the ground floor close to the stage. Albert, Laura and Kirt had seats on the top balcony. Kait, Val and I walked around the Theatre complex looking for all the world like tourists. Well, that was our plan. Circumnavigating from the other direction were Felix, Marlene, Fleur, Indy, Amina and Jem. Since they'd not been around for the tour, she was giving them a brief summary.

Visitors were a regular sight at the Festival, especially the finale. Folks had travelled for hours to get here. Especially since the Gerent was here and he was hosting. He made sure it was well worth their while. It was the best cover we could have hoped for: strangers getting lost and wandering where they shouldn't be was a card we fully expected to play.

But for now, the streets were pickled with revellers and Enforcers, and the Gerent's personal guard were thickly spread on the ground. Demons were hot on everyone's heels, enjoying the feast. Step one of the plan, our little mouse and me wife were going to slip past the rope barriers and release a mini drone into the back of the Theatre.

It was a nervous wait giving them the few minutes they needed to get into position before we started clanging our cymbals. Indy and Amina had volunteered to be our distraction. They weren't locals, had no record or technological implants, so if they were caught, or arrested for causing a ruckus, it'd most likely end up as a slap on the wrist and time out from Sardis. Although, we had tried to convince Amina it was probably best she wasn't involved. Her silver scales were memorable as were her looks. She wasn't the previous High Priestess of Ashera in Laodicea for no reason.

"All the better to lure attention, boy," had been her only response. I was not fool enough to argue with the woman, so I let it lie.

And then it began. First came a guttural blend of a scream and roar. "Get your hands off me, you ignorant oaf!'

"What?"

"I am not a piece of meat for your taking." At this, Amina had let her outer robe "slip" from her shoulders. Her scales picked up the streetlights and reflected their silver hue. The thin straps on her top hinted at the half-body coverage. Anyone who had any knowledge of Ashera—most of the breathing population—would have known what that meant. But to have seen them in silver? That was a very rare event.

Indy's tall, muscular frame and scarred face were also of note. To see this colossus of a man being confronted by a silver-scaled, stunning wild cat of a woman was a showstopper of herculean proportions. Hopefully, Kait could hear and they'd be ready.

57

KAITLYN: DEVIL'S LAIR

And there it was. Beautiful Amina and wonderful Indy had given us the gift of commotion. Jem and I were off, ducking and weaving through the shadows, under the rope, behind the guard and —after a thirty-second wait for the guard to radio his mates on the inside—through the open door. A small crowd of Theatre security were keen to see the show, making the way easier for us.

Through an old-fashioned headset I had a line to Old Faithful, but I would not be speaking unless it was an extreme emergency. Jem and I melted along the hallway to the first turn. Our little mouse knew this part of the building well, and sweet Albert had sourced an old floor plan of the temple, located at the back and under the Theatre.

I'm not too sure how Jem was feeling, but I for one had to remind myself I was the only one who could hear the beating of my heart, and not worry it was going to give us away. Praise be to the Light above, He had granted us extra Guard detail. They were fully engaged with the enemy before we even made it through the door. It was enough trying to evade human interactions without having to worry about the minions as well. They were everywhere. And I mean, the Unseen were so thick in the air and on the ground, it made it hard to see the Seen.

Once Jem and I found the old fire hydrant nook we'd been looking for, we hunkered down and I, very carefully and quietly, opened February and October's box, extracting the dragonfly-sized machine. Activating it by a slight squeeze of its thorax, I placed it on my palm and watched in wonder as it lifted, circled and took off.

We could hear laughter and cheering coming from outside. Then I had to hold Jem tight as more folk from inside the temple made their way to the back door to watch Amina and Indy's show. I felt guilty just squatting like a sack of potatoes as our Guards fought furiously for our safety all around us. But with such an audience at the back door, I did not think it was safe to try to exit. And it surely to goodness was not safe to try to find another way out.

I had Jem pinned between my hip and the wall. We were squeezed in behind the large pipe in the alcove and, with the dim lighting, we were close to invisible. I didn't want to risk giving our presence away but had to let Bear know we were staying put. Otherwise, I was confident he would do something stupid.

Leaning into Jem's shoulder, I bracketed my mouth and whispered, hoping to high heaven the girls could hear me. "Staying put. Will wait for drone. Door too busy."

February's voice came through my earpiece. I had to remind myself no one else could hear. "Copy. Will let everyone know. Out."

I didn't know how long we would have to wait, but I trusted the Light would cover us until we had opportunity. In the meantime, I went through my stretches so when it was time to move, I could. I noticed Jem trying to copy me. I patted her knee and smiled. Although I am quite positive, in this light, she couldn't see me. But, if all went well, this could be a long wait, or a short one, but most importantly of all, it would be a quiet one. So I'd keep up with the stretches.

When I'd finished, I did my best to cover Jem's body with mine, not only to keep her hidden, but to help reduce her tremors. I breathed deeply and soon she followed. We were tucked in our safe cocoon whilst all around us Warriors fought with demons, but we were safe.

Until the wolves came.

DANIEL: FLY IN THE OINTMENT

Didn't matter how much we'd gone over this, I was not going to be able to relax until these kids were back home, safe at The Wreckage. Then I would breathe easier, but I wouldn't be totally okay until this night was over and everyone was present and accounted for... unharmed.

It had been just so bleeding good to see Val again. See that she was okay, have her back in the game and by our sides.

As we got off the Pod at the heart of the Cultural District, though, what confidence I'd ignorantly held, took to the hills. The Gerent's men were everywhere. They patrolled in pairs throughout the massing crowd, the entrance to the Theatre, and the side doors where we were supposed to be.

To save time and to have less baggage to lug up the hill on the crowded Pods, we'd dressed in our Beat Band uniforms before leaving. We'd all received our virtual passes. But the kids who didn't have the tech had lanyards. We'd been up here for rehearsals but had decided to not leave our instruments. It was just one more thing that could go wrong tonight.

There was a group from our Pod heading to the stage door of the Theatre. It helped us feel like we fit in and gave us the thin security of thinking we were hidden within the process of the event. I could feel Tessa's hand shaking in mine and I saw Riah adjust her sleeve to hide her tattoo. Raph walked on my other side, holding his head high. But I could see the slight movement of his lips. He'd be reciting something to help him keep the red haze from riding his butt.

Oh Lord, help us. We so need You right now.

And just like that, an extra layer of Guards showed up and surrounded us. I felt everyone's sigh mirror mine.

I know You've got this. I know we're in Your plan. But, far out, this is doing my head in.

We were ushered through to the back-of-house marshalling area. Bright lights lit huge hallways leading us to what looked like a cavernous lounge. Couches and chairs were set out in groups throughout the carpeted space. There were three tea and coffee stations I could see and at least two banks of toilets. The place was well lit and coloured in natural tones with orange accents. Of course, I hadn't noticed this, but Tessa had pointed it out. She was right, but I didn't really care.

Because we had two acts, one mid-way through and the other at the end, we were given our own spot for the whole evening. This was purely an act of Light. It wasn't a big space, but we could leave our stuff and hang out relatively uninterrupted and un-harassed by anyone. We were supposed to be here. We were legit. So I grabbed another lounge and told Raph and Riah to each nab another comfy chair and add them to our space. This way, all the kids could sit and relax, and we wouldn't be sitting in each other's laps.

Since they weren't used to the typical luxury Sardis had to offer, we let them explore as much as they liked. Just asked that they stay within the vast room. Once we were settled, Tessa messaged Daisy to pass our update along. We were in, we were settled, and we had received the schedule, which she also forwarded to our support crew.

I had just started to relax and think we had the easy part of the night, when the main doors opened and a contingent of the Gerent's men walked through. The four of us froze. It wasn't necessarily bad news. But once the room had been scoped and secured, the man himself entered.

I leaned over to Tessa. "Grab Riah and hide out in the toilets. Raph and I will go to the Men's. If you see any of the kids on the way through, give them a heads-up and tell them not to talk about us."

Of all the contingency plans, we hadn't thought of this. Raph didn't have to be told twice, the main issue I had was keeping him from running. I couldn't message the kids because they didn't have phones. I searched the floor. The five were hanging out at a food table with bakery goods, fruit and lollies near the main doors. There was no way I was going to get their attention. And there was definitely no way I was going to walk over there, next to the Gerent, to tell them to lie low and keep their mouths shut.

Raph and I escaped and, just as I shut the door, I saw our arch enemy approach the kids. They beamed at him, nodded their heads and all started searching the room. I let the door settle in place then sent a message to everyone in our group chat.

Dan: Petition now! Gerent talking to kids!

Then I went offline whilst Raph and I hid out in the bathroom.

BALASHKA: COME TO JESUS MOMENT

"What are you doing here?" I screeched.

The Man had frightened the living daylights out of me as he walked through the wall. Through the jolly wall!

"I could very well ask you the same thing," He said.

I stared at him.

He stared back, with that pleasantly open face that had worn me down during my time in prison. It was exceedingly irritating. He waited. I had learned, many years ago, this man had the patience of Job. He could sit in silence for centuries. So I conceded. "They've all gone."

He nodded and waited.

"They've all gone off to rescue the world."

Again, he nodded and waited. His face still open, but the full force of his direct attention was a magnet compelling the ugly truth from me.

In frustration I launched to my feet, cups and plates rattling as I threw my bed covers back. "I wanted to help. I did." I turned to face him. He merely tilted his head the other way and nodded again. I started pacing. "I did go. I did help." I accused him, "Did you know that? Do you know I actually went to the temple? I helped."

He rolled his bottom lip and… jolly well nodded again.

"You know her mother isn't actually hunting her anymore. She's safe. Did you know that?"

And, of course, the infuriating Man nodded again. And sat. Silent. And waited.

I growled and ran my fingers through my matted hair, snagging a knot, which tore the final thread of my control. A volcano of acid erupted. "I want to help. I do. I really, really do." I was so ashamed. "But I can't. I'm just so scared. Terrifyingly scared. Paralysingly… scared." With each statement of truth, my voice rose until I was screaming. And all he did was sit, listen and nod. There was no accusation in him. No judgement. Just acceptance and openness.

I slumped back on the bed, cradling my head in my hands. "I don't particularly like that woman." He tilted his head. "That one who's been in jail." He raised his eyebrow. "She's a bloodthirsty harridan."

At this he dropped his head and looked at me from under his brow. I had the distinct impression I was on thin ice. "I mean to say. I am sure she is very nice. But…"—his eyes narrowed a fraction—"she is… bossy." He nodded once. "And she seems to like to fight." Another nod. "She…"—he sat very still and waited—"ugh, she's got everyone excited and amped up to go headfirst into the hornet's nest and now they've gone and now everyone is in danger and now I am stuck here because I'm too fracking scared to leave my prison and it's all her fault." There. I'd said it. I'd said it very loudly, but I'd confessed.

The Man tilted his head again, nodded slightly and considered me through narrowed eyes. "What is it you want, Balashka?"

"Courage. I want courage. To be brave." Again, with the yelling. But I was beyond caring. I was a pathetic old man, hiding in my bedroom, in my pyjamas, talking to a figment of my imagination.

He smiled. Warmth and peace ebbed through me. He stood and closed the gap between us. Warmth flowed from his hands where he'd laid them on my head. "Done."

I looked up at him in wonder. Peace still lingered and fear still reigned. "I don't feel any different."

"Don't you? Give it time."

"But I don't have time. My friends and family are out there fighting a hopeless battle and I'm here, useless… lost."

"What is it you want to do, Balashka?"

"I want to help. But I can't." I screamed at him, "I can't!"

"The choice is yours, Balashka. Always, the choice is yours." He turned to go.

"Where are you going? You haven't fixed me. I am still scared."

"I am always with you, Bal. Just call out and you will see me."

I couldn't believe he was leaving. I was being ravaged by an earthquake. An overwhelming urge to help my family was throwing itself against my wall of fear.

But at his parting words, ice sped through my veins. "I missed seeing Sweetie on my way in. I think she may have been lonely and followed Richard. Give her a hug from me next time you see her, won't you?" He stepped back in front of me, gripped my shoulders till I stood in front of him. His eyes bored into my very soul and stirred my heart within me. "Balashka." He waited till I acknowledged him with a nod. "Be strong and courageous. For I am with you, always. In me, you can do all things. All things, Balashka." His gaze intensified. I was pinned. "What that looks like, and how that plays out, is up to you. The choice is yours."

And then he was gone. He blinked out of existence. I knew he'd been real—in the absence of his support, I fell back onto the bed.

Lost, I looked around my room. The disaster area of my room. Clothes, food, dishes… my Guard. He stared at me and I could not read one jot of emotion. Then it all came flooding back. Sweetie. Richard. Jem. My family.

In a flurry, I made more of a mess looking for some shoes. I found one for my left foot, one for my right and I took off. I didn't check, but I knew my Guard was with me. So, too, was the Light.

6 0

MARCUS: TOO MANY PIES, NOT ENOUGH FINGERS

We'd received word everyone was in position, and we'd just heard that Kait and Jem were inside, safe, but waiting till the drama out here died down.

Me heart slowed to racing. I knew the Light had us, but confirmation they were okay was never wasted news. Val made her way into Amina's line of sight and gave the nod. The Amazonian finished her performance with a flurry of insults, pulled her shawl back in place, then stormed off the scene like a diva.

Indy pulled a face like Adam on Mother's Day and stormed off in the opposite direction. There was even some cheering for their performance. Thankfully, no calls for an encore. They were both so memorable they were done for the night. Before they could follow orders to return to The Wreckage, though, disaster declared itself by splattering our plans.

Through a briefly opened door, the drone had picked up frightening footage. It had taken some work, but the girls had discerned more than one captive, and had a glimpse of a terrified bloke in a band uniform clutching a butt-ugly mutt.

Our worst nightmare come to life: an unknown quantity we'd not factored in. Timing was going to be critical and staying under the radar was going to take a miracle, of proportions only found recorded in The Way. At least Bal was safe at home.

Marcus: Kait, time to come home. Traffic should be thinning soon. We'll expect you in around ten minutes.

The message was relayed via February to Kait. The return message chilled me innards.

"It may take a bit longer, someone let the dogs out and they're blocking the road. So far, we're okay, but the dog catchers are busy cleaning up another mess."

Val's iron grip almost had me on me buttooshie. She'd received the same message. As had we all. I found me feet and shook me head at her. I didn't need words. She understood.

Felix, Marlene and Fleur speed-walked to meet us. Amina under a hood, and Indie wearing a beanie pulled low, also gathered around.

With her airwaves open and everyone set to the same channel, Val started. "Indy, Amina, on my mark, take the remaining guard at the back door. Indy, take his uniform and radio and stand in for as long as you can. Amina, stay in the shadows and watch his back. As soon as you're noticed, run. Take the closest escape route. If you need a driver, take one of the cars. Do not stop, look over your shoulder, or come back. Just let someone know when you have to leave."

They nodded.

"Felix, Marlene and Fleur. You're with us. You wait at the bend Kait and Jem are currently holding. As we get hostages to you, you escort them out to Indy and Amina. Same deal. When you are identified as intruders, fight to escape, and run."

"Yes dear," Marlene answered for her group.

Val continued speaking staccato, short, sharp bursts. Time was of the essence, and we all knew it. "The Light has granted us a great number of Warriors. We will have to fight some of the enemy, but our main task tonight is getting those prisoners out. The rest is up to the Light. Understood?"

In our haste we all nodded.

"Stay low, slow and quiet. Faithful, did you get that?"

In our earpieces we all heard February's, "Copy."

"Tell Kait, we're on our way."

I did me best to look casual but me heart was champing at the bit. Until I heard the latest update from The Wreckage. "The Gerent has just encountered the teens. Our crew are hiding out in the bathrooms. They have requested petition."

"Frack." I think that was Indy, but it could have been Amina.

Our earpieces sounded again, "For now they are safe, I'll keep you posted."

"Our plans haven't changed. Move out," Val whisper-barked. To the uninitiated, you'd think she had a heart of ice. But the twitch in her eyes gave it all away. She was just as scared for our lot as I was.

The Light was with us as we began. Amina approached the man watching the back door. She dropped her shawl and Indy took him out from behind. It seemed too easy. Not that I was complaining. Indy was already wearing dark clothes, so it was just a matter of taking the guy's cap and earpiece. Amina shrank into the shadows as we entered the devil's lair.

As soon as we opened the door, we heard growling and the ring of steel. Kait and her Guard, along with Jem's Guard were holding back massive beasts. Jem cowered in the corner of the alcove they'd hidden in. I couldn't see if she was harmed, I just shot an arrow petition she wasn't. The hounds had their attention focused on the two stuck in the corner. All we could see were their powerful rumps lowered, ready to pounce.

Without taking a breath, Val was running, leaping and impaling the first with her sword, the second with one of her knives, and a third, she put in a headlock. I know from the many years I had been fighting alongside her, right now she would have wanted to release a hellish roar of her own, but she didn't. She pulled another blade and swiped it under its neck. With her interruption to their game plan, the other wolves were soon cut down by Kait and the Guards. Six in all.

The devil's dogs were still transitioning to toxic tar as I made my way to me wife. I pulled her to me, then pushed her away, running me hands and eyes over every inch of her. The slap to me shoulder was hard enough to shift me focus.

"We're fine. Just breathe, Bear, we're fine. But we've got to move. The show has started and we've got to get to the basement." Me beautiful wife then, with utmost care, turned to Jem. "Are you okay, sweetheart? You can leave now. Indy and Amina will see you out. You can go back to The Wreckage and wait for us there."

"Didn't you hear? Richard and Sweetie are here. I have to help."

All of us stared at the kid for a beat. Val narrowed her eyes as if measuring the girl's grit. She then looked to Jem's Guard. He didn't flinch but gave the smallest of nods. "Kait? Any Word from above?"

Me wife exhaled, dropped her head and closed her eyes. "Sorry, Val, nothing."

"Right. Fleur, you stay here and direct any who come to you out to Indy and Amina."

The woman didn't speak, just switched places with Jem.

Our earpieces sounded again as February commanded, "Kait, release the drone. We'll go ahead and give you eyes in the sky."

Kait turned to Jem who opened the little box, activated the retrieved dragonfly and released it. We waited a beat. "The next hall is clear. You are good to go."

"Fleur, if you need t—"

"Yes, Val, I know. Run for my life." She smiled, then sank into the recess and disappeared.

"With me." Val jogged in the dragonfly's wake. Stopping at each corner, waiting to receive clearance.

If I wasn't as tight as a sprung spring, I would have realised it was all too easy. We'd dropped both Marlene and Felix off—Marlene at the head of the stairwell, Felix at the bottom. On the lowest level we only had light from the green emergency lights. We couldn't see into the shadows but knew our Guards could. And still, it all seemed too easy.

Until it wasn't.

We'd taken the bait: hook, line and sinker.

"Drone down. Drone down. Abort. Repeat, Abort."

Too late, we waltzed straight into the arms of the enemy, waiting for us with a salivating welcoming committee.

We needed a wall to our backs to protect Jem, but we needed space to move freely to fight.

True to His Faithfulness, the Light surrounded Jem with a wall of Warriors who enabled us to focus on the enemy in front of us. I swear, Val had been desperate for this. After eight months of being locked up, she was in heaven. I wouldn't have been surprised if she'd even asked for it. But there you have it; the battle hog was happy, knee-deep in enemy skrat.

"Val." I had to yell to get her attention. "Stop playing with your food. We've got a bleeding job to do. Hurry up, woman."

Without a word of a lie, I tell you the girl growled at me. Prison had done nothing for her manners. But, back in the land of the rational, she finished the three demons she'd been toying with, and we could move on. Kait and I had dealt with the guards stationed at the door. They were now "resting" and bound, and finally we gained access to our goal.

The stench was the first thing that threw me when the door was opened. Then it was the moaning. I'm ashamed to say, I blanked out. Me brain simply could not take in what was before me. Thankfully, me Guard wasn't as dim-witted. He took out the hound that launched itself at me frozen body. I'd not even noticed Kait and Val re-engaging with another pack of the beasts. Mopping up didn't take long, but trying to comprehend what was before us did.

Stacks of crates piled three high, in rows along three sides of the room. There was no solid bases in the floors and no fresh air to circulate the stench of excrement and vomit. Dogs were on the top two rows. Humans were on the bottom.

Val was already looking for keys to free the captives and signalling the team. "We're in. There are so many. This is going to take time." She hadn't stopped searching as she reported in. Kait was checking on the captives, so I helped Val hunt for keys. In the end I couldn't wait. I grabbed a rod and started levering the wire hinges.

In our ears we heard, "The Beat Band have just performed. Our 'Reviewers' have reported no movement from their front row seats. However, the balcony reports some security action and a bit of radio communication. So far, they have seen no movement. You need to move."

Kait surprised me with her heated response. "Negative. We cannot hurry. These people are in very bad shape. This is going to take time. Get Desleigh and Audette ready."

"Copy. Sadly, you do not have time. Ground floor Reviewers report guards are on the move. Repeat. Security is on the move. Get ready. Over."

Arguing was pointless. I just gritted me teeth and continued destroying hinges to free as many people as I could. Kait was helping the victims stand and assessing their condition. Some had been in here for some time. We gave instructions to those who could walk, to meet up with our crew stationed throughout the lower floors.

A small voice interrupted my spiral. "We could take them to Bal's. I know he's skitched, but we have showers, food... and I have a stash of clean clothes. Then we could help them get back to their homes."

There was talking and pauses in our earpieces and then, "Copy. Will send someone round to check. Will start directing our trans-porters past the square. Desleigh and Audette are on standby."

"Jem, you're going to have to lead them and make sure they don't get turned around."

"I can't."

Kait took over. Just as well, I was losing me mind fighting with these bleeding hinges and worried it was all for naught.

Jem said, "Richard. Sweetie. I can't leave them."

Val had found the key in the dimly lit room and made a beeline for Richard and Sweetie's crate. "Go!"

Of course, it would have worked if Richard was operating in the same cognitive reality as the rest of us. Unfortunately, he was so disturbed and agitated he couldn't move. Kait tried luring him out with her green armour. But it was all for naught.

Jem tried coaxing Sweetie out, but Richard wouldn't release her. It was a bleeding nightmare.

In the end it was Val who served the savage yet critical blow. "Jem, you are part of our team, and on this mission for a purpose. As a guide. We are here to release and rescue. And fight. We cannot do our job if you do not do yours. Trust us, just as, right now, we are trusting you. Without your help, these people"—some of the freed were helping others as they all waited for Jem—"cannot escape without you. They may as well climb back in the crates and wait to die." Harsh but true.

It was one of the few occasions Val dropped the sharp edge of her battle-speak to a compassionate plea. "Please, Jem, we all need you to do this. We will bring Richard and the dog."

"Sweetie. Her name is Sweetie."

Val didn't quite hide the disgust at the name as she repeated it and her assurance: we would bring them.

Finally, Jem was on her way, leading the first batch of those who could walk to freedom along an honour guard of Warriors. Somehow, February and October had had another two mini drones ferried up to the temple and given Amina instructions on how to launch them. They weren't as good as the dragonfly, but enough to let us know when we could release the prisoners, when they had to wait, and when they could proceed.

What followed was a process so painful, me knickers were knotting macrame as growing grass and drying paint were taking us around the outside. In twos and threes we released the prisoners along our chain of protection. Guards, Warriors and our crew passed the freed captives much like passing buckets of water to a fire. Reeking buckets of water. I was sure the stench was going to alert the whole theatre.

But, smell aside, the biggest spanner in the works were the numbers. We'd planned on delivering one: our resource budget was blown sky-high with the multitudes. Trying to get all these people… and animals out the back door, undercover, and not raise suspicion, had us all swinging from tenterhooks by the skin of our teeth. Especially since we backed onto a very public city square.

The Light shielded our mission the whole way. But the real fly in the ointment was security. Indy was doing a great job impersonating the guy he'd knocked out. But we had to keep all other eyes off us as well, including the security cameras.

The clock was racing against us. We needed to have this place empty before anyone came down to start preparing the sacrifice for after the show. We needed more time. And we still had to get Richard out... quietly.

What we didn't need was the update that set me nerves to raging raw. "Bal cannot be found. We have someone searching his premises but, so far, no sign. We have been instructed to send our guests anyway. But guys, you'd better hurry. Our Reviewers report security is getting restless. They may know something is up. They've also connected and communicated with the Gerent's personal guard. You need to move. Now. Over."

DANIEL: IN THE EYE OF THE STORM

"We need more time." Marcus's growl sounded in my ear, which overrode the microphones and foldback. Tessa threw me a nervous glance and Riah stared at me. Her fingers still danced along the strings of her guitar, but she had a scary look in her eye that had me sweating.

Dan: Riah. Do not sing. You will reveal yourself.

It was the spark that set the storm flooding our family chat.

I almost vomited. She did the cobra head wobble. Only twice, but her face was telling us all what she thought of our demands and what we could do with them.

She then turned to my traitorous brother who was caught between a fire and stone wall. Whilst he still beat out an amazing rhythm on his drum, he shifted his back toward Tessa and me. No matter what I wanted to do and what I was capable of, there was no way I could draw this song out any longer. Our set was pretty much finished and the night was almost over.

Riah unhitched her guitar, placed it in the stand behind her, and did some rapid-fire twin speak to Raph in their private sign language.

Raph nodded once, then started a slow beat on his drum.

Dan: What the hell are you doing Riah. Raph. Stop.

Tessa: Riah, please don't do this.

Dan: Tell the crew they literally have five minutes to get out of there. We're in trouble.

Demons from all over the auditorium started moving to the stage where Sariah began dancing to the seductive beat of Raph's drum. As the crowd clapped in time, showing their appreciation, my stupid sister stepped further into her role of sensuous dancer. I swear to the Light, I was going to kill her. But with the crowd's approval and the Gerent's full attention, she dived deeper.

Dan: Are you insane? You have a chip. You are already on his radar. STOP!

62

BALASHKA: GHOST WRANGLER

I couldn't think. All I could see was Sweetie, Richard, and Jem, all trapped. Captured. Tortured…

No. I had to focus. I just needed to get to the Theatre. To get them back. I was only mildly aware of the stares and sneers I received as I rode the Pod up the mountain. I simply didn't care… couldn't care. They could do what they wanted to me. I just had to get to my family first.

You said You'd be with me. That You'd help. So, tell me. Where do I go? What do I do?

I looked to my Guard who nodded when we came to a stop in the Cultural Precinct. He then led me to the back door of the Theatre. So far, no surprises, I probably would have done that. But I had to get past the guard on the back door.

How does one enter this facility? Can You help?

I raked my hands through my hair only to remember it was a nest of knots. The pain pulled me up short and gave me a dose of reality. I actually had no idea what I was doing. What *was* I doing? I was a complete idiot. There was no way I could do thi—

I rubbed my eye and shook my head. Was that Jem coming out the back door, speaking to the security guard? She had a group of people with her.

"Jem." My relief came out in a yell as I raced across the square, intending to embrace her. She was safe. Tears blurred my vision and I ran straight into a brick wall. A woman stepped out of the shadows and almost flattened me.

"Keep your voice down. You must leave. Now."

"I will do no such thing. My family are in there and I am here to get them."

"Bal, quiet." Jem was hissing in my face. "You'll get everyone caught." She kowtowed to the Amazonian, then hauled me into the building.

"I say, Je—"

She hissed at me again. "Shut up, Bal." Dragging me into a little dark alcove, Jem grabbed my head and yanked my ear in front of her mouth. "We are breaking and entering. We are dodging security. We are fighting fracking demons. And you have to shut up."

Right. Well. Yes. "Sorry." I had the sense to whisper.

"Follow me. Now. And be absolutely silent. This is literally life and death, Bal."

I nodded. But she didn't see, she was off at a hunched jog. We flew past people stationed along the way—I assumed they were part of the mission as they all wore armour like mine—till we got to the bottom floor. Horrendous stench was the first horror to greet us.

Inside a room at the end of the hall, Marcus was pacing, turning the air blue with whispered expletives. Kait was hunkered down next to a crate, whispering, imploring. And that horrid woman from the ShellCom was glaring, with her hands on her hips.

One's eyes watered from the ammonia and offensiveness of the situation. In the dim green light, I may as well have been in the ocean. But I had no time to think. Jem was pulling me, relentlessly, till we arrived at the crate where Kait was working.

"Richard." All four people in the room hissed at me to be quiet. For goodness' sakes. We were in a dungeon. Who was going to hear us here?

Everyone froze, Jem tilted her head, then got in my face. "Bal, we're out of time. Security are coming. Get Sweetie and Richard out of there, now. Then we have to run. Or we're all going to die."

"Sweetie? Is Sweetie in there?" I folded myself to the recently vacated door and the sight broke my heart. "Oh, my poor, darling girl. Come on."

"Hello. Hello. Hello." Richard's staccato was filled with tears.

"Hello my friend. It's time to come home."

"Dog poo. Dog Poo. Dog Poo."

I leaned in and saw that, in fact, he was covered in dog faeces and urine. "Oh dear, my friend. That's no good. How about we all go home, you can have a shower and Jem can get you new clothes."

"Bang. Bang. Bang." He was weeping.

"I am sure lovely Tessa will make you a new uniform. But, my dear friend, we have to go now or the nasty people will be here."

"Catchers."

"Yes. The Catchers are coming back, we have to leave."

Richard released Sweetie and she tumbled out of the crate into my arms, a bundle of wiry legs and dog kisses. Marcus and Val helped Richard stand and we all turned to leave the hell hole.

We heard multiple heavy footfalls mere moments before security reported our discovery very loudly into a communication device: "We have a breach. All hands to the basement. Stat."

That horrid woman and Marcus pushed Richard behind them. Kait passed him to me and shoved Jem at us as well. "Stay back."

To be perfectly honest, I was not going to argue. One was very happy they were keen to take the lead. I clung to Sweetie who, thankfully, did not struggle. Although fighting off more dog kisses was becoming a tad problematic. Jem held Richard who started yelling, "Hello. Hello. Hello." Unfortunately, this escalated to screaming, "Catchers. Catchers. Dog skrat. Skrat. Skrat. Skrat."

As much as I agreed with my friend, unfortunately one did not have garden tools for him to sort, a green Jaguar for him to pet, or even the capacity to do deep breathing to help.

"What the frack?" The people who wanted to impede our escape were distracted by Richard's outburst. In turn, this was fortuitous, as that wonderfully skilled trio who stood between us and the enemy used it to their advantage. Not long afterwards, the hallway was silent and still. Sadly, I could not say the same about Richard.

"Our cover is blown, so let's just run. I'll take point. Marcus to the back, Kait with me. Jem, keep Bal and Richard moving. Do not stop. Understood?"

The nasty, barky woman didn't wait for a response, she just took off at a pacy jog. She was decidedly rude, and I still didn't care much for her, regardless of her capacity to save me and my family.

"Come on Bal, keep up. We're not out yet." Marcus patted me, forcibly, on the back. I almost tripped over my mismatched shoes but clung to my cargo and did my best. We gathered a man at the bottom of the stairs who fell in beside Marcus and a woman at the top, who took the position at Kait's shoulder. All the while the fierce woman was the head of the arrow at the front.

My dear girl, Jem, was doing a valiant effort in keeping Richard on task, whispering all the while in his ear, distracting him with promises.

When we got to the final turn, another woman materialised. She'd not been there before, but she waited till we passed then fell in beside Marcus and the other fellow.

Once we'd reached the top level, the noise of security increased. Indeed, we had been discovered and were causing quite the stir. The people escaping with me were obviously receiving information on the group chat. I did not have my earpiece so was not privy to the information. The unwelcome information. A few of them swore in unison.

The bossy woman ordered, "Indy, Amina. This is it, the last batch. See they get to a car and get them out of here. We'll meet up at The Wreckage."

Without the slightest hint of consultation, Richard, Sweetie, and I were pushed out the door into the arms of the Amazonian and a frighteningly intimidating man. Without a word they hauled us through the shadows toward the road. "Wait." I dug my heels in. "Where's Jem."

"I'm staying. We're not done."

The bossy woman was issuing orders again before I had the chance to take a breath. "You've done your job. From this point on, you'll be a liability. Go."

Even though I agreed with the sentiment, I thought the delivery a bit harsh. However, I was stunned into compliance when Jem agreed and, lamblike, joined us on our sprint across the square to a waiting car.

We were bundled inside. There was no room for our two escorts, so the driver took off with Jem, Richard, Sweetie and me, even before we had our seatbelts on. I spoke to no one in particular when giving my summary. "Well, that wasn't so bad, now was it?"

Jem didn't... couldn't? speak. She was most likely overwhelmed with gratitude that I had come to save them.

"That's okay, my dear girl. You're welcome. And now our family are safe, we can go home and rest." A stony silence filled the car. At the next set of traffic lights, I tried to reach out to her. But she turned to face the door. Then, just as the lights turned green, she leapt from the vehicle and ran. Our driver had to continue with the traffic. Silly girl. I knew she was safe. She knew this city better than anyone. I would let her make her own way back down the mountain and wait for her to come home when she had cooled off.

The driver didn't speak. But I do believe he was listening to the commentary on his earpiece. It may also have been that Richard was covered in excrement and had still not stopped his, "Skrat. Skrat. Skrat," litany.

I was just so grateful to have my family back and safe, I just let it all slide. I'd made it out. I'd helped. And I'd survived.

Thank You.

63

CONTESSA: ENCORE

When would this flopping night end? I was completely over everything. The whole crowd was clapping and cheering and hooting and whistling as my sister wove seductive magic through the auditorium.

Dan was furious.

I was all kinds of scared.

I mean, from where I stood on the edge of the stage, I could see the Gerent's box. I could see the look on his face. I could see him speak to his right-hand man, pointing to Riah. And I could see that as soon as we got off this stage we were in serious trouble—not to mention all the demon activity trembling at and leering all over my sister.

Even if she stopped now, we weren't... she wasn't... going to escape the Gerent. A one-on-one meeting with the monster. If it was the Dark Lord himself it would be just as bad.

This was bad.

So. Flopping. Bad.

And Raph was in just as much trouble.

From the Gerent that was.

And Val.

And Kait.

And Marcus... literally all of us.

And even though it was really selfish, I was also kind of scared for me. I was linked with the two of them. When he found out Riah had a tracer in her... and a tattoo, he would learn that Raph and I had them too.

The brand on the back of my hand started itching. I couldn't stop my eyes tracking every movement, every hint or suggestion of what he might be thinking, when fear mainlined my system and I almost vomited. Shuffling behind Dan, I dropped my eyes to the floor and imagined I was invisible. I was surely done for, now.

Jolena had just entered his box. As far as my fried brain could make out, the only benefit of this ghastly meet up was that the man was no longer salivating over my sister. "We need to get out of here, now." I was speaking to Dan, but my earpiece picked up my desperate plea.

Daisy: You are good to go. They're all out.

Dan: Too fracking late. Riah has thrown herself to the wolf.

There were too many messages flying into my ear to interpret. But it was enough to know that it didn't matter who got to Riah first... or second, or third, she was in for a roasting.

The beat of Raph's drum slowed and Dan marched across the stage and bent to his ear. Raph gulped, nodded once, and finished. With a bit of an ungainly twirl, so too did Riah. I can kind of understand why she didn't want to finish. She wasn't an idiot—present actions excluded. She knew severe consequences were heading her way as soon as she got off the stage... from, like, every angle.

For a moment, I contemplated running. We knew escape routes. We could leave the stage and just disappear. But the Gerent, with Jolena in tow, had already left the box and they were on their way to meet us. We were trapped and we were absolutely fralped.

To a standing ovation we dragged Sariah off the stage and into our fate. Dan was so angry he couldn't speak. The swarm of demons who'd been salivating at the front of the stage swarmed us and our poor, poor Guards and the Warriors were now fully engaged. It was a total nightmare.

    Tessa: We're trapped. We are being taken to the Wolf and the Huntress.

KAITLYN: STAGE FRIGHT

W e'd finally been able to get Richard to safety with Sweetie. We had a firestorm to get through to get to the kids, but at least the rest of our team were safe.

We didn't have a moment to breathe or even think before the enemy was upon us with more of those rabid hellhounds. Felix, Marlene and Fleur had stayed to fight alongside the three of us. Despite the darkest of circumstances, I had to admit it was so good to be standing with my sister again. Without thought or processing, we took our normal formation and started demonstrating the power and will of the Light. I was barely aware that Felix and the lovely ladies from Laodicea were doing the same.

Whilst Val was celebrating her freedom from both incarceration and being sword bound, my darling husband was releasing his frustration from the previous hour of tortuous waiting. Needless to say, I was working hard to keep up. But we'd done this before. It was how we earned our daily bread in the Light.

And that's when the message came through from Tessa, "We're trapped," and all bets were off. The fury and rage settled within me like a comforter. All three of us roared and began the mindless slaughter of everything that stood between us and our kids. The floors and walls of the "back of house" halls were bathed in toxic tar from dispatched demons.

It was a maze back here, none of us knew where we were going, but the Light had sent a Guide. He led us on the shortest route to the lounge where my worst nightmare was about to play out. But to get there we had to cross the stage. We could go behind the backdrop into the arms of the new wave of demons waiting for us.

Or, straight across the main stage in full sight of the whole audience with nothing in our way… except Jem and a sea of Darkness encroaching on her.

She was backing into the floodlights, her Guards standing at her back. Her blade shook as she pointed it to the group stalking her. "Get back," she repeated with each retreating step.

The crowd applauded. I looked out to the darkness and considered what they would see. A single girl, terrified. They quietened as she continued. "Raph said You'd be with me. Protect me." She continued, her volume increasing. "He said You'd stay with me forever." The audience was silent and the approaching demons snarled. "Raph said I just had to choose You."

"Change of plans, folks." But before Val launched herself onto the stage I grabbed hold of her pony tail, pulled the tie out, and flicked her collar up. As a curse word heated her lips, I hissed at her, "You attempt to keep yourself hidden or I will kick your butt so hard you will not be sitting for a week. Do not jeopardise your, and our future, by being reckless."

Jem, shook, gulped and yelled even louder, "I did choose You. I am choosing You. I will always choose You." Her beautiful pink armour was glinting and flashing with lightning. Her sword sparked and the enemy faltered.

Val stared open-mouthed at me, then did cuss as Marcus slapped her on the back on his way to battle. "Keep up, old girl."

Then she was free to launch herself onto the stage, kicking, punching, knifing and eventually settling into sword fighting. Don't get me wrong, we were right on her heels. I did not allow myself the luxury of considering the fact that one of our most important objectives this evening apart from rescuing potential sacrifices—which was to keep her hidden—had just been shot to pieces.

It's in Your hands. It's all in Your hands.

As we fell back into our formation and routine, I could allow some part of my brain to acknowledge more cheers from the crowd. And even more when two "plants"—Cissa and Al—from near the front of the auditorium made it to the stage. They leapt up and joined the "fun". With Cissa, Al, Felix, Marlene and Fleur, as well as a significant handful of Guards, we didn't take too long to clear the stage... of demons. Their toxic tar, however, was doing significant damage.

Once we'd cleared the way, Cissa had the presence of mind to get us, in a very haphazard way, to bow and run. We dashed past the furious stage manager who was releasing her displeasure via whisper-yelling. I am not sure whether it was for our impromptu, unscheduled performance, or the damage to her beautiful wooden stage. The stench may have also been a factor. But considering the life and death situation involving our kids, her displeasure was not a priority of mine right then.

Our Guide led us to the lounge where the Gerent, his personal guard, and Jolena confronted our children.

We weren't trying to be quiet, but our entrance hadn't even caused a flinch in the Gerent who was sniffing... yes, *sniffing* Riah's neck. His thumb was caressing the brand on the back of her right hand. The others were lined up under the scrutiny of three guards. Tessa's face glinted with tears. Raph was white. And Dan was shaking with rage. The sight forced all sense and reason from my mind and the mamma bear in me roared, "Get your hands off my daughter!"

The beast did look up then. But that may have been because I was running and interacting, with due force, with those who stood in my way.

The impudent man merely flicked his eyes and hand in my direction, like I was an obnoxious fly. I saw red. Literally. I fought my way through until I was brought to a sudden stop by a punch to the ribs.

Which was the key that finally unlocked Marcus's insanity. I heard

367

a beast-like roar which was cut short with groans. My husband's groans. He had received similar treatment to mine.

Wincing, folded in half and trying to breathe very shallow breaths with what could have been a broken rib, I turned to see Bear slumped, his arms pinned to his side and his pale green eyes promising death.

"Enough." The Gerent stepped back from Sariah but still held her hand. "I was merely congratulating this fine young dancer and her back-up band for her"—he turned his head toward her and licked his lips—"scintillating performance." He looked back to us as the others had joined me in a group. Our Guards standing around us kept the Unseen enemy at bay. "But then I realised we had met before." His hysterical giggle sent chills to my heart. "And"—he lifted Sariah's hand —"this one has previously been a guest of mine." He looked at her again, his eyes narrowed. "And yet, she lives." With a slight shake of his head he added, "Intriguing."

He then dropped her hand, turned and walked away, dismissing Riah as he stalked his way to us. Like a knight counteracting a rook, Val placed herself in front of us all. Marcus and I, now released with a warning, tried to stop her. But pulling up that particular freight train, heading toward its destination with hyper-focus, was not within our skillset.

65

DANIEL: FIRE IN THE HOLE

"**W**hat is all this fuss about?" The creep came to a stop in front of Val. "I am merely congratulating an act for an outstanding performance. I see no need for this"—he scoped each member of our group, then came back to Val—"hostility. Surely you realise such actions are worthy of death."

Tessa gasped as she clutched Riah. Raph and I were of the same mind as we manoeuvred in front of the girls.

"I have done no harm and am, quite frankly, insulted. But also intrigued." The dude looked around the room. He didn't have the Sight. Couldn't have the Sight. And yet, his gaze slowed where our Guard stood, and where the other Warriors had positioned themselves around the room. For the first time, uncertainty flashed in his eyes.

"I know this one." Vamp-woman strutted across the carpet to Tessa. She pushed me aside with a sneer, and, at her request, one of the Gerent's guards pulled Tessa out of our group. "She has done nothing but cause trouble since she arrived in our beautiful city."

"And you have done nothing but use, abuse and kill, since you tried to equal the gods."

"Shut it, Jem." Marcus tried to keep the chick hidden. But if she had a death wish, like my sister, there was little we could do to protect her.

"And, of course, I know that brat. That one I created myself."

But the Gerent wasn't listening, he was staring at Jolena. "Tried to equal the gods?" Was he jealous? He looked her over.

Under his scrutiny, she lost a bit of her bravado. "The girl lies."

One of the things I had learned to fear the most was the Gerent's giggle: high-pitched and insane. "Oh, what wonderful fun." With a flick of his head, Jolena and the four of us were marched to where our family stood in the Gerent's shadow. "I could send you all to The Games. Or"—he tapped his chin—"I could have our own version here. The room is big enough." He clapped his hands. But as his eyes circuited the periphery of the room again, he stopped. More Warriors had joined us.

Val stepped forward. "You do remember, don't you?"

The Gerent tried to focus on her, but he was becoming more agitated and distressed by the growing number of Warriors appearing in the room.

Val stepped in very close and dropped her voice. "Do you remember Philadelphia?" The man paled. "Do you remember the hand that reached into your body and squeezed the life out of your kidney?" He blanched. "Do you remember the pain? Do you remember the Warrior of Light who warned you of your fate?" Without taking her eyes off the Gerent, Val stretched her arm out around the room. "We are not alone. We are not outnumbered." The Gerent's Adam's apple bobbed. "You are interfering with things beyond your control, concern and capacity."

It was a squeak, but the Gerent found his voice. "You." He then looked to us. "You." His hand shook as he pointed. His complete attention came back to Val. Words had now failed him.

At their overlord's obvious unease, his guard stepped in, and Jolena found her backbone and tried to control the Gerent's men with a shriek: "Arrest them all."

We were surrounded. Yes, the Light outnumbered the mortals, but if you included all the demonic, we weren't the majority. As the gates of hell were opened and a new wave of the enemy spewed into the room, it was game on. We were flat out defending ourselves, let alone fighting off the confused guard.

I barely had time to register the nightmare. Whilst we were fighting the Unseen, the Seen were dragging us away. I couldn't even see what the rest of my family were doing. The sea of Dark and tide of Light blinded me to everything. Then seven spears of Light smashed onto the scene and a thunderous voice declared, "Enough!"

Everybody froze. And I mean literally. Well, kind of. The demons, the Gerent's guards and Jolena turned to statues. The Gerent and our family, however, were not bound. And neither was one of the Gerent's men. His extreme trembling gave him away. From past experience, I reckoned we were in the presence of the Star of Sardis. I felt compelled to drop to my knees. He shot me a glance and gave me a slight shake of the head and a wink.

Did he just wink at me? Forget that, just... thank You.

The Light's Chief Warrior of Sardis turned to the Gerent. The freak did drop to his knees and the Warrior didn't suggest otherwise. Nor did he do anything to stop the man's savage shaking.

"The Light's Mighty Warrior is correct. You are encroaching in waters that are not of your concern." Sweat glistened and ran down the Gerent's face. "You will not remember this family. This"—he turned to Sariah with a blank face—"act." His face scoped the room. "Any of these people. Or anything that has happened in this room. None of you will remember."

The Star then refocused his attention on the sweating Gerent. "A day will come when our Mighty Warrior will request a substitution: plain, pure and simple: one in the place of another. You will grant her this boon and on this, your final judgement hangs." The Star turned to face the guard who was also trembling. "Well met, Tobias."

The Star nodded and the man dropped to his knees then fell on his face, a litany of apologies tumbling from his lips. "I am so sorry. I am so sorry. I did not know. Please forgive me."

"Stand." The guard had no choice but obey the Chief Warrior's compelling voice.

The Gerent's personal guard, Tobias, then shuffled whilst trying to bow and kneel his way over to our family, where he finally fell on his knees again. Weeping, he repeated his apology to the four of us. "I had no idea."

The penny dropped. I realised who he was. Sariah stepped forward and slapped his face. No one stopped her. No one said a thing. This bloke was one of the men who'd held Mary and Travis whilst the Gerent had beaten them to death. At Sariah's blow, he dropped his head and wept. "I am so very sorry."

Into the silence, the Star of Sardis repeated his declaration to the Gerent. "You will have no recollection of this conversation. You still live because your purpose has not yet been fulfilled. But your time is coming and that truth will live within you." As he spoke, Warriors moved throughout the room, their hands brushing the heads of dormant guards.

The Gerent tried to speak, but as a hand brushed his head, he too froze.

The Star of Sardis moved to stand in front of Jolena, still a statue and unaware of what was happening around her. "You, however, have filled your quota of offences. You have been judged and found wanting. Receive your punishment, Jolena, slave of Dionysus."

I was waiting for something appropriate and hideous to happen to the freakoid, but she was unchanged.

"And that brings me to this evening's events." The Star of Sardis turned to Jem.

66

MARCUS: CONSEQUENCES, LONERS AND STRAYS

The Star's eyes landed on Jem and she fell to her knees. Much like breathing, it was a compulsion, you had no choice. Stepping over to her he touched her shoulder. "Rise, beloved daughter of the Light. You are seen. Your offering has been judged worthy and has been accepted. Welcome. In return, the Light has granted you this gift."

Jem's blade lit up like a beacon. A bright and blinding light... a torch. "To find your way through the darkness and as you lead others onward to His safety. Use it well for His glory, cherished, chosen, beloved."

He moved to me girl Sariah and I matched him, move for move. She was due her knuckle rap and rebukes, no denying it. But he daren't touch her, or, so help me Light, he'd be dealing with me. The Star of Sardis held up his hand and I was parked in me progress. "The Father knows your heart, Fierce Protector. Be still, be calm, His love for her is both just and boundless."

Peace settled over me burning rage as he addressed me girl. "Princess, your heart is pure. Your motives righteous. Your actions unwise." Sariah dropped her head as twin rivers flooded her cheeks. Her shoulders begged to be hugged as they shook from the weeping. I itched to hold her, but the Warrior held his hand to stay me again. Kait was a vibrating ball of energy at me side. Val was breathing like an enraged bull.

"Your actions have endangered those you love, those the Light designed to free, and the mission you were sent to fulfil."

Riah's shoulders were now fully shaking. One and all, we were tethered in our tracks, restrained from comforting her.

She dropped to her knees and covered her face with her hands. "I am so sorry." Me girl's whispered words echoed those of the guard, Tobias. Yet she had us high and dry. It was the first time I'd ever heard her speak. She'd sung, but never spoken. She looked to each one of us, her eyes swollen, red and blurry behind oceans of tears. "I am so very sorry." She shut her eyes and looked to the heavens. "I am sorry. Please, forgive me. Please let me have another chan—" Her words were swallowed by sobbing and me focus narrowed in distress for her.

From nowhere, from everywhere, we heard the words: "*Granted. Your apology has been accepted. Your punishment has been served. It is over.*" I don't know if it was meant for me or all of us, but I also heard, "*There will be no more reprisals, her sentence is served. Sariah, your burden is to remember. To demonstrate grace. To mete out the forgiveness you have received.*" We'd not needed a map nor instructions, it was understood. Tobias.

She nodded.

"*Be at peace My, child, all is well.*" There was a pause, then the Light continued, "*Tobias, before you is a dangerous and lonely road. But the choice is yours: to live freely in the Light and serve My purpose in the ranks of the Gerent, or return to the world and die within the Darkness.*"

Tobias lifted his eyes to the ceiling and nodded. It was plain as day which path he'd chosen: his body was wrapped in blazing gold armour.

"*Be strong and courageous, My son. Know that despite the isolated path you trek, you are never alone.*" Two Warriors stepped out of formation from around the perimeter of the room and stood at Tobias's shoulders. "*You are My child and I will never abandon you.*" The man's body tensed as he threw his arms and head back. A Light pulsed within him once, then settled. *"Receive this gift to assist you in your task."* Tobias shook his head then looked around the room. It was like he was seeing everyone and everything for the first time.

"Be at peace My children. All of you, again, be strong and courageous. I am with you all, My love surrounds you, My power is within you." Three Warriors approached Tessa, Raph and Riah. Each Warrior laid their hand over the hearts of me kids and Light streamed into them. *"You are Mine. The Darkness has no hold on you. The bugs have been removed. You are safe."*

"Well done, faithful ones. You have achieved your goal. As we speak, the auditorium is emptying. The square is being closed. We will give you time, but you must evacuate the building and the Cultural District. It is time for this abhorrent temple to be abolished. Go now, the time has come."

The hands restraining me... all of us, were withdrawn and we fell on those kids with love so raw it burned me eyes and scorched me throat. But our family scrum was derailed by an eruption of noise as the guards and Jolena awoke. Stoney-faced and dead-eyed, the Gerent's detail formed up around him and escorted him from the room. Our kids raced to their corner and gathered their belongings.

And Jolena started screaming. "My eyes. My eyes. I can't see." With her hands outstretched she stumbled every which way, looking for someone to help her, her panic pitched like an air-raid siren. "Help me. I can't see."

A chaos of emotions crossed Jem's face. We all paused, waiting to follow her lead. But as she turned her back on her mother, Raph approached the viper from behind. "Come with me and I will show you the way out."

As the woman turned to face us, I couldn't stop my recoil. Where her eyes had been sat two white orbs. She grabbed and grasped me boy. He allowed her. Tessa turned to stone. Jem a pillar. Raph looked to us all as he tried to lead the woman from the room. "She will suffer enough for the rest of her life. The least we can do is show her the way out."

Jolena shrieked. "What is that? I can see a light."

375

Jem snarled as her blade flashed with silver flame.

"Come on, team, we've got to go." True to form, Val's head was still in the fight and made sure we didn't dally on our way to safety.

Dan: Any chance there are some rides still available? We're ready to go.

There was silence in our earpieces.

Daisy: Will do what we can. Start making your way out and we'll keep you posted.

Originally, we'd planned to split up and rejoin at The Wreckage. But considering the battle wasn't over, nor the Dark happy, you could bet your bippy it was going to be a rough ride down the mountain. We thought it best to stick together. We allowed Jem to take point and use her blade to lead us on her hidden paths.

Raph left Jolena at the entrance to the Theatre. He reasoned someone would find and help her. But since she was one with Darkness, she didn't have to fight like we did. Trying to get the woman to stay put, however, was like trying to convince a stray dog to find another source of hope.

67

RAPHAEL: WEDDINGS, VOWS, AND PROMISES

Tiger, no longer interested in my ankles or insects, stretched out in the bed of basil. We were back at Sanctuary, in the garden, surrounded by the familiar comfort of thriving green and the perfume of leaves.

At first light this morning, we had stood with Cissa and Al overlooking the plain to the west while they repeated their marriage vows.

It was a small gathering. Jonathan led the ceremony. Harry and Marcus stood with Al; Tessa and Jem with Cissa. The rest of our families stood around them and witnessed their promises. It was quiet and peaceful. Al and Cissa wanted to have us present but did not want to steal the focus from the wedding later today of Jonathan, Overseer of the underground Community of Light in Philadelphia, and Daisy, co-leader of Sanctuary.

Harry did not stay. Friends from Laodicea and Sardis were arriving, reconnecting and celebrating while Daisy and Jonathan were getting ready. I was happy for them, but I was also heavy with sadness.

I do not know what to do with this weight. Everyone was so focused on Sariah: what she did wrong; how she discarded common sense; how she did no—

"Raph, there you are." Jet, a good friend, pulled up a chair next to me, his knee jiggling and his hands twisting a piece of long, dry grass. "So, good to see you again."

"It is good to be back."

Jet's eyes roved the garden. "Yeah, so, this crew you brought with you. Pretty cool, hey?"

"They are very nice people. We have become good friends."

His leg stilled and he looked at me. "How good-a friends?"

"You know what it is like. When you battle alongside people, you get close."

His leg started again. "So, Jem? How good a friend is she?"

"Very good." I turned to face him, hoping he might get to the point. "What is it you are really asking, Jet?"

His eyes scoped the garden, then his words tumbled over each other. "Is she seeing anyone?" At my blank look, he clarified. "Does she have a boyfriend?"

"Up until three months ago, she was in hiding, disguised as a boy. So, no."

"Sweet."

"Jet, that is not 'sweet'. She was abused, abandoned, hunted and living in fear."

"Of course, I mean, that really sucks. What I meant was, it's sweet that she is now being a girl, and she doesn't have a boyfriend."

We were silent for a while. I did not want to be rude, but I was having a conversation with the Light and I really wanted to get back to it. "Is there anything else I can help you with?"

"Actually, yes." His leg took off and the piece of grass had been twisted down to a few centimetres long.

Eventually I prompted him. "How?"

"Um, can you let me know if she says anything about me. And if she's... keen?"

The thought of the two of them together caused a fissure of light to seep into my sadness. I smiled. "I will definitely do that, Jet."

"Sweet, Raph. You're the best. Oh, and... maybe... tell her... she looks hot in pink?" And he was gone.

Thank You for our friends here. And in Sardis. And in Laodicea. Thank

You that we can be the thread that stitches them together. But... please help me. I am suspended... swinging... ungrounded. You said to Riah, and every-one, that it was over, that her dis—

Screaming broke my focus. Tiger was on all fours, his fur on end, back arched. On my feet, I searched for the threat. When laughing followed, Tiger shook himself out and I exhaled.

A high-pitched yell—"Yes!"—and more laughter preceded the tumble of two more old friends' bodies wrapped up in each other as they rolled past me. "Raph." Kelly screamed again. "Look." With one arm around Craig's waist, she thrust her left hand out in front of me. A fragment of a diamond glistened and reflected the morning light.

Warmth spread from my heart to my smile. "Congratulations. I am so happy for you both."

I had always been a bit scared of Craig, but he beamed at me, and Kelly swooped in and kissed my cheek. "You're the first to know. Oh, Raph..." Kelly jiggled, squealed, then squeezed me in a hug. Craig patted my back and they moved on. I did not feel like telling them that, by now, all of Sanctuary would know. But I was confident all of Sanctuary would be celebrating with them.

Thank You that despite all the sadness and Darkness in the world, there is still so much joy. Thank You that Kelly and Craig have given us another jewel to celebrate. But I confess, my soul is struggling to sing with them. I am lost. I was also respons—

"Raph, dear boy, this is quite an exquisite garden. Not as grand as mine, but absolutely delightful. One wonders if perhaps my gardener, Molly, might consider growing food. Charming. Absolutely charm-ing." Balashka was gone before I could reply.

Thank You that he has felt safe enough to leave his garden to join us. Please help him to continue to spread his wings. And please help me find my place again. I was also responsible for putting my family and the prisoners at risk. I am guilty of not listening to others. First and foremost I listened to my sister and put her needs firs—

"Raph. There you are." Jem took the seat that Jet had pulled close. "This is pretty cool, isn't it? Everyone here has armour. Everyone. I didn't think there were so many of us. And, I mean, have you seen those Guards? Even at the Finale I didn't see that many. This place must be pretty special." Her eyes were glued to the rows of Warriors permanently on watch.

"Yes. It is. I believe because of what happened here and the stand we took, and the price we paid, the Light has rewarded Sanctuary with peace and safety."

"That must have been pretty hard-core. I mean, I only know what it was like for us at the Theatre, but..." Her eyes were lost. She shook herself, then continued on a different tangent. "So, Jet. He's like, what? Owner of this place?"

"Nanna-May was his grandmother, his family lived here for generations. He is the last, but until he is of age, Jonathan and Daisy help him run it."

"So, he's pretty important then." Her shoulders slumped. "And, like, loaded." Her voice trailed off as she studied the dirt at her feet.

"I have told you, Jem, we are all important."

"Ha. Yeah. But we all know, some are more important than others." She started mumbling to herself. I could not hear everything, but there were some words I picked up. And they were not kind.

"Jem?" I cared about my friend, but again I was at a loss to know what it was she actually wanted. "How can I help?"

She heaved a great sigh. "Don't worry. I'm just being silly. I mean, I probably won't be back, so it doesn't matter." Sadness that equalled my own cloaked her shoulders and weighed her down.

"I do not want to speak out of place. But would it help to know that Jet asked after you?" I tried to remember his exact words. "He said, he thinks you look hot in pink?"

She sat up straight. "He does?"

"Yes."

Jem beamed and leaned in. "Thanks, Raph." She kissed my cheek and waltzed away, her feet hardly touching the ground.

Thank You for my beautiful friend and that she may find someone to walk with in the Light. Forgive me for when I put my sadness before them. And them before You. My sister before You. But how do I know when I have to choose? I thought we were helping. It was dangerous. I know that. But they needed tim—

"Do you like my dress? Daisy said I was prettier than her. But I don't agree. She has red hair. But Daddy said we're both beautiful. What do you think, Raph?" Ruby twirled in front of me. When she spotted Tiger, she leapt to him. Picked him up and rubbed her face in his neck. "Hello, pretty kitty, you smell like coriander." She turned back to me. "Oh, I was sent to find you and tell you it's time. You have to come and watch me throw petals." She dumped Tiger in my lap and continued twirling out of the garden.

Thank You that Jonathan is well, Daisy has found a family, and Jet and Ruby have loving parents again. Thank You that it does not matter when or where we are born, or to whom, You have the best family waiting for us. Thank You for my sister. That I have not ever had to be apart from her. That You have made her a constant in my life. Thank You for her bravery, and talent, and her quick thinking. She could see our family needed time. And Riah helped provide that. And I helped her. It was not the best way. But we did not have options. I see that it was a problem. I know we put others in danger, but what am I to do with the guil—

Riah bumped my shoulder. I looked up to her and she gave me a soft smile. I knew she understood my tumbled feelings. She felt them too. But she had been pardoned. I had not.

Like me, she had not changed out of her good clothes from this morning and I could see some stray goat hairs clinging to her front. Tilting her head, she offered to walk with me. We looked around for Tiger and found him hiding under the cool tomato leaves.

Together we walked to the Meeting Place where Daisy and Jonathan were to be married. There were so many things that reminded me of Dan and Tessa's day. But for this ceremony, Riah and I squeezed into the back corner behind Dan, invisible. From the stage, I looked over the crowd. Peace and joy filled the day like soap bubbles: there was no need for lookouts, or fear of attack. The Light secured our borders.

Dan gave us the nod and we started playing: Ruby's cue to begin her march, throwing petals down the central path of the packed tent.

Next came Tessa, Kait, Val—who had been speechless when asked—and Gemma, fellow member of Sanctuary and survivor of the great battle, followed by Daisy. Al, Jet, Travis and Marcus stood with Jonathan.

One of the other Community leaders led the ceremony, and, with no interruptions, declarations of war, or interference, Daisy and Jonathan were married. The meal afterward, partly supplied by our family from the Factory in Laodicea, was one we'd come to expect but our new friends from Sardis were yet to experience. The Lightmas celebration only made the day more alive, but I was glad when it was over and I could seek solitude again.

The revelry was still going, but groups were breaking off. From the back paddock under the solitary, old gum in the light of a full moon, I watched a group walk to Nanna-May's house. Jonathan walked beside Al who carried Ruby, asleep on his shoulder. Daisy and Cissa walked arm in arm. When they arrived at the little gate, Cissa hugged Daisy, then before Jonathan could take his daughter, Cissa threw her arms around him. After a pause, Jonathan hugged her back. When they pulled apart, they spoke, hugged again, then the group parted ways.

Across the paddock I saw another two bodies making their way up the hill, one in hints of pink, the other in forest green. My heart smiled.

Thank You.

A cool breeze drifted across the field, relieving the day's heat. Cattle chewed cud nearby and the scent of grass, gumleaves and soil allowed me to inhale fully. The moon was so large and full and bright, I could not see any stars. But I knew they were there. It caused me to think of how the big and showy and extraordinary is a gift, a wonder, but it cannot remain permanent. It has to fade so it can come again at its allotted time. Consistency comes from the little lights burning, shining, working in the background. On the darkest nights, they shine brightly. At the darkest times, they show the way. In the darkest circumstances, they secure hope.

Riah found me, sat by my side and leaned into my shoulder. She patted Tiger, who slept in my lap and sighed. I do not know if she meant to gift me her Peace or whether it was just what she was to me. She did not want anything from me. She did not ask anything of me. She came because she was part of me: my soul nest. Her presence allowed me to exhale freely.

I am not a moon like Riah, reflecting the glory and majesty of Your Light brilliantly. Please help me be a star: smaller but steady, not always seen, but always present. Always burning brightly for You. I am sorry I caused trouble for my family. I am sorry we brought the Wolf to our door. Thank You that You rescued us and stopped the Dark Lord's abomination. Thank You for Tobias. Show us how we can encourage and support him. But please, please...

The weight inside me was a rising tide. The sadness washed up, over and out. Riah wrapped her arm around me as I wept.

The breeze picked up, chilling my tears dry. Leaves trickled along the ground and the cattle stilled.

"Be at peace, Compassionate Healer, My son. Your petition has been heard and answered. Your heart is pure, your love is true, your gift is honoured. Before you both, the road will continue narrow and straight. Always, My Light goes before you. Seek and stay in My presence and your petition will be granted. From before you were formed, you were Mine. From the day you were born, I set you on My path. To the day you depart, you will be in My will. Be at peace, My beloveds."

"Are you two out here somewhere?"

"They'd better be, Kait. I've not seen hide nor hair of them. Not with the goats, not in the garden. Can't even find the bleeding cat."

"Calm down, you two. They'll be safe, the Warriors are on guard."

"If that be the case, sister dear, why would you be palming your blade."

"Because, old man, there is more than the Unseen about."

"We are here." Riah and I jumped to our feet. Tiger was not happy, but soon settled in my arms as our parents found us.

Kait hugged us both. "Time for bed. It has been a big day."

Val looked at my wet face and barked, "What's wrong?" The three of them went on guard. After surveying the perimeter, she pulled me close and brushed my face dry. Her voice soft and warm, she repeated, "What's wrong, my boy?"

Having her back... having her here made me cry again. I clung to her and confessed, "I missed you so much."

Riah joined us in the embrace, and we were silent for a long time. Eventually, Val sniffed and pulled back, cupping each of our cheeks with one of her warm, calloused hands. "Always..." She sniffed again. "Always I am yours. Always, I will do everything in my power to be with you. But when I can't, know that nothing can dim my love for you. It rages like an insatiable fire."

EPILOGUE

KAIT: WAR COUNCIL

O ppressive weight like a wet blanket sat over the group meeting in the glorious space at the heart of Sanctuary. We sat in stunned silence. Speechless. Thoughts, too overwhelming to wade through, bound us. The confusion was so thick, not even the fresh scents of the garden surrounding us could break the yoke of the shock.

"Was he expecting it?" My darling husband was thinking first and foremost of the poor man and what he would have gone through.

Jonathan replied in a hoarse whisper, "In a sense, I guess he did. We all do… at some point. But then? There? In that way?" He shook his head. "How can anyone expect that. Poor, faithful Amos."

Having had more time to come to terms with the facts, Daisy was shaking with rage. "They took him from within the Community. During a meeting. He was opening The Way to his people. Cuffed him. Bashed him. Then led him to the city square. The Freaky Freak himself was there. Sat on his throne in the middle of the crowd. It was all set up. A fire primed, ready to go under the bronze bull they use for demon worship." She stopped to take a shaking breath, and her eyes flicked to the Guards that surrounded us. "The Psycho demanded he bow down and worship him." Her voice cracked then. No doubt we were all remembering the very same thing happening here. At these very gates where we were held captive, made to witness the Gerent's execution of our beloved Mary and Travis.

She continued, "Amos stood firm. Said his love of the Light was too great. So, they bashed him... again, and threw him in the cauldron. And lit the fire..." She gulped and it took a few attempts before her voice came back. "And the crowd cheered."

Jonathan took over. "The faithful got us out of Pergamum where we met with Charlie in Thyatira." Jonathan smiled briefly at the man across the table from him, then the remaining light in his chocolate eyes dimmed. "Things aren't looking too good there, either. Trouble's brewing." He shook his head.

"Yeah, the numpties have invited a she-devil into the pulpit and she's vomiting lies and getting them all hepped-up and hot to trot. Blind fools." Daisy once again was on the rampage, but, taking her usual spot behind Jonathan's seat, her hand never left his shoulder. The girl was too "hepped-up" herself to sit for long.

Still shaken by the memory of the Wolf at the Finale in Sardis, I said, "That man will pay for what he is doing. The Light will not let his carnage go unpunished. But until then, let's honour our brother, give thanks for his example, and look to the Light and celebrate our many victories. It is wonderful to have you back." I smiled at the glint of Daisy's simple wedding band. "Did you manage to have a nice break before the Gerent hijacked your honeymoon?"

The newlyweds looked to each other and the warmth and light returned. Jonathan smiled again and nodded at me. "Thank you, Kait. Yes, we had a wonderful time. But I am very glad to be home." Both he and Daisy looked to the curled-up form of Ruby in Jonathan's lap. Daisy pulled Jet in closer beside her. "What news is there of the Communities?"

Cissa gave her report on what happened five weeks ago at the Theatre. It was the first time all parties had been in the same space to hear the full account. Since we fled that night into the arms of Sanctuary, she informed us of the mop-up in Sardis and the reverberations of the Light's intervention. The people were still in shock and unable to explain what had happened at the temple attached to the Theatre.

"I believe the official explanation is, 'a very localised earth tremor'." Cissa smiled at the ridiculousness of it. "Since Al and I are away too much, Arthur, Desleigh, Kirt and Laura have taken over leading the True Community of Light. We'll attend and help when we can." She grinned at us all. "And, of course, since we may have to sell our building, we are all very grateful Balashka has opened the doors of his home for our regular meetings. Outside the city wall we will still be effective, but not under the same regulations."

She returned to her seat and Felix took the floor.

"As far as the other centres are concerned, I am able to report things are... stable in Laodicea, still safely hidden underground here in Philadelphia, ever-concerning in Ephesus as the Gerent descends daily into madness." He nodded to Jonathan, acknowledging his report of faithful Amos's death in Pergamum. "Smyrna is holding strong but the... temperature is rising." He nodded to the calm man I'd not seen since our first visit to the High Council here in Philly two and a half years ago. "Since Charlie is with us, perhaps he is best... situated to give a report on Thyatira?" Felix nodded to the defrocked member of the Philadelphian High Council. He'd been the ignored voice of reason, his wisdom unwelcome, when, as a leadership, they'd debated how to respond to the Gerent's demands.

Charlie nodded to the group. "Thanks, Felix. The Community is strong. Faithful. But like all cities, we face pressure. As you know, I had to leave Sardis to take the reins of the family business in Thyatira, and I fear we stand on the coattails of Sardis's fall. We are teetering toward the same path. But the Community holds, for now..." He breathed deeply and exhaled before addressing us again. "But Daisy summed it up perfectly. A 'she-devil' is in the pulpit, vomiting lies to the blind fools." He shrugged, the weight of the world in his sigh.

Silence followed his report. There was no denying we were in tough times. All of us. Each Community was vulnerable to infiltration. The compulsion of the Word started building in my head and heart like it usually did. However, I kept silent... for now.

Jonathan took his time making eye contact with each member of the group. The man's genuine love and concern held us all captive. "I propose an alignment." He looked to Felix. "I know you are working at building an alliance between the Communities' High Councils in the Seven Cities. This is important work. Thank you for your efforts; we would have been... would still be isolated without it." At his nod, Jet encouraged Ruby from his lap and Jonathan laboured to his feet. Leaning his knuckles on the table, breathing slowly, he commanded our attention. "I propose we build an underground alliance of the True Community of Light. Any who are persecuted or in danger are welcome to shelter here at Sanctuary: to rest and recover. From here, we have hidden routes out of the city to secure freedom beyond the Gerent's reach."

Beautiful Amina demanded everyone's attention purely by standing. "Women and children can come to the Factory. We will shelter and protect. It is what we do."

Jonathan smiled. "Thank you for the continued support we have come to learn is the heartbeat of our Laodicean sisters."

Al didn't bother standing for his short declaration. "Things could get hot... hotter in Sardis. I'll pass on your invitation."

A small cough had us turning to sweet Jem. "I... um... can get anyone, from anywhere, undercover, in Sardis. I can take them to Bal's or... The Wreckage. Maybe they can be picked up from there."

Everyone beamed at the young lady. But perhaps none more than Jet. *Interesting*.

He added, "We could pick them up in Old Faithful on our regular trips to the markets at The Wreckage." The heat in their two grins raised a few eyebrows around the table.

Jonathan finished, "Thank you, friends. We have the start of a plan. We will continue to petition the Light and seek His wisdom and guidance."

"Enough talk, it's time to move." Daisy's gentle care, stroking Ruby's hair, was at odds with her tone. "Thanks for coming, folks, the urn's hot, food's out, stay as long as you like. If you need us for the afternoon, too bad. Kait and Marcus will still be here watching over things. We haven't officially taken the reins back yet. Leave a message with them. You good to go, Shep?" Her voice softened and the look of concern had us all seeing through her bluff. None more so than her husband, if the sunshine in his smile was anything to go by. It was time for him to rest and spend time reconnecting with his kids.

It took another ten or so minutes for the newlyweds to make it through their "welcome home" committee. I stood in Bear's arms and watched, remembering those early days for us, and how important it would be for them to have well-guarded, quality time alone. It wouldn't be too easy, here. But then again, with the Light's permanent provision of the Guards around their perimeter, they had a better chance than the rest of us. Especially my two.

Tessa and Dan sat quietly at the back of the group. My girl had been a bit flat lately. I suspected she was fighting off a bug. Or fatigue. We had all been so grateful to spend time here again, but she was still helping out at The Wreckage, doing assignments for Cissa, and trying to build up stock for her online store. Every day, she travelled with Marcus, Dan, Josh and Tim to Sardis, where they continued their work rebuilding homes for those hidden outside the wall.

The twins, however, were revelling in their break. They'd finished their TAVE courses, and managed to finish their final exams for Year Eleven, just in time for a quiet fifteenth birthday celebration. Raph had poured himself back into the garden, which Tiger was loving. And Riah was getting serious about fulfilling her obligation to Harry to produce a quality art portfolio for him to present to his buyers. Val, too, had been enjoying her freedom, spending more and more time with her writing.

Life here had been good. We'd all been busy, but resting and happy. It had been a good break. "I'm going to miss this place."

"What are you rattling your dags about, woman?" My beloved's spluttered response had everyone's attention.

I smiled to him, then our growing family in the Light. "Well, when we head to Thyatira, of course."

At that moment, there was a roar as a wave of attack washed against the perimeter Guards, and a flurry of movement around Val.

We all drew our swords and went on guard. Except Tessa, who ran from the Meeting Place with her hand over her mouth. And Val, who screamed as she was swamped by small, dark creatures with long fangs and whip-like tails. They appeared out of nowhere, and as she tried to cover her face and head, she went down under their mass. Before we could move, or think, the tiny beasts planted the Dark's blades deep into her flesh, then vanished.

A CONTEXTUAL NOTE

And so the team have finished their mission in Sardis and prepare for the next leg of the journey.

Thank you so much for joining me, and those encased in the Armour of Light, on the fifth leg of this adventure. I hope you have been encouraged by their victories and gracious with their failings.

If you have enjoyed this book, please consider leaving a review. It would inspire others to pick it up as well as encourage me to see the series through. Although, at this point of the game, that's a given. Four to go!

As part of my preparation for *Liberating Persecution*, I spent many hours researching the ancient city of Sardis. I found maps that offered a clear outline of what the prestigious city would have looked like and used that information as part of the setting.

I discovered many other interesting things. For example, the story of King Midas was set in Sardis. The temple to Artemis, built outside the city walls, was second only in size to the one in Ephesus known as one of the Seven Wonders of the Ancient World. However, Sardis's temple was never completed. There is evidence that, in later times, a Christian community met there.

Some of the new characters you met in *Liberating Persecution* were inspired by people we read about in the New Testament. You may have picked up Balashka's character was inspired by Zaccheus—whose name means "pure, innocent". I wondered what he would have been like after he encountered Jesus. What could his life have looked like as a follower of Christ?

Cissa and Al were inspired by Priscilla and Aquila, the tent makers Paul met in Corinth. I used this couple as a parallel story to "wake up" a sleeping relationship. There is no evidence in Scripture that this couple ever had marriage issues. I have leaned heavily into my imagination by asking, "What if?" In Scripture they stood apart from the norm due to Priscilla's prominence. The first time Paul meets them he uses Aquila's name first. After that it was always "Priscilla and Aquila". Why?

Of course, my main inspiration came from the exhortation Jesus had for the Christians meeting in Sardis: "wake up". This Church had fallen asleep and were resting on their past reputation. This tied in closely with Sardis's reputation for being an impenetrable fortress. The citizens were so confident of their safety behind the walls, they became complacent.

Throughout their long history they were only invaded twice. And those two times were because guards fell asleep. I found it interesting that, each time, hints about secret entrances were given away by lax soldiers. The first time, the enemy watched a guard retrieve his helmet after it fell over the wall. The second time, the enemy saw vultures soaring and were led to an unguarded area outside the wall where citizens would drop dead bodies.

Once the enemy gained entry to the city they met no resistance. The citizens of Sardis had no experience of warfare and didn't know how to fight; they just stepped aside.

Similarly, the Church meeting in Sardis had worked hard at fitting into and accommodating the culture around them. When the enemy snuck up on them, they didn't know how to fight or protect their faith and the purity of their relationship with Christ.

However, there was a remnant still awake, passionate and fighting. From them, the spark grew and fanned the flames back to life. There was a revival, but sadly it did not last long.

As I hope you have come to understand, though my depictions of events and some characters are inspired by historical and documentary evidence, _everything_ is fictional. If you are reading this note, then thank you for getting this far through the story... and the series. If you haven't read the previous books, may I suggest you start at the beginning—_Dangerous Salvation_.

Book 6, set in Thyatira, has some very interesting developments and deals with a "she-devil vomiting lies and getting some blind fools hepped-up and hot to trot" (thanks, Daisy). I hope you will join me, and the crew, as the journey continues.

To keep up to date with more books in the series and other news, sign up to my newsletter at donitabundy.com

Donita Bundy

FRACTURED INTERVENTION
PLAYLIST

F*ractured Intervention Theme*: Remedy – *Adele*
    Alario: Let You Love Me – *Jervis Campbell*
Jemimah: Blackbiird – Beyoncé, Tanner Adell, Brittney Spencer, Tiera Kennedy, Reyna Roberts
    Balashka: Beautiful Things – *Benson Boone*
    Kaitlyn: Home – *Harper Still, Jamie Grace, Morgan Harper Nichols*
    Marcus: Good Morning Mercy – *Jason Crabb*
    Sariah: Big God – *Terrian*
    Raphael: Rabbit & the Bear – *Josh Garrels*
    Valarie: Forty Days – *The Dust of Men*
    Daniel: Teach Me to Dance – *Jervis Campbell, Chris Renzema*
    Contessa: Stay (Gonna Be Okay) – *Seph Schlueter*
    Alario and Cissa's song: Don't Blame Me – *Etta James*
    Family: That's the Thing About Praise – *Benjamin William Hastings, Blessing Offor*

ABOUT THE AUTHOR

Donita Bundy was the inaugural Somerset Writer in Residence (Queensland Australia). Along with monthly short stories with the Somerset Writers Group, Donita blogs regularly on her website and contributes to the Gracewriters Podcast. When she's not writing or teaching, she enjoys photographing the local area as well as designing book covers.

To connect, follow her blog, listen to the podcast, check out the gallery or just keep up to date with what's going on, go to her website and sign up to the newsletter at www.donitabundy.com.

ACKNOWLEDGMENTS

To my family and support crew, thank you:

Thanks, Mum, I wouldn't be here if you weren't there backing me every step of the way.

Belinda Pollard, my friend, sister-in-arms, and editor, whose experience, expertise and oodles of patience (so when you say "pronoun" you mean... *He?*) helped me past the halfway point. Five down, four to go!

Alix Kwan, still the most amazing proofreader of all time, thank you for creating pockets of time in your very busy and stressful life to help continue the journey. Your work ensures smooth sailing and minimal typo road bumps.

Ella Green and Lee Cawthray (supplier of chocolate), the most wonderful cheer squad in the history of the universe. Ever.

Rev. Loretta Tyler-Moss and Chrissy Garwood for jumping in and doing the hard yards at the end to help me cross the line well. Thank you for the all-nighters.

Lydia Ramsay for help and inspiration shared from her years working with beautiful human beings living with significant physical and cognitive challenges at the Halwyn Centre.

Susan Pitkin (former associate and personal assistant to senior figures in the Australian justice system) and Lesley Whitteker (former ABC journalist) for helping me write a "creatively lenient" news article.

The Somerset Writers Group: a more diverse, caring, supportive crew of creative geniuses would be hard to find.

To my Community of Light, for your constant prayers, support and encouragement, thank you.

And finally, and most importantly, I give thanks to the Light, whose story I believe this is. Whilst it is told through the lens of my life experiences, it continues to be inspired, carried and created in His strength alone. My prayer remains, dear reader, you find inspiration, challenge and encouragement to keep journeying the incredible adventure in, and with, the Light.

ARMOUR OF LIGHT SERIES

Book 1: Dangerous Salvation
What if your Saviour was more dangerous than your enemy?

Book 2: Blinding Revelation
What if the Unseen was more blinding than the Seen?

Book 3: Broken Restoration
What if complete restoration requires absolute brokenness?

Book 4: Humble Insurrection
What if humility sparked the most powerful rebellion of all?

Book 5: Liberating Persecution
What if persecution unlocks true freedom?